# RAPE IN HOLDING CELL 6

BOOKS BY KYLE MICHEL SULLIVAN

General Novels:

The Alice '65
The Vanishing of Owen Taylor
The Lyons' Den
Bobby Carapisi
NYPD Blood

Fable:

David Martin

Adult Novels:

Rape in Holding Cell 6
Porno Manifesto
How to Rape a Straight Guy

# RAPE IN HOLDING CELL 6

(Books One and Two)

By
Kyle Michel Sullivan

Published by: KMSCB, Buffalo, NY

Copyright 2009 by Kyle Michel Sullivan, dba: KMSCB

New Edition containing
"Rape in Holding Cell 6, volume 1"
and
"Rape in Holding cell 6, volume 2"
2nd volume

ISBN: 978-0-9912866-1-4
Cover design by JamTheCat
Images via Shutterstock

— Acknowledgements —

Thanks to Bill for having existed — and Wayne for giving me
material enough for a hundred stories about selfish jerks.
Additional thanks to The Depraved Minds Club on
GoodReads.com for giving me so much support

# BOOK ONE

ONE      1
TWO      14
THREE      38
FOUR      52
FIVE      69
SIX      86
SEVEN      104
EIGHT      119
NINE      134
TEN      151

# BOOK TWO

ONE      161
TWO      174
THREE      194
FOUR      213
FIVE      248
SIX      262
SEVEN      281
EIGHT      300
NINE      313
TEN      325

# BOOK ONE

I saw it on a local webcast — the Right and Honorable Nathaniel Carson Gilbert, III announced he was running for a suddenly-vacant seat in the United States Senate on the Republican ticket, intending to take it in place of the half-assed-but-decent-enough Democrat who was also running and *Return this country to decency and the rule of law*.

The two-faced-hypocritical-mother-fucking-son-of-a-bitch.

I guess it's needless to say he and I have a history — and not one that was fun, lemme tell ya — but if that pompous, fatuous, silver-haired piece of shit thought I'd stand by and let him get away with presenting himself as some Holy-Joe of the law even if it *was* to be from Texas, he was crazy as crazy can get.

Okay — so maybe I oughta backtrack and explain things a little, before you think I'm some half-cocked freak that hates all judges and cops and gives the salute to neo-Nazi scum and wants to bomb anything that I don't like and all that right-wing-nut batshit. Fact is, I'm the opposite of all that. To start with, I'm a card-carrying member of the ACLU — or used to be. Just like I used to be one of those guys who, if you left him alone to live his queer life, all would be rosy and cool. And yes, I DO mean queer. Not gay. Not homosexual. And sure as hell not a queen — just queer. Or faggot, if I'm feeling especially feisty.

No, that's not true; I used to be gay and proud of it, despite my family's reaction. I wasn't kicked out of my small-town home or anything (though we did live in a smallish town); my folks just sort of nodded and gave me a few words of advice and went about their business, very quietly. As did my brothers and sister. In fact, everybody in the family got quiet. And stopped inviting me to family events. And would be nice if I called but never bothered to call me. And while mom and dad paid for my college tuition and fees, they gave me neither car nor anything for living expenses outside my dorm and meal tickets (I guess they thought they could keep me from having too wild a party life, or something). And they never came to any of the events I was part of (I was on the tennis team and we were winning medals). Nor did my brothers or sister. Nor my aunts or uncles. Nor my cousins. Nobody. It was like I'd gone from being blood to being an acquaintance-in-law who wasn't quite right for the rest of us; someone to be polite to and not one damned thing more. I guess it made sense that they ignored my declaration of faggotry; after all, we *were* in a conservative Texas town of less than 100K population not far from a *big* conservative town where some things just were *not* discussed. Plus I've always had this streak of crazy-mean in me that could explode in a nano-second if I thought I or any friend had been slighted. But I think they really just feared for the sanctity of their sons' virgin assholes and seriously believed that if I made a pass at those boys, they'd be obligated to let me do as I wanted because we were related or something and —

Okay, now I'm getting off-track, so let's offer up some clarification. First off, I'm Antony Patric St. Lazarre, AKA: Antony (and if you do call me Tony, be prepared to get coldly corrected), from a nice upper middle-class family, and who was once told by an unimpeachable source I resembled John Payne — which I didn't get since I'd never heard of him, but then I finally saw a picture of him as a boxer seated in a corner, his magnificent legs splayed open, exuding this animal sexuality, and felt thoroughly pleased. I mean, the guy was a bit darker and prettier and rounder-faced than I saw myself to be, but then his eyes were more open to fun than mine and his smile almost sweet as opposed to mine being half-cocked. Plus my nose is more Roman in structure — and I'm getting lost in nonsense, again. It's not easy to concentrate, these days.

Anyway, I'm not quite as beefy as he was, either — just lean and solid. Not skinny. Not slim. I played tennis since I could hold a racquet and fit perfectly into that look, right down to my skin being tanned (despite a ton of SPF 45) and my choice of clothes being sports casual and borderline minimal. I mean, even in winter, which can get pretty brutal in Texas, I was usually in shorts and a tennis shirt, and the cold rarely got to me. Shit, if I'd had his legs, I'd be wearing a Speedo all the time.

You know, I think half the reason I was pleased to be considered his doppelganger was who it was that told me of the similarity — Collie. Collier. Problem is, Collie's the reason I loathe and despise that fucking judge — because he's one of the bastards who got him killed.

Collier Winston-Royce — talk about yin to my yang. So smart and kind and gentle and caring and full of affection, I wanted nothing more than to just walk beside him into eternity, my body molded into his. That he and I wound up lovers was a surprise, since he wasn't exactly my type — more sunshine and light than I look for — but it fit into every cliché you can imagine from the book on finding your soul mate. And it was heaven.

I was two months into being twenty, and we met in the college refectory when he and I both grabbed for the last onion bagel. I was in a rush for media ethics class (talk about a misnomer) and hadn't noticed he'd opened the bin; he was busy dealing with a student who was being a pain. I grabbed the bagel (with paper), he groped my hand (with pinchers) and we both jumped ten feet.

"Sorry," he said. "Didn't even look."

"No, it — it's fine," I stammered out, feeling like a total idiot because I was looking into the bluest, most sparkling eyes I'd ever seen set into an chiseled face cut by a straight, manly nose and lips that looked ready to smile at even the hint of happiness in someone else. Laugh lines detailed his perfect proportions and thinning blond hair added to his aura of humanity. It didn't hurt that he had a body without a single angle to it — all round fleshy muscles covered by a layer of softness that made him achingly lovely instead of bulky, with hands that were picture-perfect and hair in all the right places (from what I could see) and then some — a buff, cheerful Golden Retriever in a button-down shirt and pair of Dockers that teased you with the brutal idea that they fitted around legs to die for. All I could think was, *Holy shit — he's gorgeous.* All I stammered out was, "Here." I offered the bagel to him.

3

"No, you take it," he said, and the hint of an accent in his voice would send a thrill down a nun let alone a sex-obsessed kid like me. "I need to drop a few pounds, anyway."

"Says who?" just popped out, without my thinking about it, because if I had I wouldn't have said it.

"Say my trousers, that're all thirty-three waist and warning me if I don't drop a few, I'll need a new wardrobe."

"Stupid trousers." And I wished I could take the comment back, it sounded so dumb. But he smiled and offered his hand.

"I'm Collier."

"Collie? Like Lassie?"

"Considering all the Lassies were actually male, yes."

His grin widened — and I realized what I'd said. Of course I blushed, and suddenly my light freckles looked like age spots.

"Antony — uh, Antony St. Lazarre."

That's when his student jumped in, eyes shooting bored darts at me. Orin Tedesco. I'd seen him around campus and dismissed him as an A&F kid who's so absolutely certain of his importance and attractiveness, he can't understand why he's not being paid attention to. No question he was hot — sun-blond hair, angular face, deep blue eyes under surprisingly bushy eyebrows, straight nose, curled lips and sharp cheekbones, all attached to a solid well-proportioned body by a neck that was just a bit too short. He wore training pants with a zipper up the leg that's only half-zipped and a hooded fleece jacket, and his calves were amazing. And amazingly hairy for a blond. But he looked like he belonged in high school (though he was a year older than me), and he spoke in a condescending *I'm being polite to you even though you're not worthy* voice.

"Excuse me," he snipped, "Professor, we're talking."

"No we're not, Orin," said Collie, still half-looking at me. "If your assignment's not on my desk by five, tomorrow, you'll be docked a grade, as I specifically stated at the beginning of the semester *and* noted in the syllabus."

"But it's not my fault!"

"We're a month into the semester and this is the third extension you've requested on an assignment. So, no. Period."

Orin stormed off. I shuddered, involuntarily. Something about him creeped me out, and I was glad he was gone. I don't know why I had that reaction, but sometimes I meet someone and I just take an immediate dislike to them. Just like I take an immediate like to others. And ninety-nine times out of a hundred, my gut's been right — as it turned out to be, about him. So I turned to my immediate-like guy and all but batted my eyes in mock-shock.

"You're a professor?"

"Creative writing. If these lads'd put as much effort into their course-work as they do their excuses, they'd all get A's."

"I gotta remember when I take your class — use my excuses as my papers."

"You plan to do that?

"Not till next year. I'm still programming."

"Computers. I'd never have guessed that."

"In a good or a bad way?" He smiled, in a beautiful way. I smiled back and continued, "No, it's really communications, but I want to be able to work my laptop even if it's freaking out in the middle of the Sahara."

"Excellent. You free tonight?"

Bam — right to the point, which made my breath quicken just enough to throw off my poor attempt at seeming cool. Fact is, I wasn't (I had a tennis student) but I said, "Yeah. Why?"

"Maybe we can get together. Have a bite to eat. I can talk you out of taking my class."

"Why would you want to do that?"

In answer, he took the bagel, split it in half and gave me a piece, then smiled and walked over to pay for it. And the way he walked — with those Dockers promising perfection underneath them — I got a boner and a half in point-two-nano seconds.

Needless to say, I rearranged my tennis session.

\*\*\*\*

We met at a Chili's. Seven sharp, though I was almost late; I spent two hours in my dorm room trying to figure out what to wear to say *Want me* but not look like I was saying *WANT ME*! I settled on a navy tennis shirt and board shorts with loafers, casual but still tight enough to show off, and I didn't care how chilly it was out.

I rode my bike over and walked in to find him wearing a simple cotton shirt, blue jeans, warm coat and — cowboy boots?! Obviously this was not gonna be a *take me home* date, not when he's wearing something that's nine kinds of hell to take off (I speak from experience, trust me). To say I was disappointed was to say the Empire State Building's tallish; in fact, I felt brutally let down. But then he saw me and smiled and my heart leapt into my crotch and I smiled back and decided to let the evening flow — and if I needed to, I'd do a quickie jack off in the men's room.

He ate the Tilapia as I chowed a burger and fries. And I found out he's from England but had lived in the States since he was five. He spoke perfect Italian because of his mother and perfect English because of his father. He had three brothers and two sisters and was the middle child. He'd been fat until he was in high school, where he'd begun to run every day and kept his weight under control by doing 5K every morning before classes. And he was just under twice my age. Woof.

I told him about my family's reaction to my coming out; my high school basically being supportive — except for some jocks who thought they could make my life miserable, until I used some Aikido on them (I'd started taking it the day after I accepted I liked boys instead of girls because I knew that would be a problem with some of the lesser-brained sorts); how I was paying my living expenses by teaching tennis and swimming because my folks wouldn't provide anything more than tuition and meals; and how I'd like to develop a Gay News Network to broadcast into homes all over the world — especially into those nations in the Middle East and Africa that liked to kill queers.

"I like tennis," he said. "We should play, sometime."

"I'll beat the pants off you," I replied.

"I figured that out already." His eyes twinkled.

"I'm going to take your class."

"Why?"

"It'll help me. I want to write as well as report the news, and anything I find that'll help me perfect my abilities, I go for."

Again, I was saying something in a way to really mean, *I want to suck your dick.*

He finished the last of his fish and leaned back. "You know what'll happen if you do?"

"What?"

"Nothing. I don't date my students."

I dropped a fry just before it hit my mouth and felt a quick scream down to my crotch. Seriously, if I'd been standing up, you'd have seen some tent-pole action, despite the liner in the board shorts.

"I — I don't date my professors," I replied.

"Then we understand each other?"

I looked at him — and those blue, blue eyes tore straight into me and that perfectly square chin emphasized the near-smile he was offering. And all I could think to croak out was, "Y'know — Chili's has the crappiest desserts."

He signaled for the waiter, paid the bill, chucked my bike in the back of his Land Rover and took me home.

Now, I know I sound like a horny little puppy here — and truth was, I was. I'd never had a relationship more serious than a couple of friends with benefits (which usually meant me sucking them off as they did me a hand-job and us never talking about it) and it'd been a month since I was with a guy (one of the University's quarterbacks, who was neither as big or as good-looking or as accomplished in fucking or sucking as he thought he was, but who was a good solid warm body, and with whom I *was* able to get off with, but whose *sessions* were built around his schedule rather than mine, and now baseball practice was underway, so...) so I was ready for some action.

But something about Collie told me he was the nesting type, and to be honest, I really wanted something like that. Needed it. I'd made no real friends on campus and was beginning to feel way too solitary in my life, so had already been scoping a couple of cute-if-lightweight classmates out as potential boyfriend material — especially a tall, sleek, golden number named Grady Lowenthaal, in Principles of Communication, who had gentle eyes and was openly gay and definitely worth going for. But Collie wiped all of that aside.

He lived in a condo near the university — one of those open, clean-looking places that felt surprisingly inviting. Gentle mixes of darks and lights. Hardwood floors. Big windows. Truly elegant.

He led me in, let me pass him as he closed the door then stopped me with a caress on my left shoulder. His fingers trailed over to my spine and whispered down it and goose-bumps danced over my skin.

"Have you ever met someone and instantly thought, *Yes, this is the one*?" he whispered.

I turned to him and nodded. "Right now."

"Are you sure?"

I spread my arms open. My first *come to papa* moment. He let his fingers drift up my sides to play with my tits and sent screaming lightning into my heart. I pulled him close to kiss him — and, sweet Jesus, what a kiss. Moist. Tantalizing. A hint of mint. A dream of perfection. Nirvana on this earth. I could have lived my life in that moment and never regretted a second of it.

I slipped my arms around him and felt how solid and comfortable he was — and how his body molded itself to mine. His hands caressed my ass — and I caressed his and loved how round and right it felt. I also felt his dick press hard against mine. Roll against it. So — he's a boxers kind of guy. I preferred the look and feel of briefs on a man's crotch, but in this case it whetted my appetite and I felt a great need to do some exploring, so I slid my right hand around his hip and slipped the back of my fingers over his crotch. Felt him move and react. Of course, all dicks feel big when they're touched this way but his — I knew I was underestimating.

He held me tighter and lifted me, still kissing, and carried me into his bedroom to toss me on the bed. I bounced back, laughing at the suddenness of it. The pure eroticism of it. My dick was pumped and ready for action and obviously so since I was straining at the liner of my board-shorts. He unbuttoned his shirt and I started to lift off mine — but he stopped my hands.

"Let me."

He pulled off his shirt to reveal a perfect chest — round and full and rich to look at, hair fanning across it like wings and curling down his smooth, trim abs to his little innie before swirling out to promise a thousand delights. His shoulders glided into arms of nearly delicate beauty, they were so neatly proportioned. He could have stood there for an hour, as is, and I'd have been happy just to lie there and look at him.

He climbed onto the bed and kissed me deeper and tickled my tits through the shirt, using pinches of his fingers to also pull it up and up and up until bare skin touched bare nipple. I was about to go crazy from the shudders it sent to my balls. And from the sensations it shot through my fingertips as I caressed his thighs. Felt the smooth cool jeans tight against solid muscle. Whispered over his crotch and traveled around and along the elegant curve of his inner legs. He squirmed as he lifted the shirt up and over my head.

The second my hands were free, I bent in to grab one of his amazingly round and brown tits with my teeth and flick my tongue over it. He gasped and ran his hands down my back to slip them under my shorts. That's when I used my Aikido to flip him onto his back and lie atop him, all so quickly, it took him a moment to realize what had happened. I used that moment to trail my lips down his hair, flicker my tongue into his belly button and undo his jeans. Then I slipped off him, knelt by the side of the bed and yanked his jeans down to his knees. He had on a pair of tight boxers that only slipped partway down his hips.

I looked at him, and from that vantage point he looked so young and innocent and open to anything, I felt a bit like a pedophile. I kissed up his left thigh — flitted my tongue over its swirls of hair as my left hand caressed his other thigh. I nuzzled his crotch. Felt his balls shift and shiver from the connection of it all. His ass clenched and I saw the bulge of his dick pressing hard against the fabric, begging for release. I got mean and ran my lips up and down it, as if to measure it.

He grabbed my head. "C'mere." Tried to guide me up to his lips for another kiss.

I reached up and pinched his tits, instead. He groaned and his dick pulsed against the fabric so hard I thought it would break through.

"Don't. Please. I'll cum."

I rolled his balls in my hand and chuckled. "No worries. You got plenty in storage."

I grabbed the waistband of the shorts with my teeth, pulled them down and let out what has to be one of the loveliest dicks I have ever seen. Thick and round and pulsing with need. A head in perfect proportion to the shaft. Veins enough to matter without being overpowering. At least seven inches and building. And though you couldn't see the foreskin at this stage, I could tell he was uncut. Which surprised me. That's something else I don't usually go for, but in this instance it only added to my desire for him.

I licked the still-growing shaft. It bounced back, almost dancing around my tongue. Lay in the thick beautiful mound of hair. Offered me promise of so damned much more if I wanted to help it. So I slipped my lips over the head and began to pump little Collie for everything I could.

"No — I'll — cum — I'll — SHIT!"

He shoved against my mouth, completely out of control. Began to grunt and whimper and let little jolts whisper from him and I felt the first taste of his semen — and he FIRED. Shot in my mouth. Shot across his chest when I slipped my lips off him and licked around the head of his dick. Fired again and again and again until he was spent.

I mean, until *he* thought he was spent.

I got wicked, again, and kept licking at his dick, even as he whimpered and tried to push my head away. Sucked his too-damn-beautiful balls out of the boxers via the fly and rolled them in my mouth with my tongue. Ran my fingers over his elegant thighs and hips and up to his tits until he was almost screaming. And I was rewarded by the beginnings of another erection.

Now don't get me wrong, here. I'm not claiming I'm some sex machine with centuries of experience behind him. I've usually just done what I wanted to do and guys seemed to like it. And that's all I did with Collie. No inhibitions. No hesitation. Nothing but me wanting to make him scream from pleasure — which he damn near did.

"Oh, shit — oh, shit — Antony." That was all he could say for a couple minutes.

I snaked up his torso to nuzzle my face in the crook of his neck. Smelled the gentle aftershave he used. The hint of some specialty soap. The first glimmers of his beard. I figured he'd shaved before he joined me for dinner, so he probably would have a five o'clock shadow, normally. And it felt so right, I rubbed my cheek harder against it.

The backs of my left fingers toyed with his right tit and my other hand traveled all over his abs and pecs, tickling the hair and tracing the lines it made. He was so fucking beautiful.

I finally rolled onto my back and pulled him on top of me. Then I slipped his boxers the rest of the way off his ass and played with the hair on his cheeks. There wasn't a lot, to my surprise; just enough to have fun with. I was rewarded with the feel of his dick hardening on my belly.

He kissed me, long and deep, then did exactly the same thing to me as I'd just done to him — but where I'd pulled down only his pants and left his boxers around his hips, he slid my board shorts completely to my ankles, revealing my manhood in all its glory (a goofy way of putting it but I was feeling goofy at the time), even though I was nowhere near as big as him. And where I'd licked and kissed the head of his dick, he swallowed mine whole and used his tongue to swirl around it like he was sucking on a Popsicle, his hands gripping my ass tight and needy and in complete control. And where I'd rolled his balls with my hands, he used his ever-growing dick to push against them and my scrotum, adding sensations I'd never known existed and taking me closer and closer and closer to the point of madness before I began to explode. And where I'd backed off after he began to cum, he swallowed every drop of mine and kept sucking at me until I was about to lose it.

But he wasn't done then. He still had hold of my ass, and as I clenched and squirmed under his touch and his still-steady sucking, he pressed his head against it. I don't usually let a guy fuck me till I really know him, so I tried to push him away then realized somewhere during his fellatio of me, he'd slipped on a condom and had it greased up and he was raring to go.

He took his mouth off my dick, lay his body atop mine, and pressed his dick next to mine. I could have thrown him off without any trouble, but the hair on his chest made my skin sing with sensation. Made my tits shriek from joy. So I let him take control. He kissed me, deep and full and whispered, "Okay? Okay?"

"Slow," I nodded. "Slow."

He shifted into position. Moved my legs to over his shoulders. Cupped my ass and somehow found my hole without the use of his hands — and began to push in.

I gasped from the pain, mainly because I'd only been fucked a couple of times due to my standards, the last being by that quarterback and he was nowhere near as big as Collie, and even then I'd all but kicked the guy out of me the moment he started pounding into me like I was a dog or a blow-up toy. Jerk.

But Collie wasn't like that. He slipped in by stages — slow, steady pushing with moments of rest as I adjusted to it then a bit more pushing, all the while caressing my ass and my legs and pinching at my tits and tickling the little hair on my abs and kissing me...and soon he was completely inside me and sliding almost all the way out and it was feeling so nice, I was grabbing his ass to bring him in closer to me — deeper into me — grinding against him to make him one with me.

He pumped faster and faster and deeper and deeper and I wrapped my arms around his powerful shoulders and he leaned on his elbows and gripped my hair and held my face and went faster and faster and he jolted and slammed harder against me and I gripped tighter with my ass and felt his whole body shake and shudder and I ran my hands down his back to hold his butt and it was clenching like you wouldn't believe and suddenly I felt a surge and gasped, "Collie", and he gripped my dick with his right hand and gave me two yanks and I exploded and I think — no, I'm pretty damned sure I passed out for a second.

Moments later, I was looking at Collie's beautiful face, so wet with sweat, hair matted to his forehead, a look of profound surprise in his eyes and I realized my board shorts were still around my ankles, binding me partially into the position he'd put me in. And I felt like such a wanton slut, I laughed.

His expression grew uncertain. I wiped at the sweat on his skin. Brushed the hair away from his forehead. Held his face in my hands. And kissed him. And said, "Of course you know, this means marriage, mortgage and more of the same."

He laughed and rolled onto his side, taking me with him. And we held each other tight. And he whispered, "Anytime, anyplace, anywhere, anyhow."

And we had nearly eight months of that beauty before all hell broke loose.

— TWO —

As that old cliché goes, the day that started the end of my life began simply. I'd stayed the night at Collie's — we didn't do much, just sixty-nined because he was tired. Seems Orin was being a prick about the *C* he got in Collie's course, spring semester, and insisting it be changed to an *A* because that's what everybody gave him. He'd caused a real scene and accused Collie of giving him that grade because he wouldn't sleep with him. But Collie stood his ground and told the spoiled brat to grow up.

"If you'd turned your assignments in on time, you might've received an *A* — but not one was."

"Nobody else cared about that and — "

"How your other professors score is up to them. I told you from the outset — for every day that your class-work is late, you'll be docked a grade. Now if you want to retake the course and try to do the work as it's assigned to you, I'm willing to let you into the next spring session — "

"I already *took* the fuckin' class!"

"Then the grade stands."

That's when Orin shifted to another tactic. He broke into tears and collapsed on the couch. "Man, don't you understand? My dad rode my ass all summer on this grade. Threatened to make me go to a school back home. The only reason he let me come here is I swore I'd get at least a 4.0 and you've dragged me down to 3.6 and he says if I don't get it back up, this semester, it just proves I'm not ready to go away for school and — and I'll do anything you want. Please."

Collie closed the door and let Orin finish crying. It took him a few minutes. Once he was back in control, Collie said, "All right, you have a good style, Orin, and a fine imagination — so tell you what — did you used to cut your family's lawn?"

"We got gardeners."

"Then write me a thousand word short story about your gardener tending to your landscaping. If you bring it to me by this time, next week, and it's on the same level as your other work, I'll re-evaluate your grade."

"Don't you have to talk to Dean Weller about doing that?"

"I'll discuss it with him before I go home. But, Orin — I will not accept the paper after five a week from today. Do you understand that?"

He nodded and rose to his feet and left the office. And true to his word, Collie spoke with Dean Weller about changing Orin's grade. And true to Orin being a little fuck, he went straight to the police and told them Collie had blackmailed him into letting the man suck him off — and lead them to believe he was underage.

I'd left for class while Collie was out on his run, leaving a pot of coffee ready and warm. He never got to it. Seems the cops arrested him as he was returning to the condo, wearing only a loose, sleeveless t-shirt, some cut-off fleece shorts over a tight pair of trunks, his running shoes and socks and booked him into the county jail. They didn't even interview him; just put him into a holding cell with a dozen other men after he called Dean Weller, to keep until a magistrate came around to arraign him and determine bail.

He wound up being the only middle-class white man there, all the rest being Black or Hispanic or biker trash and having a major hate going on for anyone who seemed above them. But if that wasn't bad enough, somehow one of them heard he'd been arrested for molesting a little boy.

Collier Winston-Royce never made it to the arraignment.

When he didn't answer to the guard's call, they went looking and found him lying in a bloody heap in a corner behind a table, his uniform ripped to shreds, his face pummeled beyond recognition, his skull fractured, both arms and six ribs broken, comatose. He was rushed to the prisoner ward at the county hospital but never regained consciousness. His parents flew in

15

from New Zealand — they'd moved there after the US invaded Iraq, they were so disgusted with America's love of violence — and they had him taken off life support after three days...and took him back to New Zealand to bury.

I was not allowed to see him. Not once.

Of course, the local media's take on the story was a child molester had been killed in jail. It wasn't considered a nice thing to have happened since justice could now not be served, but it was the victim's own fault for what he did to that little boy. When it was pointed out that *little boy* was actually a college student named Orin Tedesco who was, in reality, twenty-one years old — that changed nothing. Collie was still an elitist fag professor who'd used his position to force a fine, heterosexual young man into homosexual sex. I mean, we *are* talking about Texas, where the facts never get in the way of a good piece of hate.

Now the Sheriff's department *was* embarrassed by Collie's death. Apparently, the deputies who patrolled the jail were so used to their prisoners yelling and fighting and throwing things and using foul language, they never picked up on Collie's screams for help — or on the snarls of prisoners in adjoining cells calling for him to be fucked, again and again — or on the fact that blood was now splattered across two walls in the corner where they were brutalizing him — or that the security camera caught the whole thing on monitors that were visible to anyone but being deliberately ignored (though it later came out that the security monitors were in the middle of a glitch and no image was available for the guard to view). Such conduct was considered unprofessional and *measures to correct it would be taken, so nothing like this happens, again.*

They figured out who brutalized him via DNA. Seems the little fucks who fucked him didn't realize the cops could figure out whose semen was whose, and Texas was one of those states that requires all felons provide DNA samples, so they couldn't claim they were misidentified. They charged seven men — four black (anal sodomy), three white (two for oral sodomy, one for felonious sexual assault, which was never defined for me) — and solved nine outstanding heterosexual rapes, as well. The other five guys who just stood there and let it happen? Well, that wasn't really a crime, just morally reprehensible, so they were let off. Five of those charged plead guilty to voluntary manslaughter and were sent away for eight to twenty years while the two straight-rapists weren't given that option; they were handed three strikes and happily sent away forever.

Orin gave an interview swearing he'd told the cops he was twenty-one and just that he'd been molested when he was younger and they'd gotten things confused. That's when Assistant District Attorney Phillip Stanton stepped forward and said that Orin's report listed him as sixteen (not quite correct, but such fine points seldom matter when one is trying to cover one's ass), and he made a point of mentioning that Orin's semen had been found in Collie's office, on the couch. So Orin vanished, and no one really thought it was odd.

The matter finally died down and everyone was happy that there was one less faggot in the world, and a fat woman was brought in from another college to complete Collie's courses and the campus returned to normal.

And I nearly killed myself from grief.

Swear to God, I never knew you could feel such pain and not die from it, outright. A pain so deep in your heart, you know it's ripping in half. So sharp in your throat, you know you'll never breathe again. So tight around your chest, you're amazed you can even function. I didn't cry — not once. Maybe if I had it would have been better. I don't know. All I do know is my beautiful Collier was dead — murdered — and nobody really cared and oh sweet Jesus how I hated my life at that moment.

And how I hated the world for not caring.

And by *the world*, I mean every fucking person in it.

I stopped going to class. My father screamed about the tuition being wasted, but I couldn't even summon up the energy for a shrug back at him. My mother suggested I get away for a while — go to Canada or Europe and just do nothing till the end of the year. I'd had my own passport since I was sixteen (another step in my parents' release of me) and had already been to Dublin, Paris, Rome and Athens (Spring Break, freshman year, and some day I'll tell you which men are what in the way of fun), plus there were hints I would not be invited to any of the family's Thanksgiving and Christmas functions, but I never answered her. Neither of them could understand the depth of my anguish over the death of another man, since my being gay didn't really have relevance to them.

I moved out of my dorm room and into Collie's condo, hiding from the world and ignoring the few calls on my cell phone from mom and dad, since that was the only way they had to get hold of me, now. I lay on his bed and smelled his clothes and ate everything in the way of food in his cupboards so as to avoid having to go out and didn't bathe or shave or anything for weeks. Even Thanksgiving came and went without notice — or even contact from the family. I just kept running my life with Collie in my mind, over and over, as if thinking hard enough about it would cancel the reality and bring him back to me.

Like the trip we took to Seattle.

Collie'd been invited to speak at a writing conference in the summer and I'd never been, so we flew up together on the cattle-car airline. Had to change planes twice, but we both already knew the routines so did only carry-on bags and had a pleasant time — though he stupidly lost fifty dollars in a slot machine at the Las Vegas Airport. I warned him "Dude, you're in an airport terminal, not a casino where they want you to keep playing and buying drinks and staying the night and seeing the shows. There's no chance in hell you'll win a penny."

He'd just shrugged and said, "I'm having fun. I've never been to Las Vegas, before."

"This isn't Vegas," I snipped. "Hell, it barely counts as Nevada."

But he shrugged me off and kept playing, looking as happy as a puppy with a new toy. And I just stood there and watched him and did everything I could to keep from reaching over and pinching his left tit, just for the hell of it. A security guard standing a few yards away seemed to be waiting for one of us to do something unseemly — and I was getting more and more tempted — but then our flight was called and we headed over to our gate to get in line.

Collie likes to sit in the back of the plane by a window and get off slowly. He never did tell me why, though I think it had something to do with the journey being the most fun to him and him wanting to keep it going just a little bit longer. Me. I want out and on my way, but I let him pick where we sit, and I'd just listen to my iPod and munch on peanuts and sip a tiny cup of DP — at least, I did that on the first two legs of our journey. Between Vegas and Seattle, I decided on a different kind of refreshment.

First, when Collie set himself up by the window, I took the aisle seat and set my bag on the seat between us. He cast me an odd look but said nothing. The plane wasn't full, so no one needed to sit there. Then once we were airborne, I slipped into it, watched him gaze out the window at the non-stop desert for a moment and finally slipped my right hand on his left knee and trailed it up his leg to his crotch — then trailed it right back down. He smiled at me.

"Careful — you'll get something started, and the flight's near three hours."

In answer, I glanced around, saw the flight attendants were getting ready to hand out their meager supply of sodas and snacks, so gave his crotch a good solid grope and whispered, "Wanna be part of the Mile-High Club?"

He looked at me as if I'd grown another head — which I was in the process of doing, just not on my shoulders, if you know what I mean.

I slipped out of my seat, dragging him with me. The john was occupied but the moment we got there, it popped open and a pudgy woman exited. She squeezed past and I used her size to hide me sneaking into the bathroom and yanked Collie in with me.

Okay, even when you're in there alone, it's true that sardines have more room in their can than is offered in an airplane toilet, but that didn't stop me from sitting cross-legged on the commode, pulling Collie down to kiss me and undoing the zipper on his ever-present Dockers and pulling him out. He was already pretty much hard and a few quick strokes brought him to fullness.

"Antony — "

I shut him up by swallowing him whole. And I do mean whole. God, I loved his cock. Loved the feel of it filling my mouth. Loved how the skin glided a bit due to his foreskin. Loved the smell of him and how his pubes would tickle my nose and chin and how he'd dig into my back with his fingers, almost like a cat, kneading my skin and caressing my spine and dragging up my sides as I juggled his balls with one hand and slipped up under his shirt to pinch at his tits with the other, drifting from left to right to left to right. He really tried not to make any sounds, but some involuntary gasps and yelps came out of him and, within a minute, he was firing into my mouth. I kept it all in till I could lean over to spit into the sink. Then I stood up and leaned over him, as if he was about to carry me on one shoulder, and he found I was already primed to go so he slipped my cargo shorts down my hips, took my dick in his mouth, gripped my ass with his hands and began working me. And I have to tell you, it was fan-fucking-tastic. The sense of urgency and naughtiness adding to the whole range of emotion and sensation I was feeling to the point where I was starting to make a bit of noise and he had to stop and whisper, "Shh," to me.

Then he got back to work and finished me off within fifteen seconds and I nearly collapsed from the overwhelming beauty of the sensations whispering down my thighs and legs and up my spine, and of lying over him like a sleepy puppy that's been petted into a perfect state of bliss.

When we tried to sneak out, a flight attendant was right there, eyeing the lavatory door. So I popped some gum and strode straight out, turned her around and kissed her as Collie snuck away. She slapped me.

"What were you doing in there?" I just grinned and gave the international sign for jacking off. "By yourself?"

"Wanna join me?"

She nearly slapped me, again, snarling, "I could have you arrested."

I scooted back to my seat, found Collie in his, studiously gazing out the window. I stayed in the aisle seat, waited till the attendant slipped past and gave a loud sigh — and she actually glanced back at me with a smile. That unnerved me. I was half afraid she'd take me up on the pass I seemed to be making and I really never had been into girls, but as we were exiting the plane, she patted Collie's ass and winked at me as she said, "Next flight, make a reservation."

Fortunately, she was not on any of the flights home.

Our stay in Seattle was everything you'd think it could be — The Space Needle, The Sci-Fi Museum, the Duck Tour, driving up to Vancouver to look around, driving around the Kitsap Peninsula to look around and then across the ferry to look around, eating WAY too much fish and listening to not nearly enough music, hopping the monorail and, in general, behaving like tourists in between lectures. It was joyous and I took hundreds of pictures on my iPod to add to the hundreds more on my laptop — and that's what I was wallowing in when I heard someone scratching at the door.

I was lying on the bed, just staring at the ceiling like I'd been doing all night, every night, a picture of Collie on a ferry, with Seattle's skyline gleaming behind him, grinning back at me from the laptop monitor. It took me a moment to notice the noise, and then only because it was a creepy sound. By the time I roused myself and padded into the main room to see what was going on, the front door was open — and there stood an old man who'd already begun to wither up from years of non-stop work.

"What d'you want?" I snarled.

I scared the shit out of him, making him jump five feet in the air. He took a moment to catch his breath then said, "Bank sent me over to change th' locks. They told me it's empty."

"It is. I don't exist."

He crinkled his nose and nodded. "Smells like something died."

I chuckled, went into the kitchen and drew some water into a dirty glass. He stayed where he was, watching me. Looking at the chaos I'd brought into what was once a pristine home.

"You know the owner?" he asked.

"Knew. He *is* dead. Buried in another world."

"Friend of yours, huh?" And he asked that in a way that meant

21

he knew I was a thousand times more than that.

"Does that bug you?"

I could feel him shrugging. And my sense about people was saying, He's okay. But I didn't feel like paying attention, just yet.

"You plannin' to join him?" He got a shrug in answer. I felt him nodding. "Better do it quick. Bank's comin' in next week to clear everything out an' make the place ready for sale. May take longer'n they expect."

I looked at him. "Let 'em try."

"Won't have t' try. Sheriff'll come, put you in cuffs, take you down to county and, if you ain't nice, get you took care of."

"Forced bath?"

"If'n you're lucky."

"Luck has yet to be part of this equation."

"Listen up, son — I know folk who work down at County, and you don't wanna go there. They got some guards, they find out what you are...they'll make your world hell and won't have to touch you to do it."

"My world's already hell."

"Just — just go on, get a bath, say your prayers for what you lost an' move on. This ain't right. Ain't healthy."

"You know whose place this was?"

He nodded. "An' to my mind, judge should'a let him out the minute he was called. But there's lots of folk in this world real mean like that and — "

His words finally cracked through my hazy walls. I actually looked at him, for a long moment. I probably seemed lost. Crazy. Maybe just plain stupid. He finally sighed and started backing out the door. "I'll come back, t'morrow."

"Wait," I said. "What did you mean, *the judge should've let him out?*"

"When he got called by the guy's lawyer. They heard he was arrested an' th' bail judge wasn't comin' till three. They told the judge the kid makin' the claim was lyin'."

"How did you find that out?"

"Got a nephew who's in the DA's office. We're good Christians, don't believe in doin' stuff like that t' others. Just ain't right. An' what happened to that man — it made him damn near quit, he's so disgusted."

"Because nobody cared."

"People cared, son — just not the right ones. I'll be back, t'morrow."

"No," I said. "What's your name?"

"Ray."

"Go ahead and change the locks, Ray; I'm leaving, tonight."

"You sure?"

No, I wasn't — but I still nodded. "What's your nephew's name? I'd like to talk with him."

"What good'll that do?"

I almost said, *Figure out how to get even*, and I honestly did not know why. Because at that time, the idea hadn't really formulated itself in my brain, yet; but the impulse was already there, deep and waiting. What I did say was, "I — I'm hoping it'll help me find closure."

Talk about lame. But Ray swallowed it.

"You loved that fella, huh?" I nodded. "Well...I don't go for that — but a body cain't help who they fall in love with. Name's Tommy. I'll call, see if'n he'll talk. No promises."

"Thanks, Ray. And I mean it — change the locks. I'm going to get a shower — get my things — and leave. Here's my cell number. Tommy can call that, if he wants."

I wrote it out. Offered it. He made himself take it.

"Just not for the next hour, right?"

"Am I that bad?" Ray just sort of scrunched up his face. I smiled. "I'll get right to it. And I'll clean everything up. Collie — Collier loved to keep it nice."

Ray nodded. "World's a hell of a place, at times."

I nodded and headed into the bathroom.

I stripped and tossed the clothes in the trash bin. Started the shower going as hot as I could stand it. I stood under the water and let it pound on me for several minutes, washing away the razor-like webs that had encircled my psyche before I reached for the soap. *Neutrogena*. A light gentle scent that smelled so much like Collie, tears streamed down my face. I knew they were there. And I couldn't stop them. Didn't try. They felt right and good and were just enough of a release to get me through the shower and get dressed, again.

I used Collie's deodorant — *Old Spice* — and slipped into a pair of board shorts and one of his t-shirts. I had my top-siders to wear so didn't need socks — then remembered I'd brought all my clothes and things over. But I couldn't be bothered to change, now.

I came out of the bedroom and Ray was just finishing up.

"Shit," he said, "I thought you was black." It was borderline offensive as a joke, but I let it slide. I knew what he really meant, and I didn't have the skin color to justify getting pissed off about it. "Tommy says he'll give you a call in the mornin', after he's done with court. Should be 'round eleven."

I nodded. "Thanks. I'll have everything ready for the bank"

"They know 'bout all this stuff?" He motioned to the furniture.

I shrugged. "His family didn't want any of it."

"Ain't what they told the bank." My blank look must have been comical, because he smiled a half-toothed smile and said, "They got guys comin' in Monday to appraise it all."

"Why? To sell?" He nodded. "And the money goes to Collie's estate." He shrugged. I snarled, "You know, they wouldn't let me see him. Wouldn't let me say good-bye."

"I know some folk might take all this off your hands. Cousin of mine. Might pay a decent price for it."

"Everything?" He nodded. "Can they pick it up, tonight?"

He shrugged. "I'll give him a call."

"The bank won't care?"

"What'll I know? Place was empty when I come in."

"Cash?"

"'Course."

"Cool."

"Take care, son."

And he left. No shaking of hands. No hugs. Not even a pat on the back. He just left. And I got to work.

**\*\*\*\***

I finished cleaning just before eleven pm. Ray's cousin slipped in ten minutes later. The place was cleared out by one and I was three thousand dollars richer. Then I got online and checked my one and only credit card's balance. It showed I had nearly two thousand dollars available. I got my clothes and a few important items, piled them into the Land Rover and went straight to a motel, picking one near the airport that had free WiFi and breakfast for all guests.

Now at this point, I still had no idea what I was going to do. I figured I'd need a job, but the thought of looking for one just did not register in my brain. The fact that I was somewhat solvent lessened the need for a decision, but money don't last forever so I had to move fast.

I set my laptop up, connected and went searching for all the stories I could find about Collie's arrest and death. There weren't many, and all of them took the attitude the whole thing was his own damn fault. They were tough to read, but I made it through them — mainly because I was looking for names.

And the first one I got was the Right and Honorable Nathaniel Carson Gilbert, III — yes, the son-of-a-bitch who was now running for office. It came from Dean Weller in a tossed-aside comment regarding how hard they'd tried to get Collie out of jail — just a, "We even contacted Judge Gilbert for an expedited arraignment, but we were too late."

That bothered me. It didn't fit into what Ray had told me. I had a notebook with a legal pad in it, so the first question I wrote was, *When did Dean Weller call Judge Gilbert?*

Next was Assistant District Attorney Phillip Stanton. He's one of those sleek sharks in tailored suits who Stairmasters at the gym and exerts total control on his sons and daughter and fucks around on his wife and was aiming for a political career where he'd be in the papers and on the news even more than he already was. He took on the role of chair umpire in the battle to show how Collie deserved what he got. Meaning every chance he got, he stamped in people's brains that Orin had told the cops he was sixteen and that they didn't find out till after the *unfortunate death of Mr. Winston-Royce* that he was really five years older, but that it didn't really matter because it was still rape, even in Texas, since Orin had been coerced into letting himself be abused and on and on. I'd hated him the second I'd seen him on the news, but now I was convinced he's a bad one because he let slip one telling little comment. "You know, these homosexuals need to understand they're just as subject to the law as anyone." I saw him say it during a news conference posted on a local TV news station's site.

The prick.

Of course, that waved a red cape in front of me — as well as a few of the gay blogs and news-sites, though they took the tack it was stupid and insensitive of him to say about a gay man who'd just been murdered. Fact is, most of them saw this as a vague form of gay-bashing, which allowed the blithering idiots with the MSM (mainstream media for those uninitiated into the world of the web) to blow the whole thing off. Oh, there was chatter about calling for an investigation of the matter by the DoJ, but that went nowhere, mainly because the official line never wavered and people began to suspect they were trying to protect a mean manipulative rapist queer's reputation rather than some sweet innocent gay kid who'd been tied to a fence and left to die.

Of course, I got the same idea from the idiot's comment that most other gays had — that them fags think they's better'n the law, an' they don't know when t' shut their damn assholes — but it also didn't jibe with what Ray had said. Because the more I thought about it, the more I came to think that what Ray meant was Collie'd been targeted. For what, I didn't know; maybe it was just for punishment and the guys who did it had gone too far — but that was so totally against the law, it reeked of worse than hypocrisy; it reeked of conspiracy and cover-up.

So I found out who was in charge of the county jail — one Wilbur Nussewald, a nice fat silver-haired gentleman whose eyes were black as coal and whose smirk just dared you to slap it off. His photo was on the sheriff's website under the heading, Deputy Chief of Jail Operations. A one-time deputy sheriff with a couple of incidents involving Latinos under his belt that reeked of good-ol'-boy-racism (which were never prosecuted or even really investigated from what I could tell), he had a profile in the paper when he was promoted that included how he'd been married twenty-five years and had four sons and was a deacon at his church. But I didn't need to read any of that to get an idea of what he was about or even see him on video; I hated him the second I saw his picture. I mean, if you wanted to lay out the meaning of sanctimonious little prick, his image would be the perfect illustration for it.

I did some cross-referencing between Nussewald and Stanton and found out through news reports that they'd worked on at least a dozen cases together when he was still in the *Criminal Investigations Division*, every one of them winding up with a conviction. Now that's not so unusual, as my research quickly proved; it seems that nine times out of ten, if you're accused of a crime, you get convicted. What struck me about it was five of them were drug charges against gay men. And how did I know that, you might ask? They said so in each case.

They actually made certain the fact that these guys were gay was part of the public record, as if that made a difference in the legal aspects or ramifications of it. There went another red cape. A little more investigation showed three of the guys were still in prison and one had died while the guy who'd been busted last had already been paroled — a *former city employee* named Jake Blaine. I decided to track him down after I talked to Tommy.

Or to be honest — after I got Tommy to confirm my growing belief Collie had been targeted *for a hurtin'* (as my grandpa would've said) for no more reason than he was queer. I mean, the evidence I'd accumulated all but screamed that.

I finally crashed about five am and slept till just before nine, the thought of that free breakfast jolting me back into this world before they closed it down. I went full hog — eggs, bacon, hash-browns, toast, pancakes and a couple of pots of coffee as well as a few muffins snuck back to my room; one thing about Texas is you can feed yourself fat in a week, no matter what. I stuffed my belly and read the McPaper and relaxed and readied myself for the day.

Tommy didn't call till almost two, by which time I was convinced he'd been talked out of talking to the fag by his supervisors, though the question of how his supervisors could have

27

known he was calling me never entered my pea-brain. I knew Ray wouldn't have told anybody, and I seriously doubted Tommy would have deliberately trained their *say nothing* guns on himself. Didn't help that I was doing more research and now beginning to think somehow Collie'd been killed because he knew too much. Again, the question of what he might have known and how anything he might know could be of value enough to kill him hadn't entered said pea-brain. All I could see was, everything that lead up to his murder fell into place too neatly, which pointed to him being targeted, and Ray had said Tommy'd call by eleven and he didn't.

I'd forgotten Ray'd also said it would be after he got out of court. Or deliberately deleted it. I dunno. I don't think I was really thinking clearly, yet.

Anyway, Tommy's call did come and he agreed to drop by my hotel room for a face-to-face. I can't tell how trustworthy a person is by their voice, alone; I had to actually see him. Since the airport area catered to impermanent people, I guess he felt no one would notice or care. So after a bit of wary sparring over who I was and what I wanted to do — and me being just as cagey as him with the details — he made a date for seven and I ordered in pasta and a pizza supreme.

The food was delivered, with dessert, and five minutes after the delivery guy was gone, someone knocked on my door. I opened it and saw a chunky, shlubby kind of guy who could easily become a fat version of Ray in thirty years if he didn't start taking better care of himself.

"Tony?" he said, his voice hinting of what my grandmother called the *Lady-Bird-School-Of-Diction.*

"Antony," I said, nodding. "And you're Tommy."

He nodded and entered. He wore a suit in desperate need of a pressing and carried a worn briefcase. His tie was gone (probably vanished the second he was in his car) and the white cotton shirt looked like it had never been ironed. His shoes were cheap, to be nice about it.

"I'm only here 'cause of Uncle Ray," he said as he tossed his briefcase on the bed and dove into the pizza without asking.

"Starving," he muttered through three good bites of the thing. "Was aimin' to grab — sandwich when called you — but shit happens and — "

He swallowed it and I offered him a beer. Shiner Bock. Best fuckin' beer in the whole fucking U-S-of-A. He gulped it down and took another bite.

"Shit, I'm startin' t' feel human, again." He sat in the chair by my laptop. Saw the latest page I was reading — an article posted on a gay site about Collie's death that offered very little additional information. He nodded. "Y'know, this ain't gonna bring him back."

I nodded. "This isn't about that."

"Please don't tell me it's about findin' justice," he moaned. "There's no such thing in this world. There's just luck or chance or fate or whatever the fuck you wanna call it. But justice? That's for text books."

It's funny — but I couldn't read him. Couldn't tell if he was legit or criminal. Which spooked me. So I decided to keep it careful. "I just want to know how this happened. And so quick."

"Why?"

"Closure."

His eyes shot straight at me. "That was the biggest pile of bullshit answer I ever heard come out of anybody, and trust me — I've heard a *lot* of bullshit. Why do you want to know why? An' you better figure I'll know you're bullshittin' me."

Zing — I had his number then. He'd just tested me, and I'd flunked big-time. And it was so fucking obvious, I could have kicked myself. And what did that say? Well — for one thing, he'd let me know he was testing me, so he was one of the good guys.

"Revenge," I said.

"*Vengeance is mine, sayeth the Lord.*"

"Bullshit, right back at you."

"You don't believe in god?"

"I believe in hell, 'cause I'm in it. But heaven and all that?" I just shrugged.

"And you're gonna be an avenger, huh? Who you avengin' yourself on?"

"It's still a work in progress."

"Bullshit meter's goin' up — "

"Bullshit back. I have some names, but I don't know how it all works, yet, so I don't know who's responsible. So it *is* a work in progress."

He nodded. "What's the pasta?"

"Five cheese lasagna with meat marinara."

He smiled, and his whole face changed. "You sure know the way t' a man's heart." He dug into the lasagna like a happy child and accepted a second beer, and sat at the table to eat.

You know, I wasn't hungry until I saw the joy in his face at the prospect of being stuffed. That's when I realized I hadn't eaten since breakfast, that I'd been so obsessed with my research and prepping for Tommy's arrival and putting together what information I'd been able to gather, not even the aroma of the pizza had reminded me of my empty belly. But now I was ravenous, and I helped him finish off a meal that could easily have fed six — twenty, if you lived in Africa.

He chatted beautifully while we munched, and I quickly saw the Texas Twang was affected to throw off the opposition — i.e. the defense. The little snake. What's funny is, his caginess reminded me of that quarterback I fooled around with.

It was this little dance he did before he and I connected, and mainly stemmed from him not wanting anyone to know he was into guys. For some reason — I never was clear as to why, exactly — he'd taken a liking to me but was so low-key about it, even though I've got great gay-dar I didn't pick up on his interest — not until he started swimming with me.

Okay, he didn't really start swimming along with me. It was in October, last year, which can be a rainy month in my parts, and the University didn't have covered tennis courts. Of course, I could've just practiced my Aikido in the main gym on the mats, but I found there was always some asshole who wanted to spar and show off how good he was, and who'd get all pissed off when it turned out I was better, so I dropped that after three times. However, they did have this massive Olympic-style pool where you could do some serious laps, and that was a good counter-point exercise to the jarring on my ankles and knees from the asphalt courts. So on the days I couldn't work the racquet, I'd hop down, slip into my black boxer-cut Speedo and dive in — and after a week, he started showing up.

Now I knew who he was. In Texas, if you're a half-assed-decent quarterback who's even moderately attractive, you're treated like a god. And this guy — I mean, he wasn't *bad*-looking and he did make a couple of saves in some major games; he just had that beefy, square-necked, big-toothed kind of thing going on that's never been my fantasy.

At least, it wasn't until I was taking a breather by the starting platform and saw him pop out of the changing room in a pair of simple black board shorts with a set of white stripes whipping up the leg and connecting at the drawstring. And noticed how slim his waist was. And how solid and well-proportioned his legs were. And that he had the softest brown down whispering over his chest and washboard abs and down to where those low, *low*-riding shorts rode. And how the water clung the material to a well-shaped ass as he showered up. And how he cast a quick, intensely uncertain glance my way just before he dove into the pool three lanes down from me. And how that sent a little quiver up my spine.

There was an adult swim class taking place at the opposite corner of the pool, and a couple of other students and teachers were doing their swim-thing, too, so I kicked away from the wall and did an underwater glide for a while and watched him stroke his way to the end of his lane. Watched his powerful legs kick in perfect unison with his strokes. Watched his torso swivel and his arms pull and his chest gleam and dance through the bubbly turbulence of his movements. Watched those shorts keep threatening to let loose and actually prayed they would.

I took a breath and kept my underwater glide going. Saw him reach the foot of the pool and kick around and under the water, his arms stretched beautifully before him. He looked over at me and smiled then got back to stroking through the water. And I got that tingle in my balls that said, *Yep, he's for the asking.*

So I slipped up to the surface and finished my lap with a nice slow butterfly, during which he made another two laps. Then when

I knew he was nearing the starting platforms, I got out, grabbed my towel and dried myself off in a slow, languid manner. I never looked at him, but I could hear him stop, wait, then splash into another lap. I headed into the locker room.

The showers were of the open-style variety, no stalls or privacy to be had, and I was under one of them when I heard him return. Heard his locker close. And finally saw him saunter in, a towel wrapped erotically around his hips. His muscles were pumped and his tits looked brutally inviting — all perky and brown and cold — and when the towel came off, he revealed a nice white ass with a board-shorts tan line on his legs, but his dick was facing the wall.

At first.

I was turning off my water when he turned to let the shower pound his back and revealed a nice average helmet of a dick caught in a nice average hard-on. I'm sure he thought it was the biggest erection since Adam, but at least it wasn't tiny. I smiled, looked straight at him and headed back to my locker.

I was almost there when I felt him grab me and yank me into a side room that turned out to be a sauna. I yelped so he put a hand over my mouth and crushed my face against the wall with his body as he locked the door. I could feel his dick between my legs and he was holding me tight and pinching one of my tits and even though it wasn't very comfortable, I was getting turned on.

Then he started grinding his hips against my ass and whispered, "Ya wanna? Ya wanna?"

I twisted and spun him around and flopped him onto a bench and lay on top of him, crushing my own dick against his and getting the biggest surprised look I'd ever seen (I mean, he did outsize me by a good three inches and forty pounds, all of it muscle) as I said, "Not like that. Like this."

Then I licked his tits and trailed my tongue down his hair to his pubes and danced through them enough to get him as big as he was gonna get then took him in my mouth and began pumping. I shifted around so he could get to my dick, and he began slurping all over it and my balls and wrapped one arm around my waist to hold me in place as the other groped my ass. I returned the favor, going so far as to probe his hole with my fingers, which made him shudder and fire his load and stop sucking on me as he grunted and fought to keep from crying out as he shot over and over like he'd never done it, before. Then he lay back and absently stroked me into ejaculating. It wasn't great, but the fact is, it was better than his blow-job. Let's just say — he hadn't quite figured out what to do with his teeth, yet.

Soon as I was done, he whispered, "Wait five minutes," and left. It looked like he hopped back into the showers for a quick rinse then down to his locker to dress. I stayed in the sauna, sweating like crazy, and when I came out, he was gone. I rinsed off, too, and dressed and went to Media Crit, a bit let down.

A week later, the whole scene repeated but in an easier, much better fashion. And I started recalling how often I'd seen him around campus — walking by just as I left a lab or eating at the same time as me or showing up at the same movie as me — and how once we'd been jammed together during a free concert at the refectory and I'd thought for a second he was feeling me up but he'd apologized and moved on so I'd forgotten about it. And I finally realized in his clumsy yet subtle way he was sending out the signal he was interested.

Now it wasn't bad sex with him; I showed him some tricks on how to give good head — especially after chewing peppermint gum, which made his whole body clench and quiver with delight — and I did let him fuck me after that awkward first try. He even let me fuck him — and believe me, I took my time and felt his glorious ass up and kissed and probed and oiled him up to the point he was almost screaming before I slipped on the condom and slipped inside and did my slow, steady strokes as he lay on his back, legs in the air, hands pinching his own tits while I kept hold of his hips and when he came, it shot straight into his and my hair. Hell, we might have become a steady thing — but then his schedule made it hard to find time to be together and I met Collie and dropped him, and the next year he was doing second-string for a team that many thought would be in the Super Bowl (they missed it in the playoffs, but not for lack of trying on his part; he turned out to be a good ball-tosser in more ways than one). Now he's married and already has his second kid coming, so he'd have dumped me soon, anyway.

Anyway, that's a bit how it was with Tommy — whose last name shall remain unmentioned. Lots of subtle interplay with words and meanings and indications that could be explained away as signifying nothing should anyone pay attention or try to pin him down, but I got enough out of him to infuriate me.

Collie was arrested at 8:14. He called Dean Weller at home by 8:49, in the middle of them booking him. Weller and his attorney got on a conference call with Judge Gilbert at 9:05 asking for an expedited bail hearing, since Gilbert was the supervising justice of that area. He refused, even though it was pointed out to him that Collie had no criminal history and Orin was an adult, not underage. Dean Weller went so far as to have Orin's transcript faxed over to the judge's office to back it up, but the fucking judge wouldn't even let Collie be put in segregation until his arraignment. Apparently they argued about it for a good ten minutes before the judge hung up on them. So they called the DA and the county sheriff. Both men assured them it was just county jail, not state prison, and Collie would be fine — and refused to do anything.

Well — Collie was fine, at first. Apparently he told the prisoners in his holding cell he forgot to pay an outstanding traffic ticket, and they had a good laugh. But sometime during lunch, word spread he was really in for raping a little boy. The surveillance cameras in the corridor caught the beginning of the confrontation at 1:07, moments after the last lunch trash had been picked up. By all accounts, the attack lasted forty-six minutes.

The guards didn't find him till 3:12.

The coroner's initial report found if he'd been tended to immediately, he might have survived. His coma was brought on by bleeding on the brain that caused swelling and finally brought about irreparable damage. That was revised thanks to Stanton's objections so that all *speculative findings* were omitted, and that's the report that was released to the press.

In short, Stanton had deliberately made it seem like Collie's death was something nobody could have prevented.

I actually went cold with fury. Started shivering from it. And the room threatened to go all white on me — my danger sign. I pulled on a hoodie to try and stop it, but I just got colder.

"Know what's really fun about it?" Tommy asked, watching me the whole time. "They found out one of the rapists is HIV positive. They decided he was at the head of the line, so we told all the fuckers they might get it, too."

"Collie wasn't — "

"I know. But Stanton got it kept quiet because then they'd say he gave it to them — "

"He didn't!"

"I know! It's in his blood work. But the press don't give a shit about details. Facts are boring, so all they care about is the myth and the scandal; that's what sells papers and brings eyes to your newscasts."

"A real optimist."

"A real realist. And disgusted with it all."

"Nice of Stanton to worry about that."

"He had too many lies juggling to worry about telling the truth, on top of it. Truth is, I don't think he cared one way or the other. Nussewald just didn't want it getting around that men were being raped and given HIV in his jail, then taking it home for their wives and girlfriends to catch, so he called in a favor."

I looked out the window. It was dark and raining. I finally realized November was gone. And it was almost midnight. My twenty-first birthday had passed and I hadn't even thought about it. I was now completely, totally and absolutely legal for anything I wanted to do, and I was as lost as lost could be. No plans for what to do next. No thoughts even beginning to tickle my brain. Just a void mixed with total incomprehension at how I could have arrived at this place at this time.

Tommy rose to gather his things. "Time I was headed out."

"Court tomorrow?"

"Not on Saturday. And all my work's caught up."

"It's the weekend. I forgot."

"Yep — T-G-I-F."

"You have plans?"

"Just brush up my resume. Set out feelers. Not the best time of year to do it, but — " He shrugged.

I looked at him. "So you *are* quitting." He gave me another shrug. "Tommy — who spread the word that Collie was arrested for child molestation?"

He hesitated just for a fraction of a second before he said, "I dunno. We think it was a guard, but — "

"Bullshit meter's going. You're holding out on me."

He glared at me. "I told you more'n anybody should ever know. Be happy with that."

I didn't push it. You may think I should have, but Tommy was on my side, right then, and I didn't feel the need to make him an enemy, yet. I just shrugged and nodded and smiled and said, "You're right. Sorry."

"Yeah, well — it's been a long day. Rough day. Uncle Ray told me how he found you. Get some rest."

Again, I nodded and smiled and said, "Thanks for coming."

We shook hands and he left, then I cleaned up his mess — which was all over the room, it seemed. Which was good, because it gave me a moment to collect my thoughts.

Once the trash was done, I sat by my laptop and looked over my notes and went online, again. I'd finally realized I was going about this all the wrong way, and Tommy is the one who'd shown me. He had been leading me to believe that Collie's death probably came from a series of miscalculations that sprang from a group of middle-aged men's prejudices and who were now just trying to cover their asses so they could appear to be in control of a part of the world that was in chaos. It was horrible, what happened, but it stemmed from stupidity and shortsightedness, not deliberate intention. And I'd actually been hoping it was that.

But it was all bullshit. Tommy wasn't quitting because of a systemic fuck-up. Those happen in every business everywhere in the world. They aren't something you can run from, ever. No, he was quitting because he knew Collie'd been targeted and the ADA, the head of the jails and that fucking judge were all in on it. He'd seen something, somewhere, that shook him to his core and made him want to just back away from the cold growling evil, and the fact that he felt he'd told me enough told me a thousand times more than if he'd said that's all there is to it.

So now I knew Collier Winston-Royce's murder was deliberate and done in such a way as to hide it and I was going to find out why and by whom. And then — then I'd become the avenging devil that made that son-of-a-bitch wish to God he'd never been born.

And God himself, coming down in his chariot with his legions of angels, could not have kept me from doing it.

— THREE —

That's not to say God didn't try. For some reason, I started my investigation by tracking down Jake Blaine, the gay former city employee who'd been sent up for drugs. It wasn't easy to find him, and in the process of looking I started to see just how fucked up our society is as regards people convicted of a crime.

The news stories I could find about Jake were the usual crap handed out by the authorities. He was arrested for DUI and a few grams of coke were found in his car. He claimed the drugs weren't his, refused a plea bargain and was sent to jail for four years. He made early parole only because Texas prisons were getting overcrowded and the budget crises kept them from funding any new ones, so the Prison Board was releasing those convicted of non-violent crimes soon as they came up for review.

Of course, the idiots in the Legislature made a huge fuss over *the practice of releasing dangerous criminals back into society* so they forced through another appropriations bill authorizing more prisons and stole the money from silly things like health care for children and job training programs and aid to senior citizens, just like California had done under their Repugnican governor. I actually began to appreciate Texas' idea that politicians should not be allowed to meet too often so as to minimize the damage they could do, especially since half the people who ran for office in this state would qualify as mental patients in any other state, and every damned one of them was a Republican; I mean, yeah — the Democrats could be just as bad, but their illness could be controlled with anti-psychotic drugs.

Anyway, Jake got out and dropped out of sight. No listing for him in any of the phone directories. Nothing in the way of a location came up online. I was able to find out his parole officer's name (don't ask how because it involved some flirty talk with a female type person and a fifty) and that he was located downtown near city hall, an area undergoing a lot of reconstruction to make it "purty-er" but was really just a quasi-legal way of lining the pockets of a few of the mayor's campaign contributors since the work they were doing was as crap as crap could be. But that meant Jake was still in the area — or at least, he should be. So I decided to set up a little bit of surveillance — the kind where you sit and wait for something to happen.

By this point, I'd rented a furnished room near campus and had a wireless stick for my laptop. Got both the day after I talked to Tommy. It was too late for me to get back into my dorm room, so I wound up in a corner unit in a little u-shaped complex that was half-brick, half-wood and had an oval pool in the middle of it with nearly dead plants for decoration. I was upstairs in the back, had a cheap-assed bed, some bookshelves, a chest for my clothes, a table and chairs, and my bike to get around on. I considered keeping Collie's Land Rover to drive, but that could be considered auto theft so I returned it to the condo soon as I was moved into my new abode.

Thing was, I really could've used the car. December was being especially wet and cold, this year — probably to make up for all the drought we'd been going through — so a bike was not the best mode of transportation. But I didn't want to use the money I'd scammed to buy a clunker. Meaning my surveillance would include bus rides and finding some way to stand around out of the rain and watch the parole officer's office and hope that Jake showed up.

I found his picture attached to an article about Texas' crappy parole system — one that fought for years to continue denying paroles based on anything but the guidelines laid down by the Legislature, then told the few convicts they did release what they had to do keep their parole viable, then made damn sure they had no way of doing it. They were being sued left and right by them *damn libruls* and never mind it's the board that wasn't following the law; that's just for people who're dumb enough, poor enough or minority enough to be convicted of a crime. It was sickening.

Anyway, I found a nice little coffee shop halfway down the block and across the street. It only had a Christmas tree in a back corner for the season's decoration so I could live with that, seeing as how I was feeling *anything* but Christmas-y. I set myself up in front with my laptop and drank *way* too much coffee and kept searching for more info on the others involved as I kept an eye out and it seemed to take forever — but it paid off. After a week, I caught a glimpse of a guy who could be Jake entering the building. I was in the middle of a sandwich, so I finished eating, closed up shop and sauntered across to the entrance to await his exit, taking my time since I knew this was a place where the workers did nothing in a rush or even with much accuracy.

It had just finished drizzling and more of the same was promised, and I hoped it would happen. We'd been in drought for so long, I'd forgotten how much I liked the rain, liked the smell of it and how clean the city seemed after a shower. Besides, I had a Guinness umbrella I'd bought during the Brewery Storehouse Tour collapsed in my backpack, and that helped me keep liking it — and offset watching the sad and angry and worried and defeated men and women wander in and out of that big, stone, oppressive place.

I was outside just long enough for a guard to start paying attention to me when Jake roared out, pissed. And I finally got a good look at him — and I nearly stopped breathing. Thick dark hair cropped close and clean. Piercing black eyes under lush eyebrows that reminded you of an eagle searching for its next meal. A face sculpted into something that felt like it was moving forward, and that made you wish you could just gaze upon it, with a neat goatee to emphasize his slices of lips. His short, tight, powerful body was barely covered by a black t-shirt, light jacket and form-fitting cargo pants, with wisps of dark hair whispering over what tan skin you could see. He wore Doc Martens 9-eyes and the edge of a tattoo peeked from under the jacket's collar. Couple all of that with the padding gait of an angry tom-cat, and I could've watched him walk down the street and been content — a contentment that would last only so long as I didn't try to pet him, because while the picture he made was gorgeous, it was also filled with warning.

However, justice for Collie demanded I hurry after him.

He reached a bus stop and lit up a cigarette. I put on my most earnest face and said in a vaguely quaky voice, "Jake?"

He glanced at me then looked away.

"You're Jake Blaine, right?"

I wasn't going away, so he glared at me and growled in a low rumble of a voice, "Who're you?"

"Antony St. Lazarre."

I offered my hand. He just looked at me — and yeah — his expression was breathtakingly sexy, but it was also like he'd just as soon kill me as kiss me, and it caught me in a way I'd never imagined possible. I wanted to — I actually wanted to soothe him. Calm him. Hell, comfort him. I sat on the bench, never taking my eyes off him.

"You don't know me, but you do know Deputy Sheriff Wilbur Nussewald and ADA Phillip Stanton. I'd like to talk to you about them."

"You a reporter?"

I shook my head. Something told me, don't lie to this guy or you'll lose him.

"Can't we go someplace to talk?" Man, that sounded lame when I said it. So second-rate Hollywood.

He looked away. "I have to be home in an hour. Bus ride takes thirty-five minutes, if it ain't late, and I have to be on that route."

"How'll they know if you're late?"

Still not looking at me, he lifted his left pants leg to reveal a monitor around his ankle, resting atop the Doc Martens. He cleared his throat. "You got a car?"

"No."

"Then talk fast. I just saw the bus top that hill down the street."

My inner voice was telling me, *He's okay*, so I jumped in with both feet and asked, "Can I ride with you?"

He looked back at me, glanced me over and shrugged. And I finally noticed — well, I realized — his eyes were so walled in, it would take a sledge-hammer to break them down. And it made me sad. Here's this guy who's just a few years older than me, and it seems like he's already lived too long a life.

The bus stopped. We got on. It drove away. He sat in the first seat he found that was completely open. I sat next to him. He gazed out the window, seeming to pay me and the half-dozen other passengers no attention.

I wasn't sure where to begin, so started with the usual bullshit. "How're things going?" He just snorted an answer. "Is it hard, dealing with that — ?" I pointed to the ankle monitor. Got a shrug in answer. "How much longer do you have under — ?"

"Five months." He still didn't look at me.

"Jake," I started then jumped in, again. "I think you're innocent. I think Nussewald and Stanton set you up."

"No fuckin' shit?"

"I think they did the same thing to a friend of mine."

He looked at me, his black eyes drilling deep into my soul. "Friend?" I just looked at him. He nodded and looked away. "Motherfuckers." I waited; he finally asked, "What happened?"

"He was arrested. Then raped. And beaten to death."

Now he focused on me. "He was in GP?" I must have looked confused because he added, "General population."

I shook my head. "He was in a holding cell, with maybe a dozen guys."

"Guards didn't break it up?"

They said they didn't hear anything."

"End of the hall. Holding cell six."

"Yeah. How did you — ?"

The look he cast me shut me up. Holy fucking shit.

"Who found him?" he asked, his voice near growling.

"One of the guards. When he didn't show for arraignment."

"What excuse did they use to bust him?"

"He molested a little boy. But that *little boy* was 21 years old and lying and — "

"So? That baggie of coke they found didn't even have my fingerprints or DNA on it. But here I am." He watched the passing scenery, for a moment. "You know the reason they gave for — for doing ME in that room? I narc'd out a bro'. So I was force fed some chocolate for nearly an hour — all for bullshit. I didn't even know any blacks."

"How could they — ?"

"You ever try and fight off five guys?" He wasn't looking at me, anymore; he was staring at something that was a thousand yards away. "Took me three weeks to get to where I could shit without blood coming out. Then I wound up at Cabrillo Flats. Found out real quick it'd be an ongoing thing if I didn't work it right." He showed me his left hand. Its knuckles were covered with small scars and discoloration. "Takes a lot to convince most assholes that your asshole just ain't worth the trouble. So I signed up with a skinhead and started pumping iron — and that fixed it so nobody'd want to mess with me."

He rubbed his hand and leaned back, giving me a sensual look that would burn right through you. Without thinking, I glanced at his crotch. Saw the outline of his penis. He saw me scope him out, smiled, and it was actually a lovely sweet smile, then scooted down, lay one hand over the back of the seat and cocked his other against the window and looked straight ahead.

"Fill me in," he whispered, his voice still growling.

I lay my right hand atop his left leg. It was as solid as steel. I ran my fingers up it to his crotch. Played with the outline of his dick through the jeans. Just like he wanted. And I told him everything I'd learned about Collie's death.

I was done by the time we reached Jake's stop. I got out with him and followed him home, walking behind him, not from any deliberate decision but because I liked watching how his ass moved when he walked. And he knew it.

He led me up a street with no sidewalks that was lined with deteriorating homes and half-dead trees. Dogs barked at us from the safety of their fences, and they were the only sound. We entered an old clapboard house surrounded by weeds and overgrowth, nakedly sitting up on cedar blocks, its front taken up completely by a screened-in porch. White paint clung to most of the wood and the roof looked like it needed some serious repair. He took me through a swinging screen door into a shabby living room that could have used new wallpaper and something to hide the crap furniture.

"Home!" he yelled. No one answered. "Gramma must be out."

"This is your grandmother's home?"

He just led me into a back bedroom. It had everything my one room had along with a ceiling fan. Nothing looked like it came from a better place than Goodwill.

He whipped off his jacket to reveal more of a colorful tattoo of sweeping lines and odd symbols mixed with Celtic runes running from halfway up his left bicep to slice around to his neck; the rest of it was hidden by the t-shirt.

"Gramma's the only one who'd take me in," he said. "Give me an address. I'm confined to this house and the route to the PO's office. If I want to go anywhere else, I have to get permission a week in advance. They told me to get a job — but I can't go on interviews without permission and that takes up to ten days, and interviewers want to see you that day or the next. But if I don't get a job, time gets tacked on my parole."

"What'll you do?"

"A guy I used to be with owns a restaurant, and he put me on, so I got that route added to the places I can travel. Times I can be out. But it's only part time and he's gettin' tired of always having to fax over my schedule."

"Sounds rough," I said.

He shrugged and flopped on the bed, lay back and looked at me — and I caught a flash of the happy young man he'd once been. His right hand trailed down his body, starting at the back of his head then slipping around his neck to trail his fingers straight down to the top of his pants. His t-shirt had ridden up so I could see dark hair feathering across his lower belly. He looked like something out of an online gay porn site — the image of the college guy just before he rips off his clothes to reveal his amazingly built little ol' self.

Okay, time to pay for him letting me question him, and it was to be up front. And to be perfectly honest, I did not mind. It'd been so many weeks since my last time — with Collie — hell, since I'd even jacked off — and suddenly need overpowered any sort of sadness or guilt or moral indignation at this *quid pro quo* crap. I set my laptop down, knelt between his legs, ran my hands up his thighs and slowly, slowly undid his fly. He wore simple white Jockeys that bulged where his dick was struggling to get through. Being a kind-hearted person, I released it from its confinement.

His dick rose and seemed to look at me as if to scope me out then slowly settled back across his belly. It was lovely and thick and I couldn't help but stroke it. And lick it. And nuzzle the thick pubes surrounding it. And play with the hairs on his solid thighs. And make him damn near crazy with want — to the point where he was squirming and tensing every muscle in his body before I slipped my lips over the head of his dick and began to swirl around it with my tongue.

His legs and ass clenched and he reached down to grab me by the hair and hold my head in place and begin to fuck my mouth. I let him. And circled his legs with my arms and still used my hands to play with the hair on his thighs. He was dead quiet through it all; in fact, the only sound I could hear was from my slurping and the bed's light jiggling.

The feeling of him in my mouth was so completely different from Collie. It was harder. More insistent. Less loving and extremely wanton. Plus he was a bit bigger than Collie and his head was fatter. It was almost a challenge to keep going without choking or pulling away — well, trying to pull away. But it also felt — human and real and something I needed to do and I didn't want it to end.

Soon he was shoving harder and harder and deeper and deeper until I felt him fire into my mouth and he held my head there so I couldn't get away and I had no choice but to swallow and he kept going and going until I began to gag — and then he pulled my head back and released me and just lay there, spent.

I fell into a sitting position and leaned against the bed, brutally confused. And brutally aroused. That had been the most erotic face-fuck I'd ever had, and I realized I was close to ejaculating in my briefs from it. And *that* made me feel so completely disloyal to Collie, I nearly wept. He hadn't even been dead two months and here I was, almost brought off by servicing another guy.

Except —

I'd done it to extract information, so it wasn't sex we'd just had; it was more like a financial transaction. It wouldn't be sex until I fucked him and he fucked me. And my erection came from the understanding that I'm still a young man used to doing it just about every night, so small wonder I got hard, I'd been deprived so long. And those lies soothed my inner turmoil, a bit.

After a few moments, Jake whispered, "Tone — you give him blow jobs like that?"

"Antony."

"Tone," and his voice was harsher, filled with warning. "Did you give him blow jobs like that?"

I finally answered, "Collie? Yes. Sometimes."

"Did you fuck each other?"

"A lot."

"Did you love him?"

My heart just about tore in half. "A lot."

"Okay." And the growling was gone from his voice.

I looked at him — and the picture he made was hot, to say the least — his pants around his knees, his Jockeys halfway down his thighs, his dick still rich and full and sweeping gently to one side, the mass of pubes fencing it in, his chest still pumping deep and fast, his arms curled over his head. He was staring at the ceiling and seemed in control — but he was near tears.

I crawled up onto the bed with him. Ran my hand over his belly. Felt the hairs tickle my skin. Slipped his t-shirt up over his tits. Traced my fingers over them. Licked them. Kissed them. Sucked on them.

His hand circled my head and rubbed through my hair.

"Nussewald's so dumb, he couldn't order a number one meal at *Mickey D*'s," he said, finally. "He got where he is 'cause he knows how to kiss ass and play politics. If somebody wanted to hurt your guy, he'd carry the message — arrange for the guard to set it up — but he didn't make the decision to tell 'em he's in there for a kid. He's a dumb fuck, but even he knows what that means."

I lay beside him. Played with the hair on his chest. "So that leaves Stanton and Judge Gilbert."

"Stanton hates fags. He hated being in the same room with me

46

when he offered his plea deal. Wore this cross pin on his lapel and looked at me with this smirk — like I was scum."

"I got that impression about him. What about Gilbert?"

"Dunno. I had a different judge. Rosales. He didn't even listen to my defense. He went with what Nussewald said, like it was gospel, all 'cause the prick's a Deputy Chief."

I trailed my hand down his belly to his navel. His hair felt soft and comfortable, I let spread my fingers out to lay in the soft field of brown. He squirmed.

"Didn't you have a jury?"

"Yeah. Twelve straight middle-aged idiots who did what the judge told 'em to."

"Wait — you said Nussewald was Deputy Chief?" He nodded. "But he wasn't made that till he took over the jail."

"So?"

"So that makes him a desk jockey; why's he out arresting people?"

"He said I hit his car, which was bullshit — he swerved into me. Then he said I smelled like beer and refused to do a field sobriety test, so he busted me and that's when he — as he puts it — found drugs on me. Motherfucker planted 'em."

"Why?"

"Dunno. I mean, yeah — I was arguing over the wreck, but hell, I was in my lane and he was over the white line and — and it was so bogus to start with, I was screamin' loud about it, so it's like he had me nailed before I wound up in jail."

"Has it happened to anybody else?"

"Who cares?"

"It shows a pattern of abuse."

"The whole fucking justice system's a pattern of abuse."

"Did you file a complaint?"

"Tone — grow up. He's a Deputy Chief and I'm a city grunt." The growl was back. "Why you askin' all these questions, anyway?" And he looked at me with a funny, cock-eyed *what the fuck* kind of expression.

"I'm trying to figure it out. Nothing adds up."

"It ain't meant to." He rolled on top of me. I could feel his dick was hard, again. "You think too fuckin' much. I think I'll take your mind off it."

He groped for my belt buckle. He thought he was going to fuck me. I pushed him away.

"I already got you off, once."

He slammed back on me, grabbed my arms and twisted them behind me and managed to say, "Don't be a fuckin' tease," before I slung him halfway across the room. He landed hard against a chest of drawers and looked at me with death in his eyes — and BAM! He was back on me, laughing like a freak. He slammed a good hold of my crotch and squeezed, and I saw stars from the pain, then I found myself face down across the bed with him yanking my pants down with one hand as the other crushed against the back of my neck and his dick rubbing between my legs as if preparing for the final plunge.

I twisted and we tussled a little before I could shove him aside. I fell to the floor and scrambled back to get ready for another assault — and noticed he was leaning against the bed, laughing. He was out of breath and had to struggle to keep from choking. His pants and briefs were around his ankles, his t-shirt was torn in half and his dick was sticking straight up and throbbing red and his legs were beautiful and covered with dark swirling hair and I dropped to my knees, breathing just as hard, and realized my pants were halfway off, my briefs torn, my ass just as bare as his and I'd almost been raped — but my dick just as hard and for some stupid reason, I found myself joining in his laughter.

Motherfucker just wanted to see how far he could go with me, and now that he knew, everything was cool. Little shit.

He leaned over, grabbed the back of my neck and pulled me down to lie on the floor next to him and kissed me, long and deep and gentle. A beautiful kiss of equals in communion and love and desire and need and everything you could even think a kiss could be as he pulled me close and wrapped his arms around me and just held me. Now I knew — he liked how I could defend myself. So for a moment, just a moment, nothing existed but Jake and me lying on the floor, entwined like lovers.

Like Collie and I had once been.

BAM — I started to bawl. I buried my head in his embrace and shook with sobs. He just held me, stroking my hair, letting me finish.

I finally calmed down and he kissed me, again, and said, "It's happened to other guys. The guards know; they have to. Same thing — same holding room — over and over. Word goes out. The guy gets grabbed. The guys who don't join in stand around to keep it hidden. Your guy's the only one I know died from it."

"His name was Collier — Winston — Royce."

"What was he like?" His voice was so gentle.

"Beautiful. Big and happy and — I called him Collie, but he was more like a Golden Retriever."

"Opposite of me."

"Yeah — you — you're sort of a Min-Pin, all jerky nerves and fussiness."

He swatted my butt. "Asshole."

I looked at him. "Collie was older than you — almost forty. Taught creative writing at the university. And that little fuck, Orin, killed him over getting a *C* and — " My voice trailed close to tears, again.

Jake drew his fingers over one of my eyebrows. "Orin. Weird name. I had a run-in with one. Sort of."

What? "Was his last name Tedesco?"

"No, what was it? Willingham or something crap like that. His mother drove home one of the city cars and she wrecked it. Well, just a fender-bender but — "

"What do you mean?"

"I scheduled transportation for city employees. Who needed a driver, who got a car to drive, that kind of crap."

"When'd you start working for the city?"

"Straight out of high school. Just three days a week, but they brought me on full time after a couple months. Why?"

"You don't seem that old."

"Twenty-five next month. How old you think I was?"

"Twenty."

He rolled on top of me, smirking. "That'll get me going, again."

I grabbed him by his naked ass and flipped him under me. "Careful what you wish for."

He laughed — his face breaking into something absolutely joyous — then he kicked off his jeans and wrapped both his arms and his legs around me to hold me in place.

"What the fuck is it with you, man? I never felt so easy with anybody so quick before."

"I'm a nice guy."

"Yeah, like a coyote, maybe. Fun to look at but don't scratch the ear the wrong way."

I laughed, remembering that's what I'd thought about him. I nuzzled the side of his face and whispered, "For you — I'll play beta-dog."

He whispered his lips over my ear. "Promise? Promise?"

I just held him tighter and asked, "What happened to car-crash lady?"

"She tried to sneak it in but I noticed and made her fill out the forms. Word was, she got bawled out by her boss for doing it; she wasn't supposed to take a car home. They wanted her to pay for the damage."

"Did she?"

"Dunno." He nuzzled my neck. "I got busted a week later and lost the job. Not that I cared about that. It was shit work."

He was getting going, again; his dick riding up my belly and causing mine to do the same. I moved back, stood up and pulled my clothes together. I wasn't ready to take this to the next level.

He lay there, watching me and giving off the vibe of unbridled sex the way his legs were akimbo and his briefs and jeans hung onto one ankle and his torn t-shirt drifted away from his chest to show off his lovely pecs and his dick curled back over his pubes and across the whispery hair on his belly to give an elegant line down to his low, loose balls that all but screamed, *I'll make you weep for joy*. It took everything I had to tuck myself in and zip up my pants — and it must have been obvious that I was shaking, because he gave me his sweet smile and leaned back with his hands under his head.

"I like that you don't shave," he said with a deep breath. "That

50

skinhead I was with didn't have a hair on his body and I never got used to it."

"Have — have you had a guy since you got out?" He looked away. Meaning, No. "Jake, what happened to you was shit. Maybe worse than what happened to Collie, because he — he can't be hurt anymore while you — you're gonna hurt your whole life." He closed his eyes. "That's not right. And it makes me wonder — how many other guys has this happened to? And how many more it will happen to? And wonder how many of them'll be because they got sideswiped by some guy named Orin?"

"What d'you mean?"

"It's not that common a name."

He sat up and pulled his briefs back on, not looking at me. "You wanna ask 'em?"

I nearly dropped to the floor. "You know who they are?"

He shook his head. "I just know who knows."

— FOUR —

Turned out the guy Jake knew who knew worked at the county jail — this short, husky, round-faced dude named Enrique who had a wife, seven kids, a classy Ford pickup pimped out with *way* too much silver trim, a permanent smile (even when he was pissed off) and a dick that didn't care whose lips were on it so long as his beady eyes were closed. He gave me the once over when I met him, and I was afraid he'd want me to pay for his info in the same way I had Jake's — but then Jake smacked his ass and growled, "He's mine, motherfucker," and that was that.

It was a week later and we were at Jake's grandmother's house, again — a woman who always seemed to be out or away someplace — and the moment Enrique sauntered through the door, kitchen uniform still on, Jake had a Negra Modelo in his hand and a seat ready before a table of chips, guac', salsa, chili con queso and tortillas. Enrique's smile expanded as he sat in the place of honor — an overstuffed lounge chair covered with a light blanket to hide the tears in the upholstery — and filled a paper plate with so much food, I feared it would give way.

The first words I heard him say were "Jake, vato, you lookin' good. Put on some meat, vato," in a voice that held more than a hint of Spanish as his first language.

I had to admit, Jake did look damn good — tight jeans and wife-beater, his tattoo seeming to be even more evident. He wore cheap flip-flops and no belt so the jeans rode low.

"I've lost weight, asshole," Jake sneered back. "Tryin' to trim down."

By this point, Enrique was already piling on the food. He smirked back and said, "Don't lose too much, vato. Stats say most guys like you wind up back inside, an' more muscle you got..."

He shrugged.

"I'm not going back inside, motherfucker," Jake snarled. "I'm just waiting for the day when I'm released from parole and can get the hell out of here."

"Get your own place, again?" I asked, trying to become part of the conversation.

"Get the fuck out of this country," Jake said.

Enrique looked at him, confused. "You can do that with a record?"

"You can if you got dual citizenship."

"You ain't American?"

"Blaine's my mother's maiden name. She's American, my father's Persian and lives in Paris, and I have an uncle in Copenhagen. My birth name's Jacob Darya-Bandari. See my tatt?" He pulled the strap down to reveal it, in full. "That's *Control* written in Farsi. Soon as my parole's up, I'm heading over. As Jacob. See where I can land."

"I don't get it," I said. "Don't Stanton and them know about this?"

"They never checked. Mom registered me under her name when I started school. She didn't want kids to make fun of me. Got my Social Security number under that name, too. When I turned eighteen, my dad got me a passport in Iran; he saw how crazy this country was gettin' after 9/11 and wanted me able to leave, if I needed to. I thought it was dumb so got my own for the US using my American name. Who knew?"

"What can you do there?"

Enrique eyed Jake. "Dude, you ain't showed him your shit? I thought you said he's yours."

"He is, motherfucker, and if you fuckin' touch him, I'll fuckin' cut that fuckin' eyedropper you call a fuckin' dick off your fuckin' body and ram it up your fuckin' ass. You fuckin' got me?"

Enrique laughed and kept eating.

Jake looked at me and sighed then went into his bedroom. He came out a moment later with a large portfolio, laid it on the dining room table and let me look through it. Enrique sauntered over to take a view, his plate sagging.

"Don't drop that shit on my stuff," Jake warned. Enrique held back.

What I saw were elegant graphite and conte sketches of people's faces, bodies, hands, done in a near-Manga style, with a few watercolor images thrown in. Well-built men two steps short of superhero-style. Sleek females with full breasts and trim waists but not the monstrous exaggerations most comics have. Good sharp positions without them being ridiculous. What I especially liked were his faces — the detailed expressions despite there not being a lot of detail — sort of Yaoi without it being that simplistic. He was good — hell, he was great.

"This is all since I made parole," he said, slinging an arm over my shoulders in comradeship. "I lost the work I'd done — my portfolio — after I was busted. They tore my joint to shreds and it vanished."

"Putos pendejos."

"¡No me diga!" Jake replied then turned to me. "I had some good stuff. Professional. But being in prison for two years — I couldn't work on it so all this crap is practice. When I feel like I'm good, again — when I feel like I'm safe — I'll start in on it, serious. Maybe I'll start with you."

"My face?" He smiled, glanced me over and shrugged. Meaning more than just my face. I blushed, flattered, then nodded and said, "They're beautiful, but there's no anger in these. There's anger in you."

He smiled. "Wait'll you see the story I write. For my graphic novel. I deliberately kept the anger out of this bunch so if my PO happens to see 'em, he'll be dumb-ass enough to think I'm all fine and dandy with the bullshit they pulled on me." He closed the portfolio. "My uncle's a graphic artist in Copenhagen. Works all over Europe. He said he'd bring me on, and he don't care I'm queer."

"But your folks do?" I asked.

He took in a deep breath. "My mother has a condo downtown, six blocks from the PO's office. Here's where I live. My dad? He's sorry he got me the passport."

"Motherfuckers," Enrique muttered.

"¡Oy!" Jake's eyes let him know not to ever say that, again — not about his parents.

Enrique shrugged in answer then turned to me. "So what you wanna know 'bout jail that Jake can't tell you?"

I shot a glance at Jake. I'd thought he already told the guy what I wanted. I downed some beer and turned to Enrique.

"You know the man who was killed a couple months back?" He nodded. "The same thing happened to Jake." He shrugged. I took a moment, figured he's someone *not* to be completely trusted so kept it limited to, "Who else has it happened to?"

Enrique filled his mouth with more food, chewed on it and swallowed it with half a bottle of the Negra M. He strolled back to the lounge chair, sat and began filling his plate, again. Without looking at me, he asked, "What you two up to?"

"I just want closure," I said, then quickly added, "I've talked to someone in the DA's office, done lots of research and — and Jake's told me what he knows — but something's missing. I think I need to know more about — about the history of how this jail works. I mean — hell, you expect guys to get raped and killed in prison. Assholes make jokes about it all the time, like it's an acceptable part of an inmate's punishment; but if you try to do anything about it, those same assholes swear it doesn't happen and — and — " I was rambling. "And I'm trying to understand how it can happen in a county jail."

Enrique didn't say a word, just glared at me. Jake shook his head, took Enrique another beer and sat on the couch, next to him.

"Look, Ricky, Tone's a dumb shit from college," he said, not even looking at me. I bristled — but I was smart enough to keep my mouth shut. He kept on with, "He thinks shit through, too much. Like life's supposed to make sense. You an' me — we know that's bullshit. But he's too full of it to know we know, so he thinks he's gonna sling all this crap around and get you so caught up in his nice way of talkin' that you'll forget who you are an' tell him everything you know. An' all he's doin' is trying to hide the fact that he wants to fuck up the guys who got his buddy killed. Plain an' simple."

Enrique eyed me, wary. "That true?"

Well, Jake had spilled it all, so I stared straight back at him and said, "I don't want to just fuck up *them,* I want to fuck up the city — and the county — and the whole fucking state of Texas."

Enrique laughed. "You're fuckin' crazy, vato!"

Jake smacked Enrique on the knee and said, "He aims big, that's for fuckin' sure."

"This guy you talk to at the DA's — what he tell you?"

"The exact timing of everything. That security's video surveillance was down. They got the guys who did it. And one of them was HIV Positive."

"He told you th' video was down, vato?"

"Uh — yeah."

"So he ain't big enough in the DA's office to show you the tape."

Show me the tape? WTF. "I guess not."

Or maybe Tommy *had* seen the tape and that's what shook him into quitting. Meaning the story about the surveillance system having a glitch was crap — meaning there was some reason to hide the fact that there *was* a tape. And before I could even get to asking myself why, Enrique popped out with, "Too bad. Be nice to hear what you think on the quality." And while his voice sounded non-challant, there was an undertone of cold-bloodedness that jolted my brain into sixth gear.

"What do you mean? How bad it is? Or — ?"

He just looked at me. No, meaning how *good* it is. How fucking good of quality. I began to shake.

Jake leaned in. "C'mon, Ricky, there's cameras in all the holding cells."

"No shit, vato. Most of 'em, even I can tell the picture's crap. But in HC-6 — ?"

I leaned against a wall near the dining room, feeling cold. "That — that camera's a better one than the rest."

"The camera don't matter as much as the lens," said Jake, absently. "What the fuck, Ricky — you sayin' — ?"

"I'm sayin' — I saw how this built-up white guy got took in there," said Enrique, his eyes boring into me, his face locked in a cold smile. "By seven white guys. An' you could see 'em rip down his shirt to hold his arms. An' pull down his pants to tie his legs. An' rip off his tighty-whities to choke him an' hold him in place while another guy fucked his mouth. An' you could see how white his ass was. An' that it didn't have no hair on it. An' how it jiggled when this white dick got rammed into it. An' how that dick got red from blood, all as clear as on a DVD."

"How'd you see it?" Jake snapped.

"There's this closet in the basement, down by segregation, always kept locked," he said. He turned to me. "'Fore I got in the kitchen, vato, I was maintenance. Always sweepin' up shit. One day I'm goin' by, sweepin' the hall, an' I head somebody movin' in that room. See a light shinin' under the door. I keep on goin'. No big deal; none of my biz. Get back to the maintenance room an' hear 'bout how another guy's got popped in HC-6.

"Y'know, it's always you white guys get took to that room," he said to Jake. "By all white guys or all black guys — never the vatos. They think all of us got tiny dicks an' no ass."

"It — it was both black and white — who killed Collie — I was told."

Enrique gave me a cold smile. "First time for everything. So I go back to that room, peek under the door and I can see a laptop sittin' on the floor with two of them sticks in its side with this little blue light shinin' — what you call those?"

"Flash drive?" I asked.

"Yeah, that's it. And the monitor's got two pictures side by side showin' what went on in that cell, an' one looks like shit an' one — even under the door you can see it's a damn good picture of six guys gangin' up on that one guy. So I watch — an' I think, this is weird. So I go lookin' for my boss — takes me a while to find him — an' I tell him I need some shit out of that closet. So we go back to his office an' he digs around for his keys an' we head down an' open it up, an' there's no laptop, no more. Just shelves full of cleanin' crap an' buckets an' mops an' shit, so I keep my mouth shut. But next time I go by that room an' see that light, I look right then an' there's that laptop, again. So I go find my boss, right then — only he can't find his keys. They don't show up for nearly an hour. An' by then, that laptop's gone. An' then I hear another guy got popped in HC-6."

This ugly little thought was jabbing needles of ice into my brain, and I just plain did not want to face it, so I asked an obvious question. "But if that laptop's recording such a high-quality video, then surely the DA's office would notice the difference against the other video recordings."

Jake gave me his *what the fuck* look, but I didn't care.

Enrique gulped down more beer. "When you think they see it, vato?"

"Are — are you saying *no* one in court sees what's on the tape recorded by that camera?"

Enrique chuckled and patted Jake on the knee. "You're right — college kid. That camera's always gettin' glitches — and when it does record one, how much trouble you think it is to make a copy looks as shitty as the other cameras?"

"But what you're saying is — "

Jake sighed, long and hard, then said, "Tone, what he's saying is — is I got fucked by six black guys for some sick motherfucker's jack-off pleasure. Same for your guy — Collie, and — and, Ricky — how many others?"

"Figure an average of one a month."

"For how long?!" Jake asked.

"'Least three years."

"Jesus!" Jake went nearly white. I noticed his hands were shaking. "Dude — you sayin' I was one of the first?"

"I'm sayin', vato, that new security system went in, oh, three, four days 'fore you was busted."

Those last words had this hollow ringing to them. I heard them — but I couldn't quite make out what they meant. Because suddenly the room was white. And I was quaking from the cold. And my chest was about to explode from the hate building up in it. And I wanted — I wanted — shit, I don't know what the fuck I wanted right then except to scream in fury and tear life apart and just plain *move* — just plain *breathe* — just plain *anything* and —

BAM! Jake slapped me. Without thinking, I slung him across the dining table into a wall. Cracked it. He damn near hit the window. Enrique scurried back into a corner.

"Fuckin' shit, vato!"

I finally heard myself grunting and whimpering like a crazed animal and my head was pounding and the little light in the room seared my eyes and I was stumbling about — and then I toppled forward and —

Collie caught me and we tumbled back onto his bed. He wore nothing but his big happy grin and smelled of Neutrogena and his hair was wet, like he'd just showered. I looked down and saw I was in my black square-cut Speedo and my dick was pushing to be released. He rolled me over. Lay on top of me. Crushed me into the plush comforter. Ground his raging dick against mine. Kissed me — and his lips tasted like mint toothpaste and his breath had the hint of chocolate to it. His thumbs flickered over my tits and I dug my fingers into his ass, kneading it. I caught a light smell of chlorine and recalled we'd been playing in the condo's pool and I hadn't showered yet but neither of us cared because we were together and had been for six months and we'd been true to each other and been tested for HIV and now, now, now we were going to seal our fates to each other.

He slipped my suit off my ass and I fondled his unwrapped dick and smoothed Vaseline onto it and he probed me and rolled more Vaseline into my hole and I guided him down to me and he pressed his dick against me and slipped in so, so, so easily and it didn't hurt but felt so good and right and full that I held him closer and ground my ass against him and felt his pubes tickle my butt cheeks and scrotum as he went in and out and in and out and it made me so fucking hard and feel so fucking right, I came without him even touching my dick. Then I crushed my ass around his dick and felt him shoot into me, over and over and over till I felt full and alive and then he collapsed on top of me and I knew we'd be forever and —

Jake jolted me back to the world with a swallow of bourbon. I coughed and choked and shoved him away to roll over on my side. I was on the floor. Enrique was standing nearby.

"It's okay, vato. It's okay."

I bolted into a sitting position, still coughing but back under control — well, except for my hands shaking and my head about to split open from the pain.

"Tone — you back, now?" Jake's voice had a bit of a quiver to it. I nodded and I could taste a hint of vomit in the back of my throat. "You sure?"

I took in a deep breath and croaked out, "Yeah! Yeah." Then I figured I ought to ask, "Did I hurt you?"

"Nearly broke my fuckin' back, motherfucker," he said, still jittery. "Shit, what the fuck was that?"

"I'm a — a black belt in Aikido. Sorry. Did I throw up?"

"No, vato." I looked at Enrique. He looked back, puzzled and wary. "Dude, that was some scary shit. How close were you to the guy that got killed?"

"I — I planned to spend my life with him."

He looked at Jake. I glanced at Jake, too, and caught the tail end of a pained expression as he made himself ask, "You know the names of the other guys, Ricky?"

"Couple," he said. "Guy on the video I saw was David Hirsch. Guy before him — Andre Weir or Weil or somethin' like that. Oh, another guy's name was McNevin — his first name. Always thought that was weird, 'cause I remember his last name was kind of Italian — like Chef Boyardee or somethin'. I dunno what else I can tell you, vato.

"Enrique," I asked, "When did Nussewald take over the jail?"

"Just over three years ago. Why?"

Jake looked at me. He understood why. He grew very still.

I looked outside and noticed it was dark. I made myself rise to my feet and stand nice and tall and offer Enrique my hand.

"Thanks," I said. "You've given us plenty."

"Bullshit, vato. I didn't I give you shit, you got me? Anybody asks why I was here — you sucked my dick, is all."

I nodded. "Sorry for what happened."

He shrugged me off.

Jake pulled the remains of the six-pack of Negra Modelo from the fridge and gave it to Enrique. "You take it. I don't drink this kind of shit."

"Fuck you, bitch," he laughed — and he took the six-pack and headed out the door.

Jake immediately closed it and turned to me. "What the fuck was that all about?"

I was still standing quiet and calm in the middle of the room. "What did I do?"

"You don't remember? Dude, look at your fuckin' shirt."

It was torn. Buttons popped off. I had claw marks across my chest from my own fingernails. It was too unreal for me to accept, mental or emotionally, just yet, so I shrugged.

"You started soundin' like some animal," he said. "That's why I hit you. You were losin' it — an' then you threw me 'cross the fuckin' room. It's still hard to breathe."

"You should see a doctor," I said, my voice gentle and even and way, *way* too calm. "I may have broken a rib."

"Yeah, right, that's just what that prick of a PO's lookin' for. 'Gettin' into fights, huh, Jake? Here's six months tacked on — or maybe I'll just put you back inside.' Fuck that shit. You fuckin' owe me for this."

I nodded. I knew what quid pro quo was.

He was pacing like an angry panther. I stopped him — took him by the hand and lead him back to his room. By the bed, he started to pull off his shirt, but he grunted in pain.

I put my hands on his and said, "Let me."

I slipped the wife-beater up and over his head without him having to do anything more than shrug. I then whispered my hands down them and traced over the elegant tattoo and traveled across his nice tight pecs and toyed with his tits. He went for my belt but I stopped him and lead him to the bed.

"Lie down," I said. "Face down."

"You ain't fuckin' me. Nobody ever will — "

"I know."

He hesitated then lay face down on the bed and I worked my hands up his sides and back, feeling to see if anything was out of line. I'd been shown this trick by a paramedic when I worked as a lifeguard, the summer I was fifteen. If a rib is actually broken or out of alignment with your spine, you can feel it. A bump that shouldn't be there. A bone not in sync with the others. I didn't feel anything that wrong; if I had, he'd have to see a doctor to reset it. No, I'd probably just cracked a rib or two — I must have; he was already starting to bruise.

I went into the kitchen, found a dish rag drying by the sink and put together an ice pack. Not great, but it might help the muscles. I returned to find him watching me, waiting. Wondering if I would explain myself.

I looked at his back. The beautiful flow of it down to his elegant rear. The way his jean lay loose against his cheeks. The intricate, colorful design of the tattoo swirling up his left arm and over his shoulder and partway across his skin. It had obviously been done since he was released — and I wondered vaguely how he'd worked it out, with the restrictions on his movement — but then I figured it didn't matter. The only important thing was he trusted me enough to let me see him as his rapists had seen him — as they violated him — and that sliced into my heart.

I got back on the bed and straddled him, lay the pack where the bruising was. He grunted from the pain — but soon was breathing deep and relaxed. Then I began to gently massage his muscles to sooth the tension in them.

"Shit, where'd you learn this crap?"

"High school. I gave the football team massages."

"Just massages?"

"Yeah. Uh — none of them interested me. Too — bulky."

"You like 'em lean and mean, huh?"

"I like 'em human. Real. Honest."

"Nothing like me."

I hesitated then removed the shreds of my shirt and lay on top of him. My left hand caressed into the soft brown hair at the base of his skull.

"Exactly like you. That's what was so funny about Collie and me — he wasn't at all my type. Too gentle. Too caring. Someone you want to be like instead of just with. But you can't help where love takes you."

He sighed. "No." I nearly wept.

"Jake — you're hurt — and you're angry, but you have it under control. Me — I'm just starting to grieve — and I don't know where that'll take me."

Another sigh. "Okay."

"No, it's not okay. What happened. What I did to you, here." I touched the bruise. He winced. "That's just the beginning. I get like that, sometimes — just fucking crazy and locked into an action and — and I don't care what I do or who gets hurt — I just lash out. That's why my family got so quiet around me when I told them I'm queer. They were afraid they'd say something wrong about my homosexuality and I'd snap into one of my mental lockdowns and do some damage."

"Shit — how old are you, Tone?"

"Twenty-one — "

"Goin' on fifty, the way you talk." He rolled over to face me. "What made you so old? Not that guy's death."

"You wouldn't understand."

"I just spent two fuckin' years in a fuckin' prison for somethin' I didn't fuckin' do, lettin' some motherfuckin' skinhead fuck me so nobody else would 'cause — 'cause I had a taste of what that'd be like an' — an' you think you got a lock on bein' fucked over!? You think what you got's worse 'n that?"

I held his face in my hands. Ran my thumbs over his lush eyebrows. Ached for him and everything he'd been through. And felt the fury build inside, again. He wanted to know the whys and wherefores of my soul, and I knew if I told him, he'd be there for me. No matter what. I could see in his deep, dark, beautiful eyes that he's the type who mates for life. All I had to do to make him mine was share my innermost meaning with him.

But how could I tell him that it wasn't something that happened — that it was part of how I was born? That what made me acknowledge it was something that barely even mattered to me?

It was when I was fourteen years old — a kid I sort of knew killed himself. Not because he was gay — he wasn't; but that didn't keep some monstrous brats at school from brutalizing him, anyway. Berating him for being gay. Beating up on him for not being man enough for a fifteen year-old. And not one person did anything about it. Not his parents. Not the bullies' parents. Not the teachers. Nobody. Nobody cared, not really, 'cause he was just this skinny little fuck who couldn't take care of himself — and had nobody who'd take care of him for him — until he took matters into his own hands.

What's sad is, even I made fun of him. Because I was scared they'd start doing that shit to me. And so he was found hanging in his bathroom, one morning. And I didn't feel bad about it. I felt — better him than me.

But then I watched all the adults and all the little fucks who'd picked on him act like they'd done nothing wrong. Laugh about it. Make sick cracks about it. And that's when something cracked open inside me. Something deep that slowly built up this hideous anger. Still, I kept it bottled up, inside, afraid of it.

Until a year later. When a kid outside LA got murdered by a classmate for being gay, and hearing about it scared the fuck out of me, at first. I couldn't go to school for a week because I was sure that everybody knew that I was a fag, too, and fags kill themselves or get killed and I'd be next and — and —

And then I heard that killer's attorney start blaming everything on the murdered boy, all but brushing aside the fact that a young life had been taken thanks to hatred — and the anger boiled up, again. That some motherfuckers would make it seem like — like how you were born is wrong, and is an excuse for slaughter, and they'd make you scared to be who you are because they can't handle it — that was so sickening to me, two weeks after the murdered kid's funeral I told my mom I was gay.

She told dad and they tried to talk me out of it, of course. Said I was just confused and upset. I was too young to understand what I did and didn't like. Didn't work. So they asked me to keep it to myself. People in our town might not be so understanding. And I agreed, but for one reason only — so I could work with the football team. Because five of the suicide kid's worst tormenters were on the Varsity Squad.

You see, nobody knew at school did know I was gay, yet. And I'd already been learning about massage and pressure points and stuff from Aikido and that paramedic. So I got the job to clean up the locker room and make sure the guys had towels when they finished showering and finally got to show coach that I could rub out leg cramps and sore arms when he was too busy. And by the end of the football season, I'd rubbed each of those five assholes down good. And made damn sure every one of them got a woody. Very embarrassing for them, but I laughed and explained it away and they thought everything was fine.

Until we returned to school from Christmas break. That's when I came out to everyone and quietly told a friend (near some nosy-gossipy girls) that I'd sucked every one of the football bastards off — though the truth was, I hadn't. They were all butt-ugly to me. Of course, word was all over campus by the end of the day. A couple of the guys found out and tried to beat me up — and I got knocked around a bit; they outweighed me by twenty pounds each — but I slammed into freak-out-pissed-off mode for the first time and broke one guy's nose and another one's wrist. Then word spread that they'd been beat up by a fag.

Well — they couldn't buy their way onto a college football team, after that, no matter how much they swore it wasn't true. And that is hell for a high school football star from Texas. I'd crushed their dreams in revenge for a kid I barely knew. And I felt good about it. Which scared me, a little — because I didn't think I should have felt that way.

But that wasn't the end of it. After graduation, three of them joined the military — Army, Marines — and got sent to Iraq and Afghanistan. One was killed. Another got hit by an IED — and his parents are taking care of him, now, because he's just a couple IQ points above a vegetable. The third, I think he's on his second deployment. The other two — one's a dealer who's his own best client and the other went to Michigan State to get away from the gossip. Last I heard, he's the only one doing good — but he was never allowed near the football team.

And I still felt like this was a job well-done.

And I was going to do it, again. I knew it. Could feel the certainty filling the hole in my heart. And if I shared that with Jake, he'd help me in whatever plans I laid out. But he had plans for his life, too, and I didn't want to mess them up by him being associated with me.

So I kissed him and whispered in his ear, "You're right, Jake. I'm just pretending to be this old because I think it's cool. Because Collie was eighteen years older than me and I wanted to be as mature as he was. Guess I'm kind of locked into that."

He grabbed my hair and pulled me back to look at me. He didn't believe a word out of my mouth, and there was a lot of hurt masked by his growing sneer. Before he could say anything, I asked, "Do you have a condom?"

He sighed, released my hair and reached over to his night table, opened a small drawer and pulled out a nearly empty box of them. He held up one of the little packets, his eyes never leaving mine.

"This as honest as you're gonna be with me?"

"How does your side feel?"

He hesitated then looked away. "Okay."

I took the packet, tore it open, slipped the condom in my mouth and kissed my way down the trail of hair to his belly. I undid his jeans, pulled them away from his hips and pulled the front of his tighty-whities down to be held behind his balls. His dick was just starting to respond, so I nuzzled it, ran my lips up and down its length and around its base, felt his pubes tickle my nose and his balls contract and shift — and then his dick started expanding and lengthening and building into the glorious thing it was. And before it was at its height, I slipped my lips over its head and used my tongue to maneuver the condom over the big, round head and down the length of him with a combination of swirling motions and kissing rubs and he began to squirm and I pulled back and guided his jeans and briefs completely off — and all he was left wearing was the ankle cuff.

God, he was pretty — no, beautiful — not in that golden way that Collie'd been, but darker, angrier, tougher. Midnight to Collie's noon, better able to handle himself in the cold reality of the world. A true alley cat.

He reached up and undid my pants and we shifted around to where I was lying on the bed and he was at my feet and I let him slide the pants off me. He left my briefs on as he slipped up and lay atop me. Ground his dick into mine. Rubbed the hair on his chest

66

against mine. Wrapped his arms up under mine and grabbed my hair and held my head back against a pillow.

"Fine," he growled. "Fine."

He sat up, drew his hands down my chest and abs, took hold of my briefs — and tore them off me. Shredded them. I jolted and almost fought back, but he grabbed my wrists and snarled, "You owe me."

I nodded, pulled my hands away and lay back to grip the headboard. He finished shredding my briefs then threw them in my face and groped me — as if he needed to; I was raging hard. He pulled on me a few times, his dick right beside mine, even held both together with one hand as he stroked, then he raised my legs to rest on his shoulders, grabbed my ass, pulled me up, slopped some KY against my hole and punched himself into me in one sudden motion.

I cried out from the pain but didn't try to stop him. Then he began pushing into me — harder and harder and harder, taking his anger out on me — and I let him. Let him dig his fingers into my skin. Let him bite at my thighs. Let him push deeper and deeper and deeper as he held me tighter and tighter and his skin gleamed with sweat and his grunts and whimpers increased and tears streamed from his eyes to drop onto my face and I grew more and more lost in the feeling of it — in the beauty of the harsh, horrible fucking anger in both of us — and my dick grew harder and harder from him slamming against my balls and half-lying over my crotch and I grabbed his hair and pulled him down to kiss me and he grabbed my dick and began to yank on me, stroking harder and faster and harder and faster and suddenly I let loose and fired everywhere and I whipped my arms around him and gripped him close as he exploded into me and crushed me so tight in his arms I thought I'd melt into his body. And then he collapsed on top of me — and wouldn't let go.

And in my mind I whispered to Collie, "I'm sorry, I'm sorry, I'm sorry."

I let Jake fuck me over and over, that night, until he was out of condoms. And each time it was just as intense. And each time I was surer than ever about what I needed to do. Then as the sun was finally coming up, he crashed into a deep sleep, and I quietly rose, dressed and left.

It was only right for me to sneak off, like this. Because I loved him. Not as deeply as Collie or even in the same way, really. You see, Collie and I were like yin and yang, two opposites building a whole — like a banana-mango smoothie, for want of a better example. With Jake, it was more like — like a pair of junkyard dogs who were joining forces to face down the world. We would've fought and bonded, and he'd have caught mice for us to feast on and I'd have cornered and killed rats to snack on and we'd have traveled far and wide and been our own little pack and happy that way.

But now he needed to stay away from me. To get on with his life. Because he still had a future, and I could no longer see one for myself — since I already had a vague idea of what I was about to do. And for him to be anywhere near me over the next six months would be disastrous for him. You see, I was about to go bat-shit fucking crazy — and when that happened, somebody was going to get hurt, and I wouldn't care who was.

Not even if it was me.

— FIVE —

My mom told me a story, once — about when I was five years old. A kid took a toy of mine home with him and every time he came over to my house to play, I'd ask him to bring it back — but he never did. And on the occasions I went to his house, I asked him to give it to me so I could take it home with me, and he never did. This kept up for a couple weeks until one day, when he'd come over to play, again, and hadn't brought back my toy, again, I told him I was going to the bathroom then toddled my little self right over to his house. Didn't matter to me that it was cold and raining or that I wasn't dressed for it and his place was half a block away — I strode straight there, not giving a single solitary damn about anything but my fucking toy.

I slipped into his back yard and let myself in through a patio door, then I marched up to his room (leaving muddy tracks all over their lush white carpet), dug through his toys, found the one that was mine and proceeded to toss every one of his out the window onto the patio roof, where they spent the next two days getting rained on. Then I toddled my little self back home, dripping wet, showed him I'd gotten the toy — and smacked him over the head with it. He needed three stitches to close the cut, and did mom do a punishment on me? Wowser. But I didn't care; I had my toy back and that little shit wasn't coming anywhere near anything of mine ever again.

She told me that story when I was sixteen, right after my battle with the jocks, while I was in the ER getting my seven stitches. And she told me as if I didn't remember it. I just smiled and nodded at her, then when we got home I went to my closet and pulled out that toy and gave it to her. Without a word. She looked me over with this new expression in her eyes, like she didn't know me. I laughed, grabbed my racquet and jaunted off to tennis practice, like I hadn't also gotten a black eye and two bruised ribs. She never mentioned it, again.

What's funny is, I can't even remember what the fucking toy was — if it was a car or a soldier or horse or whatever; she never gave it back to me. I just knew that from the beginning I had this built-in attitude that nobody was gonna fuck with me if I didn't want them to. And while my folks managed to shake that out of my psyche for a little while, suicide kid started me back on the road to recovery and ever since, I've been hell to deal with if I feel dissed.

So let's be clear — what I was now about to do was nothing new to me, not really. This hard-ass streak in my being was visible even back with that kid, and it wasn't the only time it showed itself — though I do admit the first time I became truly conscious of it was with suicide kid's tormenters. And I think the only reason I noticed it then was because I was smashing up some guys who'd done nothing to me. Maybe I was doing it as a preemptive strike, announcing to the world, *I may be queer, but don't fuck with me or I'll blow you the fuck up.* Maybe I was just finally at a point where I could accept that I had this bomb inside me ready to go off at the first wrong move. Whatever the reason, from that point I also consciously worked to keep it under control. I halfway think that's why I'm a Communications major — I wanted to learn how to smack back with snap when some dickweed popped out something nasty about fags instead of just snapping and proving to that dickweed the Second Amendment don't care if you're gay, straight or like to fuck donkeys because *any*body can get a gun in this country if they go about it right, and by the way — remember Columbine?

But Collie's death shut me down. My brain refused to function outside of memory mode for over a month and it was not until I was booted into the *get even* process that I began to be able to function again. I'd learned long ago that words only work when someone else is willing to listen, and I knew without question that assholes like Nussewald, Stanton and Gilbert did not feel the need to hear anything they did not want to hear. And I couldn't be bothered with trying to deal with their wall of disdain. So my inner bomb started ticking and fuck the consequences.

The first thing I set out to do was locate the other men who'd been attacked in jail. Maybe it was just a coincidence that someone named Orin had been associated with both Collie's and Jake's arrests — it wasn't all *that* uncommon a moniker in Texas, and Jake *had* said his guy's last name was different — but I wanted to know one way or the other. And if any one of those guys had an Orin in his life in any way, form or fashion, that'd be proof enough for me the little fuck hurt Jake, too.

Now I knew one guy's name was David Hirsch, but there are literally thousands of Hirsches in Texas, a lot of them in my area. And, naturally, dozens of them came up with David mixed into their name during a quick online scan. I didn't have the time or inclination to contact each and every one, so it looked like I'd have to do more than just research. Like hack into the jail's arrest records.

Thing is, I wasn't much of a hacker. I'd done it on a low-key level to locate info more quickly than I might have been able to, otherwise, but this entailed digging into deeply encrypted information in the criminal justice system, and I wanted to do so in a way that couldn't be traced — which went *way* over the edge of my capability. So how to do it?

Well the first thing I figured was, get back in school. I needed access to the powerhouse mainframes they have and the massive information they can access — and maybe I'd even make use of the internship program to get into a position where I could get even *more* access to info. So I went to my counselor and discussed what I had to do to re-enroll.

Seems I now had five *incompletes* and had to deal with those in order to continue my degree program. I was allowed to sign up for four classes and a lab on a provisional basis, meaning I had to get all nine courses completed by the end of the semester for them to count. And the only reason she was willing to set that up was because of Collie; she used a bereavement excuse to get around all the tape crap. I agreed to everything.

I never even thought about people knowing about us, but I

guess they did — not that I cared. My campus was small enough and liberal enough to where it didn't matter except to the haters, and they weren't tolerated. So now all that mattered was me getting myself back to where I could use the power of my position in some way to quietly research anyone I wanted to.

Mom and Dad were happy enough that I was going back, and agreed to continue paying for everything so long as I lived on campus. So I broke my lease and got back into my old dorm room, and by the end of the second week of January, I was good to go. Of course, my roomie wasn't thrilled about it, but we'd already been avoiding dealing with each other (he was afraid I'd seduce his pimply ass — as *if*, to quote a famous 90's phrase) so it went smoothly enough.

I'd never given Jake my phone number (I'd always called him) and he didn't know where I lived, so being on campus also offered some protection from him looking for me. The university was way outside his accepted routes. It hurt to do this to him, but it was better for all concerned.

So now came the question of hacking. Sure, I couldn't do it, but I had an idea who could — that golden number named Grady Lowenthaal, from my Principles of Communication class. He'd been in one of my advanced computer courses and seemed a thousand years ahead of me in ability, which didn't fit because he was brutally hot — thick hair bleached by the sun flopping over a wide, happy face and big hazel eyes, golden-tan skin, shy smile, and what I knew to be a sleek, solid body under his lazy clothes. He was one of the school's diving stars, had won a couple of medals at some of the recent competitions and was being groomed for the next summer Olympics — and was so open and casual about being gay, it didn't matter to anyone but the haters. Or those who wanted to make use of it.

Like me.

Meaning I figured the perfect way to get him to help me figure out how to hack with safety was make him a relationship. So this little puppy-dog sniffed up a plan.

I remembered he'd always shown up at the computer lab at the same time when I'd been there, so I sauntered to see if he was a creature of habit. Sure enough, there he was as usual dressed in the same clothes as usual — long-sleeve pullover, baggy pants and athletic shoes, sitting at one of the powerhouse mainframes reserved for advanced students, his laptop open beside him. I drifted around for a couple of minutes then headed past the main set of terminals to *notice* him.

"Grady, hi," I said, acting surprised as hell.

He looked up at me, startled, and it took him a moment to place me. "Oh — Lazarus. Haven't seen you in a while."

Cute little play on my last name, but thinking about it that *was* how people usually remembered me — as the guy who came back from the dead.

"It's Antony, and things've been crazy, so I'm running behind. Looks like you're on top of things." He shrugged, and something about it was endearing in a bashful-boy kind of way that set my inner *Grr* to going. "So what you working on?"

"Oh — a computer model attenuated to the SAMSI Program methods for sequential decision geared to a statistical analysis of computer model data with special focus on adaptive design. It's an exercise for class; I'd do it on my laptop but that's working on methods for sub-strata sequential decisions. You'd think they'd work up assignments that're more demanding."

"Uh — uh-huh. Can you do that for anything?" I asked, using my most innocent voice. He gave me a comical grimace that all but screamed, *How backward* are *you?* and I actually laughed at the gentle attitude behind it. "Okay, I'm not as far along as you."

"Right — you're more research," he said, almost in pity.

"Communications."

"Is that like journalism?"

"Nailed it. Is this stuff what you want to do?"

"This?" He motioned to the monitor. "Absolute. I took this really cool seminar over Christmas on climate change and some of the workups they did were kick-ass — projecting eventualities using Sequential Monte Carlo Methods and the NISS project on Computer Models for Geophysical Risks — "

"Wow." And I'm sure my expression was totally blank.

He grinned and blushed, and actually looked sweet. "Sorry,

it's just — I've been a *byte-brain* since I was two."

"I didn't start till PlayStation came out, and then only when my folks'd let me play."

"I remember PlayStations. That's when I was four. They actually kept me interested for a while."

Damn, that meant he was younger than me by two years. All of a sudden I had this weird felling that I was about to do a pedophile on this innocent little kid — but it only lasted a second.

"You really that advanced?" I asked. He gave me his low-key shrug, so I leaned in close. "You ever hack anything?"

He gave just enough hesitation to answer my question before he said, "That's illegal." Which also told me he'd gotten into trouble over it.

"I get you. Was it hard to do?"

"Why're you asking me that?"

Uh-oh, a straight to the point kind of guy. It must've been some *serious* trouble he got into, maybe threats of jail or juvie since he was so suspicious. He was probably at his most curious during the crackdown after 9/11, when the government was spying on *everybody*, and got into something a bit too official, so I decided to be honest.

"I'm researching conditions at the county jail — for a paper I'm writing." Okay, honest to a point. "There's information I'm supposed to have access to because they're public record, but I'm getting the runaround from everybody. Call this department. Talk to that person. Fill out this form — oh, that's not the right form to fill out, so do this one. Wait ten weeks for us to process it. I wasn't able to get it done in time, so I got an incomplete and I'd like to clear it up and — well, I — uh — "

"And you thought I could help you."

I shrugged. "I'd be open to just getting directions on finding a way in, finding what I want and leaving without a trace — all on my own."

"What kind of data you after?"

"There — there was some trouble in the jail. A guy was attacked and killed."

"That professor — ?"

74

"Yeah."

"Whoa."

"There are indications it's happened before and I want to see what was done about those. View the reports and find out how they were handled in court. That sort of stuff."

"I could ask my mom to get it for you." I must have looked as surprised as I felt, so he gave me his shy smile and added, "She's a lawyer. Civil stuff, but she knows a lot of people over at the courthouse."

Which would throw up a *huge* red flag and that was *not* what I wanted, just now, so I said, "That might take too long. I said I'd have the paper into my professor next week. All I need is a couple of dates and what charges there were; I've already set up student access to the Bureau of Records and can get into various trial transcripts if I know the arrest reports' info to cross-reference."

"But you're all about hacking into cop's files and — "

"Sheriff's department. They handle the jail. And it's public records."

"Still ain't easy." But he was getting this little faraway look that told me he was thinking about it. Once a hacker, always a hacker. And if I'd left it alone, he might have come back to me in a few days willing to help. Sometimes the patience of Sensei works better than the jumping around of grasshopper, but I was feeling this sense of *now-now-now* so pushed it.

I smiled and shrugged then put my hand on his shoulder and gave it a slight squeeze. "Well, if you can think of any way that I might be able to do it — without much trouble — you could just tell me how and — say, uh — y'know, I'm done for the day. You wanna go grab a cup of coffee — or something?"

He looked at my hand and then at me, more than a little wary. "I can't drink coffee. One cup and I'm up all night."

"Sometimes that can be good. If you're pulling an all-nighter." Then I gave my lips a quick lick, the international sign for *sex available.*

He sighed and looked away, almost irritated. "Look, Lazarus, you're a nice guy but — y'know, soon as I'm done here, I've got practice. So nothing personal, but no thanks."

Bam — right between the eyes. No muss, no fuss, and no fuckin' way.

I shrugged and said, "Sure. See you around." Then I sauntered off, very confused and rather shook up.

The fact is, I'd *never* been turned down by a guy I wanted before. Hell, guys usually chase me. I'm good-looking, even sexy, as I've been told on more than one occasion. Didn't matter if a dude was only into girls, I could get him, too.

Like this one lifeguard I partnered with at a pool close to downtown. I'd just graduated high school and was working my ass off to build my college fund, so when I wasn't teaching tennis or tutoring beginners in English grammar, there I would be.

His name was Leon Cartucci and he was male-model gorgeous. Rich brown hair in all the right places, touched a bit with sun-bleaching. Broad shoulders, tight muscles, bedroom eyes, abs to die for, legs that strutted like a lovely prancing colt. He fit into our red board-shorts with a fluidity that made him seem to be the very guy they'd been designed for. He was in the Air Force and had just been stationed at a nearby base, and he needed the extra money to fix his car. So every weekend for ten weeks we tag-teamed at a pool that really should have had four of us on duty, considering its size and the number of screaming kids and snarly parents there were.

Now the second I saw Leon, I knew I wanted him. But he was always talking about the girls he'd fucked or would like to fuck. And whenever he was on the bench, he had a dozen giggly females around him trying to catch his attention. I knew for a fact he'd nailed at least three of them within his first four weekends, so I figured my chances were miniscule. But there was something about him that — I can't explain it, I just wanted to be able to say I'd had him. I didn't know exactly what getting him would entail, but it would be worth it, no question — even if only to prove to myself that all guys were available at the right time and in the right place, if they'd just admit it. The problem was finding that right time and place.

Which crashed into me this nice hot August day the weekend before our contracts were up. Leon and I had a major run-in with a drunk mommy who thought it was no big deal that her little precious was pushing kids into the pool, sometimes on top of other kids. He'd ordered the brat out and she was raising hell and there was a crowd growing, so I decided to call in the cops because our security guard was off smoking somewhere — or something. She saw me on my cell and, out of nowhere, punched me. I actually heard a tone ring in my ears as I toppled into the pool. The water shocked me into reality and I jumped back to the surface; by then Leon had the bitch sitting on the ground, her brat seated beside her and everybody standing back to give him space.

He saw me and asked, "You okay, T?" His voice carried what I thought was a Brooklyn accent, even though he was from Boston.

I held up my cell phone. Water poured out. "Dead."

"Get outta the pool; you're bleedin'." As I did, he turned to the woman and snarled, "Okay, that's felonious assault, lady. An' criminal mischief. Vandalism. You name it, you're gonna get it." Turned out little Leon was training to be an MP — or is it AP, for the Air Force? Whichever, he had the attitude it took.

I jumped onto the pool's side and saw drops of blood splash into the water. I immediately checked my nose; no blood coming from there.

"Check your ear," said Leon. "Her ring got ya."

The blood was coming from a cut just in front of my left earlobe, and there was a lot of it. "Shit, how bad is it?"

Leon looked and snarled, "You're gonna need stitches." He spun back to the crowd. "Okay, you guys all understand — this pool is now closed thanks to this woman an' her kid."

The crowd started to get rowdy but Leon let loose with a bellowing voice that nearly made me jump back in the water. "This pool's got a minimum requirement of TWO lifeguards, an' now one's gotta go get his face sewed up, so that'll leave just me. Thanks to her! You wanna blame anybody, blame this bitch! Then ask yourselves why you all stood 'round an' let her do it!"

Of course, it was just bullshit; the town'd gotten legal waivers so they could have just one lifeguard at a time, that's how cheap they were. The only reason this one had two was my Aunt Charla got hold of the head of Public Works and made a big deal about how it's a bigger pool and how unsafe that'd be, and tossed in a comment that if some kid drowned due to there being just one lifeguard, she'd get him charged with manslaughter. I thought she did it for me; turned out she just wanted to get a precedent set so she could make sure my cousin, Rene, could get the job in my place, next year — which he did when she also just happened to mention to that same official that I was gay when the contracts were being offered. The bitch.

Anyway, Leon was all but hopping from anger and I felt it best to let him hop. Fortunately, the cops showed up before he was done — lights flashing and in full force, thanks to my call being interrupted — and took the woman away and calmed the crowd, and Leon let me make a big show of talking him into keeping the pool open as I was taped up by a couple of hunky paramedics. Total street theater, but the crowd loved it. And this *hurt little puppy* got lots of free sodas the rest of the day — and Baracoa and guac' and chips, all the fun foods.

After we were done and had showered and changed — the damn shower stalls were the private kind, and Leon was always in and out way too fast for me to catch a good look at anything except his adorable butt — he checked my face, slapped me on the back and said, "C'mon, I'll buy ya a brewski."

Turned out Leon was twenty-three, and even though I was nowhere near twenty-one he dragged me into a bar down the street from the pool and I had my first beer on tap. Shiner Bock — which is half the reason I still love it.

The bar was dark and cool and felt so, so nice after that heat. And the beer was just the right cold. We were in a made-over gas station that had cheesy seats and Formica tables and a long bar crammed along one side with row after row of beer bottles atop the mantle. Pool and foosball tables were all over, along with old-fashioned pinball machines, and a juke box with tubes of bubbling light played music from the 50's and 60's — like Patsy Cline and Buddy Holly and a whole series of one-hit wonders wailing about dead teenagers. My head hurt but the combination of the Bock and some Tylenol made me forget about it — and feel extremely warm towards Leon Cartucci.

"You're some guy," he said as we did a round of pool.

"How you mean?" I answered. My voice was taking on a bit of his accent and attitude.

"That bitch clocked ya hard enough to knock ya out, but ya rolled with it an' only got that little cut. I was sure I'd have to dive in after ya."

"I'm taking Aikido," I said, sinking the six-ball. "If I'd been paying attention to her, she'd never have made contact."

He sank the nine. "Yeah? What level?"

"I'm at first Kyu — about to test for black belt."

"Damn. Dangerous."

"In more ways than one." And feeling very bold and kind of loaded, I winked at him.

He chalked up his cue and cast me a sideways glance as he said, "Back off, T. I'm into pussy, not dick."

Meaning he knew I was gay. Well, I hadn't exactly been subtle about it — trailing my eyes up one side of him and down the other — but I hadn't thought about trying to do anything about it till he said that. Then it became a challenge.

"Yeah," I said, "that's why I kept my hands off you. I don't think it's right to corrupt an innocent little airman."

"Airman First Class!"

"I knew that the second I saw you in those red trunks."

"Okay, now I feel weird. Guys're supposed to talk about girls that way, not guys."

"Why? Beauty's beauty. Who cares how you put it?"

"Just — don't, okay?"

"Okay. Want another beer? I'll buy."

"The hell ya will! I'm in shit enough sneakin' ya in here. We get raided, I'm fucked." I smiled at him. He blushed and snapped, "Shut it!" Then bought another round.

Two beers later, he was driving me home — and truth is, he really shouldn't have been behind the wheel of a car. So I asked him to stop in an alleyway so I could take a piss. I really didn't need to; I just wanted him off the road for a minute while I figured out what to do to get the keys away from him.

I could just take them. I figured my Aikido would overcome

his cop-combat ability — if he had any. Which he looked like he did. And if I did get the keys, then what? Knock him out? Toss him in the trunk? Take him back to my parent's home and drag him inside and tie him down and molest him to my heart's content? To be honest, I considered it.

Instead, I got lucky. He joined me for a piss.

We were in one of those alleys behind some commercial buildings that's littered with dumpsters and overgrown with weeds. I was beside a telephone pole when I whipped out, then he stumbled over and tripped and fell against me. I caught him and leaned him up against the pole and held him there as I finished. He looked down at me and chuckled.

"Man, you ain't missin' much, down there."

"Is that a good thing or a bad thing?"

"Dude, if you were into girls, they'd love ya."

He started undoing his jeans but fumbled. I began to think he was drunker than even I thought, but then he sighed and steadied himself between me and the pole and pulled himself out and began to go. He was good-sized — and even without looking at his face I could see the smirk on it.

"Big enough for ya?"

"Just the right size," I said. "I like cut cocks. They look — symmetrical, to me."

"Looks is all ya get."

Oh, yeah? The second he was done peeing and shaking, I stepped away from him. He lost his balance and fell against me. I caught him from behind, under the arms — and almost dropped him, he was so much heavier than me. I raised him back up to his feet, saw he hadn't packed away, yet, then impulsively slipped my hands around his chest, found his tits and pinched both at the same time.

"What the fuck?" He bolted away from me and tried to turn, but wound up staggering back into the pole. I grabbed his shoulders to steady him. He tried to wiggle away from me, but I had too good a grip on him. "C'mon, dude," he snarled, "that ain't my way."

"I didn't say it was. But Leon, haven't ever been curious?

Does a guy's blow job stack up to a girl's?"

"Aw, Jeez — you know how old that fuckin' line is?"

"I know girls who use it on gay guys."

"Yeah? So girls don't suck me, man, they fuck me. While I suck on their tits."

"Have they ever sucked on yours?"

"What? *My* tits?! Why the fuck would they?"

"Makes you go bat-shit crazy when you cum."

"Bullshit. You're just tryin' — "

"C'mon, Leon, don't you even want to know what it's like before you diss it? Me sucking on your tits doesn't mean anything. Shit, it ain't even sex. So just — just close your eyes. Think of the most beautiful woman you can think of. See what it feels like. See if you want to have your next bitch do it for you."

He tried to shift away from me, but I already had his t-shirt halfway up his abs. He got this deep question on his face — then he leaned back against the pole.

"Don't ya go for anything else, fucker." I just smiled. He sighed. "Okay — lemme put my dick away."

He started to shift his jeans but I grabbed his hands and put them behind the pole. I knew why he wanted to hide himself; he was already beginning to get hard.

"Shh," was all I said.

He hesitated — then closed his eyes. I released his hands and slipped the t-shirt up over his pretty brown tits. Leaned in slowly. Touched one with my tongue. Caught it in my teeth. Closed my lips around it. Pulled and sucked at it, my hands holding his hips. He gasped in and jolted back, a little, then let me continue.

"Holy fuckin' shit."

I chuckled and shifted to the other tit and did the same thing — and got an even deeper reaction, including feeling his ass clench. I glanced down and, sure enough, his dick was getting longer and thicker. I pinched and twisted his tits with my fingers as I kissed the soft down on his chest — then began to follow the trail down and down.

"No", he gasped. "No, stay away — from my — from my dick, man. Don't."

He moved to stop me, but I brushed his hands away — and he let me.

"Leon, relax. It's just like jackin' off."

His dick was already at the pre-erection stage — rich and full and flush and ready to be taken to the next level. I traced my fingers down his sides to the top of his jeans. Slipped inside them. Shifted them a bit lower as my lips drew nearer and nearer to his patch of dusky pubes. He grabbed at my shoulders to shove me back.

"No — wait — I — I can't — I'm not — "

I shrugged his hands off, guided his jeans halfway down his butt and nestled my face in his pubes then trailed my lips up his shaft, licking and caressing then fondling his balls with my tongue until I swallowed him whole and began to orally stroke him as my tender whispering fingers toyed with his tits and he groaned and cringed and clenched the muscles in his thighs and ass and pecs and I pumped and pumped and pumped.

"No — I — I'm not — I — oh — "

Suddenly he grabbed my head and shoved himself deeper into my mouth and exploded, sending spurt after spurt into my throat as he all but screamed and gasped in deep gulping waves. And I kept sucking on him, letting him fill my mouth with cum as I swirled it around to further the sensations he was feeling and he tried to pull back but I grabbed his ass and held him in place and kept sucking until he was letting out whines of near madness and I was close to choking, my mouth was so full. So I pulled back, spit everything onto the ground and cupped his balls in my right hand. He jolted tight.

"Yeah, feels like I drained 'em," I said.

He couldn't look at me. Just kept gulping in air and staring at something a hundred feet away. I looked around — and it was a cat, silently watching us. I chuckled.

"Still want some pussy?"

"Fuck, man." He slid to the ground. "Aw, fuck."

I kneeled in front of him, my legs between his, and ran my hands up the outsides of his thighs and whispered, "Maybe next time."

He just looked at me, then closed his eyes and leaned his head back, still breathing heavily. Somehow I got the feeling I'd removed his buzz and replaced it with a sense of euphoria. So I figured he could drive now.

*Next time* turned out to be three days later, after he dropped by my home in his nice, tight MP uniform that made his hotness quadruple and we went for a walk along a nearby creek and I proved to him what happened wasn't just a fluke or because he was drunk. And I kept proving it to him whenever he dropped by the university right through to the following summer, until he was transferred to Germany. And that perfect little uniform would get me off without me even touching myself, every time. We never got around to the fucking part, but he did try to return the oral favor a couple of times till I gave up and just let him jack me off. And that was more than enough.

It's funny, but I never considered that a relationship, because that's all we ever did together — no more sneaking into the bar, no movies, no sports, nothing but me sucking him off when he was between bitches to fuck and him pulling on my dick like it was his own. So he was a friend who offered nothing but benefits. And I thoroughly loved it.

Of course, that branded my brain with the idea I could have any guy I wanted at any time, and I proved it a couple more times just to see — like with my too-cool swim coach, and this buff-bear married friend of my dad's who seemed real unhappy. And both also came back for seconds, pun very much intended.

I mean, yeah, there's always the first time you can strike out — but no, that wasn't it. Grady'd shot me down hard and cold and in a way that all but said, *Don't try again.* I got to believing his dismissal of me was like he felt I wasn't worthy of him. And that pissed me off. So I stormed over to the diving boards to wait and see if he did come to practice or if that was just his bullshit way of minimizing his blow-off.

Nearly two hours later, just as my ass was about to give up and make me head on, he jaunted out of the locker room with another guy, both dressed in blue Speedos. And while his buddy was a nice, compact little critter of well-formed muscle and fine proportions whom I'd have been happy to focus upon any other time, all I could see was Grady — because he really was fucking *beautiful*. Broad shoulders, full pecs, powerful arms, even more powerful legs extending from one of the most perfect asses I'd ever seen as well as the tightest abs a man could ever have. He scrambled up the high board like a monkey, laughing, and did a triple gainer off it just for fun — and when he cut into the water, there was barely a ripple, and when he hopped out, his joy was almost intoxicating — as was the way the Speedo clung to his crotch and ass. I think I forgot to breathe, for a moment.

"He'd be fun to have, Tone."

The voice was so clear and near and perfectly Jake's, I jumped around — but there was no one even close to me.

I looked back at Grady and suddenly — suddenly I had understood that he's the kind of guy who gets hit on all the time, and he saw me as just another celebrity-junkie who wanted to make it with the reigning king of the dive sport, so he'd shrugged me off like a movie star shrugs off a fan.

And for some weird reason, that pissed me off.

Seriously, I felt a deep boiling anger surge from behind my heart. How dare that little fuck think that described me? How dare he turn down my interest in him? I'm not some superficial queen out to sleep with somebody who had something of a name, making myself somebody by proxy. I'm a good-looking guy who can have anybody he wants, and wanted him for his ability, not his body, and he'll never get an offer like mine, again. Little shit. Maybe I ought to just show him what the fuck it is he's missing, the arrogant fuckin' little queen.

I had to make myself turn and storm out the door before I went over, used my Aikido to subdue both Grady and his buddy and made him let me do what I'd offered to do as a favor, then let him know I wouldn't stop till he'd hacked in and found me the names, addresses and phone numbers of everyone involved in Collie's death. And it was hard to keep from doing that.

And that made me nervous, because this time the anger I was feeling was completely irrational and took me way too close to the point of there being no control, and over what? Nothing.

Absolutely nothing, except I made a clumsy pass at a guy who's always getting hit on — and he didn't bite.

Talk about sick.

Problem is, I only cared about it for — oh, about five seconds. Soon as I was back outside and walking in yet another drizzle, I made the decision to go after Grady and make use of him later, in some way. With him, there need not be a rush. And the fact that I'd made what is effectively a cold-blooded decision to mess with the life of a person who'd done nothing to me meant absolutely nothing in my scheme of things.

Hell, I'm an American; we do that shit all the time.

— SIX —

What my decision also meant was, I had to find another way to locate David Hirsch besides online. So I nosed into the world of Wilbur Nussewald simply because he'd be the most likely to know where the guy was located — and it turned out ol' Wilbur's world was SO easy to engage, I actually believed Jake was right when he said the man was too dumb to order food at a chain restaurant.

Antony's exhibit #1 — he's a high-ranking official with the Sheriff's department in charge of an area that guarantees people're gonna get pissed off at anybody in authority, but it seems his wife has a blog. Called Nussewalding. *Seriously*! Photos of the family vacations and outings — with Wilbur in a couple of them! Lots of info about how his sons were doing in school and what activities they were taking part in and where they were attending college along with photos of them growing up and — it just goes on and on so much detail, I wondered if he was deliberately passing out disinformation, so I checked it out — and here's exhibit #2.

According to the blog, his third oldest son is a junior on the football and Lacrosse teams at my college. The first Lacrosse game was at the first week of February, so they were practicing on the pitch every day between 3 and 5. I went to watch one in yet another cold drizzle, and there he was — Wallace Shane Nussewald, six-foot-two, two-hundred-twenty pounds of fleshy muscle packed into a loose set of shorts and shirt that hid absolutely nothing, thanks to the wetness of the day — hell, the straps from his jock all but glowed through the fabric of his shorts to outline a lovely bubble butt — with spikey reddish-blond hair atop a block of a head atop a thick neck. He was trying to grow a beard and it outlined how strong his jaw was and how bright his baby-blues were. It also made the vague sneer-like curl to his mouth seem snarlier than it was and — this is weird — I actually thought he looked Australian.

He had nice moves on the field and — well the fact is, Wallace wasn't the only attractive one on the team so I had a bit of trouble concentrating, but he was the only one where even from a hundred feet away I got the vibe, "This is not someone to trespass upon." Being in one of my contrary moods, I decided to put young master Nussewald on my list.

What's interesting is, digging into little Wally's info brought up a connection to another member of the cabal. Seems He belonged to a fraternity that one Joseph Charles Stanton had just pledged to — yes, the youngest son of Phillip Stanton, the asshole ADA who dissed Collie after he was dead. He was now a newbie with a room in the frat house and a car from daddy and well on his way to being the next asshole ADA. No picture of him on the frat's website, yet, but a lot of information had been posted — high school, sports, that he was a legacy pledge after not only an older brother but also daddy and gran'daddy, loved Thai food, cheerleaders and boutique beers. And just how does an eighteen year-old brat get to check out the various small breweries and their product, you might ask? Can you tell me one time when someone under the age of twenty-one — hell, under *any* age — has *not* been able to get hold of a six-pack? Look at how much trouble I had getting into a bar, for cryin' out loud.

Meaning he was my mainline to motherfucking Stanton.

As regards my plan for revenge — looking back, it was right about here it began to take form. That once I'd figured out what exactly the hell was going on, I should punish the scum who'd let Collie die through their boys. Put into practice the biblical standard that the sins of the father shall be visited on their sons unto the seventh generation. Those fuckers liked to use the bible to hit people like me over the head, so damn much; let's see how they liked it being used against them.

Of course, that raised a question — did Gilbert have one? Wouldn't it be just like the son-of-a-bitch to have nothing but girls?

That took a bit more research but I finally discovered through articles in the local paper that he was father to a set of twins — and they *were* female, dammit; another fantasy down the tubes — but he *did* have a son by a previous marriage who carried the same name, Nathaniel Carson Gilbert, albeit the fourth. The guy was twenty-seven, lived in another city and was doing the last of his internship at the teaching hospital there. I checked their site and found an article about him. Seems his maternal grandfather was a huge deal in medical research because he was on Dr. Jonas Salk's team and helped develop the first vaccine against polio and went on to fight AIDS, and Nat-four intended to follow in his footsteps. I actually rolled my eyes at how goody-goody he was coming across — until I caught a casual reference to his family that made wading through that garbage all worthwhile. Nat-four had a half-brother.

Named Michael Orin Tedesco.

Now I actually had a brain freeze at that. Seriously, my mind just locked onto that one little toss-away sentence at the tail end of an article about someone en route to becoming a saint, and I simply could not process the idea that locating Orin would be that serendipitous. So it had to be someone else.

Except — when I checked, he was the right age. Still, I needed more info to convince me this was more than just a fluke or coincidence of name.

There were several Tedescos listed in that town, so I Googled up Nat-four's address and saw it was in a suburb in the rolling hills of the north side. No Tedescos listed there, but quick search of the local paper's archives brought up an article in the sports section about a young master Tedesco who caught a fly ball in a little league game that sent his team to the state championships nine years ago. His team played on a field at a junior high less than two miles from Nat-four's address. Close enough to be suggestive.

The thing was, if this was Jake's Orin, his mom had to have been employed here, by the city, no later than three and a half years ago, when Orin would have been a freshman in college or a senior in high school. A quick check of the two high schools and one prep-school nearest Nat-four showed a Michael Tedesco graduating four years ago from the private school as part of the National Honor Society. Not promising, considering how dumb my Orin had been. And none of them had their yearbooks posted online. So I checked to see if there was anything about him in the papers and caught a notice listing local honorees (in a weekly freebie from his area) that included a photo. And there the little fuck was, looking as perfect and as condescending as ever. So — it looked like Jake's Orin wasn't mine.

Suddenly, all I could focus on was finding out if my Orin had vanished to live with big bro'. I found a car rental place that worked with guys my age and drove this beast of a seven-year old Malibu nearly two-hundred miles through misty rain to view Nat-four's address. Didn't have any trouble finding it; Google gives such great map.

The house turned out to be a nice big brick two-story done in a Tudor style with bay windows, a shake shingle roof, a nice-sized yard lined with thick trees and a charming mail box on a post situated at the foot of the winding sidewalk. The whole feeling was one of such inviting comfort and casual prosperity, you couldn't help but want to live there. Other homes lined the hill and winding street, each with its own style while still blending in gently with the rest — like a slice of humanity in the midst of an inhospitable world.

I parked across the street and waited — for what, I have no idea. It's just — it had worked in locating Jake, so why not? I lay across the passenger seat, its back lowered as far as it would go, and worked at gathering more info on my laptop while casting glances at the wide, slightly curved driveway that lead to the back of the house anytime I felt something move. Didn't find much more except Nat-four had graduated from the same prep school as his brother, was *Magna Cum Laude* in his BS and volunteered at a free clinic. Sickeningly perfect. And nothing happened around the house — and nothing happened — and nothing happened — until it was just beginning to get dark.

I knew I couldn't get away with staying there all night, so I was shutting down my laptop when a five-year-old Dodge Neon drove up and parked on the left side of the drive. A guy in blue scrubs got out — tall, trim, dark-haired, under thirty was all I could tell in the still-misting rain — then slung a backpack over one shoulder, pulled out a bundle of clothes and trudged into the house, looking as tired as if he'd been at the coal mines all day and night.

A light came on in the house. It looked like he was home alone. I began to wonder if I should just go over, knock on the door and see what I could glean from him, but then the front door opened and he trudged out, again. Headed straight for me!

I closed my computer and slunk down in the car, hoping he hadn't noticed I was there, then caught a peek of him digging into the mail box. I rose to get a better look and saw that he had this calm taut sense of control about him that, even from a distance, made his strong, simple features and deep eyes seem elegant if not beautiful. All tight muscle, no fat. Even his ass gave the impression of clean simplicity to it. I got the instant feeling of a long-distance runner, a marathon-man who was in perfect health and would be his whole life. And while I didn't get that good a look at his face, for some reason I knew it would be kind and gentle and open.

Because that was when I finally realized I was looking at Nathaniel Carson Gilbert, IV, who'd just come home after a long, *long* shift at the hospital. And he was such a polar opposite from Orin, I wondered if I'd done my research right.

But then a new Mercedes SLK roared up the street, swung onto the driveway and skidded to a halt, nearly hitting the Neon. And out popped Orin, dressed in slim jeans, a cotton shirt and jacket atop boots, looking very frazzled.

"Nat, I tried to catch you at the hospital," he yelled. Nat-four just looked him over and started back for the house, his gait casual and easy. Orin joined him, and they could not have looked more un-joined in any way, form or fashion. "I need a hundred bucks and I can't find dad."

"He'll be home in an hour," Nat-four said, and his voice was simple and direct. "Ask him then."

"I need it before five or I get bumped from the semester. They're being dicks about me paying everything in full."

"I thought you set up a delayed payment — "

"I did, and it's due today and I'm short — "

"Way to go, M-O. Last minute, as usual."

"You gonna give me the money?"

"Gonna pay me back, this time?"

"Cut the crap — you know dad'll give it to ya."

And at that, they entered the house and the door closed and BAM — I slammed into auto-pilot. I slipped my laptop under my seat, where it would be safe. I had no specific plan in mind when I whipped off my shirt, pulled on a hooded jacket I had with me, tore the long sleeves off the shirt and ripped its body into strips. I lay them on the passenger seat then looked over my Google map. Considering the direction Orin came from, he had just one outlet to a main street, and I could see where he had two ways to get there, so I started the car, pulled down the road — and waited.

Three minutes later, I watched Orin bolt out with a slip of paper in his hand, via my rearview mirror. He jumped in his car and spun into the street and zipped past me, heading back the way he came. I followed.

He drove like a bat out of hell, barely slowing for stop signs or speed bumps. According to my map, he was taking the short cut, so I spun onto a side street, floored the pedal, ignored the speed bumps and squealed up to the intersection just in time to see him coming. Still on auto-pilot, I popped the trunk and without a thought deliberately pulled out just enough to where a corner of the Mailbu's bumper could scrape the back fender of the SLK — absently thanking Nussewald for the idea.

Orin screamed to a halt and burst from his car, ready to kill. "Motherfucking son-of-a-bitch, why don't you watch where the fuck you're going, you cock-sucker — ?"

I was out of the Malibu in a flash — and he was out cold a second later. All it took was a quick punch to a particular area of his neck. Thank you lifeguard training.

He collapsed in my arms. I dragged him to the trunk and shoved him in, then hopped behind the wheel and quietly drove back down the residential streets to exit the direction I'd come from. It took a total of twenty seconds and so far as I could tell, no one saw me.

Man, was I riding high — and I had zero idea what I was

doing. Hell, I hadn't even thought about the ramifications that would come from kidnapping — the idea that his car would be found abandoned, and someone would raise the alarm and that might bring in the Feds and I may well have fucked up my life, completely; I just took the advantage and jumped headlong into the abyss. And call it luck or providence or fate or whatever, now I had Orin to do with as I wanted. Question was — what did I want to do?

Oh — the ideas that came to mind.

**\*\*\*\***

First thing I did was head to the top of a multi-level parking structure behind an office complex (no charge for parking in this part of town), drive around to locate the security cameras and park in a dark area away from the few remaining cars so none could see into the trunk. Then I popped it open, saw Orin was still unconscious and tied his wrists behind him with a strip of my shirt then wrapped a couple of strips around one of the sleeves, to make a ball, and used that to gag him; the other sleeve tied his ankles together. I tied his knees with the last strip of the shirt, slammed the lid closed and got the hell gone.

I hit the freeway and drove about thirty miles before I exited to hit some farm-to-market road. It was raining steady, now, and the smell of it and the rhythm of the windshield wipers clicking over the glass and the mile after mile of total darkness cut only by my headlights was almost hypnotic in its beauty. I honestly don't know how far I went before I noticed a side road approaching. I turned onto it and found it was messy overgrown gravel drive leading to an abandoned house — the kind where weeds shoot up all over and a couple of pecan trees offer shade for no reason and open fields expand in every direction. I pulled to a halt, got out and gave the place a quick once over — which was hard to do in the dark.

The building was on cedar stumps, with a dilapidated porch, doors missing and no glass left in the windows. I walked up and inside, carefully, to find half the roof was gone along with all of one wall and part of another. The floor felt solid and there was a sheltered area in what probably used to be the dining room. A bit more poking around the empty rooms provided me with some dry wood, a strip of corrugated tin and a length of old heavy rope. This would be perfect. I returned to the car, opened the trunk and looked down at my captive.

Orin was conscious. He looked up at me, shaking like a leaf. He'd been crying. I felt this odd thrill shoot into my heart, like I'd made the greatest conquest ever. I owned him, now, owned everything about him, and I loved the very thought of it. I checked his bindings; everything was still secure, so I pulled him up by his shirt then slipped my hands under his arms, dragged him from the car, slung him over my shoulder, fireman style, and carried him up into the sheltered area.

I lay him on the floor of the dining area in a corner then used the wood to build a small fire on the corrugated tin, just enough for light. I didn't have any matches, but I was a boy scout, once, so knew how to start one with two sticks. He just watched me with big eyes, unmoving. Once the fire was popping, I felt secure enough to remove the gag.

He coughed and gasped and croaked, "What the fuck's going on, man? You're not gonna hurt me, are you?"

"Depends on what you tell me," I said.

"Tell you?"

I squatted before him and pulled back my hood. He looked at me, totally lost. He didn't remember me. That would make this — oh, fun.

"I want to know what happened with Collier Winston-Royce," I said.

"Who?"

I backhanded him. Hard. Made his nose bleed. Hurt my hand, too. "Don't you fucking lie to me, again. You fucking *know* who. Tell me what happened. And if you fucking lie — "

I wrapped the rope around his neck. He began to quake.

"It — it was a mistake! He — he talked me into letting him suck me off and I — "

I pulled the rope tight. "You wanna know how easy it'd be for

93

me to break your neck, motherfucker?! What the *fuck* happened?!"

He cried out. "I'm sorry, I'm sorry! I — I'm sorry. I just — just wanted him to change my grade. But — but — he wouldn't — so I went to the cops — and told 'em — " He started crying.

"Told them he raped you." He nodded. "And that you were sixteen." He nodded. "How'd you put the semen in his office?"

He fought his way back into control and gasped, "I jacked off — into a condom. Had it with me. When he said he wouldn't do it — change my grade — I sat on his couch — and spilled it. I didn't mean for him to get hurt. I swear, I just wanted him — just wanted — "

"To get even." He hesitated — then slowly nodded. I loosened my grip on the rope. "That's a cute trick, your cum in a condom. Who taught it to you?"

"Nobody." He looked away, and I knew he *had* been shown how to do it and had probably done it to somebody before.

I kneeled and sat back. "Who showed you that trick, Orin?"

"I told you — "

I slapped him, again. "Somebody helped you set Collie up. Who was it?"

"Cousin Wilbur — he told me how to — "

Wilbur? "Nussewald? Wilbur Nussewald?"

He gulped in some air then nodded and said, "He — he's my mom's cousin."

This was too weird, so I had to ask, "Does your mother work for the city?"

He looked at me, wary. "What's she got to do with this?"

"ANSWER me!"

"Yeah! Yeah. So what?"

A question hit me like a bolt. "What's her maiden name?"

"I don't wanna tell — " I tightened the rope. He choked out, "Shit — no! Cullingham! It's Cullingham!"

Son-of-a-bitch. That was close enough to make him Jake's Orin, after all. I leaned back. Stared at him.

"You idiot," I whispered, more to me than to him, "she's divorced."

"So — so what? What the fuck's going on?"

"But you went to high school in — "

"I lived with my dad, okay!? Mom and me — we don't get along and — and he hasn't got a lot of money, so — so you're not gonna get any — "

"You wrecked a city car. Just over three years ago. Your mother got into deep shit for it, thanks to you."

He looked at me, confused. "I — I didn't — "

"So cousin Wilbur — he'd be your second cousin, right? Cousin Wilbur made it all go away by arresting the guy who reported it. And I'll bet that killed the whole mess, didn't it? Pop the guy who caught her, say it's for drugs and blame the wreck on his lyin' little self. So your mom gets off the hook — and so do you — and somebody innocent gets sent to prison. No big deal. All courtesy of cousin Wilbur. That mother-fucking-son-of-a-bitch."

Now he looked at me, confused. "Who the fuck ARE you?"

I looked at him and he flinched. My eyes must have been deadly cold as I said, "I was in love with Collier Winston-Royce, you little shit. And you got him killed."

"No — no, that wasn't my fault, man — "

"Bullshit. Cousin Wilbur knew you weren't sixteen years old. He knew fucking well the complaint was bullshit. He even set Collie up to be attacked, knowing it was all shit. Why?"

"I dunno what you're talking about!"

I yanked at the rope. "BULLSHIT! Answer me! What kind of sick crap did you two have going on here?!"

"Don't kill me, please. PLEASE! You gonna kill me? YOU GONNA KILL ME! PLEASE, I DIDN'T KNOW! I DIDN'T KNOW!"

His voice choked off. He was sobbing and twisting and trying to get away, terrified. I can't say I blame him; the look on my face probably would've scared Hannibal Lecter — because the room was beginning to go white, even though it was dark and wet outside. I was icy cold and beginning to groan. And I still had the rope wrapped around his neck. And I was all but massaging it. And I so desperately wanted to snap his thick, lying little neck. But I stopped. I don't know how I was able to — or even why I did — but I released the rope and leaned back, my eyes locked on him.

95

"No," I said. "No, I'm not." And I meant it — for one reason and one reason only. "I want to know why. Why did Nussewald tell the other prisoners Collie raped a boy when he knew that wasn't true? When he knew what'd happen to him?"

"He didn't — he — he wouldn't — "

"He did. What'd he do with the tape? Did he show it to you? You two jack off to it together?!"

"Tape?"

"Of the assault! Of Collie being raped! It happened to other men, too. What'd he do with the tapes?"

"You — you're fuckin' crazy, man. Wilbur's no fag. I — I dunno what the fuck you're talkin' about."

And you know, I actually thought he meant it, he was so obviously confused. I moved to a squat and looked at him, and even in the minimal light I could see truth in his eyes — probably for the only time in his life. And that confused me.

I took a long look at Orin, and finally admitted to myself that I was getting zero pings on my gay-dar off him. He was straight. Never really interested in a guy or anything a guy might offer, so I couldn't even begin to see him watching tapes of men being brutalized and yanking on his dick to it. He was more like those scumbags who use people's inner homophobia as a knife against anyone who didn't give him his way, because that would make the object of his contempt less human in the eyes of the world and make them more likely to give in to his demands. After all, who wouldn't believe a good-looking white boy when he said some faggot had tried to have his way with him? And that pissed me off.

He's the main reason people still hate fags, you know — snotty little cowards like him, who use the idea that being gay is awful, and use one's fear of being condemned as a weapon of control or revenge. Or destruction — like the boy who murdered his classmate and what those kids had done against that suicide boy. And what Orin had done to Collie. All because he was a selfish little prick who ran into a fag that wouldn't give him his way.

My thoughts were beginning to ramble, here, so I rose, motioned for him to stay where he was, added a bit of wood to the dwindling fire and went out to the car. I pulled out my laptop and carried it inside, protected by my hoodie. When I came back to the dining room, I noticed I'd popped a couple of buttons off his shirt and Orin's chest fur was showing. Rich and blond, fanning across a well-pumped set of pecs that flowed into nicely sculpted shoulders. My inner *Grr* went snarl, because I could finally see the picture Orin made. His arms being behind him made his shoulders seem to bulge, even under his jacket. The jeans on his legs added to the flow of his thighs into the cloth tying his knees together then seemed to emphasize his sturdy calves as they flowed down to his bound ankles. His boots did nothing for the picture; I felt they'd be better if they were off and all I saw was his stocking feet. So I removed them. And as I did, I saw how his crotch seemed to be porno-rich-and-full, ripe and ready to be eaten — and puppy began to whimper, *Feed me*.

I knew the direction this was going, I asked an obvious question. "So you don't know about the camera?"

He watched me set the laptop to his right, scared. "What camera?"

"In the jail," I said as I turned the laptop on. "In holding cell six. That records men as their clothes are ripped off. And they're fucked by several men. In the mouth and up the ass. Without a condom. Pretty Anglo men like you, being brutalized by pretty black men and other pretty white men."

As I spoke, I opened a video recording program and set it on pause. I'd been using the adaptor in the car as my power supply, so the laptop battery was full. At optimum quality, I could record up to twenty minutes of images on it as well as about ten minutes of decent video, thanks to my iPod and phone. I turned back to him. He cringed and tried to shift away from me. I straddled his hips and held him in place with my weight.

"It — it's jail, man. They got — they got cameras all over the place. Don't they?"

"You've never seen the inside of one, have you?" He shook his head, no. I smiled, pulled out the iPod and propped it on a stand to focus on Orin's profile. "Well — those cameras are usually crap; just put out enough of an image to be legal — but the one in

HC-6 has a high-quality lens. Records video sharp enough for broadcast. Or transfer to DVD. And whatever's recorded on that camera sometimes gets reworked and dirtied, thanks to cousin Wilbur, so it can be used in a trial and not raise any questions about its quality in comparison to the other videos. Why do you think that is?"

I started the iPod recording then opened my cell phone and began capturing video of his full face — his wide-open eyes — his scared expression — his chest that's visible through his shirt down to where his crotch and mine connected. Mingled with the way he shifted under me, it was like popping a couple Viagra, it got my dick going so hard. No question where I was going, now.

"I dunno anything about that, man! I — Wilbur didn't even talk to me about anything. About Professor — "

I smiled, leaned over to set the laptop to record, made sure it was focused on us — then grabbed his shirt and tore it open, revealing his tits. He jolted.

"Yeah?" I chuckled. "What about after the city car was wrecked? How'd that get set up?"

"No, no, please! Mom did that! She was drunk and she — she blamed it on me and sent me back to dad! I never had a chance to even see him or talk to him, swear to god!"

He tried to wiggle free of me, but I had too firm a grip on him with my legs — and the movement of his hips under me and his legs shifting against my ass made me nearly faint with need.

"So it's all cousin Wilbur, is it? That's just like you to blame anybody but yourself for your fuck-ups." I pinched his tits — not hard but tender, like a lover.

"No, please — please — I don't know why he did any of that and — and — don't hurt me, please — don't do this to me — " He was beginning to hyperventilate, so I toned it down, just a bit.

"What department does your mother work in?

"I — I dunno — something about buying stuff and — "

"Tell me something — does he have a business? Aside from his job? Cousin Wilbur?"

He glanced between me and the laptop, completely lost. "Yeah — I think; I dunno."

"Doing what?"

"Shit, I don't know. He's close to my mom, not me. Shit, that's why she moved back there."

"So — you've never seen the tapes — "

"I fuckin' told you — " I yanked the shirt and his jacket down his arms, revealing his strong shoulders and full chest. He cried out, "DON'T!"

"Then you never saw how scared they were. How they were held down and butt-fucked and face-fucked by several men."

I half-rose and slapped him. Twisted him onto his belly. He screamed and started to cry. That infuriated me. Collie wouldn't have cried, even as they were beating him to death. He'd have tried to reason with them. Tried to talk with them. Like they were all just human beings in need of a simple bit of communication and not animals who'd been driven mad by abuse and neglect and outright stupidity and contempt. And now he was dead and this little fuck was alive and I so fucking hated him for it.

I checked the laptop; it was still perfectly positioned — so I grabbed the back pockets of his jeans and tore at them. Ripped them off. The material split and I could just make out his stupid-looking boxers in the flickering light. I tore that split open, completely, and yanked the boxers' material aside to reveal some of his ass and left leg. He tried to kick me away so I slammed his head against the floor.

"No, please, please, don't hurt me."

I grinned. He tried to look back at me. I started recording on my cell phone, again, and asked, "What'll you give me if I don't?" And I crushed my crotch against his ass.

"Anything, anything, man please that ain't my way my dad's got money he'll pay you off and — "

"What about your brother?"

He got bewildered, again. "Nat? He hasn't got money — "

"But he's more my type than you are. I wonder what it'd be like to fuck him, instead?"

"What're you talking about? Why would you wanna do that? He's a fuckin' saint. Does everything right."

"Makes him even more interesting, sort of like how straight

boys love virgins." I leaned down to whisper in his ear. "Tell you what — I'll let you choose. I'm gonna fuck somebody over this, so I can fuck you; or I can fuck him."

"You crazy? You can't get to him."

"I got to you. And you could help me get to him. Then when I'm done with him, I could let you both go."

Orin looked at me, lost. "I — I don't get it, man — why would you do that?"

"I'm giving you a choice, bitch. Up your ass or up his. Which is it gonna be?"

He looked away. I moved the cell phone down to where it could record his face and leaned in to watch — and I saw he was actually considering it! The little fuck would've turned his brother over to me to save his own ass! I slipped my hand into the tear in his jeans and yanked at his boxers. Scraped my fingernails across his skin. He tried to jolt away.

"Why you doin' this? I'm sorry — I'm sorry, but I didn't kill your friend! And Nat — he didn't have anything to do with it — " I tore the seat of his jean completely open. "NO! Please! Nat's — but — but if that's what you want — if that'll make it okay — ?!"

That did it. I flipped him onto his back and slapped him, twice. Then as he was trying to regain control, I undid his jeans and yanked them down to his knees. I shredded off his boxers to reveal him in all his glory — and it wasn't that glorious. Well, to be honest, he was so scrunched up in his scrotum from fear, I really couldn't tell. But I didn't care; I slammed him back onto his belly, undid my pants, pulled out my dick and slipped it between his legs as I lay atop him.

He was gasping and crying and shaking, and my sense of control over him was so intoxicating, I felt like I was about to drift into a whole new plane of existence. I wrapped the rope around his neck, again, keeping it tight.

I snarled into his ear, "Now you know how Collie felt as he was held down. And his clothes were ripped away." I used my free hand to position my dick against his hole. "And strangers put their hands all over him." I probed his anus with my fingers, opening it so I could set the head of my dick up just right. "Now you know his fear — his terror — his pain — what you did to him. *You* did to him!" And at that, I pushed my dick into the little fuck.

He screamed with pain and clenched and tried to twist away to keep me out, but I keep shoving in deeper and deeper until I felt his ass against my pubes, then I began pumping into him. Harder and harder.

He grunted and gasped and tried to fight me, but the rope was too tight around his neck and my other arm was wrapped around his hips, holding him in place. And it felt so right and so good and so perfect as I slammed against him, feeling his ass quiver with every push as I grew closer and closer to the moment where I couldn't control myself, this weird sense of euphoria drifted over me and I never wanted it to end. I wanted to keep fucking this perfect asshole's ass for eternity because it made everything right with the world, again. His cries of pain were like music. The feel of his skin was like satin sheets wrapping themselves around to me intensify the sensations. Slipping in as deep as I could go was like I was a junkie sliding in the needle that he knew would bring nirvana — and pulling out was like releasing the drug into my blood to carry me away. Again and again and again and again until all I could feel was the wave building and building inside me and growing and roaring till I got to where I couldn't stop or slow down but had to punch into him faster and faster and faster until I began to explode, sending load after load of my cum into him, feeling beauty and grace and heaven sweep over me like nothing I'd ever felt before until I was almost blind with pleasure and sensation and knew I was dying — I was dying — it was too wonderful and I was dying. And I had to — had to — had to stop.

I rolled us onto our sides, my dick still in him, and felt his cock and it was hard. Not exactly raging but not scrunched up, anymore. I slipped my fingers around it, in surprise. I'd heard of guys getting erections if they were strangled a little (and the rope was still tight around his neck) so I began to stroke it — just to see what would happen.

"No — no, please — " he choked out.

I kept stroking — and within a minute, with my dick still somewhat hard inside of him, he shuddered and ejaculated. Not a lot but a nice bit into my hand.

"What the fuck? You get off on being fucked?"

"No — I — never."

I pulled out of him, rolled him onto his back and smeared his face with his own cum. "That ain't what this says, bitch." Then I looked at his dick and saw it was nice and fat with a smallish head and surrounded by a blond bush that flowed into his beautiful legs and up his too-developed abs to his rich, full chest — and I began to suck on it.

He tried to shift away, but I had too good a grip on him so he just lay there and wept. I pulled back and noticed my laptop had stopped recording. I could check it later to see what it had gotten.

I shifted up to his ear and whispered, "Now you know what cousin Wilbur was recording. God knows how many times to how many different men. Then he'd vanish the disks so nobody would see how good those videos were. Why would he do that?"

He choked out, "Please — please — just let me go — "

"C'mon, Orin, tell me. Why would he do that?"

"I — please — I didn't know — "

I wasn't going to get anything more out of him — half because he was lost in shock and half because he probably did NOT know about the videos. But he did now. He'd experienced the making of one, first hand. I'd have to send him a copy.

So I rose to a kneeling position, ran my hands over his amazingly beautiful body for a little while — tickling the hairs on his legs and abs and chest and toying with his tits and feeling up his dick and balls, and he just lay there and let me — until I started to get hard, again.

It'd been a while since I was that ready to go so quickly after so solid an explosion, and I didn't want to miss the building of it. I picked him up, propped him against a corner, face first, and fucked him standing up as I wrapped my arms around his chest and pulled at his tits. He grunted and groaned and whimpered, but his crying was over. And when I came, this time, it was almost as good as the time before.

Then I stepped back, packed myself away, turned off my phone and stamped out the fire. He stayed propped against the corner so I cut away his bindings with a piece of the tin. He sort of melted down to the floor.

"I'll let people know where you are," I said. Then I left the dilapidated house, got in the Malibu and drove away. The rain had ended and the moon was full, so my world was so clear I was able to see my way straight back to the road.

The first truck stop I hit, I used a pay phone to call the sheriff and told them where to find Orin. Then hung up when they asked for more info, snuck back to the Malibu and headed home.

And let me tell you, this little puppy was totally satisfied — for the moment.

— SEVEN —

The next morning, I scraped the little bit of paint from Orin's SLK off the Malibu's bumper, washed off the mud and turned the car in, then downloaded the video off my phone and pod onto my laptop and viewed everything I'd recorded. With sound. It didn't look like all that much was happening — just crappy images of a couple of guys fucking, albeit one of them occasionally looking scared out of his mind. Didn't look so bad, really.

I'd seen some high-quality videos from this one porn house in San Francisco that had big buff guys tied up and in chains and all begging for dick until their few clothes were stripped off and they began fucking like it was the hardest, dirtiest job there ever was. The lighting was fantastic, the cameras angled all over the place, their muscles gleamed with sweat — and it bored me silly because they all looked like they were working so hard at having fun, they weren't really having any. But in my video, I was having a blast, though you couldn't see it; the whole thing was a great profile of someone in a hoodie (you couldn't see my face, very well) lying on top of Orin, my dick slipping in and out of his ass as he grimaced and wept and sometimes gasped as if receiving pleasure while my naked little ass was busy grinding and my hands were busy groping all over his body and I was almost laughing from joy. Plus there was a great shot of me jacking him off; one spurt shot straight at the laptop's lens but must have just missed landing on the keyboard because I didn't feel anything sticky when I checked it. And I was still milking him dry when it cut out. None of me sucking on him, thought I could still make this into something truly erotic to send to his mother as if to say, *See? This is what your cunt of a son is worth. Why not show cousin Wilbur?* Just the thought

104

made me jack off, again.

That night, I watched the news. There was nothing about Orin's kidnapping on it. Looked like the family wanted to keep everything nice and quiet. Too bad I wasn't going to give them that option. Because now I'd decided — Nat-four was going to be my revenge on Judge Gilbert, ADA Stanton *and* Deputy Chief Nussewald. And I didn't care that he'd had nothing to do with Collie's murder; he was guilty by blood.

But first I needed to have a better idea of what the hell was going on, here. I started in digging for any news stories about Wilbur arresting one David Hirsh while still deputy sheriff. Came up with nothing on either name. I checked *McNevin* and still came up with nothing. Same for anybody named Andre. Just to see if I was doing this right, I checked to see what there was about him and Jake — and there were half a dozen, all holding info that obviously came from the DA's office and insisting that Jake had hit Wilbur's car while drunk and/or drugged up — until the final blurb that he'd been found guilty and the infamous comment from Stanton that echoed what he'd said about Collie, "Even homosexuals are subject to the law, you know."

Oh, the fucker.

That's when I finally remembered — with a strong mental kick for my stupidity — that Nussewald had been made Deputy Chief in charge of the jail BEFORE Jake was busted. Meaning he was no longer on patrols or in the field, so he wouldn't be arresting people. The reason he'd arrested Jake was because of the accident.

So I shifted to Stanton and cross-referenced his name with Hirsh — and struck out, again. Then checked under *Hersh* — nothing — then I had a bright idea and input *Hers* just to see what happened and came up with three that were close enough, one of whom was David Luka Hersk, who was arrested for DWI by a suburb cop. He plead no-contest, took the courses demanded, paid the fines and all was forgiven. And Stanton handled the case — which didn't make sense; he was high up on the DA's food chain so didn't have to handle simple drunk case, but he'd handled this one.

I checked out the other two guys using five different spellings of the names Enrique'd given me, and finally zeroed in on Andre Yelvin — assault, arrested by city police — and McNeal Shirripa — for back child support, busted by the Texas Rangers in another county and brought back here. I found out that both Yelvin's and Shirripa's cases were dropped by Stanton a week after they posted bail. Which was very suspicious for a strict law and order ADA to do, especially as regards child support. Oh — and all three cases appeared before Judge Gilbert — Hersk for sentencing and Yelvin and Shirripa to formalize the withdrawal of charges.

That was weird — so I checked Jake's trial. He appeared before one Judge Atelano Rosales according to one news article. I only scanned it and was about to close the link when I noticed a reference to Judge Gilbert; a bit more research showed Jake was supposed to have appeared before him but a family emergency had called the judge away and Rosales stepped in — and he was another of those idiot judges who believes everything a cop says, verbatim, and nothing that's told him by the defense without proof. So Jake was the only one who wound up in jail — which may have been because of a fluke.

Meaning it looked way too much like Stanton and Gilbert were deliberately dropping cases against guys who were raped. Which made sense — if they dropped the criminal cases as a carrot to get the guys to not file a complaint. Could that be why no one made a big deal out of it till Collie wound up dead?

But what about the rapists? This seemed just a bit too well-scheduled for them not to be in on it — yet there was nothing anywhere that I could find where anyone was claiming to have been part of the process. But you can't be certain you'd have men sexually assault someone unless you'd told them that's what you wanted or made them do it, and convicts are notorious for making all sorts of claims against law enforcement officials — and that only added confusion to the mix. I mean, maybe you can get away with that once or twice, but three dozen times? Seriously doubtful without someone spilling details. So what the fuck was going on here?

Which brought me right back to my feeling that Collie'd been set up, but now I was wondering if it actually was just to be raped on camera, then all charges would be dismissed against him and everything kept quiet or else. But no — that didn't tie in with the inmates being told he'd raped a child. Anyone who knows anything about the prison system in this country — hell, in any country — knows the vast majority of criminals were sexually abused as kids and will take their anger and frustration out on anyone accused of child molestation.

I found a BBC story about this one man accused of raping dozens of boys in Liverpool, and how a sudden jump in crimes around the city was tied to his victims acting out because no one in authority believed them or would stop the bastard, not till they were forced to. It was a nice little scandal, over there — but it went nowhere, as such scandals usually do. As for criminals having been molested, that's something cops and guards already know. So when the lie was spread about Collie, they must have known the reactions would be harsh and the guys hurting him must have known they'd be caught and punished. So what the hell was going on there?

Had Nussewald done this to end Collie's career at the university? Or to just fix it so he'd be out the rest of the term? Or could he be one of those vindictive types — yes, like me — who feel a need to go nuclear to deal with a problem? But the fact that he busted Jake built way too much of a link between him and the attacks...if they *did* start with Jake. I did some checking and found whenever people talked about the SOB — well, fellow law-enforcement officers and members of the justice system — it was with complete respect. Even his supposed run-ins with the Latinos were brushed aside as *illegals what think they got the right to do as they please in this country*. I didn't know what to think about him, anymore.

So I looked into his business dealings. Nothing came up in an online search — nothing in any way, shape or form — until I had the bright idea of checking to see if he had a DBA or was incorporated; when you do that, you have to place a notice in a local paper to announce it. And there it was, placed three and a half years ago in this nice quiet little business weekly distributed just in the downtown area to no one who'd care — an incorporated entity

107

called *Greco'd* was established by one W. S. Nussewald. I searched the company, online, but all I found was a basic web page for something based in Europe, which had a notice that I had to apply to be a member to get past the intro window. That didn't sound right, so I figured he just didn't have an online page — not all businesses do — and dropped it.

What I *was* able to find out by digging through the public files on incorporated businesses is, Nussewald had three shadow partners, none of whose names were required to be publicized. Raising the question, if Stanton and Gilbert were two of them, who was the third? I hadn't seen anyone else's name come up in conjuncture with them often enough to be suspicious. And if they had this business and it was tied in to these videos in some way, how could they keep it so secret?

Now all this info was grabbed in the space of two days, using the school's library and its massive connection to the whole university system's research materials. And despite the nagging questions, I was feeling pretty pleased with myself as I headed back to my dorm room, with all of this stuff I'd hunted and gathered and noted and annotated and safely ensconced in a folder in a notebook in my backpack. So pleased, in fact, that when I saw a couple of men waiting down the hall in suits by Men's Wearhouse, all I noticed was one of them looked like Adonis, and the other could have been a cable-movie grandpa — oh, and that both wore white cowboy hats and black boots.

"Anthony St. Lazarre?" asked Grandpa.

"Antony — no 'H' in it," I smiled — not at him but at Adonis.

"I'm Officer Thomas and this is Officer Marquez. May we ask you a few questions?" Then he showed me an ID with a "star in circle" badge. Holeee-shit — Texas Rangers! ZING — heart in throat time. The Tedesco family wasn't keeping this quiet, after all. Shit.

I took in a deep breath and made myself smile and unlock my door, saying, "Sure, come on in — but don't be shocked at the mess. I'm playing catch-up from last semester." And I hoped they didn't notice my hands were shaking.

Adonis did, and glanced from them to Grandpa. Then he

looked at me with this deliberately blank look on his face, and I realized he'd already made up his mind that I was guilty. No discussion with me. Don't even need to bother telling me why they're there. Just slap the little faggot in jail. Like they had Collie, who'd done nothing to anybody. Like they do every day without any thought or consideration. That's when this — this calm came over me, and my smile became a grin.

Okay, motherfucker, you wanna play? We'll play.

I opened the door and lead them in, saying, "You guys want something to drink? I've got DP, sparkling water or coffee — though you'll have to have the coffee by yourselves; I'm so juiced on it, I'll be up all night and that's with putting milk in it. Which'll come in handy since I have to have one of these papers in by five, tomorrow. Either of you know something herbal to counteract the caffeine?"

I was deliberately chattering to play up the caffeine rush. I dropped my backpack on the bed and unfolded a couple of card table chairs I'd stolen from somebody's trash somewhere then dove into the fridge.

"Oh, you're in luck!" I squeaked. "My roomie's got some tomato juice and I have lemon. If either of you have a fifth of vodka, I'll make Bloody Marys."

"You old enough to drink, son?" asked Grandpa as he sat in one of the chairs.

"Don't you already know?" I shot back before thinking. *Not the direction I wanted to go with these two.* So I gave a goofy grin and added, "You're Texas Rangers. Don't you have dossiers on all us liberals now, thanks to Homeland Security?" Then I batted my eyes.

He just looked at me.

I sat on the bed and cast my eyes over Adonis, who was standing by the window, looking out. He had that smoldering Latino thing going on — so much so, I had a pretty good idea he was brought along deliberately to throw me off my game. So — now I knew the rules; now I could mess with them.

"Are you from Brazil, Officer Marquez?" He looked at me. "Because I'll bet you'd look perfect in a Speedo on a beach in

Rio." He tensed.

Grandpa huffed. "Careful, son."

"Sorry," I said. "Didn't know it was illegal to pay one of you guys a compliment. So what do you want to ask me? My roomie's got a lab till seven. We got plenty of time. And I'm happy to help you in any way I can."

I could feel Grandpa glaring at me, but I kept my eyes on Adonis — and he was feeling it. He started glaring back — so I deliberately traveled my eyes up one side of him and down the other, resting them for a few special moments on his crotch.

"Okay," Grandpa sighed, "I need to ask you some questions." I shrugged an okay. "Do you know a Michael Tedesco?"

"I know an Orin Tedesco; met him last Spring."

"Have you seen him, lately?"

"How lately?"

"The last few days."

I looked straight into Adonis' eyes and said, "Yeah, we had sex. What's it to you?" Adonis looked away, irritated.

"So you have seen him?"

"I'm sorry, am I muttering or something?"

"Where?" Something about that question made me look at Grandpa. My expression must have been seriously confused, because he leaned forward and added, "He's missing."

What the fuck? That must have been the expression on my face, because Grandpa nodded, sympathetically, obviously of the opinion I was shocked at the idea of Orin's disappearance. But I wasn't; I was shocked at how obvious the bullshit was.

You see, I took a class last Spring dealing with media criticism, and part of it dealt with the disconnect between TV dramas and real life. One aspect of that had been how readily TV cops and FBI agents and lawyers gave up information while initially interrogating suspects, when in reality they won't tell you jack shit. They just want questions answered, period. So Grandpa sitting there telling me Orin was missing meant they'd found him and he'd told them what happened to him — and most importantly, who'd done it. So now he and Adonis were here to get me to implicate myself in Orin's rape and kidnapping, and were doing it by lying to me.

Except — if they believed him, then why weren't they just arresting me? What I'd done *was* kidnapping and rape, even in Texas. Maybe they were after something more and felt the best way to get it out of me was to let me think Orin was still in that empty farmhouse in the middle of God knows where. Which also told me all they saw sitting on this bed was some dumb twenty-one year old college twit who didn't know a fucking thing about anything and they'd have complete mastery over him in a heartbeat, all because one guy probably looked like his grandfather and the other filled out a suit very, *very* nicely.

Oh, this was gonna be fun.

"What do you mean?" I asked, a hint of a quiver in my voice.

"Just tell us — where'd you last see him?"

"At his home, after I dropped him off. He called me about noon and begged me to come there."

They tried to cover it, but I could tell that mixed up Grandpa's game plan, a bit. "Why?"

"He and I'd been talking. About Collie's death. He was sick about it — "

"Wait," said Adonis, with the hint of an accent to his voice. Maybe he *was* from Brazil. "Who is Collie?"

"Collier Winston-Royce," I said. "He was raped and murdered in the county jail, a few months ago. Orin's the one who put him there."

That brought a glance between them. All their little suppositions were suddenly poised on the windowsill ready to fly away. Apparently Orin didn't mention that particular little detail to them.

"You telling us you went all the way to his home to talk with him about another man's death?" asked Grandpa.

"I had to. I'd been working on him to talk face-to-face about it, for weeks. He was finally willing to so — so I wasn't going to miss the chance. It was a pain, too; I had to rent a car and it rained the whole way, and I hate driving in the rain — "

"When did you get there?" shot Adonis.

"About two-thirty. He said he'd be there around three, but he was having some trouble at school and said he might — "

"When DID he arrive?" Adonis was glaring at me, as if he knew I was lying.

I looked straight back at him, though I still cast some deliberate glances at his crotch. "I dunno — four, four-thirty, something like that. His brother'd shown up — and he said if he did then we'd have to go someplace else and — "

"Where'd you go?"

"A parking lot behind some office building. He didn't want anyone to see us, together. He's afraid somebody'd recognize me and it'd get back to cousin Wilbur."

"Cousin Wilbur?" This came from Grandpa.

"Nussewald," I told him, in all faux-innocence. "Deputy Chief — in charge of the county jail?"

Zing! All suppositions had just flown south for the winter. Grandpa leaned back and exchanged a long look with Adonis. Apparently that had *also* not been part of what Orin told them, and now their kidnapping-rape was mixed up with something they weren't sure they either understood or wanted to know about.

"What did he tell you?" asked Adonis.

"I don't understand what this has to do with — "

Grandpa cut me off. "Just answer the question, please."

"Fine. He had Collie busted because he was jealous. The bad grade was just his bullshit excuse to — well — "

I jolted into silence as the picture of Orin and Collie arguing by the bagel stand had slammed into my brain — and it cut into my heart. Suddenly memories of Collie were crashing into me, and I couldn't make them stop. Our months together. Our making love. The trip to Seattle and the Mile High Club. A thousand other moments that he and I had shared, all destroyed by that little shit and his fucking relatives — and I couldn't have this — not now!

My hands began to shake and my voice quaked as I made myself continue, "He — he was upset — that Collie chose me over him. But you see — he was in one of Collie's classes, and Collie didn't date his students and — "

The pictures kept coming. I bolted to my feet, near tears. Yes, half of my reason for doing it was to further my act, but half was a

rage against Orin and cousin Wilbur and these two fucking
Rangers who were so fucking casual in their attitude that what
happened to this faggot was nothing important outside of it
messing with their stupid little plans — a rage that flowed over my
heart like a flood of molten rock and I didn't want these two to see
that — and starting to pace was the only way I could hide it well
enough to keep them off-center.

Adonis almost caught it. "Did you blame Tedesco for this
guy's death?"

"I don't know!" I said. "Maybe. What I really wanted from
Orin was — was to — to understand."

"Did he tell you anything that helped?" asked Grandpa.

Okay, I still had enough awareness to know I had 'em hooked.
Time for some real lies, so I nodded and told them, "He said he
called his cousin and asked him to keep Collie safe. He knew
what'd happened before and he didn't want — "

"Before?" asked Adonis.

"Yeah, a couple years ago. Another guy was busted for
something Orin did — and sent to prison. Orin didn't want that to
happen to Collie, too. But cousin fucking Wilbur didn't do a
damned thing — not one fucking thing — to protect Collie, even
though he knew he was innocent and — "

"How do you know he knew that?"

I had to take a moment to calm down; right now I was more
afraid of losing control of myself than I was of them. I made
myself stop pacing, finally caught a deep breath and said, "The
complaint had Orin down as sixteen. Nussewald knows he's really
twenty-one. So he'd know the whole thing was bogus."

Grandpa stood and said, "That's stretchin' it, a bit." But I
could tell he was wondering what the fuck was going on here.

Adonis had also backed into questions about Orin and his
story. "What happened with you and Tedesco?"

I stood still and looked out my window. The wind was
blowing. Looked like a Norther coming in. I could already feel the
chill. I spoke softly and absently.

"He left his car on the street and we drove over there —
parked in the shadows — and talked. He was really cut up about

Collie's death. He said he'd talked Collie into having sex with him, but I didn't believe him. Collie wouldn't have done that."

"How do you know?" It was Grandpa asking.

I glared at him and said, "I told you, he didn't date his students."

"You were one of them."

"No — I was never in one of his classes."

"Stretchin' things a bit."

He stood there, smirking. He wanted me to get angry, the fucker. I turned and leaned against the window.

"So you're one of those kinds of cops," I said. "All fags want is dick and they don't care whose it is. And you use any excuse to think badly about them. You think the same way about straight guys and the pussy they get?"

"Watch your mouth, son."

"Collie liked adults, not grown babies. And that's all Orin was — a child in an adult's body. My grandmother would've called him *hateful*. He couldn't have Collie, so he was going to punish him for rejecting him — and he got him into a situation where he got killed and now he's thinking if he says he's sorry often enough, it'll all be okay. Only he's finding it isn't! He's scared and his dreams hurt him and his cousin Wilbur's threatened him to keep him quiet and he can't think and his new school's jumping on him for not paying his tuition and isn't life hard and please feel sorry for me and — and — "

I was close to ranting and had to shut myself down. Now my hands were shaking from anger and my voice quivered from the strain of not screaming. And both Grandpa and Adonis could see it, plain as day. And I didn't give a shit.

"You said you had sex with him," said Grandpa.

I gulped in several deep breaths and nodded. "I — I didn't plan for that to happen. But he was crying — and like a dumb shit, I felt a bit sorry for him — and held him — and I hadn't been with anybody since — since — and it just happened. And it made me sick, afterwards."

"This was in your car?"

I looked straight at Adonis. Saw the disdain in his eyes. I all but snarled, "Yes. Do you want it described in detail? Or would you like a blow-by-blow re-enactment?" And I deliberately licked my lips at him.

The son-of-a-bitch bolted over and damn near hit me. "You cut that shit out on me, faggot!"

"Benny!" Grandpa stopped him then guided him to the door. "Wait outside, Benny."

Adonis glared at me, straightened his suit and stormed out to the hall. I almost wondered if what I'd just seen was an act for my benefit.

Then Grandpa turned to me and said, "You shouldn't provoke an officer like that." I just looked at him. "How much of that story you just told me was true?"

I sighed and shook my head. "Believe what you want."

"I don't believe things," he said. "I look into them."

"Do you?"

He smiled and slowly approached me, his eyes never leaving mine. "You really think you got this all figured out, don't you? Son, you ain't even got a clue." I didn't budge. He nodded. "I will say you're good. Ain't many guys can get Benny to lose his temper, like that — you just ain't as good as you think you are. You see, I've dealt with punks like you for thirty years, so any trick you think you got that's just too slick for this old bastard, trust me — I've already seen it."

In response, I held out my hands, wrists together, daring him to cuff me.

"Don't tempt me. I've got enough to send you away for thirty years."

"Except — ?"

He sighed and relaxed. "You put enough shit in the water to foul it. Now how much of that crap you handed me was true?"

"Every word."

"Bullshit."

It's funny, but my inner filter was saying, He's good; he's cool. Saying it loud and clear and just a bit too happily. Just enough to where I'm thinking, "He ain't kiddin', he knows what's what. Motherfucker's playing me." So I broke eye contact first to give him a small victory. Then I decided to keep playing the game.

I cast Grandpa a sideways glance. "Bullshit right back at you. Orin's not missing. He's still feeding you lies, and you're swallowing them like a hungry catfish."

"Listen, you little shit — "

"Fine, don't believe me!" I snarled. "Check it out. That's what you say you do. DO it! Check Orin's complaint to the cops against his statements to the press. Check out his teachers and see how many times he's gotten decent grades even though he didn't do the work. Check out how many people he bitched about Collier Winston-Royce to. And while you're at it, check the semen they found in Collie's office. It's Orin's. He told the cops Collie sucked him off there. But I'll bet you fifty bucks there's latex residue in it, or maybe a spermicide. Because he admitted to me that he jacked off into a condom, snuck it into Collie's office and spilled it when Collie wouldn't give in to him. So check all of that! Then come back to me and tell me you believe a single solitary word out of *his* fucking mouth. Or are you the type who believes anything a supposedly-straight white boy says and thinks all fags are liars? That we all oughta be put away to keep innocents like Michael Orin Tedesco safe from us turning them onto our darkest desires? That's what Adonis thinks — your little partner, Marquez — he thinks if I look at him wrong, he'll go queer for dick. You believe that shit, too? You really one of those assholes?"

Grandpa glared at me then took a step back. From the look in his eyes — if he was still playing me, he was way out of my league, because he now had questions in there. His voice grew wary.

"Did Tedesco tell you all of that?"

I nodded.

He leaned against my desk and looked at me for a long, long time. He finally sighed and said, "I get the feeling you're still lyin'."

"Check it out."

"I will. And I'll be back tomorrow night. Same time. And you better be here, or I'll have a warrant sworn out for your arrest. And trust me, son — there ain't no place you can go to get away from

116

me."

And with that, he left.

I went to the door and watched them walk down the hall to the stairs. No elevator for these men. But I had to admit, Grandpa'd impressed me. I wondered if he would look into things — and halfway wondered if I should have told him in detail about what happened to Jake to bolster my story. It might have lead to Jake's exoneration.

But then I was glad I hadn't, because something about the visit with Grandpa and Adonis shook me up — like I'd just gone from AAA to the big leagues of liars and manipulators — and I started feeling what he really meant was he'd be back later that night with a search warrant for my place. So the second he was gone, I downloaded my notes off my computer onto a jump drive then burned a CD-R then dumped everything on my laptop into the trash and wiped it out. It could still be retrieved, sure; but I wasn't going to make it easy. I then slipped the disks and laptop into my backpack and headed for an a twenty-four hour diner I knew. And I stayed there in a back booth and worked all fucking night, downing coffee like it was speed and assembling all my notes into order. Then I burned *another* CD-R and, soon as I could, hit the post office near campus.

I put each disk and drive into a padded envelope and sent it to my dorm address, my old apartment address and my home address via registered mail, restricted delivery — the slowest method possible — but I put Dean Weller's return address on them. Now I had some protection in case Officers Thomas and Marquez came back and decided to keep me someplace for some serious questioning. Registered mail required the signature of the recipient to be released, under Federal law; and if it was unclaimed, after fifteen days it was returned to sender. Once Dean Weller got these, wondered what they were and opened them, if I had disappeared into the Justice Department's American shadow prisons, like some Americans and Canadians had done, I might not be allowed to just stay there. Then I went to the library and napped till my first class.

I wish I could say I'd known what was going to happen next and that's why I'd taken the precautions, but reality is — I was only being paranoid. At the time. But that paranoia proved to be my saving grace, because as I neared the building my first class is in, two campus cops and four sheriff's patrol cars roared up and surrounded me. They all jumped from their cars, some with pistols drawn, screaming, "Down on the ground! Face down! Get down! Now-now-now!"

I got.

The cops swarmed around me, yanked away my backpack and whipped those flex-cuffs around my wrists, behind me, and pulled them *tight*. I actually screamed from the sudden pain and the two assholes sitting on my back, making it so damned hard to breathe. Motherfuckers.

"What's gong on?" I croaked, even though I had a pretty good idea.

One fat cop snarled, "Anthony Lazarus, we have a warrant for your arrest for kidnapping and assault. You have the right to remain silent..." and on and on, but I wasn't listening. I suddenly realized I really was in deeper shit than I'd expected — and it wasn't because I finally knew which side of the fence Grandpa stood on, the son-of-a-bitch.

No, I was now headed for county jail — and that scared the fucking shit out of me.

— EIGHT —

I was driven straight to jail in a sheriff's cruiser — no passing go, no collection of my two-hundred dollars — and while I've read a lot about the place and seen photos of it, I'd never actually understood how intimidating the reality of it was. Seriously, one minute you're driving through this area of run-down buildings and vacant lots cleared of trees when all of a sudden you see this pair of long, four-story brick buildings that looked like they belonged on a secret military base, thanks to the tiny slits for windows and the outer wall separating them from the area. Then you drive past this well-guarded entrance, zip down a sharp, small incline between the two buildings and get backed into a small space that looks way too much like a loading dock at the mall — minus the dock. And every second of it is meant to impress upon you just how powerless you are — which it did a damned good job of doing to me.

Two deputies lead me from the car through a thick metal door and down a short bland corridor to a large, open room with two doors in every wall and a single countertop sort of desk in the middle of the room. Two more deputies sat at computer terminals behind the counter and a small shelf jutted out at about belly-button level all the way around. I was shoved to one of the terminals, where a fat bored slug ignored us both.

"Anthony Lazarus," snapped one of my deputies. "Warrant for transport."

"Got nobody on the manifest by that name," came the dead-as-can-be reply from the slug, who didn't even look at me.

"Here's the fuckin' warrant." He slapped a slip of paper in a brown wrapper on the top of the counter.

119

Slug took it with a sigh, looked at it and sniped, "S*aint* Lazarre, Landon. Shit, can't you fuckin' read?"

"I fuckin' got him here, Herrera. Rest is up to you." Then he cut off the flex-cuffs.

The Slug-Known-As-Herrera finally looked at me — and I have never been so creeped out by someone's eyes, before. They were this ice-cold grey without a shred of humanity behind them, and when they swept over me I felt almost violated. But that wasn't the worst of it. He said, "Empty your pockets," in a voice that had lost all of its deadness and sounded almost like a cat who's seen the canary that's about to be its supper. Then he added a hint of a smile to his lips and I nearly bolted for the door. "Name?" he continued, still with that little purr still lacing his words.

"Antony Patric St. Lazarre," I replied, not even trying to keep my voice level and smooth. I knew they wanted me scared, and I wasn't going to let them think for two seconds that I wasn't — not till I could be to myself, assess the situation and kick-start my how-do-I-get-the-fuck-out-of-here senses.

He input my address, age, description, social security number, waist size, shoe size — you name it, they wanted to know it. So a warrant *had* been issued for me for Orin's kidnapping and assault (nothing about rape in it, surprisingly) and I was to be held until someone could be sent to ferry me back for arraignment. Which they had up to seventy-two hours to get around to, and wasn't it just awful how slowly the wheels of justice can turn? All this info came from Herrera, offered up in a voice that just dripped with joy, disdain and ice-cold menace. I was then taken to a small room with a block of concrete jutting from the wall that served as a bench and handed a jail uniform by a short, squat man who looked so much like a movie version of a don't-give-a-shit jail guard, it was almost comical.

"Strip," was all he said. I did while the motherfucker watched in as bored a manner as he could — but when I got down to my briefs he said, "You can keep those, but put them down at your ankles." I did. "Bend over." I did and he proceeded to make sure I didn't have anything shoved up my ass in the most boring manner possible. "Put this on." He pointed to the uniform and a pair of cheap flip-flops. I did. Then he put restraints around my ankles and wrists, lead me to another room and stood me against a wall next to a height ruler to snap a mug shot and take my fingerprints — all electronically, which surprised me; no ink. Very modern in comparison to the hundred year-old manner of everything else.

After that, he herded me back to the intake desk. Herrera wrote down the number on my uniform's jersey and had me sign a printout for everything I'd handed over, trying hard not to smirk the whole time. I read it and without thinking said, "You misspelled my name. There's no H or K in it."

He looked in my wallet, saw how my name was spelled on my driver's license and shrugged. "Sign it."

I did. And my hands began to shake. Because I had a pretty good idea that if everything wasn't perfect as regards your name on a warrant or any other legal piece of paper, it was possible to get it dumped in the trash. Meaning I wasn't meant to make it to transport back for Orin's charges. Meaning this nagging little scream in the back of my brain — that I was about to find out exactly what had happened to Collie when he'd been through all of this — became a deafening roar.

"HC-6," whispered past Herrera's almost snarling lips. And my stomach nearly did a flip.

Sure enough, Bored Guard lead me through another thick door to a hallway that lead past a series of thick-barred cages backed up to a concrete block wall, with thick-barred sliding doors cut horizontally by a narrow slit for meals or something. Each was filled with an assortment of scary guys awaiting arraignment or transport or just being held till it was decided which area of the jail they'd serve their short-time sentence, all of them a mixture of black, brown and white with the occasional Asian. They yelled at me and made so many lewd comments I honestly wished I'd had a note pad to write some of them down, they were so *promising*. That kept up until we got to the last cage — from which there came this dead silence in counterpoint to the nastiness of the boys.

This holding cell was at the end of the hall. Which slammed up against a stone-block wall painted a dead shade of blue. With a three-foot section of stone blocks jutting out to meet the bars and sliding door. Which, along with the two concrete walls meeting at the inside corner, added to the feeling of being isolated. And enclosed. Almost private. Like the other cells, it had two concrete slabs atop braces built into the floor that served as tables, with four concrete blocks for benches and an exposed toilet in one corner. And like the others, despite a sign above it that said "maximum capacity 8" there were twelve men in it, all in the exact same uniform as me and most of them seeming more experienced at being in here than I was. But unlike the others, all of them were white, Anglo-Saxon and probably Protestant — though religious preference is probably not something one should bring up at a time like this.

So, Antony, looks like we'll be having no racial-mingling in your rape video, thank you. Apparently, they only do that with buff Englishmen and cute transportation schedulers who work for the city. But didn't they know one of my fantasies was to be used and abused by this one particular actor who's in that black, gay vampire series on cable? Huh, motherfuckers?

Bored Guard told them to, "Step back." They did, then he slid the cage door open, undid my restraints and nodded inside.

I stepped in, doing my best to keep my shaking under control. Then I noticed the camera window in the ceiling corner and there was no question in my mind — this *was* the room where Collie and Jake had been attacked. And I was about to have the pleasure of being next on the menu. Boy did survival mode kick in, then.

I stood ramrod straight. Didn't look directly at any of the other men, even when Bored Guard slammed the sliding door closed and sauntered away. No need to initiate a confrontation, yet; I wanted time to see if I could figure out who was going to lead the pack and who would follow — and who would just stand there and let it happen.

The guys broke down into four basic categories — biker trash, nervous junky, White-Collar criminal, and a muscle queen. And unsurprisingly — not a one of them was in any way, form or fashion ugly or homely or even unattractive. The best-looking was this one biker with shaggy brown hair, a rattler tatt on his left forearm and a goatee in need of a trim, who was taller than me and more tightly defined than an A/X model (from what I could see) but who hit me as so straight I couldn't see him doing anything like initiating the rape of a man, especially in front of his biker buddies. One of them shadowed him, had a bright red semi-Mohawk, was dead-faced to the verge of being stoned without quite making it there and had both arms covered in ink.

The other pair of bikers sat in a corner, watching each other's backs, both looking like ordinary guys in their twenties — albeit with buzz cuts and bitchin' tatts — who'd be happy to knife anyone you wanted in exchange for a cigarette. One was square-featured, blond and beginning to go bald; the other was husky, had a round face and a wicked grin that almost made him sexy. Their arms suggested strength and the way they just glanced at me then looked away suggested they were could be a problem, but I figured I could take them if it was just those two.

The White-Collars were less troubling. There were four of them — all with the preppy looks and clear faces that're so big on Wall Street, all with the feel of guys who played lots of handball with each other and football on the weekends and kept themselves in a vague sort of shape because it was expected — and they were obviously scared shitless. They huddled together to one side, like a pack of wary AKC puppies, and I had the feeling they were the ones most willing to do anything to keep out of jail. But I still felt I'd only need to beat up one of them to intimidate the rest, so they weren't the ones who concerned me. What's funny was, one of them looked familiar — this sandy-haired guy who was shorter than me and had narrow shoulders — but they were so generic, I figured he just looked like someone I'd met once.

As for the junkies, one had sad, lovely eyes and a slim, sloping body with an elegant feel to it, and I had an idea his legs and ass fit him just right. In fact, both the other junkies looked like guys who'd kept themselves trim enough to probably sell their mouths, butts or dicks on the street for a decent price if they needed a fix. I could take all three in a fight, if it came to that, so I doubted they'd be the leaders in any attack on me.

No, the closest any of them came to feeling dangerous was

that juicer of a muscle queen who had the chipmunk cheeks one gets from steroid use. Everything about him spoke of power and certainty, and I'd bet that once they were pumped up, his thighs were probably as big as my waist. Plus, I'd heard how juice-boys had nasty tempers, so if he did start things, he'd be the hardest to stop. But something in his eyes told me I wasn't built up enough to be worth noticing.

So much for me figuring out who was what. Shit.

I kept my back against the bars of the door and set my mind to defensive mode — meaning one wrong move by any of these motherfuckers and I'd break their fucking neck — and used my peripheral vision to get a better sense of the room. It was about fifteen by fifteen with a twelve-foot ceiling, oddly warm fluorescent lighting and a much lighter shade of blue on the enclosed walls. Better to reflect some light with, I guess. The camera was set up at a perfect forty-five degree angle to the table to my right, where the bikers were seated. I caught a couple of them casting glances at me but felt nothing more than the usual malevolence from it. Anywhere. The fact that I couldn't sense anything about anybody, coupled with the non-stop silence of my cell-mates despite the non-stop verbal screeches from the other holding rooms, made me just about certain I'd been set up to be taken by all twelve of the fuckers and they were just waiting till the signal came.

What made this a special kind of hell was knowing Jake and Collie were raped on top of the table to my right. Or slammed over one end of it. In perfect line with that camera. Perfect line to catch someone shoving their dick into them. I could now see how Enrique could have seen so much detail during the rapes; the fuckers'd have access to beat their fuckee from all sides as they held him down. Shit, I could see them doing it. Seriously — pictures of Collie and then Jake being grabbed and their clothes torn away and being slammed face down on the table, screaming for help and pleading to be left alone ripped into me and — and I started to get physically ill from this loop of images blasting through my brain, but I couldn't stop them. Couldn't stop them. Couldn't stop them. I wanted to pace, just to give myself something physical to do and break the cycle of hate and hurt building up in me, but I didn't dare move till I absolutely had to — so I stood there and clenched my hands and my jaw and my heart for what seemed like hours and hours and hours.

The fact is, it couldn't have been much more than thirty minutes because I was slapped in here about eleven-thirty and Herrera'd mentioned something about lunch being at noon. And there came Bored Guard escorting somebody down the hall with a cart of box lunches. And over the hollering and complaining and screeching of the other prisoners, I could just make out this familiar voice yelling back, "All I got's chicken, turkey or cheese, vatos. You don't pick, you get what I give ya! What the fuck you expect? It ain't like you guys pay taxes or shit." And then I saw him — fucking Enrique and his non-stop smile.

I stayed by the slot in the door and waited for him to get to my room, then before he saw me I said, "Cheese."

He looked up and his smile froze for a fraction of a second, then he dug into his cart and pulled out this half-box with a cold sandwich wrapped in paper, a tiny box of juice and an apple — not enough to feed a first-grader, let alone a grown man. I took my meal and stepped back. He did a quick scan of the other guys as he said, "Put your trash back in the box. I'm comin' for it in half an hour, and if there's any crap on the floor, you *all* get points against ya."

Then he saw something and drew in a deep breath. He cast a quick glance at me and snarled, "Goes double for you, Rattler."

"Don't you fuckin' call me that!" snapped past me from the direction of the corner table. "You ain't got the right!"

Enrique shrugged. "Don't wanna clean up your mess, again." With that, he headed back down the hallway, Bored Guard in tow.

So — Biker Trash Rattler was the lead. Shit, they must have something major to offer for him to get it up for a guy's ass, because I still didn't get that *possible* vibe off him. I surreptitiously watched him and his buddies take up residence at the table under the camera to eat — and two of the White-Collar guys sat with them; the Sad-Eyed junkie started to but realized there wasn't enough room so sat with his buddies and the muscle queen along with the other two white collars at the other table.

So — just seven to one? Still not good odds, even for me.

The sandwich was made of white bread, mayo and a slice of that pre-wrapped processed cheese. Tasteless, but I still wolfed it down, gulped my juice in two swigs and munched through the part of the apple that wasn't bruised in the space of a minute. I wanted to be ready.

Sure enough, soon as he was done eating Rattler started casting me looks, as did the biker boys. The white collars at his table focused on their food. So I started looking closer at him — not directly, just quick glances to get a better idea of who was about to come at me. His face was sharper than mine, more feral-looking thanks to the goatee and beginning to look a bit gaunt. Maybe malnourished or in need of hydration. His neck was so tightly muscled, you could see the cords in it. His arms were sharply defined and virtually hairless, and his hands were hard and strong.

Fact is, his buddies weren't nearly as powerful-looking as him — though Husky had arms that could give muscle queen a run for his money for size, but they were fleshy, not muscular, an aspect that was almost hidden by the ink all over them. He also had a bit of a tummy and legs like tree-trunks, as made evident by how the uniform pants stretched against them. Not in top shape.

The Blond one was as slim as Rattler, but in a wiry way that suggested he could hold his own in a fight. What was funny was, his expression was almost welcoming, like he just wanted to be buddies. It made him attractive in a *best friend* kind of way, and his smallish mouth kept whipping into a smile that was almost lovely.

As for Mohawk, he was one of those dumb-as-dirt types who just does shit and doesn't worry about it 'cause he's usually stoned, dude. He had nice eyes and purty lips, but he also was verging on sloppy, now that I got a good look at him. Probably a meth-head doing it 'cause it'd get him a fix or two.

And then it hit me — not one of these guys was over the age of thirty. In fact, most looked like mid-twenties. More like central casting for a porn movie than a jail call.

I actually stared at the two White-Collars. One was dark-haired, one had thick blond hair, and both were a bit on the beefy side. They had the bland good-looks of frat boys en route to having suburban mortgages with bland wives, one-point-eight children and an ever-expanding waistline. I wondered what had brought them to the point where they'd be willing to participate in another man's sexual assault.

Of course, by this point I'd pretty much figured out how this thing had been choreographed. Half the guys would maintain a wall of separation while the others stuck themselves into me, all to be captured by glorious video. I wondered if they actually knew the camera was recording it in Hi-Def and if they'd signed waivers to participate in another jack-off movie. I doubted it; nobody'd gotten me to sign anything about —

Wait one fuckin' minute. I'd signed that property form. Three times!

Holy shit — maybe we'd all signed one without knowing we'd signed it. Maybe they didn't know about the camera. Maybe they thought they were doing this to make some cop happy and nothing more — and suddenly I had all sorts of ideas screaming through my brain, and I had no choice but to laugh.

They all looked at me, but it was just Rattler who asked, "What the fuck you laughin' at, bitch?"

I looked straight at him and sneered, "You, bitch." Then while he was getting over the shock at my response, I slipped off my flip-flops and strolled over to him. "Fucking idiots. All you guys at this table, you're fucking idiots. You think you know what the fuck you're doing, but you got no idea!" And I laughed some more.

Rattler bolted up and slammed me into the corner, and his body pressing against mine was suddenly, amazingly, impossibly erotic. There wasn't an ounce of fat on this guy, and every muscle was perfectly defined. I could see why he was chosen as lead dog. He snarled, "You think you can make fun of me — ?"

I slammed my heel against the top of his foot, breaking some bones. Probably collapsed his instep. He screamed and dropped to the floor, and I stomped on his stomach. He began to gasp and choke and retch.

Mohawk jumped up to hit me but I just ducked and pulled his fist into the wall hard enough to snap his wrist. He screamed. I slung him aside, jumped the dark-haired White-Collar guy and yanked him to the floor between the table and the wall, with me. I dug my fingers into his eyes and he screamed like a child. The others jumped up to back away from me and I laughed.

"Okay, bitch," I snarled to my White-Collar boy, "you're gonna tell me what the fuck's going on. I know the outcome — Rattler picks a fight, you guys at this table gang up on me and fuck me. But why? Why're you doing it?"

"I dunno what you're talkin' about! I dunno — "

I dug my fingers deeper, enough to hurt but not yet do damage. "I'll fuckin' rip your eyes out, cunt, so you fuckin' tell me!"

Now by this time, the other prisoners in the other holding cells knew something's going on and were hollering and making enough noise to bring the guards. And the junkies and the other two White-Collars were at the bars yelling for help. And my guy was screaming, "No, no, don't, don't," at me. But the muscle queen was just watching me, waiting — and I realized he had no idea *any* of this was going down.

So I smiled at him. "You want to find out what I'm talking about?" I asked. "I need quiet. And time."

He nodded and bellowed, "SHUT THE FUCK UP! NOTHIN'S GOIN' ON, HERE! NOT ONE FUCKIN' THING — that the GUARDS don't know about." The noise abated just as the door at the end of the hall was opened. Muscle queen glared at the junkies, bikers and White-Collars and quietly said, "Finish your meals."

They saw me ready to rip the eyes out of whimpering White-Collar, saw Rattler and Mohawk moaning in pain at the head of the table and saw the glare in muscle queen's eyes — and did as they were told.

The guards entered, gave the cells a quick once over, didn't see anything they didn't want to — and left. All without a word.

I held White-Collar closer, wrapped my legs around his and caressed his chest with my left hand as his body lay against mine.

It felt like he still had some baby-fat around his nice-enough pecs and ass. The fingers of my right hand pressed against his eyes as I whispered, "What's your name?"

"Travis," he quaked out.

"Travis, you're going to explain to me exactly what Rattler set up. What you were expected to do."

"You say a fuckin' word, you fucker, and I'll — " Rattler started.

I whipped my hand back and cut him off with a punch to his broken foot. He hollered in pain but listened as I snarled, "Next time, I'll send two of your ribs right through your heart, motherfucker, so shut the fuck up." He shut. "Now, Travis — speak."

Travis whimpered then said, "Me — me and my buddies — we're up on rape charges — but the bitch's lying!"

"Trav!" That came from the blond White-Collar.

"Shut up! I don't give a fuck *what* you did; I just want to know how they got you to agree to do this to *me*! Now keep talking, Travis."

"Charges'll get dropped if we — if we do it."

"All four of you?"

"Yeah."

"Rattler told you that?"

"I can't — " I dug my fingers deeper. "YES! Yes."

"That's all I need from you," I snarled, then I kicked him off me, jumped to my feet and matched the glares from the other bikers. "And you cunts decided to go queer with him — why?"

"We're not queer," said Husky.

"We — were gonna hold you down, that's all," said Slim.

"In exchange for what?" I asked. No response. From any of them. I sneered. "You wanted to fuck me, too, you cunts. Get your rocks off in a way that doesn't mean anything and maybe score some points with the sheriff's department, right?"

Husky and Slim bolted up to grab me, but Muscle Queen just grabbed their jerseys and yanked them back onto their seats. Then he took the remains of their meals and ate them.

During all of this, the junkies cowered in the corner between the bars and the toilet. Behind them, I could see into all the cages down the room, and every one of them had guys gazing down at us, trying to hear what was going on. It was so surreal, I had to laugh, again. Talk about a captive audience.

I looked at Sad-Eyes. "Why were you doing it?"

He jolted and actually looked almost childishly innocent. "I wasn't — we dunno what they were up to — " I just eyed him and he looked away. "We were just gonna stand around. Not do anything. Just — keep it hid." I kept staring. "And if somethin' came up about it with the guards, say it was your fault. You — you came on to Rattler."

"Why do it?"

"He's my — our — " He looked at Rattler and I understood; he got his junk from Rattler and would have been cut off. Well — I guess I couldn't blame him. Besides, he didn't look like he could have gotten it up unless he ingested a case of Viagra, which was sad; he had such an elegant look to him.

I turned to Travis. "And you'd say I asked for it, too?"

"Part of the deal," he said, tenderly massaging his eyes.

I turned to the blond one. "What's your name?"

He jumped. "Bryce."

"Who's Rattler to you?"

"Nobody — we didn't — I — " I grabbed his ear and nearly yanked it off. He hollered then said, "We — we bought some stuff from him!"

"Drugs." He nodded, and then it hit me. "Roofies! He sold you some roofies and you got a girl junked up on then and fucked her and now he's got enough shit on you to make you fuck a guy so you won't go to jail." They couldn't look at me, so I was right. I laughed — and then it hit me. I spun on the sandy haired White-Collar and said, "You! You were at a frat house, on campus. *That's* where I know you from! Holy shit."

He backed away from me, but I knew I was right. I went to a party there, my freshman year, and got lucky with the guy who headed the department that signed up pledges — and Sandy-Hair'd been one of the frat's officers.

"So you're all clients of Rattler's?" I turned to the little fuck and smiled. "So he's the one who chose you — the best-looking boys in his clientele. Looks like Rattler-baby's the one who's going to tell me who's behind all this."

"Fuck you."

I laughed. "Wasn't that your plan?" And as I was looking at him, lying on the floor between the head of the table and the wall, rubbing his foot in pain it suddenly hit me — Enrique'd recognized him. Enrique had known he was the leader. He'd done this before. And not just once. "How many times?" I asked.

"What the fuck you askin' me?"

"How many times have you set up another guy's rape? How many times have you forced some buddies and clients to help you with it? Or coerced others into joining in? How many times?"

Muscle Queen looked at me then frowned at Rattler. He noticed.

"I dunno what the fuck you're talkin' about," he snapped, but he was getting nervous.

I squatted next to Rattler, still smiling. "Oh — I get it. You're queer for it, ain't you?"

"I ain't fuckin' queer, motherfucker!"

"You get off on it, and your buddies in the Sheriff's department know. They want somebody punished, they call you. You pull together some guys you're attracted to — guys you got something on. Promise this'll make the cops happy. Maybe your buddies even bust some fresh meat to help you out, in case you can't get enough guys to join up. Then once it's done, you got even more on everybody — and you can tell what to do whenever you want — and you got your rocks off with another guy in a way that means nothing to nobody but you."

"You're fuckin' crazy!"

I looked at Husky. "Am I? Have you been here to do this, before?" He looked at Rattler, confused — and shook his head. I turned to Slim. "You?" He'd already put two and two together and come out four thousand and ninety-seven. He shook his head.

And Rattler could see it. "Wolf, Nails, you know this guy's bullshittin' you! He's makin' shit up and — "

"Makes sense to me," snarled Muscle Queen.

I glanced at him. "How'd you wind up in here?"

"Assault," he said. "No promises; no meetings; nothing." I waited. He finally added, "I hit my girl friend 'cause she got pregnant. She said she was raped in jail. By a couple guards. I didn't believe her. She didn't tell nobody or file charges or nothin' — so I smacked her around. But now — ?" He grabbed Rattler up by the shirt and front of his pants and slapped him face up on the table, like he was lifting up a doll. "Now I feel like an asshole."

"Pun intended?"

"Shut the fuck up," he snapped, but he was almost smiling when he said it. He turned back to Rattler. "How many times you set something like this up?"

"I DON'T set it up!" Rattler gasped out. "I — I get busted and I get told! Like Travis. If I — if I don't do it, my probation gets revoked and I go to prison."

"Now who's bullshittin'?" I laughed. I turned to Mohawk and asked, "When'd you get busted? Same time as Rattler?"

He held his wrist, still in pain, and looked away. Answer? Yes. Meaning he most definitely *was* Rattler's backup bitch.

I looked at the other two bikers. They glared at Rattler, which I took to mean *after*. I eyed the White-Collars.

"He was here when we were brought in," said Travis.

"I thought it kind of weird, seeing him in here, too," said Bryce.

"Us, too." That was Sad-Eyes. "He laid it out when we were all here but before this guy was brought in." He nodded to Muscle Queen. "I was afraid he was the mark and — and — "

"So you were all gonna fuck me," I said, stepping back so everyone could see me. I pulled off my shirt. "Am I your type? Is this what you faggots get off with?" I pulled at one tit and gripped my crotch. I was so glad I still had my briefs on, because I was already getting hard as a rock and that would have hurt the effect.

"No, we had to do it, dude," said Bryce. "I can't go to jail."

"Should've thought about that before you raped that girl."

"Bunch of little fuckers," said the Muscle Queen. Then he looked at Rattler. He still had hold of the man's shirt. "Not you — you're a big fucker." He suddenly yanked the guy's shirt up to his neck to reveal his six-pack and a pair of hairless pecs that were nicely pumped up.

Rattler tried to stop him. "What the fuck you doin'?!"

Muscle Queen smacked Rattler's face a couple of times then yanked his shirt the rest of the way off, tearing it a little. "Still kind of skinny, but better'n you," he shot at me. Ow! But compared to what he thinks is hot — justified.

"You gonna break him in, Nick?" asked a chunky guy in the next holding room.

Muscle Queen looked around, snarling. This spooky ripple of low-key laughter whispered through all the cells. Rattler's eyes got as wide as could be. Now he knew if he ever did go to jail, he'd be the snitch who gets dragged into the showers every night to get taught a lesson by half a dozen inmates at a time. Starting right now.

He tried to fight us, but it was hard to do with a broken foot. He screamed for the guards, but Nick the Muscle Queen whipped a choke-hold on him and I shoved my shirt into his mouth. I snapped at Husky and Slim, "He set you up! You gonna just stand there?"

Each grabbed one of Rattler's legs to hold him.

Nick the Muscle Queen looked at me and asked, "You wanna do the honors?"

"After lunch," I said. "That's when it was planned for — so there'll no interruptions. I say we stick to the schedule — and fulfill the contract." Then I ran my hand up Rattler's right thigh and fingered his crotch. He struggled but could not break free. I quickly found that he was going commando — which gave me an idea. "And I think I'll start by proving a point."

Nick eyed me, wary, but I just smiled, first at him then at Husky and Slim, then at the White-Collar boys and finally at Sad-Eyes and his buddies.

I wasn't just gonna fuck Rattler; I was gonna fuck him up.

## — NINE —

When Enrique came back for the remains of the lunch, he couldn't help but remark, "Damn, vatos, you did it. All of you, so fuckin' neat. Shit. Oughta have more of you white boys in here. Teach some of these animals a lesson in manners."

I yelled after him, "School's in session," as he headed out the door, Bored Guard in tow. We'd used Husky's shirt to bind Rattler's wrists behind him and Slim's shirt to hold in the gag, then they'd held him down behind the table and the rest of the joint kept noisy enough to grown out his grunts and whimpers. Mohawk didn't say a word. I'd put on Rattler's shirt to greet Enrique, and Bored Guard hadn't noticed a thing. It was classic. Once they were gone, Husky and Slim lifted Rattler back onto the table.

Then the lights flickered twice. The signal. Playtime.

Rattler squirmed about as I positioned him so his head pointed to the wall and his legs pointing at the bars. Travis and Bryce held his legs as Husky and Slim held his arms and Nick braced his head so he couldn't move too much. And looking at Rattler like that — with his naked chest and abs pumping from fear, and his hips shifting about on the concrete table, and his arms and legs straining to be set free — I could feel my own chest contract from the eroticism of it all. I yanked off the jersey, just to show off for the video, then positioned myself at his feet.

"Now, class," I said with absolute grandeur, "I'm about to show you how to tell when a man likes to have sex with another man, no matter what he says. Travis, Bryce, pull him down so his calves are over the end of the table and hold him there."

They did. Then I slipped my hands up Rattler's legs, felt his powerful muscles straining at their captors, took hold of the elastic band around the waist of his pants and pulled them down to expose his dick. He was soft and cut and had a nice pair of low-hangers. His pubes swept into hair that swirled down his legs to emphasize how nicely formed they were. And everything bounced around as he struggled, making me tingle deep within. I groped him. He all but screamed with fury, and even though you couldn't make out what his words were, exactly, I knew they weren't pretty ones.

I began whisking my fingers around his balls and up his dick in quick firm motions, first my right hand, then my left, then my right, then my left, over and over and over — and within a minute he was beginning to respond.

"Travis," I chuckled, "get your buddies to pinch his tits."

"DJ, Kev, c'mon. Fucker's gettin' off on it."

The other two White-Collars came over and looked down at Rattler. They hesitated.

"Just feel 'em up," I said. "Like you would a girl's."

Rattler threatened them with his eyes and snarling growls, so Nick grabbed the tits and yanked at them, hard. Rattler cried out, in pain.

And his dick got harder. And harder. And his balls started growing tighter and tighter.

Husky and Slim were fascinated at the realization a man could jerk off their so-called friend and controller. Same for Sad-Eyes and his buddies. Their eyes bounced up and down with my hands as I shifted into a pull then reverse sort of motion — going up with one hand as I went down with the other, over and over and over as he got harder and harder and harder.

I focused on my stroking, fighting the urge to lean down and take him in my mouth. That would have broken the spell — made the whole moment way too queer in their eyes and given Rattler a chance to regain control. But now, with all eyes locked on the man's dick — a dick that was really quite lovely when hard, its trunk thick and round, its head bright and full and beautifully shaped, my fingers whispering up and down him — it made for a mesmerizing show.

Rattler began to whimper. Tried to shift away from me. Tried to shift away from Nick's steady massaging of his tits. Tried to shift onto his side. But it was no use — suddenly he grunted and bucked and shot a long stream of cum into the air that slapped onto Travis' face. More spurts followed, some hitting me, some hitting Nick and Husky, some landing on Rattler's own face. And in moments, he was whimpering at my very touch as I kept stroking him.

"And that, children," I said, "shows just how desperately he wants to get fucked. So who's first?"

Rattler shook his head and tried to twist away. No one else seemed to move.

I looked around at them all. "He was using you. He told you lies and forced you to do what he wanted. You're not the first guys he's used like this. Why let him get away with it?"

"Because they're sheep," snapped Nick as he released Rattler's tits and rose to his full height. I noticed he was also going commando, because he had some tent-pole action going on. "Put him on his stomach — at the foot of the table." When no one moved he snarled, "NOW!"

I helped them flip Rattler over and position him so his ass was fully exposed, then I took Nick's position at Rattler's head and held him in place. He was still fighting and shifting and his ass was looking so fucking right and inviting from this angle, I hated myself for letting someone else have first crack at it (pun intended) but then Nick had his hairless dick out (and that whole idea about building muscles to make up for the lack of something else appeared to be true), so maybe it was better he went first. He grabbed hold of Rattler's ass and pushed himself in and Rattler screamed bloody murder, even with the gag in his mouth, as Nick began to pump and grunt and shove and the guys in the next cell started calling out encouragement and making suggestions. But Nick took none of that in, because he came within two minutes. And for some reason, the whole scene was a real turn off, for me.

Then Travis nudged Nick and they swapped places. Travis pulled down his pants and showed off a decent-sizer, with a nice mushroom head and shaved pubes. And he slapped Rattler's ass a couple of times before he pushed into him and began whipping in and out like a rabbit in heat as he muttered, "Motherfucker,

motherfucker," over and over until he jolted and came and gripped Rattler's ass cheeks like they were melons. Then he took Bryce's place holding Rattler's other leg, and Bryce proved he was a natural blond when he pulled his dick out over the top of his pants — this one was NICE in size and shape — and stuck it into Rattler and went slow and easy and steady and moved more like strokes instead of punches and gripped Rattler's hips to stop him from trying to twist away and I could tell from his ease with it all that he'd done this before, albeit with a willing partner, most likely, and it took him several minutes to finally get off and when he did, he pulled out and spurted onto the small of Rattler's back.

Then DJ (quick and rabbity) and Kevin (who couldn't get it in so just jacked off on his back) took turns, almost giggling for joy. I'll bet they raped that girl the same way, and the expression on Travis' face made me sure of it, he was so embarrassed.

By this point, Rattler wasn't struggling, anymore. So while Kevin was jacking off over him, I went to Sad-Eyes and lead him over.

He resisted me. "I — I dunno — I can't — I — "

I put a finger to his lips and said, "Think about it." I closed his eyes. Drew my finger down to his pants. Slipped them partway down his hips. He wore briefs — cheap bikinis. I grinned. "Just think," I said, "This is what he wanted you guys to do to me." I tore the briefs apart at the hip. He jolted. "Or he could've been doing it to you, instead." I slipped my hand under his balls and shifted the torn bikini's material away then gently guided his dick out over the pants. It was a pretty one, in an odd way. Multi-colored with a whitish ring around the center of it that I realized was a birthmark. It sloped, just like he did, with only a few veins and a head that was just the right size for it. Here's another dick I'd have loved to suck on, but I didn't. I slipped his balls out over his pants, too. Then I lifted his shirt up and over his head to reveal his curvy, sinewy, hairy torso and his lean solid shoulders and his casual arms and the hints of hair on the small of his back I thought, "What a waste; what a fucking waste."

I pulled him close. Whispered into his ear, "If you keep fucking up with drugs, the next time it *will* be you on that table. Is that really what you want? Do you really want someone to do to you what we're doing to him? Because he would have, if he'd been told to. He'd have ripped off your clothes and held you down and hurt you. Scarred your psyche. Destroyed your soul. Do you really want to keep heading for this?" I stroked him as I spoke, and he began to get hard. He swallowed, tightly. "What's your name?"

"Sean — Sean — " he gasped back.

Without thinking, I leaned in and kissed the side of his neck, then whispered, "This is what'll happen to you. If not in prison, then on the street. You're worth more than that. But this guy — he took away your self-worth. He made you into nothing but a commodity. Why don't you take it back from him? Or do you want more of this?" I tore his briefs completely off.

He jolted and looked at me. I was still stroking his dick and using my movements to guide him closer and closer to Rattler. He was damn close to hard. Slim was fucking Rattler, now, grinding in long and slow and making every slide and glide count to the max. From what I could see, he was the biggest of us all, so far. Then his slim ass clenched and he jolted and slapped up hard against Rattler's butt and grunted and his dick popped out and he shot his wad down Rattler's leg and I finally saw he wasn't so much big and fat as damned LONG, just like a snake. I felt my heart go pitter-pat at that view.

I was still fondling Sean, so he pushed my hand away, stepped up to Rattler's ass and looked at it — and hesitated — and then slipped himself inside. Rattler grunted and squirmed, a little, but didn't do much more. Then Sean began grinding into him, deep and complete and as harsh as he could. Going faster and faster. Slamming harder and harder. Taking more and more control of the situation.

I stepped back to get a better look, and it was like watching porn. Sean's pants slipped down to his ankles to reveal a beautifully-shaped pair of thighs that swooped from a smooth sloping ass into a thick pair of calves, dark, rich hair swirling around them and up over his cheeks as his muscles clenched and shoved and moved him faster and faster until he grunted and jolted and slammed himself hard against Rattler's shapely butt and he lay across him, as he fired at least twice more into Rattler's anus. And the picture of his sweeping body lying atop Rattler's muscular one damn near made me cum in my shorts.

Then Nick looked at me, a question in his eyes. I smirked and nodded. It was time to really fuck Rattler up.

"Flip him," I said. They rolled him over and it made an even lovelier picture — him lying on his back, his pecs still pumped and inviting, his belly gliding down to his pubes and his dick sloping to one side, surprisingly full, his legs half-hanging over the end of the table, his head shaking back and forth in a vague sort of *no*. I hoped they'd gotten everything on the video and were fucking enjoying this. Now came the real show.

I pulled off my pants and briefs and climbed onto the table to straddle his chest. My dick was raging hard, so I pumped it up even more and let it bump against his chin. He tired to focus on me, but he was too out of it. Perfect.

I untied the gag and pulled my shirt out of his mouth. He mumbled and muttered and kept shifting his head from left to right. I gripped his ears to stop the shifting, then I touched his lips with my dick. He grunted and muttered, "Wha — " which opened his mouth enough for me to slip my dick inside. It fit, perfectly — so I pumped in and out as fast as I could — in and out and in and out.

It took him a moment to realize what was happening and focus enough to understand and try to spit me out, but by then it was too late. The instant he ejected my dick from his mouth, I began to cum. I fired into his mouth, making him gag. I fired all over his face as he tried to wiggle free. My dick bounced against his cheeks and his eyes, making me ejaculate even more semen out onto him. And I leaned back and fired more onto his chest and played with his tits and rubbed my ass against his dick and was rewarded with it beginning to get hard, again, so I scooted back and lay my dick against his and rubbed my balls against his and pulled at both our dicks with my right hand as I played with his tits and he got hard, again — and in the space of a few moments, he ejaculated, again, mingling his cum with mine. I caught enough of it on my hand to smear some on his face and into his mouth. Then I used my shirt to wipe myself off and jumped to the floor and dressed myself as fast as I could while everyone else just exchanged glances and tried to figure out what the fuck had just happened — and how the man they'd let manipulate them into to raping another guy had been fucked by them and jacked off twice, once after being raped.

Then the door to the main room opened and Bored Guard sauntered in yelling, "Vernon Tidwell! 2924483!"

From the *Oh, shit* expressions on Husky's and Slim's faces, I figured that meant Rattler — who was definitely in no condition to be seen, right now.

The other prisoners started making noise but Bored Guard ignored them and kept on coming.

I motioned for them to hide Rattler and figured since I was dressed, I'd just tell him the guy wasn't here. Which was stupid. Then they'd probably do something like a count and find him and find out and then my life'd be REAL hell — unless —

I jumped over and looked at Rattler's face. With his hair back off his face — aside from the scraggly goatee, he could almost be mistaken for me. Not as attractive but — but I had on his shirt. My hair was shorter than his and neater, but if I messed it up and kept it in my face and kept my arms in tight so no one would notice I wasn't tattooed — y'know, with this guard, it just might work.

I yanked out some of Rattler's hair and used the still sticky cum to paste it to my upper lip and chin, then I mixed more into my own hair and messed it up.

"What the fuck you doin'?" asked Nick.

"When's the magistrate due? For arraignments?"

"Three," said Wolf.

"I'm gonna buy us some time. Clean him up."

"How?" asked Nick.

"Toilet's got water. Use that and my jersey. Keep him hidden as long as you can — till you're out of here, if possible. Tell the guards he went batshit crazy on you and you didn't realize what'd happened till I was gone."

"That won't work," said Travis.

"Try it," I said, then I went to the barred door's slot to wait. "And if they call bullshit on it — threaten to reveal what Rattler was up to — but do it through your lawyers."

Then I shut up, because Bored Guard had stopped before me. He gave me the least of glances, noticed the number on my tunic and said, "Hands through the slot." I did as he asked, with my palms up to keep my forearms somewhat hidden. He slapped the restraints on my wrists and said, "Stand back."

Nobody moved; they were already away from the door.

He opened the door then lead me out and closed the door and put restraints on my ankles, never once looking any closer at me. The other guys watched me go, nervously. I sent a quick wink back at them and let Bored Guard herd me down the hall. The other prisoners still made their comments as I passed, but this time they seemed more tender than when I'd first arrived. I was almost saddened to be leaving them behind, like we'd just shared in a life-altering experience and didn't want to let go of it.

Of course, that only lasted like — five seconds. The moment I was out the door, I was so ecstatic, I almost smiled.

Bored Guard was joined by another deputy, and they lead me into an elevator and we went down a couple of floors, then we shuffled down a corridor that was so faceless and unchanging, I felt like I was going through a time warp. And I could also feel my faux moustache beginning to come undone, which would not be pretty. I tried to keep from shifting around too much, but it was just getting worse and worse.

We finally hit an elevator, entered and went up at least three floors, maybe four. Then I was shuffled out into a nice reception room where a pleasant-looking secretary glanced up and nodded to a set of double-doors. They guided me through them and into a relatively plush office with cheesy wood-paneling, a thick rug, a couch with a matching set of chairs, a single desk that was kitty-corner near a couple of vertical slit windows and a wall full of framed photographs and documents.

A nice fat silver-haired gentleman in a blue suit, whose eyes were black as coal, sat behind the desk, signing letters. He looked up as he said, "You can leave him — " Then he froze. And his black eyes glared at me. And his ruddy face got ruddier. And he snapped, "What's this?"

The Bored Guard lost all his bored, right then. He snapped to attention and said, "You sent down for Vernon Tidwell, sir."

Those black eyes turned on him — rested for a moment — then turned back to me. "What's your name?"

"Antony Patric St. Lazarre, Deputy Chief Nussewald." And I delivered the line in an amazingly calm tone, even though I knew that I'd — as my grandmother put it — jumped from the frying pan into the fire.

\*\*\*\*

Nussewald's black eyes glittered with anger then he punched a button on his phone and picked up the receiver. "Check HC-6." A beat. "Don't reboot the system! Check the holding cell!"

So — the security monitors WERE shut down during the rapes. I wondered how they could do that without anyone noticing the repetitive timing? Something to look into if I ever got free.

I was jolted out of my thoughts when Nussewald slammed the phone down, stood up and stormed around to me. "What do you think you're pulling, St. Lazarre?"

Fuck waiting till I'm free to find out. "Is that how it works? The security system malfunctions so nobody at the security desk sees what happens in holding cell 6?" Talk about jumping in, feet first, before checking the water. *Big* mistake. Those black eyes stopped glittering and turned into something as cold and vicious as a jackal's.

He leaned back against his desk, his eyes locked on me, then he snarled at the Bored Guard, "Get out."

Bored Guard scooted through the door and closed it. Now it was just Nussewald and me, and if you think I was nervous, you'd be understating the situation. I was scared shitless. But the thing is, that's when my inner animal kicks into gear and I think with a clarity I can't seem to find except when I'm pissed or petrified.

"I have an insurance policy," I said. No response. "It pays off if I disappear."

He crossed his arms. "What does it cover?"

"Enough to put you in these." I held up the restraints.

"Nonsense. What you did to Orin was illegal and you're going to prison."

"Sodomy laws were overturned by the Supreme Court, or hadn't you heard?"

"You're still claiming it was consensual? I'm hearing kidnapping, rape and assault from his side along with a great deal of evidence to support his version."

"Bullshit. It's his word against mine, and he's got a track record going back three and a half years. And his versions include causing the death of a man who'd done nothing to him. Which he told me happened with your help."

"Nonsense."

"Oh? You didn't show him the trick with the condom?"

He slapped me. Hard enough to slam me to the floor and send my mind reeling into space, for a moment. I actually bounced and wound up on my back. Shit, who knew the fat guy could move like that? And now he was moving to kick me in the balls! I automatically rolled and all he connected with was my left thigh — which still hurt like hell; that's when I noticed his boots had gleaming chrome tips. He aimed to whip another kick at me — and I was ready to snap his fucking knee when he did it — but the phone buzzed, so he had to force himself to back away and grab across the desk for it.

"Yeah?" He snarled and glared at me. "Are they broken? Okay, get 'em to the infirmary, and no one in the holding rooms gets released until we — " He tensed and stood upright. "Which ones?" He slowly walked back around his desk, his mind whirring. "I know him. His firm represents the kid's father."

Holy shit, sounded like some of the White-Collars had protection from on high. Halleluiah. I scooted over to a chair and used that to help me get back on my feet. My leg would love to have buckled under me, it hurt so much, but if you think I was going to let that asshole think he'd scored anything against me, you don't know me very well. I stood straight and proud and *damn* the pain.

Nussewald sat at his desk. "Tell him I'll be right down. And assure him we'll get to the bottom of what happened." He punched another button and said, "Send the guards in." Then he turned his black eyes on me.

I looked back, waiting, but he said nothing as Bored Guard and his buddy entered. They flanked me, nervously.

"Segregation," snapped Nussewald.

"But the magistrate's called for — " said Bored Guard.

"He's being held for transport. We want him kept safe."

Bored Guard nodded and yanked me to the door.

"I have the right to make a phone call," I said over my shoulder.

I heard Nussewald say, "I know." And then the door closed.

They took me down, limping and across by the same route, but this time instead of going back up the elevator I was lead down another corridor to a hall lined with a number of doors. At its head was a desk positioned before a wall that held eight monitors, each showing a small room, half of them empty. A trim middle-aged guard got up from behind the desk to meet us.

"Anthony St. Lazarre," said Bored Guard. "Deputy-Chief wants him kept in isolation."

"I've got nothing here about that — "

"Just do it, Orosco! Nussewald's pissed off enough!"

The other guard chimed in, "Paperwork'll come." Somehow, I didn't believe him.

Orosco shrugged and buzzed open a door halfway down the hall.

"I'm due a phone call," I said.

Orosco eyed me as Bored Guard lead me to the door, removed my restraints and shoved me inside.

"I'm still due a phone call!" I yelled as the door closed on me. I slammed a fist against it and screamed, "I WANT MY FUCKING PHONE CALL!!!" Which did me not one damn bit of good.

So — I was now in segregation. Which was a single room with no window, a slab of concrete jutting from the wall for a bed, a stainless-steel toilet jutting from the back wall, a single florescent light in the ceiling, and nothing else. There was a slit in the door which turned out to be for food and for when they wanted to put restraints on my wrists. And later, Orosco brought in a long block of foam to sleep on. But I got no sheets or blankets or books to read — nothing except myself to keep me company or occupied. My only break was half an hour to shower and change clothes in a bathroom near the elevator.

I was kept there for three days, which gave me plenty of time to think and remember and dream and second-guess myself. And I went through all stages of that, believe me. I finally began to understand what Officer Thomas — I still wanted to call him Grandpa — meant when he said I didn't have a clue. He was only half right — but half right's enough to hurt your confidence in this sort of situation. Because the fact was, I had vanished from the face of the earth, and if no one wanted me to be found, I wouldn't be.

It's mind-breaking, realizing you have zero control over a situation. I was trapped here while Nussewald and Stanton and Gilbert had time to rework what happened in HC-6 to their advantage — building new scenarios, destroying evidence of their crimes and making me into the worst offender to walk the face of the earth since Hitler, if they felt like it. And there was no question in my mind that was exactly what Nussewald wanted to do, if only to keep people from finding out what he'd done to help cousin Orin, all of it with the backing of a system of justice that favors scum like him.

But hell, that's how it's always been in this country — in *every* country's system of justice. Money and influence mean more than justice. Look at how Bush-2 and his slime perverted every law they could, not just in America but across the world. And has one gone to jail, yet? And to show how his crap was just a perpetuation of policy, look back at Ulysses S. Grant's administration and how he handed the country over to the rich and powerful — and was too stupid (or drunk) to even profit from it, himself. Makes Bush-2 look crafty by comparison.

So here I was, now — no lawyer, no access to communication of any kind, no way to spread my story except via a couple of disks I'd made that I hoped would get into the right hands. But I'd been idiot enough to let Nussewald know I had my insurance policy so they were probably rooting around like crazy to find out what it was, and I was sure that by now they'd seen a notice in my box at school that I had a registered letter waiting for me, and they were moving heaven and earth to find a way to get hold of that envelope. And maybe they'd think of hitting my folks to see if there was anything else. And if they got the envelopes, they'd see Dean Weller's name on them and maybe go after him and — shit.

So there I sat with nothing to do but wonder if I'd screwed up a number of other people's lives, yet. And wonder what Rattler told Nussewald to explain away how things had turned on him. And wonder if the guys'd had a chance to clean him up before he was found. And wonder what lies Husky and Nails and Travis and Nick and Sean had told to protect themselves — though if it *was* Travis' daddy's lawyer there backing him up, he probably wouldn't have had to say a thing. I wondered what the video showed and if you could tell who was doing what to whom on it, and if Nusse-baby'd already snuck the laptop out and fixed that *glitch* in the system. I wondered if Enrique knew what was happening to me, now — or if he even cared; Orosco brought my food tray and picked it up, every time.

What's interesting is, all of this was still too abstract for me to connect with, emotionally, except for one thing — Jake. I was terrified they'd find out I'd actually contacted him and use that to send him back to jail. Without question that would destroy him, and for all my hate and anger and need for revenge and worries about my family, that was the one thing I knew I couldn't live with. So I did everything possible to focus on the chaos I'd caused Nussewald's nasty world and avoid even thinking about Jake. Sometimes the steps you take are the ones that break your back.

On the fourth day, after a dinner of especially cardboard meat loaf, extremely powdered potatoes and way-over-cooked green beans, Orosco lead me to the bathroom to shower, as usual. And, as usual, I tried to get him to talk to me.

"So, Orosco, when do you get a day off?" No response. "I mean, you're here all the time. Breakfast. Lunch. Dinner. Bidet. Spritz. Shits. Are you an indentured servant?" Not even a look at me beyond making sure I wasn't trying to escape. "You know, I'm still due a phone call," I reminded him for the umpteenth time —

then I gave up, with a sigh.

I undressed and he laid out a fresh uniform. No undies; mine had vanished into the jail's laundry system after the first change of clothes. I stepped into the shower and set it to going. And the hot water took its usual time coming forth — but soon I was into the soaping process. And letting myself luxuriate in it. If this was to be my one moment of pleasure in the day, I was going to make it the finest experience I could. I was covered with suds and contemplating how long it might take me to jack off with them because my balls were loving the way the soap's bubbles tickled over them when I heard, "Anthony Patric St. Lazarre?"

I looked around to find a tall powerful man in a thousand dollar suit with a shiny gold cross on his lapel standing by the door, looking at me. Of course, I knew it was Stanton the second I saw him and he'd brought my Rangers with him — both Grandpa and Adonis, dressed in their usual Men's Wearhouse suits and boots and white hats. I figured he'd set it up to meet me like this, thinking it would give him an advantage, what with me being butt-nekked and all; maybe he even wanted to show off a little for the Ranger-boys. But if that motherfucker thought I was that fragile, he'd not done his homework. I turned to face them and started rinsing off the soap, enjoying not only the hot water but the fact that my dick was nice and full and sort of pointing at them.

"Hi, guys," I smiled. "What took you so long?" Then I focused my eyes on Adonis and gave my dick and balls a few extra rubs. "Come to wash my back?"

"Don't be vulgar, St. Lazarre. I'm Assistant District Attorney — "

"Phillip Stanton," I chimed in. Then I looked at Grandpa and sneered, "You see, I *do* check things." He looked away, not pleased. That was a surprisingly hopeful sign. I turned back to Stanton. "You owe me a phone call."

"You'll get one," he replied. "I'm here to inform you, your arraignment will be tomorrow morning. We're charging you with rape, conspiracy to commit rape, assault, attempted escape and assault on a police officer." Man, they're offering me a full plate. "These offenses can bring you prison time of up to a total of two-hundred and thirty-five years."

I don't know why, but I actually laughed. What he was telling me had absolutely no effect because it was so over the top, I couldn't believe he meant it. I turned my back on him, turned the hot water up and let the steam begin to billow around me. If I was going down, it was going to be as the cleanest little sacrifice possible.

"Did you hear me, Mr. St. Lazarre?"

I turned to let the water pound on my neck. The way it was cascading down my back and over my shoulders and caressing my tits before it flowed down to encircle my dick and balls was so erotic, I was able to get hard without even touching myself. So I looked at Adonis, again.

"My name is Antony, Phillip. No H in it. Nor is there a K at the end of my middle name. Make sure you get that right. I'd hate for anything you want to do to me get overturned on a technicality. Wouldn't look right for either of us, really."

"You think this is some kind of joke? Do you have any idea how much evidence we have against you?"

"So you've seen the tape, huh? How was the quality?"

He blinked. Obviously, I was not following the expected path of fear and intimidation. "The video surveillance system wasn't working at the time."

So *that* was going to be their take on things? I smiled. "Well, considering the price of the cameras — especially in HC-6 — I'd say the city got fucked by the contractor."

"What're you talkin' bout, son?" asked Grandpa.

"Stay out of this, Thomas," Stanton snapped. "This has nothing to do with — "

"Three and a half years ago the city put in new security cameras, Officer Thomas," I said, loudly enough to be heard over Stanton. "The same camera in every cell — except for HC-6. *That* one was special."

"That is complete nonsense — "

I cut Stanton off with, "It's a matter of public record! All you have to do is check." I shot that last line at Grandpa.

He stepped forward. "Why would you look for something like

that?"

"You questioned me about Orin Tedesco's claim that he was kidnapped and raped. I told you about his connection to Collier Winston-Royce's murder. Did you check it?"

Grandpa hesitated. "What's that got to do with — ?"

"Collie was murdered in HC-6. And researching the history of that unit — to see if it'd happened before — led me to Orin being connected with another guy's arrest. Three and a half years ago. Just after the cameras were installed. It sounded weird, so I checked into it. A city employee named — shit, what was his name? Blake or Blair or something; if I had my notes or my computer, I could tell you. Oh, oh, wait — I already told you about that. And you guys have my laptop, so you must've already gone through my notes — "

"What about him?"

"He was arrested by Deputy Chief Wilbur Nussewald, Orin's cousin. Something else that sounded weird, because Deputy Chiefs don't usually go out and arrest people. So I dug into it some more, and you know what was even weirder? Orin's mother worked for the city. I think in the department that okayed the order for the cameras. And she had a run-in with the guy who Nussewald arrested. And our Mr. Stanton sent him to prison."

Stanton's eyes were locked on me, now. And Grandpa didn't seem so deferential. Even Adonis had a confused look on his face.

"I — I don't see what this has to do with your situation, Antony," said Stanton.

"My grandmother had a saying," I replied. "If it happens once, it's a coincidence. If it happens twice, it's a trend. If it happens three times, it's a personality trait. And look at this — I'm the third guy Michael Orin Tedesco's had busted for supposedly messing with him."

"The charges I mentioned to you have nothing to do with the Tedesco complaint," said Stanton. He was still fighting. "That has been withdrawn. These complaints deal solely with actions perpetrated by you after your arrest."

"Which brings us back to the camera," I shot back. "Why is it HC-6 is the only cell that has a camera with a lens that gives it high enough quality for transfer to DVD? And why is it I was slated to be raped and, maybe, killed in that room while being recorded by that camera — ?"

"What're you talking about — raped and killed?" asked Adonis.

"Ask Rattler — or should I say, Vernon Tidwell. He admitted it for everyone in those holding cells to hear. Didn't he mention that?" The hot water was dying out, so I turned off the shower and began to towel off. "Then ask Nick. He's the only guy in there who wasn't recruited by Rattler to attack me. The others were blackmailed into doing it. Apparently a man in a suit whose description sounds an awful lot like Deputy Chief Nussewald told them if they didn't, they'd go to jail." A little embellishment, here — okay, a *lot* — but I figured it didn't matter at this point in time. "Oh, and in case Nussewald didn't tell you, this will all become public — in just over ten days."

Grandpa frowned and gave Stanton a cool glance then said, "Get dressed."

"Now just a minute, Thomas — " Stanton said.

"We're not discussin' this here, Stanton," Grandpa snapped. "I want an interrogation room and a tape recorder."

"This man is still under my county's supervision — "

"Marquez, you wait here. I'm goin' up top to call the AG."

He started out the door but Stanton stopped him. "Are you serious? You're taking this man's claims at face value?"

"I don't take jack at face value," Grandpa shot back. "I check things out."

"And I'll have lots of details to give him," I said, sweetly, then let my inner dog growl, "You think for two seconds I'd say this shit and not be able to back it up?!"

Stanton was outflanked so went for a delaying tactic.

"Fine," he said, "I'll arrange for the interrogation room."

I'd been dressing as they talked, so I held out my hands to be cuffed. "Ready when you are, honey."

"Cut it out," snapped Grandpa as he grabbed me by the arm and guided me from the room. Stanton and Adonis followed us.

I was starting to have fun, again.

— TEN —

I won't bore you with the details of the interrogation that followed — I mean, I told Grandpa and Adonis and Stanton everything I'd learned up to that point — except for one thing; when Stanton asked me if I'd met with Jake, I said, "I can't find him. He's vanished into this black hole called probation. I wish I could have — so I could tell him I think he was set up by Orin and cousin Wilbur."

"We can find him," said Grandpa.

Now you're probably wondering why I would have given up Jake's name in this since I was so scared he'd be hurt by it. It's because that voice in my head that says this person or that's all right was finally calm enough to let me trust Grandpa. I still didn't like Adonis — and rightly; he's the fucker who turned me over to Nussewald. And even though he said he was sorry, it felt like he still thought of me more as a fag in need of being put in his place than a human being in need of justice and protection and was only apologizing because he'd jumped the shark. The shit.

So another name got added to my list of fuckers to fuck with.

But the deal is, I also trusted Jake to be aware enough to keep quiet about him and me. And let his anger get channeled into what Orin had pulled. And I wanted him to know — shit, I wanted *everybody* to know what happened to him was just plain evil. And now was the time to start the process — so I started it.

The Attorney General came in with his crew and kept me in my own little cell while they dug into my story — not one of the holding cells, but a private one on the top floor with a view of downtown and books to read and better food to eat. I even signed the notice for one of the registered letters so they could look over the info I had on the disk, though I didn't tell them I'd sent three. A little withholding never hurt anybody — especially since I was doing it to protect myself.

This continued for another three days, until Grandpa dropped in on me. He was somber and had removed his white hat. He sat on my bed — a much nicer one with sheets and blankets and everything — and asked, "You ready to leave?"

"Where we going, today?"

"You're bein' released." I froze. "Things still ain't completely settled, but the water's so muddied up, right now, there's no way we'll get it cleared up anytime soon, and your folks've got a lawyer screamin' in my ear about Habeas Corpus and all that crap, so — you're gettin' a hearin'. Bail and all. But I gotta ask you one thing — don't say a word about what we're lookin' into. Just make your plea, let bail get set and go home. Can you do that?"

I swallowed. And nodded. He nodded back.

So my clothes were released to me, I dressed, was hauled before a happy little judge and had a tall, smooth lawyer named Angelo Castillo stand at my side. I plead *Not Guilty* to all charges, had my bail set at twenty-five thousand dollars (it seemed small, considering, but I didn't complain) which mom and dad posted and I walked out of that jail with them. And through it all, this sense of disbelief surrounded me.

Castillo didn't even talk to me; it's like he already knew everything he needed to know at that time — though we did set up an appointment for me to give a deposition in his office later in the week. Then mom and dad drove me drove home, and on the way they told me they'd had a hell of a time tracking me down. Herrera had entered my name as Anthony Lazarus in the system. No surprise there. I laughed about it. In fact, through it all I felt like I was doing a damn good job of handling everything, just like I had at the jail.

I felt that way as we drove up to the house. And as we got out of the car. And as we walked to the door. And then I heard, "Tone," and spun around. And saw this guy sitting on our porch swing.

"Jake!" He stood up. I started to tremble. "No — this is *way* outside the area you're allowed in and — "

He lifted the leg of his jeans. No ankle monitor! He pointed from it to me. "You did this?"

"What? What?"

"They took it off, yesterday."

Mom and dad headed on into the house; apparently they'd known he'd be waiting here for me and hadn't said a word, as is their way — but for once, I was glad for their silence. It gave me an odd sense of protection.

Jake started walking to me. "Word is, they're gonna clear me, Tone. Stanton got a judge to revisit the case and they acknowledged the evidence didn't warrant a conviction — 'specially with what's goin' on with Nussewald. I may be gettin' a full exoneration."

"What — what's going on with Nussewald?" I asked, fighting to regain control.

My mom came out with a couple of cold DP's and asked, "Didn't they tell you? He's under investigation. There's talk of a Grand Jury to indict him for corruption."

I looked at Jake. "So you're safe?"

"You shouldn't of dropped out on me like that, Tone." He was standing right before me. "I'd of backed you up."

"Are you safe? Tell me you're safe. Are you safe?"

"Dude, yeah. I'm fine. Your folks asked their lawyer to rep me, too and — "

"You're safe. You're safe."

Suddenly, all of my hate and anger and vindictiveness dissolved into nothingness. Suddenly Collie's death released its grip on my soul and drifted into the clouds like a gentle whisper, leaving wounds behind that could now heal into scars. Suddenly all I could see was Jake's beautiful hawk-like eyes boring into my heart and his wary smile offering me comfort while his good, strong hands held my shoulders as if to brace me against this answered prayer. Suddenly the only thing that mattered after all I'd done was he was all right, he was safe, he was here with me and my shaking flew out of control and everything exploded inside me and suddenly I was bawling.

153

He pulled me close and stroked my hair and whispered, "it's okay, Tone, it's okay," over and over as I gulped and sobbed and soaked his jacket with tears and gripped him so tight I was probably squeezing the life out of him, but I was so afraid he'd leave me and I wanted to be with him and if I let him go I knew he'd vanish like everything else had. But he stayed there. And held me. And helped my mom guide me into the house and up to my old room and lay me on the bed and he lay down beside me and let me cry myself to sleep in his arms.

I dreamed while I lay there. Collie was with me, again, but we stood apart. His happy eyes sparkled and his grin cut into my soul and he whispered the lyrics to this goofy little song his mother used to sing to him.

> "Dreams are the roads you follow;
> The past a forgotten line.
> So you hold my life in your hands, my love,
> Please never forget you're mine.
> My wishes are there forever,
> Wherever the road may wind.
> So my heart will always be yours, my love,
> Please never forget you're mine."

"I won't, Collie. I can't." My thoughts seemed to float from within me. "You were my first true love, the first man I wanted to spend my life with, the one I would be true to forever. And when you were taken, it nearly destroyed me. But it also strengthened me and made me truly aware of just how vicious and casual the hatred was in this world. I'd always known it was there, but had never paid much attention to it beyond the occasions where it came too close to me. But now?

"Now I can see it everywhere. Can see how it nearly crushed Jake. And how it may have crushed others. And how I used it as a method of vengeance that crushed those who would crush me and mine. I can see it all, Collie. But now I can see it with clarity and calmness and distance, without emotion. I can see how fragile love is. Since Jake is safe, I can face the casual cruelty and figure out better ways of fighting it than exploding into chaos."

I knew all of this as I looked into his eyes and he sang to me, over and over, and I understood that it was all right if Jake came into my life, now. The love I had for Collie would never leave me; it was caught in a chamber of my soul, forever. And while the love I have for Jake could be just as strong, it would always be different. And that would be fine. And I knew it. And what's even better — Collie knew it.

So he ended the song and kissed me and stepped away from me. And sun blossomed around us and the light filled my eyes and hid him and I said, "Collie."

"It's okay," said Jake.

I opened my eyes, and he was lying beside me, still holding me. It was dusk and no lights were on and the room had that glorious stillness that grows with the coming of night. I wanted to stay like that, forever.

I finally sighed and said, "Jake, I hated hiding from you."

"Shh," he whispered. "It's okay."

"I didn't want 'em to know we'd talked. I was afraid that — "

"Tone, you don't have to tell me shit. Not till you feel like it."

"Did Enrique tell you where I was?"

"Didn't even have to buy him a beer or feed him. You spooked the shit outta that guy."

"Cool." He squeezed me. I nuzzled his neck. "Jake — how do you feel about me?"

"Easy." He said it without a thought. "Right."

"Why?"

"'Cause you're the only asshole who's held his own against me. And 'cause I trust you." He took a moment then added, "An' you trust me."

"You heard from the Rangers."

"'Bout a week ago. Day after Enrique told me 'bout you. Took me till yesterday to convince your folks you were in jail."

"How'd you find them?"

"Called every St. Lazarre there was in the state. There ain't that many."

I propped myself up on one arm and looked at him. "Wait — they talked to you a week ago? Two Rangers? Old guy and young one?"

155

He nodded. "You send 'em?"

I shrugged. "Did they ask you about Orin?"

"Nope. Nussewald. I told 'em everything."

Meaning Grandpa'd already talked to Jake before he came down with Stanton. Meaning he'd been putting on an act for Stanton's sake. Meaning Jake hadn't said a word about me meeting him. God, I was happy to be right about him. About both of them. But there was one last thing that bothered me.

"Are you still moving to Denmark?" His face grew somber. I understood. "Can I be with you till you go?"

"That what you want?"

"I want to be with you as much as I can."

"Come with me?" I blinked. He took in a deep breath. "Am I a fuckin' idiot?"

"No. It's just — I dunno if I'll be able to."

"Right. Right."

"Jake — I want to be with you. Can't you stay here? You'll be exonerated. They may even give you a settlement to make up for all that time in — "

"C'mon, Tone, you're a big boy. You know what's what. This country's fallin' apart from hate, and it'll just be time before it crashes down on us. You an' me. Leavin' may not be the perfect idea but — "

I nodded. And I kissed him. And my heart threatened to break in two until I said, "If I can, I will."

He held his breath. "You will?"

"If I can."

His face lit up. He grabbed my hair and pulled my head back and his eyes shot into my soul. "Don't you be fuckin' with me, bitch."

I grabbed him by the hair, right back, and snarled, "That's *exactly* what I want to do with you, cunt."

He burst into laughter and his glorious smile made my world soar and we kissed — and the touch of his lips against mine was like fire and the feel of his tongue with mine was like heaven. And we hugged and to have his strong arms around me and his body against mine was perfection, so I lay on top of him and he held me close and I nearly wept from the beauty of it all.

He was still in his jacket, so I slipped it off him. His t-shirt was all holey. I tore it open. He jolted, laughing, "What the fuck?"

"I have a drawer full of new ones," I said, then I surrounded his left tit with my mouth. Felt the hair around it tickle my nose and chin. Smelled him and how clean he was.

He grabbed my butt — slipped his hands under my jeans to caress my skin and pull me tighter against him. Tighter. Tighter. Kissing the back of my neck and across my shoulder as his legs wrapped around me — intertwined with mine.

I pulled off the last shreds of his shirt and worked at the button of his jeans. He let me go and lay back.

"Tone — your folks — "

"Shh," I whispered. Then I sat up, unzipped his fly and pulled his jeans down to reveal his briefs. I could already tell he was ready for action. I slipped him out and let him lie there for a moment as I drank in the view, then I leaned in and began to give what has to be the gentlest, most elegant blow job ever in the history of the universe. To put it crudely, I flat out worshiped his dick with my lips and my tongue as my fingers caressed his tits and danced over the hair on his chest and belly and toyed with his hips as I drove him close to madness from the sensations I offered up. But not in sacrifice — no, this was a joyous occasion. This was ecstasy and nirvana and the making of love eternal — and I stopped before he was the point of no return.

He looked at me, breathless. I pulled off my shirt then leaned down to nuzzle his neck and guided his hands to my jeans. He undid them like a tentative lover might and slipped them away from my hips and down my legs and ran his hands over me, and I wrapped my arms around him and leaned back and pulled him with me, so he was lying on top of me and his erection was playing with mine and his balls were dancing on mine and his arms were wrapped around me and he looked at me, uncertain.

"I don't have a condom," he whispered.

In answer, I shifted and guided him to where I wanted him to be. And he gasped and kissed me and slipped into me and filled me and made complete and total love to me and, oh dear God, I would have died for him, right then. I'd never understood that phrase, even with Collie, not till I'd seen how easy it is for someone you love to be snatched away by madness or chance or stupidity. I now could see how a parent would become a *tiger* to protect their child — how soldiers would die to protect their comrades — how the very idea of *you are too important to me to let anything happen to you* could explode out of nowhere. I loved Jake. Loved him so deeply and completely and madly, I'd have destroyed the world to keep him safe. And it scared me — and exhilarated me — and made me decide, no matter what, I would be wherever he was.

Isn't there something in the Bible about that — "Whither thou goest, I will go. Whither thou stayest, I will stay" — something along those lines? I'm trying to remember my Sunday school classes (mom and dad being Presbyterians who didn't believe in pushing a religion on you but did want you to know something about one should you decide to go that way).

Anyhow, that's how I was with Jake. I wouldn't do anything that might endanger him — not now. And if he decided to live in fucking China and eat rice and eels, I'd join him — hell, I'd cook the fucking things. He was my world, now. My sun and my moon. My gentle breeze and warm breath. The blood in my heart and the strength in my soul. And if the motherfuckers had just left us alone, that's where it would have ended with him fucking me and me loving him and him loving me and nothing else in the world mattering a damn as he kissed me and tightened his arms around me and pushed into me and came in me and filled me with everything he had and I held him close and never, never, never, never, never wanted to let go.

But being stupid sons-of-bitches — they didn't.

They fucking didn't.

# BOOK TWO

I awoke to being slapped and the immediate thought in my head was, Jake better have a damn good reason for doing this, because if he doesn't, I'm gonna sling his ass across the room. In fact, the only reason I'm not slinging straight off was how good things had been between him and me the last year. No, not good — fan-fuckin'-tastic, in every way you can think of.

Seriously — I never thought I'd ever find that again, not after Collie was killed. Collier Winston-Royce. Dear God, how I'd loved that man. He was gentle to my razor-sharp attitude. Comfort to my rock-hard ego. Sunshine and Light to my Midnight Monster. And since I insist on being repetitive — Yin to my Yang, in every clichéd meaning of the phrase. His buoyant British bluntness always kept me off-center enough to where I could never get angry about anything if he was around, while his sparkling eyes and cheeky smile always seemed to be telling me, *You're such fun to be near, it makes me happy just to know you.* And losing him nearly sent me careening into cloud-cuckoo-land (although a lot of people would say I *did* fly there, first class).

But Jake had taken his place so completely, it's as if my time with Mr. Winston-Royce had been naught but a most excellent dream. A fantasy of what life could be like till I ran headlong into this perfect specimen of reality — and Jake fit that description in every way, even though he was Collie's polar opposite. A moonless night in comparison to Collie's noonday sun. Sleek and tightly muscled in comparison to Collie's beefy beauty. A bad boy with a sliver of black in his heart that made him as volatile as me, but never with me, in direct comparison to Collie's heartbreakingly even temper.

I loved how Jake could tan in just five minutes of sun a day, even in a Danish winter. I how loved his thick black hair, cropped close and cool, edged sharply forward around a smooth forehead to counterpoint the neat goatee that seemed a natural extension of his elegant lips and clean eyebrows. I loved how his dark, hawk-like eyes hid his darkest mysteries. I loved how his body was put together in perfect proportion by God and not just by some weights in a gym. I mean, yeah — he worked out; but his slavishness was to his art and his art was something he expressed through his graphics work, not through hours and hours of sculpting himself into the vision of an untouchable god. But most of all, I loved how right his dick was — thick and straight and cut and nicely sized and nestled into unshaved pubes that fanned out across his belly and thighs; once again, the opposite of Collie, whose was like a hose that grew to reveal itself in a manner almost shy until it knew it could trust you then would shove aside all vestiges of a foreskin.

Y'know, I could just sit and watch Jake shower. Happily witness the sensuous trails of water as they cascaded down his rich golden skin, the hair on his arms and chest and legs flowing with it like willowy reeds caught in a quiet river's steady current. I'd never done that with Collie. I mean, I tried to, once, but he'd pulled me into the shower with him, and after we'd had some nice, raw, very wet sex that kept going till the hot water ran out, he said he didn't like to be gazed upon while doing anything he felt was private. I'd reluctantly respected his wishes. But Jake? He didn't give a shit, and the vision of him wet and clean and steaming always made my heart race as much as it enchanted my dick.

I know he loved me, too — not because he told me so but because he showed me in little ways. Like insisting I pose for him so he could sketch me into an ad he did for his uncle's firm, a male version of the Arrow Shirt Man from the beginning of the Twentieth Century. The final image was far more romantic than I'd ever seen myself as being but his response was, "Don't matter how you see you, Tone; matters how I see you." (He was the only person I'd let call me Tone; with anyone else, it was *Antony* or *Mr. St. Lazarre*, nothing in-between.)

I knew he loved me by how he'd put on a little show as he bathed, slowly soaping his sleek arms and buff chest and flat belly and exquisite crotch and just-round-enough ass and all the way down his beautifully-formed legs as steam filled the room and suds cascaded by in gentle waves. I never got the feeling he needed the attention; it came across as him being happy that just seeing him pleased me. Then he'd invite me into his world and wash me in the same luxurious manner, lingering in places just long enough to let me know what he wanted to do that night, and I'd accommodate him every time.

We never fucked in the shower; it was all deep kisses and hands caressing and nipples touching and dicks sliding against each other and legs maneuvering until we were close to madness, then he'd turn off the water, grab a pair of thick towels and we'd dry each other in sexy ways that still amaze me and wind up on the bed and I'd crush him so tight against me it's like I was melding him into my body while he roared in his need and flipped my legs in the air and pushed himself into me and pinched at my tits as I let my hands drift all over his body and shoulders and arms and ass, driving him even crazier until he exploded inside me. Half the time, I'd cum with him; the other times, he'd whisper his lips over my dick till I shot — and it was always like the first time we'd been together.

I know he loved me because one night, after we'd been together for six months and were celebrating that he'd finally gotten word he was legally free and he' d made a definite date to leave for Denmark, after he finished inside of me instead of trailing his lips down to my hot and ready dick, he lay atop me and ground himself against it and kissed me and whispered in my ear, "If you wanna."

Now this was a big deal to Jake. After what'd happened in that holding cell and in prison, he'd sworn he'd never let anyone inside him, again. But that night, it seemed to finally sink in to him that he'd soon be in another part of the world and I might be trapped in Texas, never to see each other, again, and he wanted me to know I wasn't just his, he was mine. And I could almost hear him thinking, *This makes it forever*. But lying there, wrapped in his arms, I couldn't think. All I could say is, "Not tonight. But if you still want to, tomorrow."

"I will," he replied. And I could see in his eyes how deeply he meant it.

That night was the first time in eight months I didn't dream about Collie.

And twenty-four hours later, he let me lead him into the bedroom and undress him in my own slow way, my fingers lingering on every part of his body as I unbuttoned his shirt and slipped it off, to be followed by his jeans and socks and finally his briefs, tickling the hair on his arms and chest and legs and belly as I went, getting him as hard and ready as I was. I kept my clothes on, this time, doing little more than opening my pants to let my dick loose before I guided him down to the bed. This is where I always begin my Jake-worship, using my tongue to dance over his pubes and increase his need to the point of explosion. His dick was so lovely when it was hard (or soft or in-between, didn't matter) and I'd work on him and I'd kiss him and I'd take him right to the brink before backing away, making him all but growl in frustration.

Finally, once neither of us could handle another moment of toying, I lifted his legs onto my shoulders, positioned myself, ran my hands over his body and arms and thighs and ass and gently asked, "Are you sure?"

He smiled and nodded, a bit tense but obviously willing. It was time to meld together. So I entered him. Slowly. Gently. With plenty of lubrication. Steadily working his dick with my right hand. The first few moments, he nearly froze up; but locked onto my eyes and saw nothing but love for him in them, so ran his hands down my back and under my jeans to grab my ass and let me keep going until I was in all the way. He didn't grimace once. Even as I pulled back and slipped in and pulled back and slipped in, all so carefully and steadily and finally erotically he couldn't help but get caught up in the moment. He pulled open my shirt and played with my tits, sending screaming lightning down to my balls and before I knew it, I was exploding inside him. What made it perfect was, he howled and whipped his arms around my waist and crushed himself against me and came at the exact same time.

I couldn't move, it was so wonderful. I didn't want anything to change the beauty of that moment, so I even kept my eyes closed for fear I'd see something less than happiness in Jake's face. But then he reached up and slipped his hand around my neck and pulled me down into a kiss — and from that day forward, I fucked his asshole as much as he fucked mine. And what made it even better? He loved that I put it so crudely; Collie would've shaken his head and smiled in a way to let me know I could have chosen my words more carefully.

We didn't use condoms, Jake and I. We'd both been tested and were negative and planned to keep it that way, forever, because after that night I knew there was no one else I could even think of being with besides him. And I never once caught him looking at another guy, not even this one gorgeous student of mine, who had the perfect tennis-player's build (like me) with sharp colt legs and trim hips and a back-hand that would make Roger Federer weep with envy — and whom I'd caught sending out the signal, once, that he'd be open to doing whatever Jake wanted. But my man had done nothing more than plant a long deep kiss on me the first chance he got, and cast me a look of such naughty sexiness, I'd had trouble finishing that student's lesson. It was heaven...and we deserved it after all the hell we'd been through.

So yes, Collie had been completely different from Jake — a Golden Retriever puppy to his wise old Black Lab...which was a funny way to put it since Collie'd been almost forty when he was murdered and Jake had only recently turned twenty-seven. But age is not determined by numerical equations; even my own mother once suggested that I was born with a fifty year-old soul. No, it's who you are and what you know and how you've suffered or not that matters, and Collie'd been sheltered from the casual brutality of the world up to the day it destroyed him while Jake had been touched by that cruelty from far too early an age. But it had made him a rock, someone you could count on and believe in, and now I could no more imagine myself without him than I could imagine not having two legs or a pair of eyes.

We lived in Denmark, in a quirky little town outside Copenhagen. His move came six months to the day after I went head to head with the great and fucked-up state of Texas; it took the powers-that-be that long to finally acknowledge that this son-of-a-bitch named Wilbur Nussewald, a deputy-chief in the sheriff's department, had been setting up men to be raped on video in the county jail, and that Jake had been his first victim. Why he was doing that had yet to be answered — well, to me, anyway; the Texas Attorney General probably knew and was just keeping it quiet till the trial. And there would be one; Nussewald had been very publicly indicted by a Grand Jury, along with his cousin-in-crime, Loreen Cullingham, while some of their victims' lawyers were now sniffing around for lawsuit gold. It hadn't been a fun time and there were more than a few moments where I thought I'd wind up in prison for things I'd done...and the brutal fact is, my situation wasn't completely settled, yet.

But Jake's was. Because the state had finally, publicly acknowledged he'd been convicted for a crime based on falsified evidence...evidence that was obviously shaped by the Nusswald's need for revenge against Jake for doing something that was right and correct. Evidence that everyone now agreed really should have been much more thoroughly vetted. What that meant was, Jake got a nice settlement from the state's innocence fund and as soon as it was in the bank and he had documents proving everything, he headed for Copenhagen. His uncle Ari lived here with a wife, six kids and a thriving graphic arts business catering to the Iranian community scattered around Europe.

I joined him a month later, two weeks after my lawyer got my charges dropped and even though I really wasn't supposed to leave the country. The pre-trials of Nussewald and his pack of rats were still being battled out, and Jake and I were key witnesses in both of them. But I didn't care; I wanted to be with my man. Once I was here, I told the AG that I'd return with him when needed, and while the AG had a fit there was little he could do short of file for extradition. He didn't, though he probably *would* have me arrested and my passport confiscated once I was back. Let him; I applied for Danish citizenship the moment I landed, as had Jake, and we hoped to hear back about them before we had to return.

We stayed in Uncle Ari's penthouse till we found this upstairs apartment in a nice little duplex overlooking the Baltic Sea. It wasn't cheap, but it was worth every Krøna. Real wood floors and paneling. A vaulted ceiling. Furnishings by Ikea (I know, but they worked and were cheap enough to afford). A downstairs neighbor named Mrs. Honingen, who was older and either deaf or didn't care about Jake's and my bedroom antics (or was turned on by them; if only there was some polite way of asking her). It would've been the perfect *Ozzie and Harriet* existence if we'd had two hot teenaged sons.

Jake churned out artwork for ads and industrial pamphlets and the like, and he worked on his graphic novel the evenings he was able to let go of the day job. He'd hop the *S* train after the morning rush three days a week and work at home the other two. He loved windows, so I set his drafting table up next to the doors leading out to a small balcony that offered the perfect view of passing ferries, and some nights he'd step outside, even if it was freezing, to mentally work through a design problem or figure out a better direction for his novel (whose plot he refused to divulge). The first time he'd done it, snow was drifting down and I'd damn near dragged him back inside, but something about his whole attitude said, *Just let me alone for a second*, so I'd made hot cocoa, instead. He came in a few minutes later, just as I was pouring it into the mugs. I dropped in marshmallows and handed him some without a word. He sipped it, dipping his whiskers into the thick brown liquid, then grinned at me, hints of chocolate dancing around his lips, and I reached over, wiped it away from his mouth and licked it off my fingers. And he kissed me and the taste of "Swiss Miss" mingled with his mint chewing gum was the perfect flavor. I could have died right then and been happy.

I kept up my end of expenses by teaching both tennis and American English to a number of kids and young adults in the area. Students from the local schools, college kids, even businessmen wanting to better their mastery of the language. And what was really great? The Danes didn't seem to care one single solitary damn that a fag was dealing with their precious little Edi or Steph (so long as I didn't try anything) and I even got a couple of referrals since I also knew *Texan* (trust me, it's a language unto itself). So together he and I were doing okay, and that's without

167

touching a single penny of his settlement; he didn't want to till he'd had it three years, for some reason, meaning it was accruing decent enough interest in a couple of CDs spread across a few different banks. I didn't mind that; I rather enjoyed being independently dependent with him. We were even learning Danish while he also brushed up on his Persian, for his uncle's sake.

Oh, and his Uncle Ari — big and burly and as brusque as they come, with dancing eyes inherited by all his children. His lovely wife rarely spoke, but I was able to get enough words out of her to know she a) knew very little English or Danish and b) was deeply in love with her husband. Which I could understand; so far as I could tell, he treated her like a queen. And all their kids were going to be heartbreakers, with one boy out to break other boys' hearts, if my gay-dar was correct. I hoped Ari would take it better than Jake's father had.

I told him so as we headed home on the train, after a perfect dinner at his uncle's.

Jake nodded and slipped down in the seat to rest his head on my shoulder. The clean little car was deserted but for us and I felt like it was our own private chariot wheeling us back to Valhalla.

"Uncle Ari ain't like dad," he said, finally. "He loves people; my father expects things from them."

"If he had any sense, he'd be prouder'n shit about you."

"If I had any sense, I wouldn't give a shit about what he thought." I just looked at him. Caressed his chin. I knew his parents' banishment had cut him deep, and he'd speak when he was ready. Which he finally did. "I called him. Let him know I was here. Left a message with his secretary. Three times."

I sighed. "Well, looks like you got your smarts, talent and decency from your uncle."

"Cut it," he chuckled and nuzzled closer to me. It was chilly out but warm in the car. And oh so silent. You could barely hear even the sound of the wheels clicking along the rails. I held him tight. For a moment I thought he'd drifted off to sleep, but then he whispered, "Uncle Ari gave me the address of his office. It's in Paris — in the Défense area."

Oh, shit. "You planning to go and show?"

He shrugged. "Most of me says, Fuck him. But — but he is my dad and — "

"If you do make the trip, wait till April. Paris is lovely then."

"You been there?"

"Spring Break. Middle of March, when it was cold and wet."

"Then how d'you know — ?"

"That's what everybody *told* me." He chuckled and poked me. I jostled him back. "Y'know, je parle un peut de français — just enough to get myself into trouble. And I made damn sure I did a few times, just for the hell of it. I gotta say, the French are usually really nice if you'll just *try* to talk to them in their own language. Well, that and apologize for Bush, which I had to do twice as much since the SOB's from Texas, too. I even said I was sorry about the *freedom fries* bullshit."

He looked at me, only half smiling. "I never can tell when you're shittin' me."

"I'm not. Nor will I ever." What a whopper that turned out to be.

He shifted to lay his head in my lap and look up at me. "If I go — you gonna wanna come?"

"Only if you let me dress as Lady Gaga."

"Oh, that'd be perfect — show up with a mean queen."

I leaned down and touched my nose to his. "Wherever you want me, there's where I'll be."

He just smiled and closed his eyes and we rode the rest of the way with me gazing at him.

That'd been a month ago and everything had been just like it always was...until the last few days. He'd started acting strange — no, just plain weird, and he wouldn't tell me why. He'd go into work early, some days, then get home really late. He'd head out the door aiming for the train depot then shift down a side street or hail a taxi or just turn around and head the opposite way down the block. The only reason I knew this was a new English student had called asking directions to my pad and I'd told him I'd be outside waiting for him so he wouldn't get lost, again, and noticed Jake passing behind the house across the street from us headed away from the station. Then I saw a taxi cross the intersection down from us heading for Copenhagen, and he was in the back seat. Jake was paying for a cab to go to work instead of train fare? When he hated spending money? Forget that. And that's when I started watching him and noting his odd behavior.

Now I mean it when I say that I don't nag Jake or ask him questions until he lets me know it's all right to. I trust him enough to tell me what needs to be told, but this was making me nervous. Not about us; when he was home he seemed to melt into my arms as much as before, if not more, rather like a cat that needs a bit of petting. No, I was worried about him.

Then last night he called to say he was running really late and I said, "Do you want me to meet you?"

"Meet me where?"

"At the office. Have a late dinner. Ride home together."

"C'mon, Tone, I — I dunno if I'll have time."

"Then I'll wait in the break room. I have a couple of English papers to go over — this one guy swears he wrote his essay in Texan and — "

"Tone, I'm not seein' anybody else."

"I know that. I *know* that. I'm just worried. About you."

"Why?"

"That — I do not know. But I'm hoping you'll fill me in, sometime soon."

He sighed and I could all but hear him thinking — almost had the impression he was talking to someone else — before he finally said, "Stay home. Tonight. Just stay up. I — I'll tell you, tonight. When I get home, I'll tell you."

Holy fucking shit, Jake never stumbled around like that unless it was something massive. But I held back my questions and said, "Okay, I'll be up."

So I waited. And he didn't show. And he didn't show. And long after I knew the last train had come in from the city, I called his mobile phone but he didn't pick up, so I called the office number and got the message center. I went outside to look around but the town was shuttered down and fast asleep. I considered calling the cops, but what was going to tell them? My boyfriend's working late and he won't answer his phone? Hell, it sounded dumb to me. So I finally just sat in a chair to wait and drifted off to sleep, really upset, and now Jake was slapping me awake, the little fuck, apparently pissed off that I'd tried to question him and we were about to have a monster fight at God knows when in the morning and I twisted to get away from him — and didn't move. Hell — *couldn't* move!

Smack! A backhand, this time. I could taste blood in my mouth and my ears rang and every part of my body began to ache. "Fuckin' shit!" I grunted.

"He's awake," this gentle, accented voice said. A voice I did not recognize. Cold water slapped into my face and I choked and coughed. Gasped for breath. "Anthony, do you hear me?"

I gulped twice, breathing hard, then grumbled, "It's Antony, motherfucker."

Thwack! Another slap brought ringing to my ears.

"Stop." The voice said it softly but there was brutal strength in its gentleness. "Now...Antony...do...you...hear me? You may nod your head if so."

I nodded and finally realized I was sitting in a chair, and not the chair I'd gone to sleep in. I pulled at my hands but they were tied to it, as were my legs, and this was not some flimsy dining room chair; it was as solid as a concrete floor.

"What the fuck?" I gasped out, trying to open my eyes then finally understanding I was blindfolded — and all the aches and pains in my body vanished into this wave of adrenalin. I heard something scrape up in a hideous squeal then clunk in front of me; my guess was Gentle Voice had dragged a chair over to sit on, one that was not as solid as mine. I coughed, not so much because I needed to but because it gave me an excuse to keep acting like I was out of it.

"Antony," Gentle Voice said in a tone that forced me to focus on him. I still couldn't place the accent but I knew it wasn't Danish, German or French. "I represent some gentlemen to whom you owe a great deal of money."

Oh, the stupid fucks; they'd grabbed the wrong guy, because I didn't owe anybody jack shit, not even my MasterCard. "What you talkin' 'bout?" And I kept my voice shaky as I kicked my mind into gear.

"Texas," he said, as if I should understand.

"Guys, Texas has fifteen, twenty million people in it and just 'cause I'm from there — "

Bam! That hand smacked me in the back of the head. I saw stars, it hurt so much.

"Don't play games." The voice was still in front of me. "You ruined a very lucrative branch of my clients' business, forcing them to refund a great deal of money in advance fees and harming their reputation. It has been decided that you will help replace those funds and the trust my clients once enjoyed, doubled to make up for the trouble you have caused."

"You talking about what went on in the county jail? Are you fuckin' crazy — ?"

BAM! Another smack to the back of my head. I nearly wept from the pain, this time. I think he used something nastier than his fist on me.

"Stop." I heard the bastard step away, beside me, then I heard Gentle Voice stand, pushing his chair back a little. "Antony, you can do as we ask, or it can be done to you. The choice is yours. Normally, these are not the options I offer, but your escapade in that holding cell impressed one of our clients and he'd like to see more of you committing the same actions. I promised I would at least give you the opportunity to do so. But whichever way you decide, I will see to it enough is done to recoup our losses. Think about it."

I heard him walking away. "Hey — you know I'm due in court next week. In America. If I don't show — "

"Oh, yes — Deputy Chief Nussewald suffered a massive coronary and died in hospital — what? Two days ago? When Ms. Cullingham realized she would be left to answer to the charges on her own, she took a bottle of pills and is now under a coma. She is not expected to awaken. The few others involved are of no importance."

No importance? Oh, fuck, oh, fuck, oh, fuck. "What've you done to Jake?" burst out of me along with a sick fear.

"Make your decision, Antony."

I heard a door whisper shut then something "clicked" and my hands and legs were freed. I yanked off the blindfold and sure enough — the chair I was sitting on was solid steel and attached to the floor by thick bolts. Electronic cuffs had locked my wrists and ankles in place, like this was some idiot James Bond movie. I realized I was still in my clothes (but for some reason they didn't feel right on me, like I'd shifted around in them) and blood trailed from my face down my torso to stain my shirt. I looked around at four blank walls, the outline of a door in one of them, all barely illuminated with soft lights from sconces placed near the ceiling, fifteen feet up. It was maybe ten by twenty and had a rise in one corner of the floor that was just large enough for the brand new foam mattress that rested atop it. A toilet sat in the opposite corner, a sink next to it. There was nothing else in the room, not even that chair I'd heard Gentle Voice sit in. It reminded me so much of that segregation cell I'd been kept in, back in Texas, I began to shake. I was in the deepest, darkest fucking prison I'd ever even thought I could be in, and to say I was scared would be an understatement; I was fucking petrified.

— TWO —

Hours that seemed like years later, a slit in the bottom of that next-to-nothing door opened and a paper bag of food whispered in. I was lying on the mattress, trying to calm the pounding in my head, and was back to aching all over while still trying to figure out how the hell I'd gotten here and what was going on. I mean, how'd they been able to grab me without me waking up? They'd have to break into the apartment, find me and jump me all before I noticed, and I'm not *that* heavy a sleeper. Plus I'd dozed off in a chair; not the most comfortable of places to nap. So I figured they must have had a key and so much chloroform, it caused my brain to seize up and blank out. Sounds lame and very "B" movie-ish, but that's the best I could come up with. And how might they get a key? Lots of people had one to our place — the owner, the management company, we had one at Uncle Ari's office and his penthouse, hell, even Mrs. Honingen had one in case she needed to get in while we were away. I could not keep track of all the fucking keys...and to be honest, I hadn't thought for a second that I needed to — which now seemed dumb on my part, being the paranoid freak I supposedly am. Plus I had marks on my body that looked as if I'd been wrapped with rope or rolled up in a carpet, like some cheesy gay porn novel from the 70's (one of Jake's older buddies in prison had told him all about them as a way to laugh and pass the time; jeez, some of the stories he'd tell).

So I was actually pondering how absurd this whole situation was when I heard the bag of food slide in — and I mean barely heard it, they were so damned quiet. Hell, *everything* was quiet, like I was in some sound deprivation chamber. Nothing to give my location away except a slight movement to the floor, a nearly imperceptible shifting from side to side that hinted I was on a boat anchored in still waters. Which might be good. If I could get out of this room and out on the deck and could see land, I could swim the fuck away. The trick was getting out. The only path to the open world was through that one fucking door and there was no way I'd ever be able to open it without plastic explosives. So my only option was subterfuge.

Problem was, I had nothing to work with. I couldn't fake illness; that would be so obvious not even fucking Nussewald would've fallen for it and he was an idiot. Well, *used* to be an idiot, if Gentle Voice was to be believed; I wasn't ready to accept his word, yet. I had no tools. Nothing to make tools from. Nothing to fake a suicide with except my pants or shirt, and nothing to hang them from. I mean, I guess I could've pretended to tie them in a knot around my neck and to the base of the toilet or that chair then pulled it tight — but again the obviousness of it sprang to mind. Guess I had to wait till they came back for me and use my brilliance then.

Only I'd been coming up zeroes as regards a plan, outside of hit 'em over the head and run or pretend to agree to whatever they wanted. And the latter plan was the only one that offered me even the barest chance at success. Which is what I'd settled on when the food arrived.

Now the thought did cross my mind that I'd be better off *not* eating, doing the hunger-strike thing, but I was starving like I hadn't eaten in days and food in me was a better idea than a hunger headache adding to everything else and messing with my thought processes. Meaning I wolfed it down. And it's not like it was much — a turkey on rye with potato chips and a dill pickle, like what you'd find in a deli. No utensils needed, thank you, you fucks. At least it was better than that crap I got in jail, except there was no juice box; it was nothing or drink from the faucet in the sink to wash it down. I chose nothing. And what was even more irritating was, the paper was waxy so I couldn't even begin to do my boy scout thing and find a way to start a fire; I'd done that once with a paper bag and napkin wrapped around a plastic straw (which had taken forever but got me my fire badge and showed up the scout master who'd sworn it couldn't be done).

That actually seemed like an idea — maybe set the mattress on fire — so I started shredding the bags and sandwich wrapper, rubbing off the wax as best I could then rolling them into little sticks and wetting them to make them a bit harder when they dried...but then I heard this soft hiss, like air going out of a tire, and I got sleepy...that quickly turned brutally sleepy. I was being gassed and in a flash realized that's how they'd gotten to me. It was a cold night and Danish homes are very well insulated. Shit. So I stood up and aimed for the mattress but before I could make it there, I passed out.

I woke up groggy and trapped in that chair, blindfolded, yet again. But no slaps, this time; just some stench blasting into my nose. I jerked away from it and Gentle Voice said, "He's awake."

I coughed. "Yeah — yeah, I'm awake, motherfucker, and want to know — "

"What is your decision?"

"About what?"

"If you do not say yes, I will take that as a no."

Oh. Okay. "Yes."

"Good. Remove the blindfold."

It was taken away and what I saw before me was a trio of computer monitors set up on a rolling table. The first one showed a buff guy in a camouflage uniform, pacing in a room that looked exactly like mine. He was blond and I got the idea he was Russian, with the square head, sharp cheekbones and wary eyes of a soldier. The second monitor had a slim dude in a room identical to the Russian's, dark haired, big eyed, looking like a college kid who played nothing but *Extreme Combat* on his computer or TV. I probably outweighed him by twenty pounds but for some reason he didn't strike me as skinny, just lean and tight. He sat on his bed in the Lotus position, keeping very calm. I actually wished I'd thought of doing the same thing, even though I'd never been into Yoga. The third monitor showed Jake crouched in the corner of a bed in the exact same type of room — and the feeling I got from him was fear, the way he was hunched over and refusing to move.

I think I actually snarled when I saw him. "If you've fuckin' hurt him — "

"Choose which of the other two men you will be with first." Gentle Voice was behind me, and the only hint of a reflection I saw was his silhouette on two of the monitors. "We have the same order for both types. Mr. Blaine will be released unharmed when you complete your end of the bargain."

"You're lying. Why's Jake crouched in a corner like that?"

"He was brought here and put in the room, nothing more. Apparently he is claustrophobic and the absence of windows builds on his fear. So the sooner you are done, the better."

What bullshit. If Jake'd been freaked out about that I'd have known it, but I had no choice in the matter, right then, so I said, "What do you want me to do?"

"What you did in holding cell six."

"With how many other guys?"

"Merely you, on one."

"How many times?"

"That depends on your performance."

"Will you let both me and Jake go?"

"Yes."

The lying fuck; what else was he going to say? "Just to be sure I understand, whichever one I choose now, the other one comes later." (Pun *not* intended.)

"Yes."

"The little guy." I didn't want to do it to him; he looked rather sweet and innocent. But I was still a bit shaky and figured he'd be the easier one to control, right then. I'd try and make it as easy as possible on him, but the fact is — I'd do anything to get Jake away from these fucks...even if it meant murder. Of course, the second that thought hit me, I asked, "I just do what I did in holding cell six, right?"

"Yes. With as much pleasure as you achieved there."

"There were several guys involved."

"Which means you will have to be inventive or repetitive. I have no doubt you'll know what to do to lengthen the time it takes." Meaning play with him like a cat plays with a mouse. Shit. "Do you wish to change your mind?"

177

I looked at the blond guy, again. Probably Russian military. Knows how to fight. And judging from how tight his uniform was, outweighed me by thirty pounds, all of it probably muscle. Yeah, I knew Aikido, but I hadn't practiced it for over a year. No, the little guy was a better choice to start with, so I shook my head.

"Here is fresh clothing." A tall, cold-eyed Arab-looking man with muscles that had muscles on their muscles and wore a t-shirt and pants so tight they seemed like a second skin dropped a full setup of clothing before me, right down to a pair of deck shoes. "Shower, first. You have twenty minutes."

I heard a door whisper closed behind me, noticed the first monitor shut off, then the second and got one last look at Jake before they closed his down, too. Then the restraints popped open and I was free.

Except for Mr. Muscles and two buddies who were just as big. He motioned to a door to my right. I gathered my clothes and went through it to find an open room made of tile with a drain in the center. Buttons in one wall; nozzles in the ceiling. A shelf to one side held a sink with soap, washcloth, towel, a toothbrush and those tiny travel-size containers of deodorant and toothpaste. Guess they wanted me to smell nice and have minty-fresh breath when I fucked up Geek-Boy.

Mr. Muscles and company weren't going anywhere, so I tossed everything on the shelf, pulled off my clothes and hit the buttons. In the mirror, I caught him giving my ass a serious once-over with his eyes. Something to file away for later use.

Water streamed down in gentle sprays from above, and it felt so fucking nice and real and human and memories of Jake in the shower crushed into me — so I focused on soaping up and rinsing off and getting done. It took me a minute to dry off, another minute to brush my teeth. Then came the clothes — tighty-whities, a pocket t-shirt, slim-fit jeans with strategic holes in the ass and knee areas, and no socks to wear with the shoes. No belt, either. But everything fit very nicely, so it didn't matter.

Throughout this, I tried to psych myself up for what I had to do. But it's one thing to go after somebody who's messed with you or is planning to, like I'd done with Orin and Rattler; those two deserved it. And yes, I'd thought about going for some other guys — Judge Gilbert's son, Nat-four; Nussewald's younger son, Shane; Joe, son of that fucking DA, Stanton — but I'd shoved all that anger and need aside while I was with Jake, because to be honest, I'd been spooked by what I'd found out about myself after my two rapes — that I enjoyed it. Kind of sick, yeah, but that truth wormed its way into my soul. Only being with Jake had given me strength enough to return it to the shadows. But now I was being forced to let it out, again...and I didn't know if I could still control it, or if I'd even want to before I was done.

You see, I have no illusions about my nature. I'm like one of those mean-assed cats that'll let you pet it till you're feeling all nice and safe — then'll whip around with the teeth and claws to draw blood. It had popped up too many times in my life for me to ignore it. Yes, I know it was a form of defense mechanism, but against what? My upbringing had been nice and decent, with no more than the normal scars inflicted upon me. which made me wonder why I'd developed into this "scorched earth" type that roars when threatened and won't stop till he's destroyed everything he can to feel safe, again. Collie and Jake had given me the choice to continue that or be civilized, and I'd made the subconscious but deliberate decision to go their way. Now I'd had the decision taken out of my hands and I had no idea how to kick whatever it was I needed into gear to show me a way out of whatever the fuck this idiot situation was.

Of course, that could be a problem — me just not being able to my dick going to make this rape-porn video for some sick fuckers who order it like you order a pizza or books from Amazon while using guys I wasn't even angry at. Plus I was pretty sure that Russian-dude did *not* want to be here. The expression on his face, the way he strode around the room, it all spoke of fear and nervousness, like me. Geek-Boy was harder to read, but the logical assumption is he was there against his will, too —except for his calmness in the face of the unknown. How they'd been brought here and why and what it truly meant in the scheme of things — shit, I had to shut that part of my mind down. It was all just too damned freaky to face, right then.

So I was ready in fourteen minutes and thought I'd spend the next six minutes talking myself into making this as good and as sexy as I could and just hoping that Geek-Boy could handle it. Mr. Muscles and company had split in the middle of my bath so I thought I'd be alone, but they returned the second I was done and motioned for me to follow them. Which told me they'd been watching and probably taping my shower. Guess I was giving up a full course meal for whatever pervert they had a contract with. Well — I hope I live up to the sick bastard's demented dreams.

\*\*\*\*

I was led down a short, dark, blank hall where a door silently opened and Mr. Muscles shoved me into the room. The door whispered closed behind me. Everything looked the same as on the video except there was a mattress in the center of the floor and the lighting was nice and bright. Before I could even think to look to find my victim, I was slammed in the neck, and I felt EVERY FUCKING NERVE IN MY BODY FREAK OUT! I crashed to the floor, jolting and screaming from the pain. Then I felt someone's hands grab my wrists and twist me around and I couldn't even think about making any Aikido moves before my hands were bound behind me and my ankles were caught in some cuffs chained to a bar, keeping them spread about two feet apart. I coughed and spit and cursed and finally got enough past the still tingly freakiness of my skin to look around and see the Geek-Boy — about my age, maybe a couple years older — standing there looking at me, his big eyes laced with a frown.

"Shit, that was too easy," he muttered to himself in a vaguely Southern US accent.

"What the — ?" was all I could get out before he slapped a strip of duct tape over my mouth.

"Keep it quiet," he muttered, his voice low as if he knew we were being taped and he didn't want anyone to know he knew. "I'll make this as quick and easy as possible."

*He'll* make it quick and easy? What the fuck — that wasn't the deal! Was this *Alice in Wonderland*, where nothing made sense to anyone except the people making the comments?

Then he patted my face, grabbed the bar between my feet and dragged me over to the mattress. I scraped along on my ass, fighting to keep my body up so I wouldn't crush my arms against the floor. He pulled me across the damned thing and fastened the bar to an eyehook at the head of it. I flopped around on it, realized it was just a block of foam covered by a fitted sheet and propped myself up on my arms. My t-shirt had ridden up a little, exposing my lower abs, and the jeans had come close to giving me a wedgie.

The guy stepped back to view his handiwork and I finally had sense enough to get a really good view of him, and he looked — hell, he *did* look like a sweet little college geek. Shorter than me by a good four inches (and if he was more than one-thirty dripping wet, I'd be surprised). Big brown eyes under a high brow of thin dark hair, a nose that was a bit too large but actually worked with his face and a crooked near-smile on lips that could promise tenderness or cruelty, all highlighted by a touch of scruff on his round chin. He wore a plain black t-shirt that fit tight to a lean torso and smooth arms along with blue jeans filled out by what looked like a surprisingly sturdy pair of legs and a perky ass. I revised my estimate of his weight up to one-forty because those legs...while not beefy were definitely solid; they were probably the reason he was so much stronger than he looked. He wore deck shoes and his jeans bunched at the ankles, making him seem younger than I'm sure he was. And on his hip sat a Taser. In a holster. Like this was an electronic version of *The Wild, Wild West*. Shit, no wonder I hurt; that's a torture tool. And for the first time, I was really nervous.

He didn't like what he was seeing, so he tried to flip me face down. I refused to let him. "C'mon," he said, "don't be an ass."

I muttered, "Go fuck yourself," through the gag, and enunciated so he understood every word. Because now I saw this whole thing had been Gentle Voice's set up. *Go rape this kid for us and we'll be on the road to happiness,* when he was really prepping me to be this *kid*'s toy for an entirely different situation. Maybe Geek-Boy was a client and had paid for the privilege of forcing himself on me, and their way of getting their investment back was to provide him with toys and videotape it. Made for a more realistic reaction on my part, I guess, though GV could be getting *his* happiness from fucking with men's brains instead of their butts. Which made me wonder if he'd been planning the same scenario with the Russian or if that was supposed to be a "Whoever comes out on top" kind of deal, like wrestler porn. Well, Jake mattered more to me than my being used and abused by some geek for a while, so I figured I could take it; I mean, how rough could this nice little fella get? Still that didn't mean I had to be nice about it, and I let loose with a verbal barrage that was almost funny in its word combinations — the *father-fucking ass-licking son-of-a-cunting-whore* kind of things.

Well — he nodded at my cursing, grabbed me by the hair and twisted. I cried out and tried to jerk away; instead, I wound up face down with my ass in the air, so to speak. "Nice," said Geek-Boy as he gave my butt a slap then said, "Now stay there."

I did.

He sat on my back and began exploring me with his hands. First came my ass, and I'm not saying I've got the world's most perfect butt (I'm too much on the flat side for my liking) but he was feeling me up like I had a pair of melons in my jeans. Then he drew his hands up my legs, molding his fingers around my inner thighs as his thumbs kept digging into me. He slipped them around and under my hips to grope my crotch, nodding as he said, "Feels nice." He was really rough about it so it didn't feel nice to me, the way he nearly crushed my balls and actually grappled through the jeans for my dick. Then he shifted around to lay atop me and slip his hands around to pinch at my tits through my shirt — pinch hard.

I didn't even think — I grabbed at him with my hands and, even though they were bound, managed to get hold of his jeans and flip him off me. Then I rolled back over to snarl at him and give a muffled scream of, "You fuckin' leave me alone!"

He laughed then bounced back to me and shoved me down, and my arms felt like they were about to tear out of their sockets. "Be cool or you get some more of this." And he pulled the Taser from its holster. I eyed it and deliberately made myself come across as subservient. He liked that.

He set the Taser aside then felt up my pecs, erotically. Massaging the muscles. Pinching at my tits. Bending down to try and kiss me, but I twisted my face away so all he got was cheek. He slipped his hands down my belly to slide my shirt up then pinched my tits...and it sent shock waves down to my groin — hell, to my dick. Which I could not fucking believe!

I mean, yeah — I was going to let him use and abuse me, but I'd figured anal only. I never considered even for a second that I might be taken off by it, but my dick (which occasionally can have a mind of its own) was taking notice and wanted more. And that jolted my brain and my creature within.

He sat back on my crotch. Seemed to feel I was getting hard. Ground his butt against me and smiled and said, "Oh, yeah, this is perfect," then he grabbed my t-shirt and tore it open from the neck down, exposing my chest.

I jerked and flipped him off, again; the bar at my ankles kept me from sending him too far. He chuckled and jumped back on me, and this time he held himself tight against me by crushing his legs to my sides so I couldn't get the leverage to send him flying, again. Then he continued running his hands all over my torso and toying with my nipples as he whispered, "Fuck, you're beautiful. Just what John would've gone for."

Finally, he shifted down my legs to sit on my knees and slid his hands down my sides to grab my jeans, right at the point where my hips flowed into my legs.

He chuckled. "Fuck, you feel so fine and smooth." Then he worked his hands around to cup my ass inside my jeans and got back to kneading my cheeks.

I tensed but only struggled a little. If I'd fought too hard, I'd have dislocated my shoulders. And I have to admit, I was getting to where I was liking the idea of him using me instead of me having to use him — and that made me really start to get hard, as if this was something my body would enjoy (and didn't care that it *was* fucking with my mind). Of course, then I began to hope he was all I'd have to handle, because I could just see Mr. Muscles and his queens coming in to partake if they saw me seeming to have fun.

"He's on a roll, girls, so have at it while you can." Shit.

It's funny, but some synapse in my brain clicked off and I stopped seeing this as rape, even though it was. Rape was what happened to Collie and Jake and God knows how many other men in that jail cell. It was *not* what I did to Orin and Rattler; theirs was punishment for what they'd done or agreed to do. And this? It had, quite seriously, turned into rough game playing where I could go with the flow and give Geek-Boy and his peeping toms *all* they wanted. I'd still fight some, to make it look good, but I could justify my dick going along with it by telling myself I was putting on a show to make them let Jake go...or at least leave him alone. Plus it would give me time to figure out what to do next — so it wasn't like I was cheating on Jake; I had good solid reasons to let this guy pop me off as he popped off with me and focus on it just being a — shit, a porno play.

Of course, that all depended on this guy being what I thought he was — a quiet guy out to have some real fun instead of just role-playing on his monitor at home, with a bag of Cheetos and 2-litre bottle of Mountain Dew on hand as his fingers flew across the keyboard in Sim-Sex. He had those kinds of hands — long fingers and clean nails. I figured he'd do some grabby-crap, pinch and bite a little and treat me maybe a little harsher than he already had, but nothing like I hadn't been through already.

The first hint I got this was more than just a sex game was when he tore the holes in the knees of my jeans wider and shoved his hands inside them to travel up my legs and maul my balls from within. Since my legs were spread apart, I had no way to stop him as he gripped and twisted them through the cotton fabric, sending pain shooting into my sides. I jolted around, almost doubled over. He smiled.

Then he slipped a couple of fingers inside my briefs at the hip, shifted them around to my ass, and probed between my cheeks for my hole. The muscles in my ass reflexively clenched and tried to shift me away from him. He laughed and tore the jeans open wider.

"Man, you're gonna be perfect."

He stood up and pulled off his shirt. Oh, he was thin to where you could see his ribs, but he had enough beef on him to keep from being called skinny. A dusting of hair whispered over his pecs and his little brown tits were pointed and hard, plus his right one was pierced and held a small gold emblem. Uh-oh, not exactly a guy averse to pain. But what really made me nervous was, he had a tattoo. That's something I'd never even thought of doing to myself because the idea of a needle jabbing ink into my skin thousands of times a minute just freaked the fuck out of me, not to mention the hurt of it. I mean, yeah — Jake's Persian tatt was beautiful and I'd admired it, but he'd done it before I met him. When he'd raised the possibility of adding to it, a couple months back, I'd freaked and said, "No fucking way," because I knew I'd suffer for him ten times more than he'd suffer for himself and — and now this little fuck had one — of what looked kind of like a flowing Japanese character in deep black on his pale olive skin. Meaning his Zen thing in the cell wasn't an act; that's how he dealt with pain — by accepting it! Shit.

He strolled over to the sink and grabbed a little digital camera then strolled back and took photos of me lying there, propped up on my arms, my t-shirt torn open, my legs spread apart, my jeans ripped open to reveal some of my legs. His jeans rode down his hips, revealing a treasure trail of dark hair as they rocked back and forth with his casual moves, and the simplicity of it was — shit, it was surprisingly sexy.

He zoomed in and out and shifted left and right and close and away, taking picture after picture after picture. But as he shot, I noticed he had a tiny pair of needle-nose scissors in his right hand, and that really came close to freaking me out.

To keep from losing it, totally, I snarled, shook my head and muttered, "What you think you're gonna do — sell these to a fag rag?" as I stupidly tried to scoot away from him, even while keeping my eyes on him the whole time.

Finally, he knelt on the mattress, between my legs and groped my crotch, again, this time massaging it more gently. "Don't worry. Just want better access." Then he set the camera aside, grabbed the right leg of my jeans with one hand and used those little scissors to cut from the tear up along the inside seam, aiming straight for my crotch.

I crushed my eyes closed. I could still hear them slice into the fabric...*shhp, shhp, shhp*...and feel one sharp tip of the scissors glance against my skin and the hair along it. Up past my calf...over my knee...along my inner thigh...sometimes nearly digging in to cut me but never quite making it, until they all but kissed my balls and seemed about ready to bite into the CKs when he stopped, took a couple more photos — and did the same to my left leg.

"Damn," was all he said, over and over and over.

I finally looked down to see my legs completely exposed along with some of my briefs. He took another series of photos then knelt between my legs, again, undid the button on my jeans and unzipped them to reveal the area of the CKs that held my dick and balls. He rubbed his hand over them, snapped more pictures then cut through the zipper on both sides and pulled the jeans away from me, completely, and spent a good ten minutes feeling up not only my crotch but my legs and body in every way you can think of.

And I started getting harder.

This time when he got up, he went crazy with the pictures. Took dozens from every angle, including as close as he could get to my briefs, aiming to get the best view of how my growing dick lay against my balls under the white cotton. He groped me a lot more. Felt me up almost non-stop. Pinched my tits. Shoved the t-shirt off my shoulders. Pulled my briefs lower on my hips. His hands happily exploring wherever and whatever they wanted. Then he cut away the t-shirt, completely, and rolled me onto my belly, where I could only listen as he took more pictures and I grew closer and closer to screaming at him to get on with it — until he knelt between my legs, again, felt up my ass then grabbed my briefs and cut them at my right hip.

I sensed them drifting away from my ass, slowly, as if reluctant to let go. I heard more *clicks* from the camera before he rolled me onto my back and I tried to twist away from him, but of course I couldn't. I could feel the cotton material still clinging to half my dick and one of my balls. He took photos of it. Lots of photos. Adjusting the briefs so I'd be better covered then pulling them away to reveal me, completely. I think I actually whimpered when he did that, because by this point I was close to losing it, thinking he was going to do really hideous things to me with those scissors and that Taser, if those were the only toys he had, and not even for Jake's sake could I handle this much longer.

But finally he stopped and whispered, "Oh, fuck." Like he'd just realized he was seeing me in the flesh and not in pixels.

My eyes were closed, at that moment, so I felt him get back on the mattress and position himself between my legs, again. Then I felt his fingers tenderly caressing my pubes, whispering around the base of my dick and dancing over my balls. "Oh, fuck." He ran his hands up my abs and the moist warmth of his lips kissed the head of my dick. "Oh, fuck." Encircled it. Engulfed it as he slid down to the base of it and swirled his tongue around me.

I was neither hard nor soft at that moment, but the gentle touches he now gave me shot electricity across my tits and into the nerves that made up my entire being, and in less than a minute I was solid and ready, thanks to his sucking, swirling mouth. His fingers flicked against my tits and I shuddered. His chin nudged my balls and I gasped. He drew one hand down to caress them and toy with the hairs on my thighs and tickle over my own treasure trail as his other hand jumped between my left tit and my right one, and every move shot as much electricity through me as had that fucking taser.

Shit, this guy gave a blowjob like I'd never felt before. Like I'd like to learn how to give, myself. His tongue velvety and consistent and all encompassing. No ebb and flow to the fire it was adding to my crotch but a steady building burn taking over the whole shaft. The movement of his lips rhythmic as he pumped me. The lightness of his touch everywhere else. He finally settled on toying with my right tit, somehow sensing that one was the most connected to my pleasure point. Within minutes, to my absolute shock — and I *do* mean absolute — I was close to firing.

I must have said something like, "I'm gonna cum," because he pulled away. And I was left with a near-release that made me crazy with need. He chuckled, "Not yet, buddy. Not yet."

He took a hundred more photos then gently guided me onto my belly, maneuvering my dick so it jutted out between my legs along with my balls, adding to my sense of vulnerability. A couple of strokes along my dick. A dash of tickling on my balls. A few more pictures snapped. Then he lay on top me, molding himself into me. I heard a *zip* and then I could feel his dick pressing against my ass, and I wondered if I should revise my estimate of his weight up by a good five pounds because it felt massive. He rubbed it between my cheeks and whispered, "Yeah, buddy, yeah. How's it feel, Chris? How's it feel?"

I felt him pull back and reposition himself at my hole. It felt like he slipped on a condom before he began to lube me up and probe me with his fingers. I clenched my butt against him but it did no good. He pushed his head in with a quick, painful jab.

I cried out at the suddenness of it, actually wondered if he was going to tear me open with it till he lay on top of me and said, "Relax. Push back against me. Makes it easier."

He's telling me how to help myself get butt-fucked? Shit, did he think I was a virgin? Or straight? Was that his fantasy — raping a straight guy? What kinds of lies had they told this little shit?

I tried to grab at him with my hands, but he'd curved himself down to me in some way that kept him out of my reach. Plus his legs were proving strong enough to keep me from twisting away from his hard-on — so he pushed in some more — and it felt fuller and still hurt — and some more — and it still hurt — and some more till he was at the hilt and I couldn't take anymore — and he began to pump into me, deeper and deeper and deeper, and harder and harder, his hands gripping my hips, his thumbs pressing into my cheeks, my anus stretching and accepting the fullness of him, grunts beginning to emit from deep within him like some sort of animal as he fucked me.

And from within me. Even through the pain of it.

I started to breathe fast — hell, hyperventilate, it was hurting so much, because the moment his plowing into me started to feel acceptable, it's like he knew and would up the intensity — once, twice — and then he pulled out. And moved off me and flipped me onto my back and got between my legs, again, and pulled my ass down so he could spear me with his dick — and he shoved himself into me — even deeper — left hand gripping my ass to hold me in place as his right one pulled on my dick. And I really responded, this time.

Meaning, yes — the fucking he was giving me started to feel nice — erotic — shit, it was feeling good, and the motherfucking-son-of-a-bitch knew it — because I got hard as a rock as he yanked on me and his pubes brushed against my balls and his grunting grew deeper and growlier and I started to whimper at being so completely out of control and then I felt a surge from deep within me and cried out, despite the gag, and let loose with a load of semen that shot back over my head and slapped against my face and chest and clenched my ass so tight, I nearly ripped his dick off, making him growl and ram me harder and harder and gasp and pull out and yank off the condom and unload himself onto my belly and chest and face, mixing his semen with mine. And I finally got a good look at his dick and thought, *Shit, no wonder I couldn't relax.*

He folded himself on top of me, almost purring like a happy cat — rubbing his dick against mine, smearing our cum across both our bodies — and hugged me as he whispered, "Oh, fuck, oh, fuck, oh, fuck..." over and over and over.

As for me, I — I couldn't think. My mind actually went blank and I stared at the meaningless ceiling. Any thoughts of justification for this act of rape vanished into the shadows. This guy lying on me was the only reality of the moment, and the vague understanding that he'd made me enjoy it, participate completely in it and cum as if it were my first time ever — that was rocking me, deep within.

Seriously, I had totally gotten off on being tied down, stripped and sexually assaulted — and the first truly coherent thought to dance across my brain after experiencing a — hell, an exquisite orgasm like that was, *Hmph, guess a little rape never really hurt anybody,* and I felt less guilty about what I'd done to Sad Eyed Sean, once upon a time.

It almost made me laugh. In fact, the only reason I didn't was, I didn't want it to be on tape. I wanted Gentle Voice and his motherfuckers to think I was destroyed by the experience, since I was ninety-nine-point-nine percent sure that's what they were hoping for.

And then it hit me. This guy who'd just fucked me to within an inch of madness — who'd just let loose the monster of my shadows and happily petted it and it had played ball with him — had said something like, "John would've loved you," and "You like it, Chris," or words to that effect. I looked at him. He looked at me. His brown eyes were even larger than I thought, and kinder, and almost loving.

He nuzzled my neck and carefully peeled the strip of duct tape away from my mouth. Then he rolled up to kiss me, and I made myself kiss him back. Let it be a deep kiss, our tongues doing their own little dance as our breath mingled, because my heart was racing with a sudden idea. He finally pulled back and looked at me with such caring compassion, I knew I was right; his game was written all over his face. I now had whatever justification I needed to excuse my part in this carnal exercise because it showed me how to get back on top.

My expression went hard and I sneered, "So — you do *your* rapes by proxy."

He looked at me, confused. "What?"

"I'm the substitute fuck you don't have the balls to do in reality."

He frowned a little and said, "I dunno what you mean."

I snorted and shook my head. "I'm somebody else to you. Somebody you haven't got the nerve to tie down and fuck, so you did it to me, instead. How's it feel, being a wimp?"

He propped himself up on his arms, his eyes glazing over with wariness. "Should a trick talk to his john, that way?"

"You think I was paid to do this?" More confusion entered his eyes. Oh. Obviously, he did. "I'm here 'cause I did my rapes against guys who actually *did* fuck me over."

His jaw almost dropped to the mattress. "You WHAT?!"

"I fucked the fuckers who fucked with me, not some guy in a secret room you pay by the hour for."

"Bullshit. If you'd of done that, you've of gone to jail."

"It's on tape. One I made. One that was made of me."

"Made of you? How?"

"Get 'em to show you. You'll see."

"Why?"

"Why what?"

"Why get 'em to show me what you've done? Why would I care about that?"

"To show you how to do it up right. For next time."

"There — there isn't gonna be a next time," he said as he sat up.

"Yes there will. Maybe not for a year or two, but you'll get back to wanting this, again. Shit, *needing* it."

"No, I — I just wanted to get off — with a guy and — "

"Who's Chris?" He jolted. "I know he's the one you really wanted to do this to. I'm him for you. So who is he? Why'd you rape me so you could think you were raping him?"

"I didn't rape you! Not really!"

"Why ME and not HIM?"

"You — you can't rape him," he said, a bit too quickly. "He — he's a character in this video game and I liked how he was drawn and that — I mean, I — I — "

"Bullshit. You came here and fucked me 'cause you don't have the balls to go after him. Same for John."

He froze, for an instant, then started blabbering, "You really are working your imagination. That's Gacy. John Wayne Gacy. Raped and murdered thirty-three guys about your age. Just like this — just like what I did, here — but some of 'em didn't get hard and cum, so he'd choke 'em till they did — like in auto-erotic strangulation — and — and — I wanted to see what it was like, that's all. And — and I was told that you liked that and you wanted me to do it to you, but I didn't have to 'cause you got off and — and that's all there is to it. I'm just havin' a little fun pretending to be this famous serial killer but that's all — just pretending and — "

"All by proxy," I cut in. "All of it bullshit pretend shit 'cause you're scared. You think it's hard to rape a guy. But it's not. It's easy. And all my guys came — and I didn't need to do anything more than what you did here."

He eyed me, his mind clicking a thousand miles a minute. Something was building in there and I was hoping it was what I wanted — desperately wanted him to think, *Say...maybe I could go*

191

*after this guy who hurt me and use this dick as my mentor.*

Now before you go thinking I'm presenting myself as some brilliant brain or manipulative mind, let me tell you that I wasn't trying to do that when I started. All I was trying to do was jolt some information out of this guy that I might be able to use against anyone else who came at me — or even try and get away from this place. I'd already figured out Gentle Voice would never keep any agreement he made; he'd proven that by setting me up as this guy's trick and lying to this guy by telling him I was being paid to do whatever he wanted, if Geek-Boy was to be believed. It's just, he had gotten me into it way more than I'd expected so I hadn't had a chance to do any truly coherent thinking, yet. Throwing his little comments back at him gave me a breathing space, something to make him jump off course and let me finally see what the hell was going on here — and I mean *really* going on.

But now — now I could see a possible plan. If I could get back to the real world — even if it meant promising another sexual assault on some innocent dude — I could always find some way to get away from this freak. I might be able to get help and save Jake that way. And since this character probably knew our location, I could keep working him till I knew, too, and then called Interpol or the UN or the fucking Marines, if necessary; just tell 'em they're al Qaeda with American hostages and they'd storm them with choppers and cruise missiles and drones and everything they could, no matter where it was. Hell, Americans love to shoot first and ask questions later.

But first I had to get the fuck out. And I finally saw a glimmer of the possibility in my rapist's eyes.

He rose to his feet and I realized he'd never taken his jeans off, just undone them enough to get his dick out, and even flaccid he was impressive. And I was happy to see he was cut. He tucked it away and zipped himself up as he said, "You really think it'd be easy to — to get to Chris? The real Chris?"

"I've done it," I said. And I propped myself up and made myself look as sexy as I possibly could, considering how dirty I felt. But I figured this is how he pictured Gacy's victims looking at the end — bound, naked, sticky with semen — and it would crater his logical thought processes. "Twice. They have copies of the tapes. That's why I'm here. I messed with the wrong guy in the second one and they're getting even. Get 'em to show you. Decide for yourself."

He used my briefs to wipe off his belly and chest, and something about that picture just looked...right. Looked porno and nudged something behind my heart...which pissed me off at myself for even considering it. He picked up his shirt, pulled it on, grabbed the camera, took a dozen more carefully composed shots of me lying there to give himself time for serious thought about what I was suggesting, then he said, "Be right back," and headed for the door. It opened without him having to do a thing, and he did not seem surprised.

I knew it. He did know they were taping. That or he thinks this is a new *Star Trek* movie and I'm the latest incarnation of Spock.

I lay back and closed my eyes, then shifted to my side since my arms were killing me. It wasn't comfortable, either, but it was better than flat on my back. Then I thought, *Shit, they've seen my ass plenty*, so I lay on my stomach since that worked better than anything. And I started trying to work up a plan C if need be...but nothing was coming to mind. Guess all my hopes and probabilities were riding on a Geek-Boy with big eyes being as hungry for some fucking revenge as I was.

Pun intended.

Still — not much of a bet, to say the least.

— THREE —

I lay there about half an hour, maybe longer, counting one-Mississippi, two-Mississippi to keep track of the time. I figured if he wasn't back in an hour, it hadn't worked and I'd have to reconfigure. Besides, if they took longer than that, I'd have to demand the right to pee — or else just work my way around to figure out how to unhook that bar and make my way over to the toilet to do it — or I'd have to wet the bed, *none* of which appealed to me. But finally in came Mr. Muscles and his boys, who freed me from my chains and half-carried-half-carted me out of the room bare-assed nekked and back to the shower, where a new stack of toiletries and wearables awaited. He held up his hand showing *five* and left — meaning, *Be quick — and I don't speak English.* I got the water going as hot as I could stand it, just let the piss out to flow down the drain with it...and let me tell you — I don't know if girls feel this way, but to most guys there is *nothing* like a good long elegant piss when you've been holding it for way too long. It's almost as good as an ejaculation — almost. Once I was done, I soaped myself up then rinsed off three times — and for some weird reason I wanted to go for a fourth but I knew that would take too long. I'd just started drying when they came back for me.

"Done in a minute," I said, wrapping the towel around me like I had any reason to be modest, anymore. Mr. Muscles just grabbed the clothes and his buddies grabbed me and I was dragged back and tossed into the same room, wearing nothing but the towel. Everything else was tossed in after me.

The mattress had vanished and all that was in there now was a small chair. A sleek man in a five-thousand-dollar suit sat in it, looking like something out of *Details Magazine*. His face was as hard as carved granite so his features seemed unreal even though they were deeply attractive in a Mediterranean sort of way — meaning he could be anything from Spanish to Egyptian. Geek-Boy stood behind the table, still dressed the same, looking nervous — only I really couldn't call this guy *geek* anymore, not after what he'd done to me, so I asked, "Do either of you have a name?"

My rapist — what a funny way to put it, like *my bodyguard* or *my car* — he almost spoke but was cut off.

"I am told you have offered to help this young man personalize his needs. Is this to be believed?" So...this was Gentle Voice.

I almost snapped back with, You heard everything, you sick fuck, you tell me — but the shower had enlivened my brain so I grabbed the jeans and as I pulled them on said, "If you'll let Jake go."

"How many do you agree to participate in?"

"He was talking about one — " but I noticed Geek-Boy had raised his hand to show the "Peace" sign so I added, "Two? Oh, both Chris *and* John, right?" He nodded, a sweet, slightly crooked and surprisingly shifty smile on his face. I turned my gaze back to Gentle Voice. "Fine — both of 'em."

Gentle Voice nodded and barely shifted to speak to Geek-Boy. "You say you have two cameras?"

"Yeah. High-Def. One's a little better'n the other, but it gets just as good of shots in the right light and — "

"You will need two more," said Gentle Voice, cutting him off, again, in his low-key don't-fuck-with-me tone. "I will tell you where to focus them. Send us all the footage you shoot; we will do the edit." They both acted like they were discussing the latest porn shoot in the San Fernando Valley.

"Will that be enough settle things?" I asked as I grabbed the shirt off the floor and slipped it on.

Geek-Boy looked at me, frowning. Gentle Voice made no move. "For Mr. Blaine — yes."

"His last name is Darya-Bandari."

Gentle Voice still didn't move. "An additional one and your obligation will be complete." An additional one? Shit, he'd upped the price. Then he finally shifted his granite-stare straight at me. "Of course, this depends on the quality and detail of the product."

*Quality and detail*; such a nice way of saying, Nothing wimpy, you little shit. I made myself smile. "Understood."

He offered me a card. All it had was the website for Greco'd. "Upload the footage here. You have forty-eight hours from your release for the first one."

Geek-Boy jumped. "Wait, we need to plan it out — "

"Fine by me," I said, slipping the card in my pocket.

Gentle Voice eyed me, probably suspecting I was up to something, but since *I* had no idea what I was up to there was no way he could figure it out, so he said, "If you do not meet your full obligation, Mr. Blaine will meet it for you. I have two bids for him, already."

The cock-sucking-mother-fucking-needle-nosed-prick-son-of-a-bitching-asshole was really trying to get at me. Probably lying, but I smiled even wider and nodded my understanding.

After a moment, he returned the nod and Mr. Muscles came over with a vial holding two small pills, and I wondered which one makes you smaller and which one makes you tall, and if mother actually has any to give me, at all.

"Take either one," he said. "Your deadline is midnight, the second day after you awaken — and we will know when you wake."

I popped the pill dry, without a thought. My rapist hesitated then took his, as well. He needed water to get it down. Maybe I would go back to referring to him as a geek, the little fucker — and smirked to myself, enjoying the pun. I sat on the floor, remembering how quickly the gas had slammed into me. Geek-Boy came over and sat next to me, gripping my hand as if we were Butch and Sundance about to jump off that cliff. I let him, not from feelings of solidarity but because I wanted him to be as open as possible with me. It's only by having him at least a little on my side and access to lots of information that I knew I'd be able to figure out my next move. So I also made myself smile at him and lean over to kiss him and that's when the shit hit me and I slumped to the floor and —

I was with Jake and Collie, both — sandwiched between them, Jake in front of me, Collie molded to my back — but I couldn't really see their faces and something felt off. Both were caressing me and kissing me and I was doing nothing in response, just feeling Jake's tight, naked body against mine as he reached around to fondle Collie's rich naked ass. Jake focused his lips on my tits, sucking at them, light and wet, gently pulling at them with his teeth in exactly the same way Collie had used to do. And Collie slipped his strong lovely hands around my hips to fondle both Jake's and my dick and balls, massaging them together like Jake had so loved to do, and I could feel Collie's elegant hard-on slipping between my cheeks, up and down, and then into me without a hint of pain even as Jake's exquisite hands cupped my ass.

We lay out in the open...in a *Sound of Music* type meadow...by a soft, gurgling brook under a weeping willow tree...thick green grass smelling so alive beneath us...blue sky dashed with soft clouds above us...birds singing happily to charm us...and I knew I could be like this forever and never want it to end.

We floated up and I turned over and both of them were gone but someone was servicing me, orally, and I could not move to see who it was — not at all — but by the feel of his velvety tongue I guessed it was Geek-Boy. And once again he took me to the point of explosion before pulling back and rolling me over and slipping inside me. Again, without pain. The grass and meadow were gone and I was in a room so beautifully appointed for comfort and joy, I never wanted to leave it, and would have tolerated being fucked face down for as long as was necessary to be allowed to stay. Then I was guided back and onto my knees, Geek-Boy's dick still in me, and fucked as I sat on his lap and he'd gotten so strong and in control and he jerked me off to where I shot wave after wave of cum up into a bucket that was suddenly before me, filling it even as he filled me with his own cum and

I drifted up and over, again, and I was being bathed under that shower, washed erotically by Mr. Muscles and his queens — and the Russian was with them, as big and buff as I'd feared, and each took his turn lingering over my ass and crotch as the other held my hands in place as each crouched down to suck on my dick and balls and then slip his tongue in my ass and I tried to shift away but the others wouldn't let me, and they kept at it one after the other after the other after the other until I was wild with want and was bent over to have their dicks slip into my mouth, one after the other after the other as each took turns fucking me from both ends, like I was on a spit, and cumming in me and me finally getting so lost in it I came, too, and the shower finally ended and I was dried off and —

My eyes opened to a dark quiet room, a chilly breeze drifting in through a window. I was on a bed, lying atop the covers instead of under them, and I was still dressed in that set of t-shirt and jeans but I could feel myself with a piss hard-on and a hint of stickiness around my dick along with a satiated sense of wonder that didn't connect right. Fuck, I hadn't had a real wet-dream in years, and the fact that I could have one that included the scum who were helping fuck me over made me a bit ill.

Of course, I was still refusing to acknowledge what Geek-Boy had done to me even counted. It's like it was all part of a movie I'd been in — not the porn thing they probably shot but something out of Hollywood, where I'd done the method crap and gotten deep into character and had yet to get back to me. After all, if it hadn't really happened then it didn't matter how I felt about it and it had nothing to do with Jake. Except it had happened. I was still sore in places neither Jake nor Collie had EVER made me sore and my shoulders still felt a bit out of line.

On top of it all, my head was fuzzy — but I could move around without much discomfort...just a hint of nausea that could also come from me being hungry as hell. And I could have drained one of the Great Lakes and still been thirsty, it felt like. I wanted to just curl up in the covers and go back to sleep, but I smelled food and hunger forced me to my feet. I was wobbly but sturdy enough to find the bathroom, take a piss and cross to the door — until I realized people were talking on the other side of it. I stopped, but then the door opened and two amazingly gorgeous, dark-haired male models in the latest of sleek menswear saw me. One popped over his shoulder, "He is awake," and his voice carried a strong accent that I couldn't place. He and his buddy opened the door wider, obviously intending for me to pass through it, so I did.

Turned out we were in a massive suite of rooms on the top floor of a hotel that looked out over an elegant city that was surrounded by snow-capped mountains. The non-stop furnishings were ridiculously rich-looking, with flowers and magazines and crap all over the place to add to the comfort level. And seated on a couch across a glass-topped coffee table was Geek-Boy, talking to a man who would be the perfect image of a 40-ish Air Force General on some TV show where they used nothing but the beautiful people from Central Casting. He looked at me with grey eyes that sparkled with intellect and were the perfect compliment to his grey-flecked hair and high-class moustache.

"Mr. St. Lazarre," he said, his voice carrying the same accent, "how good of you to join us."

I swallowed, suddenly thinking I may have gotten into something more than I expected. Surely I wasn't about to find out that this was *Chris* or *John* and I'd been flipped, again. But then I saw the room service tray and smelled the food still steaming under a stainless steel lid and the only thing I could think to say was, "Is that for me?"

He nodded, so I jumped on it — roast beef in wine sauce with buttery potatoes and asparagus — and I didn't say another word till I'd actually licked the plate clean and swilled it down with a bottle of Perrier and two St. Pauli Girls. They waited for me, patiently working on their iPhones and iPads and laptops and such, never once looking at me or giving off anything in the way of impatience.

When I'd finished the second beer, I smiled at the guy who'd spoken — who was clearly the Boss — and asked, "Okay, so now what?"

He looked back at me, not smiling but not cold or wary. "Do you know where you were?"

"Guys, c'mon, I already told you I'd do what you wanted me to, so why the bullshit?"

Geek-Boy rose, his whole demeanor suddenly different, more in control and self-assured, almost seeming military in his bearing. "Antony, we're not with them. What we're trying to figure out is how to get *to* them."

I looked at him, wary. "So who are you?"

"I'm Matthew — uh, Matt — and these guys — "

Boss Man said something in what sounded a bit like German...and then I remembered this guy I'd met in Paris, an intern who let me get into some major trouble of the fun kind with him, who spoke not only French and English but German, Spanish and Yiddish — and suddenly I realized, "Aw, shit — your tattoo! It's not Japanese — it's the Hebrew sign for life!"

Boss Man blinked at that. "You think *la Chaim* looks Japanese?"

Well, now I felt like a dumbass. "I — I wasn't really thinking about it; I just — just thought — " Oh, holy fuckin' shit. "Are you guys Israeli? Oh, fuck, oh, fuck, oh, fuck — are you Mossad?!"

Boss Man rose and strode over to me, still even and cool. "We never said that. And do not repeat it, please." Then he took me by the arm and guided me to the couch. I floated down into the thick cushions as he added, "And we need to know if you knew where you were."

I shook my head, verging on shock. "I was out cold when they took me there — and when they brought me here."

Boss Man sighed and nodded to Matt, who sat on the couch's arm.

"You see?" Matt said. "That's how they work it, so nobody knows where they are or how to get in or out."

"Then we need a contact." Boss Man turned to me. "You came the closest to discovering someone in their organization. Tell us how you did this."

I started to freak. "Whoa, whoa, whoa, guys — what the fuck's going on here? Are you gonna screw things up for me and Jake?"

Boss Man looked at me then at Matt — and finally nodded. Matt sat beside me and said in a voice that was startlingly tender, "Antony, we need to get in there, fast. We think they have an Israeli soldier and the brother of a Palestinian that Hamas wanted punished, and are doing the same thing to them that — well, that — "

"That you did to me," I snapped, not even thinking.

He blinked and cast his eyes down. Looked like I cut him, deep — and I actually thought, *Good.*

"Mathieu, perhaps it is better that I explain," said Boss Man, then he turned to me and added, "You may want another beer."

I nodded and started on the third of four St. Paulis that I'd ingest before he was done with his story. All without the hint of a buzz, dammit.

Apparently Greco'd *was* connected to what happened to Collie in that holding cell. It was a secretive company that catered to discerning ladies and gentlemen who wished to have more than just the typical sexual experience. If you were a member, you could access their library of video porn, which was reputed to have several thousand different scenes available, most of them male on female or vise verse. More upscale associates could order various scenarios in which they could participate or just have "acted out" for them. An even *more* select group — those willing to pay from one million up to five million dollars — could special order their own private video, which apparently meant anything from fetish to brutality to a real rape to rumors that suggested snuff territory, both gay and straight, with male and female victims. Specifications were agreed to, the order was dispatched to a subsidiary and either it was recorded or the person chosen as victim was brought to someplace like I'd been, for the client to use like Matt had used me.

Two weeks earlier, an Israeli Defense Force outpost near Lebanon was attacked by Hezbollah. One soldier was killed, another was wounded but escaped by pretending to be dead, a third was taken hostage. After days of arguments back and forth between the Israeli Government and the terrorist group, the IDF's intelligence sources isolated two stories about what had actually happened to the missing soldier — he'd died of his wounds and been buried by Hezbollah, or he'd been sold to a shadow group that used attractive young men for sex toys. The IDF dismissed the second claim as ridiculous and concentrated on regaining their soldier's body.

But a week ago word began to circulate that the younger

brother of a man in the Gaza Strip who was suspected of feeding the IDF information about Hamas had vanished — and word was he'd been handed over to the same demons connected to the story about the soldier in exchange for a number of weapons; seems the kid was damned beautiful. And this time the information matched up with what various spies were hearing elsewhere. On top of that, the story and Greco'd's name came from a believable source — a major member of Hezbollah who thought what had been done was evil and immoral and didn't care how it was stopped. So the powers that be started looking into it...and soon learned something similar happened in Chechnya two days later, where a young Russian soldier had vanished and first the rebels had said they captured him but then said they hadn't and his body had yet to be found.

I stopped Boss Man with, "I saw him."

"Describe him," he said. One of the male models quickly pulled up information on his laptop.

"Beefy, well-built, blond. A lot heavier than me. Cheek bones that would cut ice. I think his eyes were brown. He was next on my list."

Right-hand guy looked at Boss Man and nodded.

Boss Man sighed and continued.

After days of intense, secretive investigation, they'd ferreted out all they could about Greco'd — including my encounter with them — and also learned the only way to even be allowed to apply was by referral from a current member along with a million dollar non-refundable fee. Other than that, they'd had no luck tracking down where the company was located or how they worked or how many members they had or anything. Even their hackers couldn't get past the firewalls Greco'd had erected on their site — not without a lot more time...and time was not plentiful if they wanted to get to this Palestinian kid and the Russian before they'd been brutalized beyond repair; the sub-text being they believed they were too late for their soldier. A stroke of luck lead them to a member of Greco'd in Miami's Cuban community, and some blackmail made him agree to refer one of their people for a membership — Matt.

"I do I-T work," Matt slipped in, "and I was on a kibbutz just out of high school. Plus I was the only openly gay Jewish geek they knew about in Florida."

"Do not denigrate yourself, Mathieu," said Boss Man. He turned to me. "We learned he had already done an excellent job saving the man from a disastrous encounter with a hacker. Prevented millions of dollars in costs and liabilities, so rather than take the time needed to secure him a membership, we asked *our gentleman* to *show his gratitude* with a one-time encounter. His fantasy with you cost over a million dollars."

I looked at Matt, who blushed. "I didn't know," he said. "I would've freaked out."

"You mean, I wasn't worth it?" I asked.

Matt blinked. "That — that's got nothing to do with it. I was just really on edge. Shit, they actually investigated me. Checked out my FaceBook page, my friends, made sure I was gay and open to the services they offer and — and could keep from yapping it up all over the place."

Okay, Matt was back to being non-geek, and a bit scary. "How'd you know they checked you out?" I asked.

"We monitored his sites," said Right-hand guy. "We even traced them back to a service here."

"It was spooky," added Matt. "And if I hadn't passed their inspection, they wouldn't have given me one minute with you."

"So where's *here*?"

"Zurich. Switzerland."

Dammit, this was starting to sound like a Richard Ludlum novel. I just sat there and let them keep on with the tale.

"Obviously, I got the okay," said Matt. "But I had to meet them in Geneva, like right then."

"Part of the deal," said Boss Man. "When an invitation is extended, you must be at the location they determine within twenty-four hours or the invitation is withdrawn."

"Who met you?" I asked Matt. "The guy with the gentle voice?"

"Who?" Matt asked. "Orin?"

What the fuck?! "Orin?!"

203

Boss Man showed me a sketch and asked, "Him?"

It was Gentle Voice. "He calls himself Orin? Seriously?" Boss Man nodded, and then it hit me — Matt helped them make a sketch. I spun on him. "Dude, how long've you been awake?"

Matt frowned. "I was dropped off yesterday morning. You didn't show up till a couple hours ago."

"You appeared in the room below ours, lying on the bed. Apparently, two men walked you in, then called Mathieu and left. We brought you up here."

Holy shit — maybe that wet dream wasn't a dream. "What day is it?"

"Thursday, the twenty-third." It'd been a week since I was grabbed. That fucking Gentle Voice *had* taken even more of my flesh to service this debt, the motherfucker, maybe even before I woke up the first time. If I ever got my hands on his ass, he'd wish to God he'd let them use him instead of me because — oh, fuckin' shit — that meant Jake had been in that fucking room for a week — if he'd been grabbed at the same time as me. But what if he'd been grabbed before? What if the reason I couldn't get hold of him that night was he'd already been taken and was in that room and — OH, HOLY FUCKING SHIT!

I bolted to my feet and stood on a balcony to look out over the city. And it sure as hell *did* look like Switzerland, from the old-roofed buildings to the tiny streets to the cars and busses and trolleys and the cold night breeze. A silvery lake just past some squat white structures with sharp roofs. I started to shiver — not from the cold (though it *was* freezing) or the sense of dislocation but from this hideous gnawing fear in my belly at finally understanding what had happened.

"I was taken last Thursday," I gasped out.

Matt came over and put a sympathetic hand on my shoulder. "We know. That's when I was told to get ready." He nodded back to one of the male models and added, "It only took Eli half an hour to connect everything. That deputy-sheriff's heart attack and Jacob Darya-Bandari vanishing then you — "

I jolted. "So Jake *was* grabbed before me?"

Matt nodded. "He was in Paris — "

"Oh, shit. In the La Défense district."

Boss Man eyed me. "How did you know?"

"His father. He'd been talking about trying to see him." His nerves those last couple days now made sense. He wanted to face daddy on his own to see how it went. Probably was in Paris when I called his mobile phone. May have still been trying to work up his nerve to face the guy and — and — it all came crashing in. Those bastards at Greco'd didn't give a shit about Jake; he was just the first dude they fucked around, and he'd gone on living his life. I'm the son-of-a-bitch who'd fucked things up for them. I'm the bastard they wanted to get even with. I'd brought them back to Jake and they were using him to get to me and — and —

I started to pace, fighting the urge to scream. "Aw, shit, aw, shit, it's my fault. I fucked things up. I fucked it all up. I should've let him go. I should've let him go it alone. If I hadn't come to live with him — if it hadn't been for me, they'd never've gone after him and — "

"ANTONY!" Boss Man's voice sliced into my spitting, growling, whirling fury, so I stopped pacing and fought my way back into control. "You're correct — Jacob flew to Paris that morning, took a meeting with his father then was seen no more."

"Not till I saw him," said Matt, "when I was offered my choice of — well..."

"Your choice of who to play your fuckin' game with? Thanks for choosing me, motherfucker, it was the smart move. Pickin' the guy who can handle this shit and — and — "

Except I was still freaky about the whole situation and what had happened with him and still too close to going bat-shit crazy, so Boss Man yanked me back to the couch and shoved me down in it. Then he got hard in my face.

"You want your friend to be saved? Help us find a way to him. Help us find a way to that Palestinian boy, and that Russian. Then when we have finished this filth — *then* wallow in your self-pity." The look I cast him must have shown that he'd misunderstood what was building in me and that it was anything but self-pity. He almost frowned then backed away, just a little, not a hundred percent sure of himself for the first time since I'd met him. "We

205

need to make contact with someone who is part of the main organization. Using a member has proven to be a waste of resources. You actually connected an individual to those who control this company. Your research suggests two others were part of — "

I stammered out, "Guy named Stanton and — and a judge. Uh, Gilbert."

"We've looked into them. The only connection we can find comes from the cases they handled — " I started to speak but he just raised his voice, " — that appear to have set a number of men up for assault. But these can easily be blamed on a dead man." Fuck, Gentle Voice was telling the truth about Nussewald. Shit. "We need something definite to work with."

Something definite? And they were expecting this to come from me? What'd they think I knew or who or — son-of-a-bitch.

"Marquez," I whispered, just making a leap from A to X. "A Texas Ranger. He — he turned me over to that fat fuck, even though his supervisor didn't want to. And he did it in a way that'd make me disappear for a while."

Eli frowned. "Texas Rangers? You mean like cowboys?"

Matt chimed in with, "Cops. Rangers are like state cops. Guy I used to date had some run-ins with them in this town north of Houston. They all but ran him out of the state."

"And — and — and the Texas Rangers were connected to the arrest of one of the guys who was raped in that holding cell and he — I didn't check to see who the arresting officers were and maybe — maybe — "

"This is something to consider," said Boss Man, "But he sounds too low-level to be of worth."

"But how's he paid?" I asked. "It couldn't go through Nussewald; that'd be too easy a link to check. And no smart cop'd take a bribe unless he knew who it was coming from and how he could get around it, and Rangers tend to be sharp. And I think his supervisor, Thomas, is good. And honest. So how was Marquez paid? Could that lead you back to somebody?"

Boss Man looked at Matt, who said, "I didn't check into him or Thomas, at all. They're Texas Rangers."

"My — my check was only cursory," said Eli. "To verify they were whom they claimed to be."

"Then have it done, and as quietly as possible," said Boss Man, a bit irritated. "Then we can decide if he is worthy of attention."

Matt scurried over to a laptop set up on the dining table as Eli began clicking away at his own, and suddenly the only sound was the two of them ticking at their respective laptops. Boss Man focused on a folder of papers and the other male model rolled the dinner tray out into the hall. Suddenly, I felt as if I'd been dismissed.

I rose and returned to the window to watch the city grow darker and the silver of the lake grow brighter in comparison. I slipped my hands in my jeans' side pockets and felt something press against my ass. I fished out my passport and wallet from a back pocket, cash, my Texas DL and my MasterCard with them. My kidnappers thought of everything to make my passages all nice and legal-looking, the bastards. I put them back and caught Matt casting me a guilty glance. I jerked my eyes away, suddenly furious and feeling my stomach start to churn. I began gulping in deep breaths of the icy air. Boss Man noticed and came over to me.

"Antony, Mathieu had no choice but to do what he did."

And enjoy it so fucking much? And make me fucking enjoy it? And fuck with my mind doing it? "Yeah, right."

"You need to understand, when we asked him to help us, all we expected him to do was act as — well, as a homing device, so we could pinpoint where these men were being taken. Since he was meeting them in Europe, we thought this is where they will be located and it will be easy for us to — oh, take matters into our own hands. It was a foolish assumption on our part."

"What — you — you guys were gonna storm in like — like a SWAT team?"

He just smiled a non-smile.

Oh.

Shit.

Then he said, "Unfortunately, the homing signal failed and Mathieu was left to get himself out of the situation — which he did by — by fulfilling the fantasy he'd told them about. Then you gave him a path to gain both your freedoms."

Meaning he hadn't told them how much he got into it. Or how much I had. And how sick that made me feel — shit, *makes* me feel. But that still didn't make sense. "All I did was tell him what I'd done."

"Rape one man and turn the probable rape of you around on another," he said. "They showed him part of both videos. Allow me to tell you something: we think the reason he was accepted into Greco'd's game is, his FaceBook page shows a — a morbid fascination with serial killers of all natures. He even brags about owning one of John Wayne Gacy's clown paintings." I cast Matt a wary look. "Not an original, just a facsimile, but he used this to validate his — fantasy."

Gacy killed his victims. Shit. "What was Matt's fantasy?"

Boss Man looked uncomfortable. "I would rather not — you should talk with him to — he should explain this to you."

"But it included rape."

Boss Man took in a deep breath and said, "Yes. And once he knew your history — something we had not shared with him — he figured he could get you both out. He did not know about your friend until yesterday."

Parceling out the data, huh? Boss Man sounded a bit like the same type of controlling bastard Gentle Voice was. I glanced at Matt, now even more wary of him. "Kind of freaky — being so locked into a guy who killed for pleasure."

"Is that something you should criticize?" Boss Man's voice was gentle but sharp as a knife. "It is one thing to be fixated on death and destruction — it is quite another to actually *do* what some of those men have done...unless coerced."

Bam, straight to the gut. Judge not, ye little fuck, 'cause you've already shown how, with just a little effort, you could wind up like Gacy or The Green River Killer or Ted Bundy or be the inspiration for some TV cop drama. And I'll bet every serial rapist or killer had his own warped justification for the rapes and murders. My one positive was, I hadn't killed anybody — not yet. But I knew that little demon lurked within so I had no counter-argument to his logic. It was too damn fucking correct. Dammit.

Boss man continued, "Mathieu brutalized you, yes, but by doing so, he showed Orin a man who was serious about his fantasies and used that as a bargaining tool. He also had the intelligence to try to get the price of his fantasy refunded in exchange for him videotaping the — encounter, playing the cheap little Jew to perfection." Said without irony, which seemed odd, coming from a Jewish man. "Orin, being the man we now know he is, saw the other possibilities on his own."

I looked away from Matt. No way could I see him as a geek, now, and not so sweet, either. Partner in psychosis, maybe? I almost smirked.

"So where were we that you guys couldn't get to?" I asked. Boss Man just looked at me. "C'mon, the signal died? Bullshit. That crap can be picked up by fucking satellites from anywhere in the globe. Shit, they find black boxes from plane crashes under ten-thousand feet of ocean, and your shit'd be just as good as that. We were someplace you had no way in to. Where?"

"Dubai," he said, finally.

Fuck, no kidding they locked out. There was no way in hell a Moslem government would let an Israeli SWAT team storm a building in their kingdom. Not after having accused Mossad of an assassination on their soil. The jihadists would go nuts.

"You know where in Dubai?" I asked.

He smiled. "Have you heard of that immensely tall building they have in their city?"

"Shit — we were up near the top."

"Oh?"

"The floor had this slight sway to it. I thought we were on a boat in a harbor, but the wind against the building — "

"That would put you above floor one-hundred, making it even harder to deal with."

No shit. "So how're you gonna get Jake out?"

"We must convince the government of Dubai to do that for us. Which I am certain they will do since having it known such an organization is set up in their little kingdom, after all the negative publicity of recent — it would be devastating to their position in the Arab world. But first we need irrefutable proof. Something they will believe, even if it's brought to them by a Jew."

"You want your *Orin* to tell them."

"It would be foolish of me to say anything more. All I ask is that you understand, what Mathieu did, he did to protect you both."

"Y'know, that shit I said — it really *was* lucky he chose me instead of Jake. 'Cause he — "

"Not lucky. We told him to. Your looks fit better with the fantasy he requested — " Which didn't sound quite right. What little I knew about John Wayne Gacy, he'd gone after blond guys who were younger and slimmer than me — more like kids than adults. "We also knew what had happened to Darya-Bandari in that jail cell and prison. We did not wish to inflict that on him, again."

Son-of-a-bitch. "You knew there's a possibility he'd have to go all the way." Boss Man nodded. "And Matt knew." Not a hint of movement from the guy, meaning, Yes. Meaning I was designated the sacrificial lamb, if need be. The cold-blooded bastards. "I was the fucking *Plan B*."

"Once again, Mr. St. Lazarre," he said, "you are hardly an innocent young man. I hope you will take into account how necessary it was to have not only a Plan B, but also a Plan C, D, E and F."

He headed back to the couch and made a call, talking in what sounded like Hebrew. I watched Matt work, and he was so focused on what he was doing, he lost all wariness and uncertainty and fear and instead became this model of purity happily tracking down anything he could to help his buddies do what they needed to do to save — hell, not just one of one of mine but two of their enemies. His elegant fingers flew over the keyboard, the lean muscles in his arms offering a gentle dance in perfect synchronicity, ankles crossed under the chair, big brown eyes lost in the information flashing before him. He was almost like poetry, someone gentle and deep with meaning.

Of course, I'd caught the hint from Boss Man was that I should consider what Matt'd done to me to be rape against him, too. If you're forced to commit a crime to protect yourself or a loved one, isn't that crime being perpetrated against you, as well?

What I'd done had been simple revenge, punishment against those who'd wronged me and someone I loved, but even as I was doing it I'd known, deep down, Collie would not have approved. Because of him, I'd become aware of the world outside my own little sphere of existence. Because of him, I'd been learning about things more involved than tennis and English. Because of him, I'd begun to feel a bit of compassion for others, even those members of my own family who'd cut me off from their lives. If he'd lived through his ordeal and learned of my plans, he'd have stopped me and done so in a way that forced me to see how much like an animal I was becoming. 'Cause that's what animals do — when they're hurt, they lash out and don't care who they shred, even when you're trying to help them.

I think this was the first time I started to wonder if Collie and I would have lasted. He was so good, so decent, so fair, and me — shit, I was closer in temperament to Jake. If you get hit, hit 'em back — and if you can't, deal with it in some other way and fuck being nice about it. I'd kept that aspect of myself in check for the eight months Collie and I were together and I like to think it was because I was becoming a better person with him, but the truth is I hadn't been crossed or had anyone piss me off enough to lose control. His death is what unleashed the hounds within and it had lead directly to me leading Jake straight into hell, again. And I had to deal with that.

And now Matt was going to have to deal with what he'd done to protect himself. And deal with how much he'd enjoyed it, because no matter what the little fuck might tell Boss Man and Eli and his friends and all, he'd really gotten off on the role-playing he'd set up...just like I'd had fun with mine.

Yes, it's time the absolute truth was acknowledged here — I'd more than enjoyed what I did to Orin and Rattler...and even to Slim Sad-Eyed Sean, molesting him to get him to participate in Rattler's fucking...I'd luxuriated in it. Loved how it swept over me and carried me down a path of self-satisfaction.

And another truth? I wanted to do it, again. And again. The beast was out of the shadows now and commanded a sacrifice or two or three. And I was already planning my next one —

something that would strike at the heart of Texas' fucked up sense of justice and right.

Oh, and this was gonna be a beauty.

— FOUR —

They caught Officer Marquez as he was running along the trail by Lady Bird Lake. I don't know how they knew where he was; truth is, I didn't bother asking. I just know that they dragged him into the warehouse we now occupied, his hands bound behind him, gagged and blindfolded...and I had to admit, now that I was seeing him outside of a suit, he looked even hotter than I'd imagined. He wore a pair of cut-off sweat pants and a wife-beater, revealing perfect shoulders and chest muscles, solid and smooth and gliding down tight abs to a trim waist and lovely butt that flowed into a pair of the most beautiful legs I'd ever seen. He was nearly hairless, but I think that was natural with him, not shaved. His powerful arms were pumped from fear and anger and his pecs heaved against the flimsy cotton of the t-shirt as he struggled against his captors.

We were in a cinder-block building on the south side of Austin, off Congress and 290. It was an area of junk yards, railroad tracks and old warehouses, with ours down a small rutted drive lined with overgrowth that passed between a fence that tried to hide stacks of old appliances on one side with a tin-roofed excuse of a structure whose walls were metal sheeting on the other. Inside, it was open and empty with nothing but blank walls, except for a table jammed next to an industrial sink in one corner. The place looked so lost and uninterested in anything, I wondered if it even had an address.

We'd flown into Bergstrom on a private jet and hopped in a huge Chevy Suburban that already had a driver, then headed straight here to get ready. How or why they'd picked this location was not explained to me, nor did I ask. By this point, I was ready to get something done and fast; we only had till midnight to get some footage off to Gentle Voice (I just could *not* call him Orin). Matt had already sent him a message telling him we were working on Central US time and had gotten a cryptic "Time OK" message back.

Boss Man's guys moved the table to the center of the room, set up bright lights all around it and this too-fucking-butch guy fastened a sturdy wooden chair into the cement floor next to it, using drills and joints that I'd never seen before. Sure enough, when they slammed Benny into it and bound his legs to the chair's legs, with his arms behind its back and rope wrapped through the cross bar then around his lower torso to secure him even more, it didn't even budge. Sort of a low-tech version of the chair I'd been held in while Gentle Voice talked to me. Only when Benny was solidly roped did Boss Man nod and his boys remove the gag — but not the blindfold.

And the first words out of Officer Marquez's mouth? "What the fuck's going on? Are you people fuckin' crazy? Do you know who you've kidnapped? I'm a cop! A Texas Ranger! I keep a schedule and I'm expected on duty and — "

Boss Man squatted before him and said in a tone so even and calm, it sent chills up my spine, "We understand you've done work for a company known as Greco'd. Who do you deal with?"

"I dunno what you're talkin' about. You got the wrong guy! I'm a cop! A Texas Ranger and — "

"Office Benjamin Marquez, twenty-eight years old, undergraduate degree in Criminal Science, joined the police force straight out of college and shifted to the Texas Rangers three years ago. Your immediate superior is Officer Arlen Thomas, who's been with the Rangers for nearly thirty years. Excellent decision on their part, having an experienced officer mentor an inexperienced one. And so far as I can tell, he has no blemish on his record."

"I don't either! Who the fuck are you?!"

"I am the one who asks you for your contact at Greco'd."

"What're you talkin' about? Never heard of 'em!"

"You received three substantial payments via a subsidiary of that company — the first, just over a year ago for thirty-thousand dollars; the second, ten days later for twenty-thousand dollars; the third, last month for twenty-five-thousand. A total of seventy-five-thousand dollars in the space of little more than a year. It also appears you've interfered with the state's investigation into another part of that company — a subsidiary that operated in two different Texas cities."

Two?! Shit, there was another one?

"You dunno what you're talkin' about! I never killed any investigation! I got no control, like that! So you got your facts screwed up. And that money — that's from an inheritance, from my grandfather. The money's bein' handed out in bits — in sections — "

He kept jabbering on, swearing the money was legit and he'd never done shit and we'd better quit and just let him git — uh, get. And as he jabbered, Boss Man showed me copies of his bank statements and how the money tracked back to an account set up to handle his grandfather's estate and could have come from sales of stocks over the year, stocks that were purchased by a subsidiary of a subsidiary of a subsidiary of a company headquartered in Paris and *not* named Greco'd. All handled through a bank in Miami — so, Benny might be Cuban, huh? It fit. And it did look legitimate. And I could see Boss Man didn't want to start any *enhanced interrogation techniques* without something more substantial to go on.

Now the truth is, the only reason I suspected Benny is he'd turned me over to Nussewald, who'd had me busted. It could've been a legitimate piece of professional courtesy. *Look, we talked to this guy and I think he's the one who fucked your cousin, but my partner's playing careful, so here's where you can find him.* Which damn near got me killed, but he might not have known that.

Except...he did. I'd laid it out about Nussewald. Sure, half of it was bullshit, but there was enough truth behind it to make any cop worth half a shit take a step back and want to know more about the situation before acting. And Thomas *had* been willing to do that. So there was something else going on — and then I found my proof (well, proof enough for me) on the bank statement.

I handed it back to Boss Man and softly said, "Let me. Matt?"

He came over, a palm-sized HD camera in hand, and I whispered, "Did you tape them bringing him in?" He cast a quick glance at Boss Man and gave me his crooked smile, hidden from their view. He had sneaked a shot, the little shit. I could've hugged him. "You got everything we need for tonight?"

He looked at Marquez, his big eyes even bigger. "Won't they know who he is?"

"Not if we call him Chris."

"But he could call 'em and tell 'em and — "

"He won't. Trust me."

He looked back at me, wary. I nodded. He almost smiled. "I'll have it all ready in five minutes."

He bolted from the room. I smiled at Boss Man and added, "You and your boys may want to leave."

Boss Man just shook his head. He didn't want to chance me putting any marks on this cop, in case it I was the one full of shit. I shrugged and waited for Matt. He set three little HD cameras up, all focused on our captive, and initiated recording.

I took a moment and let the cameras get some nice long images of Benny bound and struggling and still spewing his crap about his innocence, then I slipped up behind him, leaned over to wrap my arms around him and rested my chin on a shoulder.

"Hi, Benny," I whispered. "Remember me?"

"What th' fuck — what're you doing? Who is this?"

"I'm the faggot you turned over to the cops."

"What? Who — ?"

"The faggot who's supposed to have been fucked and killed in holding cell six? The college dude you almost hit 'cause he's just too queer for you?"

He cocked his head, startled. "Lazarre?"

"*Saint* Lazarre!" And I flicked my thumbs over his tits.

He jolted and began to struggle. "What the fuck, man? What the fuck're you doin'? Why're you back here?"

"Oh, just to finish some business with a guy I really think is hotter'n hell." Then I grabbed his wife-beater and tore it open.

He cried out. "No! Fuckin' shit, man, I didn't do shit to you!"

"Oh? Well — in the world of remarkable coincidences, your

first payment came on two days before I was arrested — which seems just a bit *too* coincidental." And I pinched his tits.

He screamed and twisted to one side. "What're you doin'?"

"Having fun." I walked around to squat in front of him, careful to keep out of the way of the camera. "I'm gonna prove you're just as big a queer as I am."

"No, no, no — I'm no faggot!"

"Bullshit, cunt. You liked me looking you over in my room; that's why you had to attack me — to prove you weren't like me. But all it proved to me is you want my mouth on your dick and my dick up your ass. And if you think I can't prove that, you're a fuckin' idiot."

I slid my hands up the inside of his shorts, gliding them along his thighs like Matt had done to me, and found he had a nice layer of down along his skin. He tried to wriggle away but he was too tightly bound to the chair for him to do anything more than shift around in it.

"Motherfucker, I didn't do shit to you! Fuckin' shit, leave me alone! Stop it!"

My fingers reached his scrotum to find smooth material mixing with thick pubes and traces of sweat. I chuckled. I could see why Matt liked doing this; it was like exploring and finding hidden treasure. I caressed Benny's balls. "Nice and full. You've got enough for more than one milking."

"No! NO! You're not gonna do that to me! No fuckin' way! I'll fuckin' kill you, if you even try it!"

He struggled even harder, his muscles pumping up rich and full, his tits round and brown and tight as they peeked from behind the torn shirt. The rope around his belly had kept it from tearing completely apart and one strap had slid down his left bicep, allowing his left pec to be revealed, and the lower part had ridden up a little to let me see the beginning of the treasure trail that flowed from his navel. Sweat formed on his skin, making him almost gleam. I stepped back to gaze upon him, and he suddenly remembered this Argentine porno god. He had the same trim, smooth beefiness about him to match his gorgeous face with lips perfect for a blow-job. Talk about fucking erotic — I had to look

217

away or I'd lose control and have a go at him.

I noticed a pair of scissors on the table and strolled over to get them. They were big, sharp and surprisingly clean. I bet Boss Man and his boys had brought them in for some use of their own, but they'd never figured it'd be for this.

I glanced at them. Boss Man was watching me, wary, while Butch and the boys were looking away, not wanting to see what they knew was about to happen. Matt's eyes never left me.

I strolled back to Benny. He was still spitting and cursing and swearing he'd get me if I fucking touched him, again. And he was so fucking gorgeous as he snarled out his words...and he kept snarling them till I touched the cold steel of the scissors to his left tit.

He jolted and whispered, "What's that? What the fuck — ?"

I just went, "Shhh," then moved the scissors down his belly and across his leg to his knee then sliced them through the left leg of his shorts, whispering the material away from the smooth tanned muscle of his thigh to let me see the barely visible hair dancing around its perfect shape.

"No, no, don't," was all he seemed able to say as the cold steel cut and cut into the material. Man, the feeling behind my heart as I went — remembering how Matt had done it (and thanks for the idea, motherfucker) — made it hard to breathe as I got closer and closer and cut through the waist-cord and the shorts drifted open to reveal a pair of flimsy, striped bikini briefs.

He began to whimper, "Please, don't. Don't. You don't know what you're doin', you don't know what you're doin', I swear, I swear I — I — I didn't know what that fat fuck was planning, I swear to you."

I glanced over at Boss Man. He'd both perked up and seemed irritated. Probably at his boys for not zeroing in on Marquez. I smiled and began cutting up the right leg.

"Swear to God, I didn't know! It was just a phone call! All they wanted to know was what you told Thomas! That's it! I swear! Shit, motherfucker, I'm fuckin' tellin' you the truth!"

Snip — the shorts were gone and the only thing protecting his dick from me was those cheap little briefs. Which surprised me, since I figured him for the tight-white-CK kind of guy, though the basket they held looked promising. Too fucking promising. My breath actually grew shallow as I reached down and groped it. Swirled my fingers around the fullness of his balls. Sent screaming lightning from my fingers to my chest.

"NO! SHIT! I'm tellin' you the truth!"

Boss Man stepped forward. "How did it work?"

"My — my grandfather'd just died. This guy, he — he said some of Poppo's stock was undervalued, but they'd be happy to buy it at true value if I — I'd just tell them what this — this fuckin' faggot told Thomas. That's all! It didn't seem like all that big a deal and — "

I squeezed his balls. He cried out. Then I snarled, "Both times?" I was starting to shake.

He began to hyperventilate. "Both — both — ?"

"In my dorm room and in the shower, over a week later?"

He hesitated, trying to think. The little fuck, he was still lying. I grabbed the left side of the briefs and tore them at the hip, revealing his dick and one of his balls; the other one stayed trapped in the material. He wasn't that big — though that could come from his being scared — and, as I'd expected, he was uncut, just like that Argentine porn god. And from the looks of it, his foreskin was just as thick and ugly and that lessened the roaring I'd begun to hear in the shadows of my heart.

Look, I don't mind a guy being uncut; shit, Collie hadn't been and I'd loved his dick. There were times I'd even play with his foreskin to make him crazy with need. But I've always had a preference for circumcised cocks. They just look right to me, probably because mine was. And I agree that it's just one of my own peculiarities, one that I can easily ignore if the guy hits me right. Hell, there was this one beautiful blond porno god named Pavel with a never-ending dick and foreskin that I'd have *loved* to have got hold of, mainly because his eyes held so, so many secrets. But this one — this one just looked lumpy and — hell, and thickly there. So I just concentrated on his balls, whispering my fingers around them, encircling them, over and over and over.

Benny started gasping, "No, no, no, no — I — yeah, I talked

to him both times. But they called me; I never had a way to contact them! Never!"

Boss man asked, "Did you recognize the voice? Anything about the voice?"

"No — shit — stop it!" I kept fondling his balls, actually liked the feel of them, they were so fat. "I — his accent — shit, his accent — I think he was Cuban."

"Like you?" I asked.

"I ain't fuckin' Cuban! My family's from San Juan! Shit! Get your fuckin' hands off me! I'm tellin' you the truth!"

I glanced at Boss Man. He looked at Matt, who absently shook his head.

"That guy in Miami — I didn't meet any of his people." Obviously Matt was having a bit of trouble concentrating.

Boss man nodded then called over his shoulder, "Find out more." Butch pulled out a cell phone and went off to a corner to talk, probably to Eli. Boss Man turned back to Matt. "Stock sales?" he asked.

Matt grimaced. "Too — uh, too easy to trace and cross-reference. Even back a — a dozen levels."

"So it would need to be something more carefully hidden."

"Or deliberately obvious. Three different sales — I can probably find a pattern to link to. Do some triangulation — "

"No, you stay with St. Lazarre."

"But — "

"Yo, dude!" I snapped. "We have to upload something by midnight or they'll — they'll — " I couldn't continue. Just the thought of what might happen to Jake sent daggers of fury and fear into me and I wanted complete control, right now. "Besides," I added, "this guy's not being completely honest with us, yet."

"Bullshit!" Benny shrieked. "I am! I am! Swear to God!"

Boss man looked at me and then at Benny, and for the first time I had the feeling he hated making a decision. He finally nodded and turned to Matt. "He's right. We have enough to begin with but see what else you can learn. Or is this a situation you no longer wish to be part of?"

The full implications of what Boss Man was saying slapped

into Matt. He cast a look at Benny, and I could tell he was torn. He wanted to be more directly helpful to Boss Man, and I think he was afraid of what had happened with me — of how much he'd wrapped himself up in it. But the sight of big, bad, beautiful Benny struggling and the reality that my caressing of Benny's balls was having an effect — what promised to be an impressive effect, despite the situation — tickled his prurient needs. And I could see in the way his eyes flashed between me and a certain ever-expanding dick that he had his own wild dogs howling in his shadows, wanting to spring into action. Wanting to make Benny his next *Chris* proxy. He looked back at Boss Man, still unsure.

The man put a fatherly hand on Matt's shoulder and spoke softly and deliberately. "I will want no details when you make your report."

Matt licked his lips...then nodded.

Without looking at me, again, Boss Man and his boys quietly left the room. But Benny must have heard the door close.

"Oh, shit, please, I told you what I know. That's all I know. I don't know anything else. Please, don't leave me here! Don't let him hurt me. Just lemme go. Please. Please. Don't do this to me. You don't know what you're doing!"

I just kept running my fingers around his balls, watching his dick shift and flop about and slowly, slowly continue to grow. It could have been a lovely dick, aiming to be fat and perky and curved in just the right way, its head promising to be exceedingly juicy. I was actually beginning to re-evaluate the look of it, so I pulled back the foreskin — just to get more info to make my decision. Honest. And I was right — perfectly shaped and just begging for the caress of someone's lips, so I leaned in to make it happy.

Matt went over to one camera and zoomed the lens in on me sucking Benny's cock. Then he jumped. "Shit, I've got the other camera in the car," and he raced outside.

Benny heard him. "Camera? What the fuck — you're taping this?! You sick fucking freaks, you're fucking taping this?!"

I pulled back from his dick and whispered, "Just like your buddy, Nussewald, did in holding cell six."

221

"I — I didn't know about that. Dude, really — "

"He got some wonderful video of dozens of men being raped and sold it to the guys who paid you." I tickled the fingers of my left hand through his pubs. His dick gave me a hint of a joyous jump. "He even shot video of a man I loved — being raped and killed." I caressed up the length of his growing shaft, just medium hard but getting fuller. "The same thing was supposed to happen to me, thanks to you. All by special order."

"I — I didn't know. You think I'm that kind of scum? You think I could do that? I didn't fuckin' know! I didn't!"

"Bullshit!" I snarled, then I softly bit at his left tit. He tried to twist away but this time I gripped his balls hard enough to hurt, then I whispered, "You wouldn't have done this without knowing who you were doing it for. You'd have had to have a name. Do a face-to-face. Be able to check them out. You'd have had to be sure this wasn't a set-up by some ambitious attorney general out to get a corrupt cop."

"Please, no — I — I'm telling you — "

I grabbed the hair on the back of his head. It was wet from sweat. I held him in place and I planted a kiss on his lips, gripping him too tightly to twist away. Then I added, "But it doesn't matter. You see, those guys that grabbed you — they don't know I'm working for Greco'd, now. The guys that paid you gave you to me in exchange for a friend of mine. All I have to do is give them a videotape of it."

"Bullshit — they'd never do that — not to me — "

"Why not? They got another special order."

He gasped. He knew. He fucking *knew* what that meant, the motherfucker.

"No, no, no, please don't do this to me, please, please, please, don't hurt me."

"Don't worry," I said. "That's not part of this deal. You just have to make me happy. But if you do...I'll make it go very, very easy for you."

Then I kissed and licked my way down from his lips to his chin over his throat and across his chest to along his abs and into his groin to nuzzle his pubes. He'd grown soft and ugly, again, but

I now knew that'd be easy to remedy. I got back to circling my fingers around his balls and nuzzling my lips around his shaft and along first his right thigh and then his left, nipping at the soft hairs there. He tasted vaguely salty and smelled musky and his balls were honestly just too fucking gorgeous, so I licked them and sucked them into my mouth and gently rolled them around with my tongue — and sure enough, he started growing, again.

"You — it's being taped?" Benny whimpered, sounding confused. "They're gonna see it? They — they're gonna hear everything and — and — shit. Motherfuckers."

He kept growing and I kept working him, and I didn't stop till he was at full staff. But that fucking foreskin still covered most of his head. Oh, it slipped back easily to reveal the beauty of him and a quick flit of my tongue against the slit told me he was getting into it, whether he wanted to admit it or not. Like Leon Cartucci had, only better because this time I was in complete control and could go as far as I wanted.

I remembered Matt was supposed to be part of this scenario and looked around to see he'd set up the fourth camera and it was taping. I hadn't heard a thing. I wondered how long he'd been doing it — hell, how long *I'd* been diddling around with Benny.

I leaned back, looking at Matt. He was breathing quick and shallow, his expression tentative, his eyes as big as I've ever seen them. He was wearing casual pants and a button-down shirt, and it made him look like something straight out of a frat house, the last place I'd think he was even interested in. Then I looked at his crotch, and he had a nice bulge starting up —something I knew would be fun for Benny and even more fun for me to watch instead of participate in — which I didn't really understand but preferred not to deal with, just yet. So I gestured him over. He approached, warily, his eyes dancing between me and Benny's now full dick.

"You like?" I asked. He nodded. "Ever had a virgin before?" He shook his head. "This one's for you."

Benny moaned and gulped, still trying to think as Matt knelt beside me, his breath still quick and shaky. I stroked on Benny's dick with one hand as I pinched at a tit with the other. He groaned. Then I gripped Matt's shirt's collar and pulled him closer to the massive shaft as I shifted the foreskin back. He licked his lips then kissed its head.

"Oh — oh, shit." Benny's voice was strangled. He grunted and tried to shift but Matt now had a grip on his balls.

Matt encircled the head with his lips then drew them back over it. Benny groaned. I gently whispered my fingers around his tits. Matt took him deeper in his mouth, this time. Put his other hand around the cock. I reached down to trace up Matt's right thigh and brush against his crotch. He was as rich and full as Benny was, and the image of that in Benny's virgin ass took me close to the edge. Matt shifted to give me better access to his crotch so I ran my fingers the length of his dick, once — then froze. I couldn't move until I whispered, "Save it," and shifted back to Benny's legs to hide my sudden inability to touch Matt more.

I began sucking on Benny's tits and caressing his thighs. He was more still, now, allowing us to do as we liked. His breath was still shallow and ragged, half from erotic need, half from fear.

I rose and stepped back to make sure the cameras were getting everything, and they were perfectly aligned. The first one was still focused on Matt's blow-job, getting the beautiful motion of him pumping his head up and down Benny's shaft, his lean clean fingers mimicking his lips...and I had a damn good idea of how much effect that velvet tongue of his was having on Benny's nervous system by the way the guy's stomach tightened and his ass tensed.

The second camera was a wider shot that showed all of both of them, and it was elegant. Benny blindfolded and tied to the chair, hands behind him, his shirt partially torn away, the one strap drifting down his left arm to reveal his torso, the other strap barely in place atop his right shoulder, his chest heaving in reaction, his briefs half torn apart, the material still wrapped around his right leg, riding up and down as Matt tucked in on himself and sucked on him, faster and faster.

The third was a head and shoulders of Benny's face, capturing every twitch of his lips and jerk of his chin. The fourth was tightly focused on Benny's pecs, pumping up and down and unable to move about very much, giving Matt all the access he wanted to

Benny's tits. By now my own dick was screaming to be let out — so I obliged it.

I slipped up behind Benny, lay my erection on his left shoulder and reached down to play with his tits (because they were the one part of him I could fondle without getting sick), giving Matt the freedom to focus on the guy's balls and legs as I whispered, "This is what happened to other guys, with your help."

"No...no..."

"Oh, yes."

"NO! NO!!"

Then I realized he wasn't responding to me; he was jerking, close to firing. I gently reached down to caress the top of Matt's head. He looked up at me, lost in his own erotic haze, his hand still pulling at Benny's massive dick, and I blinked. How the hell Matt got his sweet little mouth around that thing was a question for the ages, because its amazingly fat head had swelled to the size of a Georgia Peach, it looked like. The foreskin was still up around part of it so I pulled it back to reveal the whole knob — and that was just enough manipulation to make Benny gasp and jolt and let the first spurt explode from its slit.

Matt jumped and dove in to lick at the shaft as another spurt fired out — followed by another and another. Even just leaning over Benny's shoulder, I could feel his muscles tensing and pumping and he all but screamed as he shot, yet again.

Matt tumbled back to land flat on his butt, in shock at the sudden beauty of it all, his face covered in semen, his big eyes wide and in awe. I laughed and reached down to keep stroking Benny's dick, and was rewarded with one more spurt that smacked against Matt's mouth. He laughed.

I kept at it until Benny was drained and whimpering. He sat slumped in the chair, as slumped as he could be, his breath ragged and shocked, his head shifting around as if trying to understand the meaning of his new reality. He'd just been sucked off by a fag, and he'd cum big time, and I knew that was truly fucking with his brain.

What he didn't realize was, we were just getting started.

\*\*\*\*

I used Benny's sliced up shorts to wipe my hand off then guided Matt to his feet and cleaned his face with them, like you would a child. He was still chuckling, almost in shock, hints of confusion in his eyes.

"It was good, wasn't it?" I asked.

He nodded, gulping in air. He started to shake. He was going to back out of doing anything more, I could feel it. This moment had been too glorious and it scared him. So I pulled him close and kissed him, deep and full and as tender as you kiss a lover. He tasted of semen and salt, a different taste from when I'd kissed Collie or Jake after they'd sucked me off. It wasn't — hell, I dunno — it just wasn't right. But before I could pull back, he slipped a hand up around my neck to hold me in place as he kissed me back, his grip filled with hunger and need and fear. I held him close and he hugged me, tight, almost whimpering.

I kept my voice calm. "It's amazing, isn't it? What just happened."

He nodded and shakily whispered, "Overwhelming."

"Like a drug." He nodded, still shaking. "Did you feel that with me?"

He gulped in more air and sighed, "Yeah."

"When you came in me." He nodded. I caressed the back of his shoulders, soothing, tender. "It'll be even better when you do it in him."

"No — no — " He almost pulled away. I held him too tightly. His shaking increased.

I nuzzled his ear. "Matt — what happened to you? What did Chris do to you that hurt so much?"

"Name wasn't — Chris. Really is — character in video game."

"What did he do?"

He slowly lay his head in the crook of my neck, breathing quick and deep, and finally, finally whispered, "He made me love him."

"Made you?"

He nodded. "We'd wrestle — in the dorm room. And he'd hold me down and — and it wasn't like he needed to do that but it — it was part of the game. Till somebody found out and asked him about it. And he — he hit me. In front of our friends. Over and over. Called me a faggot. Told me to stop telling stories about him." Motherfucker. "But I hadn't said anything. To anybody. Then — two weeks later he snuck into my room — and made me love him, again, till people asked him about it, again."

Shit. I held Matt closer and asked, "How many times?"

"After the fourth repeat, I — I popped a bottle of Tylenol PM." I stroked his face. "That was so fuckin' dumb." I kissed his forehead. "All it did was make me sick."

I let my hand drift down his neck. "I'm glad it didn't work."

He held me a bit tighter. "You ever feel like — like — you know — the pills and — ?"

I pinched his unpierced tit through his shirt. "C'mon — haven't you figured out by now that I'm too much of an asshole?"

He chuckled, his throat thick and on the verge of tears. "Antony, I — I'm sorry for what I did to you, but I — I was scared. I had to make it look real 'cause I told them I wanted to make you come and — I — I never thought I'd really have to do it but — shit, something in me took over and — and — it got to where I couldn't stop and — I was drowning in it when I was done and I felt — I felt — "

"Peace."

"Yeah." He held me tighter.

I kissed him. "It's okay. It's okay. I understand. And I meant it — I *can* handle it." And I was beginning to believe I could. I slowly unbuttoned his shirt. He let me. "Y'know, my mom once told me I was born with the soul of a fifty-year-old man, because of some of the things I'd say or do around her." And then let me shift the shirt apart slowly...slowly revealing the light hair on his chest. "And I really don't remember ever being a kid." Revealing his nice brown tits. "I remember being somebody who was way harder to deal with than people expected." Revealing the gold emblem. I twisted it. He groaned. "And I never really understood any of that crap, until the last year." Revealing the soft treasure trail and the smooth skin over his belly and his trim sides. "But I guess now people're catching on. Your Boss Man — he knew I could handle it."

"He did?"

"He knew there was a possibility you'd have to go all the way. That's why he told you to pick me."

"He — he said you'd be more believable for a Gacy freak."

"He was right." I tickled my fingers over his treasure trail. He squirmed just a little. "Jake's too old — hell, I'm too old, really; Gacy liked 'em young, didn't he?"

He nodded. "Teens. Blonds more than brunettes. Guys he could control."

"See — that's not me."

"You got a nice butt," he whispered. Ran his hands over it. "The guys, they were supposed to show as soon as I got in," he sighed. "But they didn't come and they didn't — "

"They couldn't, right?"

"Yeah. I guess. You — you know how they — they were tracking me? This." He toyed with the emblem around his tit. "It's got a transmitter. For all the good it did. It really hurt, getting it pierced and the tattoo — that's fresh too." His voice was still shaky and scared.

"I'm sorry," I said, slipping the shirt off his shoulders. Letting it drop to the floor. I surreptitiously checked to make sure we were in camera range. We were.

He tried to pull away from me. "Antony, please — I — I can't do anything more. It was too — it'll be too much — "

"Shh." I kissed him and undid his belt then unfastened his pants. Slipped my hands under the waistband and inside his briefs and around to cup his ass. He felt solid and round, almost pert. My fingers tickled against some light down. He gasped. I crushed my crotch against his. They fit each other almost perfectly.

"No — no, you don't understand — "

"Don't I?" I kissed him, again. "You're afraid of the animal that hides in your shadows. The beast you could become." He looked at me, startled, not sure he knew what I was talking about...but wanting to believe he did. "It's there in all of us, you know, ready to pop out for some reason or other. Did they show you the videos?"

"One. In a jail — " He tried to twist away. I wouldn't let him, the little liar. Boss Man said he'd seen both videos.

"Well — I've seen my beastie more than once, and I'm still here," I said. He licked his lips, unsure. I slipped my right hand around to fondle him.

"Don't — "

I nuzzled the crook of his neck. "Tell me — what did this non-Chris look like?"

"I — I — can't do this — "

"Tell me." I slipped my lips down to the tit with the emblem. Played against it with my tongue. He gasped.

"Dark — dark hair. Curly. Grey eyes. Played baseball. Just the right — the right body for it. So beautiful."

"He never let you fuck him, did he?"

"What? No way he'd let anybody do that. Not to him."

"But he fucked you."

He almost chuckled. "Part of the game."

I slipped his pants down his hips. Pulled his dick out over the top of his briefs. Stroked it. I knew he was big and cut and nicely shaped, already. What I didn't realize was he had a great set of hairy legs to go with it, as if his upper and lower body had been put together from two completely different molds — lean and boyish from the waist up, built for stud from the hips down.

As I slipped his pants and briefs to his ankles, I let my lips trail down his chest to his belly to his crotch to encompass his dick — and while Jake's was larger and Collie's more lovely, it didn't matter. He was a nice fit and I actually liked sucking on him — but not gently, no — no, the little fucker got it hard and steady and fast and so fucking intense, his ass clenched at each stoke of my lips. And he loved it. His muscles jolted in his groin and he ground his hips forward and started shoving against my mouth. Shit, he was ready to explode, and I was almost past the point of caring, so I stopped and stood up and backed away from him, smiling.

He watched me, confused...but not for long.

I positioned the table before Benny. He was lost in his own

fog when he heard me move it. He jolted back to reality.

"What — what's that?" he asked. Damn, that blindfold was good.

I untied the rope holding his torso to the chair then slipped my hands under his arms from behind and guided him to his feet. His ankles were still bound to the chair's legs and his hands still tied at the wrist, so when I pushed him he had no choice but to flop forward onto the table. He landed hard and was now prone across it, his ass no longer covered by the torn briefs, his legs splayed apart by the chair.

He cried out then snarled, "Fuckin' shit! What the fuck? You're not gonna fuck me! You're not gonna fuck me!"

"Time for round two," I said, almost kindly.

Benny jolted back to reality and snarled, "You fuckin' think you're gonna fuck me? You fuckin' think you can — ?"

From my position, I could see his balls hanging between his magnificent legs. I had no choice but to reach down and give them a tickle — then I slapped his ass, hard, and tore the briefs completely away. He screamed, as if he wasn't already completely exposed.

"Benny, you're getting fucked. At least once. The only question is whether or not you get fucked twice or three times or in the mouth or — "

"You put your fuckin' dick in my mouth I'll fuckin' bite it off, you fuckin' understand me?!"

I slapped his ass, again. "You'd have to be able to close your mouth, and I got a tool here that'll keep it open."

"Fuckin' shit, motherfucker, you can't do this to me! You can't fuckin' do this!" He squirmed. Made the table shift.

"Okay, tell you what — you don't wanna get fucked, tell me who contacted you."

"I fuckin' told you — it was a fuckin' phone call!"

"And I fuckin' told you, that's bullshit."

I went back to Matt. He'd been watching me and Benny, silently, warily. His dick was getting soft, so I kneeled down and licked it as I slipped his briefs down to his ankles, guiding his feet out of them and his pants as my tongue did its gentle caresses, bringing it back to a state of nearly solid. Then I rose, saw Matt was naked except for his socks so removed those and slipped my hand around his dick to guide him to Benny.

He almost hesitated. "Antony — "

"He never let you fuck him — non-Chris didn't. That's why you got off on fucking me. How much like him do I look?" He was beginning to be scared of me, so I put a smile on my face. A gentle smile. "How much?"

"A — a little," Matt finally said. "You're slimmer."

"How much does Jake look like him?" He couldn't answer, which told me everything. "And Benny here?"

He looked the fucker over, his breath getting faster and stronger. "Pretty close."

"So he'll do as a proxy, won't he?"

"What're you doing to me? I — I told you — "

"Shh." I pulled him closer, my hand still wrapped around his dick, still massaging it, still making it grow harder and harder. I wrapped my other hand around his neck and dove in to kiss him, but only barely, this time. Then I whispered, "You know, the animal in your shadows — he's not to be feared. He's your protector. He's your life. He's why you took Tylenol instead of looping a noose around your neck. He's why you fix on people like John Wayne Gacy. That motherfucker was powerful, was a guy who acted and did what he fuckin' wanted and didn't care about anything but feeding his own little animal. He's why you went along with choosing me instead of Jake, so you could keep one last level of distance between you and what you really wanted to do to fuckin' non-Chris for fuckin' you around for so long. And what you really want done to yourself for letting him do it. Think about it — if you had chosen Jake, it would've been too close to reality and you'd have lost yourself in the hate you feel for that little fuck, and you might have killed him. The animal's what really turned you to me. The animal's what kept you under control for so long. He's not to be feared; he's to be embraced. He's to be fed this man instead of the one you truly hate, so you can continue to step back from the anger and pain and live and not wind up slaughtered in some crazy need for vengeance." Because death begets death while

231

sex only begets shame."

He seemed mesmerized by my voice and the soft, gentle words I was using. It was easy to lead him to the chair and guide him into stepping in between Benny's legs and caressing Benny's wide-open ass. The fucker struggled and shifted and spit out curses like I'd never heard before, including a *lot* in Spanish, but it did no good; Matt was giving in to his beast.

"He's a virgin," I added. "Just for you. And it's okay. Even your boss said it's okay." I glanced at Benny; he kept trying to free himself and rise back to his feet. I shoved him back to the table. "Everybody says it's okay. Take him like you would Chris. Take him like you would the man who made you so hate yourself, you'd rather have died. Take back your life, Matt."

I climbed on the table to straddle Benny's back and hold his ass in place and watch as Matt's hands rubbed up and around Benny's flesh and his thumbs found Benny's hole and his dick caressed over and back along the crack between Benny's cheeks and then positioned itself and toyed with the idea and grew harder and crueler in size as his head kissed against Benny's opening and finally, finally he let himself push it in, slowly, deliberately, his sweet face showing signs of the demon he was unleashing as he dove in deeper and deeper.

Benny screamed and tried to twist and fight, but he couldn't get the leverage, and in seconds Matt's dick was all the way in, his pubes tickling Benny's butt, and then he was gliding in and out of him and all Benny could do was grunt and curse from the pain.

I got down off the table, shifted the cameras to make sure they were getting good angles on what had to be the most glorious fucking since the term had been coined then returned to the table and squatted before Benny's face. He was red and sweating and I seriously think the only word he could think of for those first few moments was "Motherfuckers."

"Okay, Benny, listen to me. You want this to be the only fucking you get, tell me who your contact was. Tell me, or I'll fuck you next. And I'm bigger than this guy." And to prove it to him, I took my dick out and slapped him in the face with it.

"No — motherfucker — no, don't. Stop. Stop. Please, it

fuckin' hurts. It fuckin' HURTS!"

Matt kept slipping in and out of him, grinding his hips and pumping away. His hands gripped Benny's ass cheeks like they were basketballs, and I liked the image that made. Shit, loved it. Felt my own animal howl in agreement so reached over to toy with Matt's tits, making him grunt with joy.

Benny's curses and grunts grew quieter and quieter, so I checked under the table and smiled at what I saw. His dick was getting hard, again. Was he actually getting into this? I groped him and he jolted.

"What the fuck?"

"Don't be so repetitious," I snapped as I pulled on his dick. He got harder.

"Oh, shit — no — oh, shit — "

I ran a hand up Matt's leg. He gave me the barest of glances, his eyes glazed over in lust.

"Benny likes it up the ass, buddy," I said. "Take your time." Matt snarled and actually did slow down his actions. Then I slipped back to grab Benny's chin. "A man's fucking you and you're hard as a rock. Told you I'd prove you like guys."

"Please — make him stop."

I looked at Matt. He was pushing harder into Benny's ass. The table was shifting in a steady rhythm. "He's almost done," I said. "Then it's my turn. I got a feeling I'll be able to get you off, again. That ought to make everybody happy."

"Motherfuckers — you stupid motherfuckers — don't you get it? Fuckin' shit!" His voice dropped low, barely audible. His grunts more like whimpers, his hands clenching and unclenching in pain. "They set me up. They fuckin' set me up. That motherfuckin' judge, he — oh — oh, no. FUCK! NO! FUCKIN' SHIT!"

Matt was slamming into Benny and grunting and then he gasped and his mouth flew open and he shoved himself deeper inside and gripped Benny's ass so hard I thought he'd tear off some skin and he jolted a couple of times then slowly, slowly lay down atop Benny, his chest heaving, vaguely whimpering.

Well — I guess he'd just cum.

\*\*\*\*

Benny was whimpering, too. And shaking. I kneeled beside the table. Lay my head atop it to look straight at him. And I quietly asked, "The judge set you up?"

"Motherfucker. Motherfucker."

"BENNY! Are you telling me a judge arranged for the payment and transfer of your information? Benny?"

He fought to regain control. Fought to keep from bawling. "Motherfucker vouched for that fuck. He vouched for that fuck."

"Which judge?"

"Motherfucker vouched for him. Met with us both. Fuckin' vouched for him. Had it all set up, motherfucker."

I burst into a roar. "WHICH JUDGE?!"

Matt jumped and looked at me, still a bit fuzzy. Benny was closer to bawling.

"Fuckin' judge. Fuckin' Gilbert. He vouched for the motherfucker."

Gilbert? Judge Gilbert? The son-of-a-bitch who'd left Collie in jail to be killed? No fucking way. Did I really have the motherfucker? "When?"

"Day — two days before we met. You, me, Thomas. Two days before. Hotel. Outside town. Motherfucker."

Motherfucker was right. Fuckin' Judge Gilbert arranged for a meeting between Benny and a guy at Greco'd? Gilbert was in it up to his balls and somehow had hidden it so well, not even Mossad was able to connect him to it? Motherfucker was totally right.

"Why'd they pick you?" I asked.

"Said you like guys...like me. Like that guy — you're with. Said I could use it — to get info — to mess with you. But you — you messed with me. Fuckin' pissed me off. I fuckin' hate fags, you fuck. Hated 'em since a priest — since a priest — " He started to sob.

Son-of-a-bitch, he'd been molested by one of the Catholic Church's saintly-scum. And I'd bet Gilbert and company had known that and used it to play with Benny's hatred of gays and this was just too fuckin' rich and it fit so perfectly and — and — wait a

234

minute.

I stood up and stared at Benny. His broad back heaved with sobs and his fingers twisted and worked at the air, helplessly. His lovely ass added to the eroticism of the moment and yet — something about it was wrong.

I looked around and realized Boss Man had taken all the paperwork with him — but Matt's laptop was still here, its USB modem plugged in its side. Matt was slumped in the chair, naked, his hands folded awkwardly against his chest, his gaze focused on something un-seeable a thousand yards away. I went to him and took him by the arm. Tried to guide him to his feet but he just looked at me, bewildered. I squatted beside him.

"Matt," I said, careful to keep my voice low and soothing. "I need some data off your laptop." His glazed expression did not change. I caressed his face. "C'mon back, buddy. It's okay. It's all okay. Antony's here. Your critter's all fed and happy. So let him sleep. Let him sleep."

He shook his head then reached over to caress Benny's ass. The bastard clenched his cheeks and shifted away as much as he could. Shit, I wondered if I went too far with Matt, making him do something he was so afraid to do. Thinking back on it, I didn't remember him saying a word as he fucked Benny. I wondered if the beast had taken over. Well, one way to find out.

I flicked the side of his head with my index finger, sharply, and snapped, "Matt!"

He jolted and looked at me, still a bit hazy but more focused. He swallowed. "What?"

"Does your laptop have the Marquez data on it?" He thought for a long moment then nodded. "Pull it up for me."

He let me guide him up and step out from between Benny's legs. He shuffled over to his laptop, and watching him go like this — I mean, he wasn't my usual type, but he had an adorable little ass shifting atop those nicely-shaped legs, his slim back flowing down to meet them — so I felt something stir inside and thought, *Maybe you and I'll really settle scores, later*.

He awakened the laptop and in seconds had pulled up Benny's folder. I had him open the bank statement for a year ago — and there it was. The deposit cleared two days before Thomas and Marquez came to my dorm room. The little fuck was still lying to me.

But how? I mean, if his reaction to getting screwed by Matt was an act, he was fucking brilliant. No, he'd really been freaked out about what happened. Shit, this was getting too weird — too confusing. Time for my inner asshole to take over.

"You better get dressed," I told Matt. He looked at me, as if he didn't understand. "You've had Officer Marquez. He's mine now."

Something flitted across Matt's eyes that sent a warning straight to my brain, like I was trying to take a dog's bone away from him. Man...I was even more certain I'd rattled his cage a little too much. But finally he just nodded and began looking for his clothes as I returned to Benny.

And I picked up the scissors as I went.

Benny heard me approach and turned his head to face me. "So — so what're you gonna do? You gonna let me go, now?"

"No," I said, squatting before him. "I still need to find out how much of that story you told me is true."

"I fuckin' told you everything, motherfucker!"

"Officer Marquez, I'm going to give you one more chance — tell me the truth, the whole truth and nothing but the truth."

"I HAVE!"

"Bullshit!" I rose and circled him, running the scissors over his beautiful back...his most excellent ass...his powerful arms. "I'll bet if I ask Officer Thomas, he'll tell me you asked to come with him to investigate Orin Tedesco's rape and kidnapping. No, no, wait — that'd be too chancy. How could it have worked? How could it have worked?"

"What worked? What the fuck're you talking about?"

"Somebody caught on that I was investigating Collier Winston-Royce's murder. And I was pulling together too much information, and easily. Very easily. I'd already found Jake Blaine and knew about three other guys who went through the same thing, so I wasn't just a threat; I was showing how easy a trail it was to find. So how to stop me and shut everything down without it blowing up and exposing Greco'd — oh, dammit, which *is* what happened once you turned me over to Nussewald — but that — no, that was a controlled explosion. Like bringing down a skyscraper with a series of charges. Not much damage or — " And then it hit me, slam, like going ninety into a telephone pole. Oh, shit. "Oh, shit — Collie's death was a mistake."

I was facing Benny, now, scissors still in hand. I snipped at the air, finally understanding. Collie was *not* supposed to have been killed. Nussewald *had* deliberately set him up to get even for what he pulled on Orin, but things had gone too far. The guys running this operation weren't so stupid that they expected a man's death to be passed over by everyone, even if it was a fag accused of child molestation. Too many questions were left unanswered. Gossip was already beginning to spread. What Enrique told me...and what he'd told his boss. Ray's nephew, Tommy, quitting. Maybe the AG was already sniffing around, smelling something rotten, and that's why the Rangers were on top of things so quickly. So the big boys set Nussewald up as the main fall guy with Gilbert as their Plan B if that wasn't enough — and it hadn't been. So somehow Marquez was selected as the one to deliver the latest sacrifice, probably because he was a Ranger and not your typical corrupt cop.

It made a lot of sense. Maybe they knew about Mossad's interest. Maybe Nussewald had started making threats to get himself freed and they needed to end the connection, completely. Maybe they were using me and Gilbert as their Plan B diversion, with Jake in the mix to kick my ass into gear. Gentle Voice had agreed to Matt's and my plan pretty damned easily. Well, yeah, I could understand why Matt had gone along with my suggestion but — wait. Wait, exactly *how* did I know Boss Man and Matt were telling me the truth?

Okay, I know what you're thinking here — Well, Antony, isn't that an *obvious* question? Did they show you any ID? No. Did they do anything to prove they were who you thought they were? No. Hell, I'm the one who labeled them as Mossad and was so happy they were as worried about Jake as I was I didn't think beyond that and — and maybe I should have questioned it more. But shit, if Boss Man and his boys were acting, they had the whole routine down tight. They'd have to be part of the cabal.

I looked at Matt. He was dressed and trying to slip his sneakers back on but was still foggy. If *his* was an act, it was even better than Benny's. So...maybe he wasn't part of it. I mean, how hard can it be to find a gay guy who'd been fucked over like he had? Who'd probably discussed it on his FaceBook page. Who'd jump at the chance to become heroic, even if he was only on the periphery of the action. Who'd love to actually live one of his video games. Shit, I could picture it — gay, geeky Matt's visited by a gorgeous man from central casting who says, *Hi, we need your help*. What fag in his right mind would refuse a guy who's appealing to his dick as well as his head and heart? Shit, I wouldn't have. Okay...that — I could find out for sure, later. Maybe there wouldn't be any reckoning between me and Matt, after all.

But Benny just plain didn't add up. He didn't give out Gilbert's info till after he'd been fucked, and he'd hated every second of it. Why wait to spill it? What the fucker up to?

I removed Benny's blindfold. He jammed his eyes shut at the bright lights. I crouched beside the table and lay my head on my hands, waiting. He finally looked at me, squinting. I caressed his face with the scissors. He flinched.

"Please, man — please — I told you everything I know — swear to God, I — "

"Officer Marquez," I whispered, gently, "how long does it normally take a wire transfer of funds to clear an account?"

"What?"

"How long does it take money to be wired into a bank account — and clear?"

"How the fuck should I know that? I'm not in finance."

"Me, neither, but that's how my folks gave me money for my classes. My account was in a different bank, so the beginning of each semester, they'd have their bank transfer in as much as I needed. Usually took a couple of days to set up and finally clear. And that's over a space of less than a hundred miles."

"Okay — so?"

"So, Benny — can you see the future?"

"What're you fuckin' talkin' about?"

"The first payment cleared into your account the day after I attacked Orin Tedesco. Meaning it had to have been set up a couple of days before. The second payment was three days after I was released from jail. About the right amount of time for the wire to have been sent. So — you were already on their payroll. The fact that I jumped somebody just gave you and the fucks you work for an excuse to set everything in motion. I could be killed in jail and have it all blamed on Nussewald, the stupid fuck. Only I turned the tables on Rattler and got out of it. But that didn't matter. They just had Stanton slow things down for a week, giving them time to set everything up so BAM — Nussewald and cousin Cullingham get hit. And then conveniently kick the bucket."

"That — that's bullshit, man. You're just makin' shit up like it's — it's some movie."

"Am I?" I glanced at Matt. He was seated by his laptop, looking at me like I was from Mars or something. "What do you think, Matt?"

He opened his mouth then turned to his laptop. "The third payment. It's a month ago. How would that figure in?"

A month ago. Jake? "Can you tell if Benny's left the country, since then?"

"I don't have the access, but Eli might."

He pulled out his mobile phone and was about to call when I snapped, "Don't!" He looked at me, totally confused, and I realized he hadn't caught on that Boss Man wasn't Mossad. He wasn't helping Israel get back one of her soldiers or anybody else. It was all just one big setup and something more floated into my brain to prove it — Boss Man had known I didn't know Jake was in Paris. When I mentioned the Défense district, that first time we were talking, he'd asked me how I'd guessed that's where Jake had gone. How could he know I didn't know?

Son-of-a-bitch, he *was* part of it.

I looked hard at Matt. And deep inside my critter said, He's too confused; he still trusts those bastards. This could mean he's okay...so I decided to make the leap of faith. "Did Boss Man ever show you an ID proving who he is?"

"Well, yeah — I — he showed me — shit, it was some kind of ID with his picture on it and — "

239

"What's his name?"

"I — I didn't catch it. Nobody ever used it — "

Nothing specific. Just, Hi, I'm with Mossad and we want your geeky ass to help us. Ya wanna? And maybe he'd batted his eyes. Shit, no wonder Matt had jumped at the opportunity.

No question now, I was being played. Matt and I *both* were, the motherfuckers. That's why it'd been so easy to get Matt in. That's why they'd told him to go with Plan B and choose me. That's why Gentle Voice had gone along with the program. That's how they'd been able to grab Benny in the middle of the day in a park. Hell, that's why Matt had been able to get off some footage of him being dragged in. And that's why Benny'd waited till he was fucked to give out his information. They wanted me to end Gilbert and were giving me every reason to believe them.

But there was one question left to be answered. "You've never been fucked before, have you, Benny?"

"I fuckin' told you — I'm no fuckin' faggot."

"No, I guess you're not. But you still agreed to let us do it, for some reason."

"Bullshit — you — you're fuckin' crazy!"

It was the hint of hesitation in his voice that let me see I was right. I mean, seriously — I'm working on a deadline to video a rape and a gorgeous guy is brought to me, bound and gagged? When I'm already known to have brutalized two men? C'mon, he had to have known. For some reason — probably another nice payment being wired into his account even as Matt fucked him — Officer Marquez had agreed to let himself be fucked, to let that be what *made him tell us* about Gilbert, to absolutely convince me the judge was to blame for everything.

But why would they need Jake for that? They could've just grabbed me and still got me to focus on Gilbert, so how did Jake figure into this? He'd be a witness. He'd be a danger to them. So why would they need him? Just to give me greater motivation to follow what Boss Man and Matt told me? To fuck with my mind and keep me off balance? To make use of before they killed him? Was he already dead, maybe? Jesus, just the thought of that made my heart drop — until I — I wondered if — if he — could he —

could he be part of it, too? They'd needed a key to get in the place. He'd told me to stay home, that night — insisted on it. Then never showed. And they had a key. How? Unless they had his key and he was — he was — ?

I felt something sick and furious in my belly. They knew I hadn't known he was in Paris. And Jake would never have spilled it if he didn't want to. So how else could they've known he hadn't told me unless — no — no, Jake a part of this shit? No way. No, he'd never do that to me. No, no, never! Never!

But still — the question wouldn't go away. Kept gnawing at me. It fit too perfectly to be ignored. It all but screamed in my ear, He told you to stay home, you dumb fuck, then he never showed. He fuckin' told you to stay home. Insisted on it. So they'd know where you were. But no! NO!

My heart was racing. I could barely breathe. I glared at Benny. He flinched. I must've had the demon in my face, right then, and the truth is — I was going bat-shit fuckin' crazy, because I had to know what the fuck was going on, and he was the only person I had access to who could tell me.

I HAD TO FUCKING KNOW!

I grabbed him by the hair and yanked him back off the table, making him slam into the chair. He stared at me, terrified. "What? WHAT?"

My voice caught a low growl. "Who's your contact, Benny?"

"I told you everything I know! I fuckin' told you — "

I kicked the table away. Got in his face. "Who's your fuckin' contact, Benny?!"

I vaguely noticed Matt rising. "Antony, dude, calm down."

"I'm tellin' you the truth! Shit, I'm fuckin' tellin' you everything and — "

The lying motherfucker.

I let go of his hair, grabbed his dick, pulled it by his foreskin and sliced the scissors through that part of his flesh, all without one conscious thought. He shrieked in pain as blood spewed and slammed against the chair, horrified.

"Fuckin' shit!" Matt cried out. "Antony!!" He jolted over but I shoved him back. He landed on his ass.

241

I slipped the circle of bloody skin onto the scissors, snarling like a maniac, then tapped them on Benny's head a couple of times. He was bawling, near hysterics.

"Who's your fuckin' contact, Benny? Or do you want me to cut the rest of your dick off?"

It took Benny a few moments to get to where he could quietly choke out between sobs, "I — I don't know — his name. I don't know — his name. Oh, God, please — I'm tellin' you the truth. Please."

The pitifulness of his voice cut right through the beast in me. I finally noticed he was bleeding like crazy. I stepped back, realized the blindfold was still in my hand so wrapped it around the wound. Then I held his head in place and said, "Look at me. Look at me, Benny." He was still bawling but not as much. I slapped him, twice — and I wanted to keep hitting him — but I forced myself to stop. "Look — look at what I've got. BENNY!"

He forced his eyes open and saw me holding up the scissors, his foreskin still looped around them...but I don't think it registered in his brain. He just choked out, "What — what?"

My voice shook. "All — all I did just now was circumcise you, and yeah — it hurts like a motherfucker but it'll heal — if you see a doctor. Now, one more time — what's his name?"

"He — he never told me. He never told me." And his voice was so achingly soft and real, I actually believed him.

"Describe him."

It took him a while, but Benny managed to whisper, "Older. Fifty. Black hair — with grey. Olive skin. Sharp eyes — brown. Hawk nose. Your height. One-ninety and solid. Looks Arab — but French accent."

French accent? Really? "Why did you trust him?" And I kept my voice as soft as his.

"Gilbert — said to — "

"Gilbert *did* vouch for him?"

He nodded. "Still didn't want to. But my — my sister — she's into drugs. And shit. They had video of her. Shootin' up. Turnin' tricks. Were gonna send it to my mom. She's old. Sick. Would've killed her."

Oh, shit. "Were you really molested by a priest?"

He shook his head. "Never said I was. My sister...she'd been fucked up ever since." He looked down. Saw blood staining the blindfold, even though it was wrapped around him, several times. "Aw, man — am I gonna lose it — ?"

"No," I said, suddenly exhausted. "No."

I turned to Matt. He was seated on the chair, again, his hands curled against his chest as if he didn't know what to do with them. His big eyes never left me.

"Okay, Matt — we — uh, we're on the Southside of town, off Congress and 290. Step outside. There's a street sign about a hundred feet down the road. Get our exact location and call a cab."

"I — I'm supposed to call — Eli when we're done." Jesus, his voice sounded young and scared.

"Don't."

"But the guys'd come — come pick us — up." I just looked at him. He finally nodded. "But — but you think — Antony — dude, you really think — that they — they aren't — ?"

"Matt — let's talk about this later. Right now, I want to be sure we're both safe."

"But — but why would they pick *me* for — for this?"

"Probably your FaceBook page."

He actually looked bewildered. "Nothin' on there that's so — so — " His voice trailed off.

So awful? Just worship of a serial killer? Yeah. Right.

And that is when everything began crashing horribly into place. That is when I finally understood — they wanted me dead. I *was* supposed to have been killed in that room. And I knew and why Matt had really been chosen. The Gacy shit.

"What? C'mon, that's just crap. Fun shit to freak people out and — and lots of guys and even girls do it — pretend to be bullshit crazy over some fuck like Gacy or Ted Bundy or — "

"But that's what gave them the idea how to kill me."

"Kill you? They were gonna have me — no, c'mon, they — they thought I'd — you think I — I could kill anybody and — and — ?"

"You didn't need to," I said, in this distant voice. "You told me Gacy liked to choke his victims to make 'em hard and you wanted to have fun like he had — so I bet they figured you'd do some of that. Didn't have to go all the way. Just some video of me being strangled — even just a little by you — and then that big fuckin' muscle queen comes in to finish the job. And guess who gets the blame?" And I looked straight at Matt.

He backed into the idea, slowly, horror dawning in his eyes as he looked at Benny, deeply shaken. His thousand-yard stare threatened to take him over, so I went to him and lifted him to his feet and held him close and stroked his head, tenderly. He was shivering like a Min-Pin in need of attention. "No, Matt, stop — stop — we'll talk about this later. Go call a cab. As we're leaving, we'll call an ambulance for Benny. Okay? C'mon, dude, you can do this. You can do this."

It took him a few moments, but he gained enough control to nod and head for the door — then he stopped.

"Antony — the upload." He motioned to the cameras. They were still taping.

"We'll do it, tonight," I said as I went around and turned them off. "Go."

He left.

I powered down the cameras then squatted before Benny. "Do you know your blood type?"

He slowly nodded. "B — positive."

"You'll need some." I used his blood to write it on his chest. "I suggest you not tell anybody what you told me. Not even Thomas. And you better assume they have their own cameras recording everything that just happened. I don't know if they worried about getting sound — and we were probably talking too softly for them to pick up our voices very well — so if Boss Man and his dogs come sniffing around, let 'em know — you told me Gilbert was behind it all and I'm going after him. And that this is what it took to convince me. Tell 'em I dragged Matt along with me. Forced him to leave you so we could save Jake, and — and I — I said something about Gilbert's son, Nat-four. Be smart, Benny. Protect yourself."

"You think they'd — kill me? They're that — fuckin' —

stupid? I — I'm a cop — "

"Do you really think Nussewald died from a heart attack? Or that cousin Cullingham tried to kill herself? Seriously?"

He looked away from me, slipping into shock, I bet. I hoped he believed me. I hoped he was smart enough to put two and two together and see he yet another sacrificial lamb meant to keep me focused on the story they wanted.

Matt came in and said, "It'll be here in five minutes."

"Pack away the cameras." Then I washed off what blood I could in the sink. What I couldn't get off my clothes, I smeared with dirt from the floor to hide it.

We had everything outside moments before a cab appeared down the road. As Matt waved for it, I put through an emergency request for the paramedics, told 'em a guy was bleeding to death and needed help now, now, *now*! Matt told me the address as he loaded the cab. I heard the sirens approaching as we drove off, and saw a patrol car scream around the far corner at Congress just was we turned left to return to 290. I figured Benny'd be safe — for little while, anyway. Considering what I'd learned, I was actually sorry for what I'd done to him.

I had the cab take us to Bergstrom Airport, then bought two one-way tickets for Chicago on the cattle-car line. But rather than use them, I found an ATM, withdrew six-hundred dollars, went out to the rental cars, got one by way of a cash deposit and drove us to a motel north of town that had free WiFi. Then using Matt's laptop, I cut the videos just after the point where Matt came. As he was uploading just the section showing the rape — and I was impressed at how he was able to make himself handle that — I bought pizza and fresh clothes and we pigged out while I filled him in on why I thought the whole thing had been a setup. He finally agreed maybe I was right, and the hurt in his eyes just verified in my heart he was a good guy.

The ten o'clock news led with a story about the vicious attack by *drug gangs from Mexico* on a Texas Ranger. Benny'd fed them a line Texas cops and reporters love to hear and hate to question, so I knew he'd be safe. Matt and I took a long, *long* hot shower together, collapsed on the bed naked — him still a bit freaked out but willing to let me soothe him into sleep as we spooned, me ready to drop into slumber land the second he was gone — and we didn't wake till nine the next morning, getting up just in time to feast on the fat-making breakfast that came with the room. By ten, Matt had gotten a message on his e-mail that said, *Accepted. Want you both on next one. 2 days.*

So far, so good. So Matt looked at me, still a bit shaky, and asked, "So now what?"

"We split up," I said. "I need you to do some serious hacking and spying, here in Texas."

"What do you mean — like what?"

"Scope out the next victim. And I want you to grab more info for me, info I can't get. I'll be back in two days."

"You already got a guy picked out?" I nodded. "Do to him what we did to — to — dude, you gotta be kidding — "

He was starting to hyperventilate. I drew him close and rubbed his back. "We won't have to *do* anything. This one's a feint. And keep telling yourself — Benny was there to be fucked. He knew he would be. You didn't do anything more to him than he expected. He didn't like it, but he expected it."

"You don't really know that — "

"Oh, yes I do. He admitted it. And he's going to keep it quiet because that's the only way he'll stay alive. So you just focus on the next guy. We need his schedule and video of him and — in fact, let's do this with two guys I know. Let's give the bastards a choice, like they gave us. See what they say."

"Just — just videotape them and gather data?" I nodded. He took a deep breath and said, "Okay."

"You sure you can do it?"

He finally nodded. "I — just can't wrap my head around the idea they thought I'd kill somebody or — "

I slung him onto the bed and fell on top of him, lying face to face. "Matt, listen to me — they didn't. They just wanted somebody who'd go real far, with me. Like you did."

He gave a soft, hurt laugh. "Made you cum."

"Big-time. To where my own little critter was purring, you so got me off. But you know what's funny? You being a decent guy

246

— that's what fucked up their plans. So they had to come up with this crap."

"But they got me involved before I even saw you and — "

"And when you didn't even start to choke me, they adjusted their plans. It's like improv on a stage or something."

"Fuckin' shit." He finally accepted it. Let his hands drift up over my ass. I ground my crotch into his. He looked gentle into my eyes. "I really did get you off."

"Me and Benny both." And I kissed him. "Real power trip, isn't it, stud?"

"Yeah. It was." He looked away, lost. "It wasn't really that easy for you, was it?"

I was surprised he'd seen through my bravado. I decided to be honest. "I don't know. It was — shit — it wasn't."

He nodded. "Never gonna happen, again, is it?"

I nuzzled his neck. "Let's see, when I get back."

"But this Jake guy," he said, turning back to look at me, "you belong to him."

Did I? "Right now, I don't belong to anybody."

"So why you gotta go? Why not stay and — and be with me and — ?"

"Because," I whispered, "I have to see a dog about a man."

— FIVE —

La Défense is one of the smartest things the French ever did — jamming towering skyscrapers of a hundred different designs together on the west end of Paris instead of allowing them to be sprinkled throughout the city, like in London. Yeah, there were a few other tall buildings around the town, but they were the exception that proved how brilliant the rule was.

What was even nicer — the area had wide plazas dotted with trees and sculpture and breathtaking vistas, so as the workers scurried from one towering wall of glass to another they could feel a bit human instead of totally animatronic. And the humans of France — man, I could have stood in the middle of it all and done nothing but watch Parisian men in their too-cool suits race about with the crowd. I don't know what it is about les hommes français that gets me going — maybe it's just how absolutely casual they are in their own attractiveness — but the last time I'd been here I decided I could spend my life chasing after any of the guys I saw (well, the good-looking ones; every country has its shlubs and France is no exception). But at that particular moment I was on a deadline and didn't have the inclination to dawdle and drool and dance around the pretties that were so in evidence (hey, being loyal to Jake don't mean I can't look) because I was headed for the office of Faraz Darya-Bandari.

Yes — Jake's father.

And I was *fucking* pissed.

I'd bought a prepaid phone soon as I landed at De Gaulle (via a nonstop flight from Texas that took just over nine hours) and called Matt, first, to get some of the info I asked for then punched in Uncle Ari's number to get Faraz's address. I figured if I hit him before he'd had his morning coffee, he'd be easier to handle. No such luck.

"Antony, where the hell you are been?" he blasted soon as he heard my voice. I loved how he mangled the English language, and I grinned until he added, "Jake is crazy worried for you."

And the one little question I was going to ask him vanished from my brain. Jake was worried about me? Ari had talked to him? Was he free and roaming around? Before I'd fulfilled my end of the bargain? That didn't make sense. No, what Ari's words indicated was, Jake was at home — and my fucking brain immediately jumped back to the question that stabbed like ice into my soul, Was he a part of it? Because what the fuck? What the *fuck*?

Fortunately, all that came out of my mouth was, "What?" Not very eloquent, but seriously — what the man had just said was completely without foundation in my current state of being. Because what Ari's words made it sound like Jake was not now, nor had he ever been, in a cell in Dubai freaking out, meaning for sure Gentle Voice had lied his ass off about him and that Jake was in Copenhagen worried about me and that didn't fit any scenario I could think of and, seriously, what — the — fuck?

"For to be vanish like that is wrong! Very wrong! Why you treat him so bad? Is what he does so bad for you?"

My mouth finally kicked in and I sputtered, "Ari, Ari," a half dozen times before he finally shut up. "Where is Jake?"

"He is at your flat. He will not come into the office to wait for you. He thinks you leave him, and because he only takes this stupid trips — "

Stupid trips? Ari kept rattling on but I locked on to those two words and lost half of what he was saying. Stupid trips. *Trips*? Oh, fuck. So he really *had* gone to Paris. To see his father. So they *weren't* lying about that. Shit.

"Antony, he is sick with worry. He does not eat. He does not work. He calls me four-five times a day to see if you have called. Why you do this to him? Is the trips so bad? He does not tell you for many reasons and now I see why."

And this is where my brain started screaming, Gimme a

chance to catch up, asshole! Shit! *Shit*! The only way to shut this down was to end the call. Then I punched in Jake's mobile phone number. It rang once. Jake's voice popped onto the phone thick with sleep and fear, "Tone? Is that you?"

Oh, fuck, oh, fuck oh, fuck — what the fuck was going on?

"Tone!? Who the fuck IS this!? ANSWER ME, MOTHERFUCKER!"

"Are you at home?" I was finally able to ask.

"Tone! Jesus Christ, where the fuck are you?! You know how scared I've — ?"

"ARE YOU AT HOME!?"

People in the terminal looked around at me, because no matter what language you're speaking in, my voice carried enough anger to make anybody want to be wary of me.

"YES, motherfucker. Where the fuck else would I be, you vanishing on me, like this? Again! Fuckin' AGAIN!"

I looked up at the screen showing departing flights. SAS was leaving for Copenhagen in twenty minutes. "Hold on."

"Hold on?! Is that all you got to say to me?!"

He was launching into a major rage, so I ended the call and ran to the SAS ticket counter. They had a seat available in first class (950 fuckin' Euro to go 600 miles, shit) but I snagged it because it also put me at the head of the line for security. The moment I was through and running for the gate, I called him back. This time when he answered, I think he was ready to kill me, his voice was so low and barely in control.

"You motherfuckin' asshole, how the fuck could you do this to me? Not even a fuckin' note?"

"I didn't," I snapped back at him. "I'll be in Copenhagen in about two hours."

"What d'you mean 'in Copenhagen'? Where are you?"

"Paris."

"Aw, shit, Tone — look, I know I should've just told you I was sneakin' off to see my dad but — but he said — shit I thought — I mean, I still came home every night and — "

"Jake, Jake, JAKE, listen to me. You are not listening to me. I did not leave you."

"Then where'd you go? All your clothes're gone. You won't answer your phone and — "

"My clothes're gone?"

"STOP FUCKING WITH ME, TONE! YOU WANNA QUIT ME, FINE — DO IT LIKE A MAN! FACE TO FACE! Not this fuckin' sneakin' off in the middle of the night all because I won't tell you every fuckin' thing I'm doin' every fuckin' minute — "

"JAKE, I...did...not...leave...you! Listen to what I'm saying."

"But you're not makin' any sense! Make some fuckin' — some fuckin' — sense..." His voice lost its edge and was filled with confusion. "Wait...did that Texas AG have you extradited? Is that it? Did — did he have you taken back to fuckin' Texas? Is that what happened?"

He didn't know. He honestly did not know. His voice was real. I knew it too well. There were no lies hidden in its crevices. And suddenly I couldn't move. Maybe he was still mine. Maybe he was. I'd come so damned close to believing the worst about him and based on what? Some confusing details in a very complex narrative — and now I was so fucking ashamed of myself for being so paranoid because this...this guy I was talking to — he was still Jake, he was my Jake and he'd never been anything else and — and I was so fucking stupid for even considering he could have been part of this bullshit and I started blubbering, "No, no, I'll explain when I get there, but Jake, Jake, Jake, please believe me, I didn't leave you, I could never leave you, you're my rock, you're my world, you're my life and I could never do that to you and — and — "

And I was halfway down the corridor to the plane and leaning against the side, and the gate attendant was coming down the aisle to get me since the plane were ready to take off. So I forced myself back in control and waved her away and started walking and said, "I'll explain everything — when I get there."

"I'll meet you at the airport," his voice wary.

I gave him the flight information as I sat in my seat then shut down the phone and started trying to make sense of what I'd just learned, because to be perfectly honest, my brain was still careening all over the place because the details did *not* add up.

I mean, for Christ's sake — I'd seen Jake cowering in that room! I had *seen* him. And he'd told me to stay home, insisted on it and it was apparently — too fucking apparently — so the assholes with Gentle Voice would know where I was to grab me. And obviously they'd had a key and been able to take their time, so they must have known he wouldn't be coming home soon, even though he'd told me he was. It didn't make sense unless he was part of it.

But he was also saying they took my clothes, like I'd left him. And they'd taken my mobile phone, too. And to back that idea up — they'd stuffed my passport and wallet (with cash, Texas driver's license and my one credit card) in my jeans while I was unconscious in that hotel room. So — so could Jake be feeding me a line? Acting out his part in this ludicrous play?

No. No — his voice was too real for that. The hurt and anger and confusion — they rang so true I couldn't even begin to think he wasn't desperately freaked out over my vanishing.

Shit, I don't know who's directing this piece of crap but nothing's holding together. None of it matches up.

I mean seriously, if they'd wanted me to go after Gilbert, that wouldn't have taken a bit of manipulation. I'd seen the web announcement that Gilbert was running for Senator as I was showing Matt the information I wanted him to dig up, and that alone had brought out so much anger, I'd made Matt nervous. And the fuck'd apparently announced it ten days ago, so all those shits would've had to do is let me know that and I'd have gladly flown straight home to rip the motherfucker a new asshole, problems with the AG or no problems. He was as guilty of Collie's death as Nussewald or Stanton or even the men who'd actually committed the murder, and if anybody thought I'd have stood by and let him cloak himself in this morally-superior crap he was handing out, then they didn't know me too well.

Oh my God, the absolute fury and disbelief I'd felt that he was presenting himself as a champion of law and order and *true justice*, as he fucking put it. Yeah — justice for those who can afford it. All others should abandon hope, for the Right Honorable Nathaniel Carson Gilbert, the Third had no concern for the less-monied crowd, the motherfucking-son-of-a-bitch.

Poor Jake. He'd had to deal with my rantings about the bastard so many times the first months we were together, it amazes me he didn't toss me out in the street during one of my bouts of psychotic hate and — wait. That's when it hit me — Jake *would* have known how easy it'd be to get me howling after Gilbert. He and I — we had this symbiosis going, where it took only a word or touch for either of us to make the other happy and bring us out of sadness, and knew when to leave the other alone when he needed it. If he'd been helping them, they'd have known, and none of this double-dealing bullshit story would've had to be played. Benny wouldn't have had to go through what Matt and I put him through to get me focused on him. But they *didn't* know any better. Gentle Voice had honestly thought I needed to be twisted and turned and led to my glowing hatred of the prick like some idiot child who didn't want to take his cough syrup. So they were playing it on the fly — making it up as they went along and *that's* why everything jolted from one set-up to the next — to adjust for changes I'd unwittingly forced on them.

And there was my proof positive. They did not know me. Jake hadn't told them anything about me. He wasn't with them. He really was with me. The reality crashed in on me like one of those monster waves on Hawaii's North Shore and nearly made me explode with joy. And as I gazed out the window to watch the Baltic Sea whisper past, far below, I let the beauty of the moment wash over me.

Jake was mine. All mine.

Now I had only to be ashamed that I'd doubted him.

\*\*\*\*

I saw Jake the instant I exited the airport's secure area — light jacket, low black jeans over his boots, a t-shirt under a white cotton shirt — and he saw me at the same time. Jesus, the circles under his eyes. The lines on his face. He'd been hit by my vanishing. I strode up to him, his eyes locked on me, then he took my face in his hands and looked hard at me, wary. I couldn't speak — having his hands on me, again, killed any thoughts I had in my head — so I left the moment up to him.

Finally, he whispered, "Tone — what happened to you?"

I hadn't thought the events of the last few days might already be etched onto my face, but the worry in his expression and the dawning horror in his eyes filled me in. I pulled him close, wrapped him in my arms and the thought, *Your father*, slammed into my brain — and I barely kept from saying it.

To be honest, until that moment I had had only the most basic idea that somehow Jake's dad was part of this catastrophe. Exactly how, I hadn't figured out in my mind, but that's why I was in Paris — to understand. But the instant he spoke to me, it all made perfect sense. From the fucking beginning, it made sense. And I went weak at the knees at the implications.

Jake had been sneaking off to see his dad. He'd said he still came home every night and Ari'd use the plural for trip, meaning it had been more than once or twice. So he'd been popping down to Paris, probably on tickets dad's company paid for — or maybe even a private jet. He told me later his dad *wanted to quietly repair the bridge in their relationship*, not knowing all the while it was being done in such a way as to drive a wedge between us. Done in such a way as to keep Jake from believing anything more had happened than I'd gotten pissed off and left him, like the nut-case I was. So no one would go looking for me, and if I'd wound up dead like they'd planned, people would think I got what I deserved for fucking around on a great guy.

Which brought me to the final conclusion — Jake's father was the third backer of Greco'd. And what was truly sickening was, it meant they'd deliberately chosen the town where his ex-wife lived to set up one of their little operations. It was where his disgraceful fag son lived.

Holy fucking shit — it meant Jake had been chosen to be the first lab rat for this new venture, and his own father had been in on the decision. That he'd been sent to prison may or may not have been deliberate, but it was immaterial. After him, adjustments where made and no one else wound up as totally fucked over as he had been (and forget anything about a pun, here) so he'd served his purpose. But then a man had died thanks to Nussewald going a couple of steps too far, and to kill the track of this — this diseased setup back to him, the father of the man I loved was using me.

Oh, Jesus — I couldn't tell Jake that. I couldn't be the one to verbally destroy that hope of reconciliation in him. Not now. So all I said was, "I just had a glorious encounter with the scum at Greco'd. I — I thought they had you, too."

"Me?" I gave him a moment to absorb the full implications. "But why would you think I was — ?"

"I saw you on camera — in a room. Crouched on a mattress in a corner. Nothing but blank walls. You wore these same jeans. Same shirt. Your cowboy boots."

"My first trip to Dad's office. I — I got in an argument with a couple security guards. They said I wasn't authorized to go up and see him, and the French fucks wouldn't even call him. They kept me there an hour 'fore Kazem showed to release me."

"Kazem?"

"Dad's assistant. Errand boy. I dunno. It's a bullshit job; he's married to one of my cousins and — " He stopped and stared at me. "How'd you see that?"

"Someone must've gotten the security tape. I was in a room just like it. They said if I didn't do what they wanted, they'd — " I cut my voice off. I didn't want him to know what was up, yet — but too late; his eyes grew wary and sliced into me.

"Tone — you're here — now. What'd you do?"

"Nothing," I stammered. "I'm supposed to be in Texas."

"What'd they *want* you to do?"

"Send Judge Gilbert to jail. He's running for the Senate and I think they're afraid the scrutiny'll shine too much light on them. So they're using me to shut him down."

"C'mon. They had to threaten me to get you to do that?"

My heart leapt for joy at hearing him say that. "You know me; these idiots don't."

"So now you can tell 'em to fuck off."

"I can't. I'm leaving on the next flight to Paris. Will you come with me?"

"Tone, why can't you let go of what that asshole did?"

"No, I *have* to get back; I'm not the only person caught up in this, now." Questions shot into his eyes so I quickly added, "I'll tell you everything I can on the plane. Thing is, you'll have to pay for it. My card's nearly maxed out."

"What the fuck's with Paris? Why were you even there?"

"Jake, I swear to you — I'll explain it on the plane. Will you come with me?"

He looked at me long and hard, could see he wasn't getting anything more out of me, so bought himself a ticket. And did he grumble about it having to be first class. I loved it — the guy's got three million dollars in the bank and he's whining about a few hundred euro. I nearly kissed him for being such a cheap-ass.

We got adjoining seats and I kept my word — I told him everything I'd been through since that night and the deal I'd made with Gentle Voice and what I'd figured out, keeping my voice low and the details minimal and going nowhere near my belief his dad was behind it all. There was time enough for that, once this was absorbed. I also stopped before mentioning how far we'd gone — I'd gone with Benny and emphasized how Matt had been tricked into helping me.

Jake eyed me, wary. "What're you holdin' back, Tone?"

How Matt had raped me. Jake would never've stood still for that. "I've told you all I can, right now."

"You said you'd tell me everything!"

"Everything I *can*! Jake, please believe me — I'll tell you everything else when the right time comes."

"That means never."

"I promise you, it won't be that way. I swear. Right now, I have to focus on following through with what I agreed to do," I said, exhausted by reliving it all. "If I don't, they'll take it out on Matt and still come after both you and me. Better to end this now. Cut it off."

His voice was tight with anger and a hint of despair. "It'll never end, Tone. Once shit like this gets started — "

"I can minimize it to where they can't do anything more to us." Then I added, "But that's why I need to see your father."

"Why? What's he got to do with this?"

"I — I don't know. It's pretty coincidental this happened when he was asking you to keep your trips secret from me."

"Don't get all carried away. Dad's just a control freak — has been ever since he left Iran. Ask Uncle Ari." I let my eyes ask him why, instead, and he gave me a nearly French shrug. "Something to do with the Shah. Our family supported him but dad was one of the students that set up protests and he got arrested, and once he was released, emigrated to France. For a while, there were stories of Persian expatriates being targeted by Khomeini's supporters — and I think he still thinks they're out there after him. It's paranoid bullshit, but — "

"Did he tell you why he didn't want me with you?"

He nodded. "His wife — she's real religious. Thinks all fags oughta be hanged. If both of us'd shown up — well, she'd of found out and raised hell, maybe cut him off from my brothers and sisters for darin' to allow 'my filth' near him."

Excuse me? "You have brothers and sisters?"

He nodded. "None of 'em know about me — so it's like I don't really have any. It's weird."

"You never said anything about that."

"Oh, an' you tell me everything?"

He had me there, so I raised the seats' arms and lay my head on his shoulder. "Sorry."

"No, man, I'm the sorry ass sittin' at home for a week thinkin' you're a asshole and all the time — you're — "

"Stop it." I kissed his hand. He was shaking. God knows what was going through his head, but I could pretty much figure it out and see the direction it was going — he'd blame himself for being a part of my life and getting me into this mess, even though it was really the other way around — and the only thing I could think of to kill the progression was to tell him, "You know, they tried to convince me you were helping them."

He jolted and looked at me. "Bullshit."

I looked straight back at him. "Look at what happened. Somebody made it look like I split on you. And they tried to make me think you'd told me to stay home so they could grab me."

"But — how would they know I wouldn't be there? I was all

set to take off when dad's plane had problems, and by the time they told me we weren't goin', all I got was your voicemail when I called. And then I got home and everything's gone and — " He looked away. I squeezed his hand. He took in a deep breath. The announcement came on that we were beginning our final descent into De Gaulle. He finally looked at me. "Besides, who the fuck cares if we're together?" He must have seen the answer in my eyes because he froze — then he looked away, and the words, "You think my dad set it up," whispered out of him.

Yes. "I don't know. That's why I have to talk to him."

"He won't see you. Not even if I ask."

Wanna bet? "I have to try. And you're staying out of it."

"The hell I am — "

"I mean it, Jake. You'll jeopardize becoming part of your family if you rub everyone's face in our relationship."

"That's — that's not part of the equation. His wife — "

"Will love you when she meets you. Who couldn't love you?"

He rolled his eyes and I kicked myself. Right — his own mother. He smirked. "Don't matter; dad won't see you."

"If he doesn't, he doesn't. We'll head to De Gaulle and I'll catch my plane. It leaves at seven."

"What're you gonna do? When you get back there?"

"Shoot Gilbert down — metaphorically speaking."

His dark eyes sliced into me. "You're keeping too much hid from me, Tone. I don't like it. I'm going back — "

"No."

"Just fuckin' try and stop me."

"Jake, you want to know why I vanished on you the first time?" He hesitated then shrugged the barest of nods. I'd been so tight-lipped on that, he still had no idea what all I'd pulled. "Because I didn't want you to get hurt. And if you'd even been in the periphery of what I was planning, you'd never have been considered for exoneration by that fucking state. They'd have used that as their excuse. Might have sent you back to jail for violating parole, that's how morally bankrupt Texas is. If you go back with me, they may not let you leave, again."

"Jesus Christ, Tone — what're you gonna do?"

"I told you — put a fucking end to this."

"How?"

"I — can't tell you that." Because I wasn't really sure. I just knew I'd do whatever had to be done.

He looked at me for a long, long time then asked, "There's times I wonder if I really know you."

How could he, when half the time I didn't know me, myself? But I gripped his hand and said, "Everything I am with you is honest and pure. I hide my past, but not the here and now."

"Aw, listen at this bullshit you're handin' me."

"Okay, okay — I'll make you a promise. When I come back, ask me anything you want — I will tell you the absolute truth."

"Why not now?"

"Dunno what it'll be, yet."

"You — you're not plannin' to come back, are you?"

"Jake, if I have to drag myself out of a grave, I'll return to you. You may not want me in that condition, but — "

He snarled. "Aw — you drive me fuckin' crazy, you know that? I never put up with this much bullshit, before. Not with dad, not with mom — nobody!" I couldn't help but smile at his frustration, but he knew just how hard my head was when I'd made my mind up. And he knew I was right. And he knew I was going to do something that he might not — or...he might *have* approved of; you never really know till it's done. And I knew he was trying like crazy to figure out some way around all the walls I'd put up. All I could do was nuzzle his neck to show how much I appreciated him. And then he said, "I'll give you a week. If I don't see you. In our home. One week from today. I'm comin' after you. And I don't give a shit what you say or what you've done or what it means to me, I'm comin' after you." Then he held my hand close to his heart. "And fuck the consequences."

His words slipped into my heart and I felt such pride that he was mine, I almost lost it. "You shit," I said, "don't you make me cry; I will *not* face your father with red eyes."

He cast me a wicked nasty grin. "So face him like this." And he slipped his hand between my legs and tickled my crotch as we touched down, making more than just the plane jolt as the wheels hit the runway. But what's weird is, it also was a bit uncomfortable.

Then he caressed my ass as we waked up the passenger corridor, making me feel a bit drunk. And a bit sick.

Then he pinched my tits to pull me into the men's lavatory and shoved me into a stall and crouched on top of a commode and groped my ass as he used his teeth to undo my belt and pull down my zipper and lick at my crotch through my briefs and I felt both an intense need for him and had to fight to keep from pushing him away. The confusion nearly sent me over the edge — until he got me past the point of giving a shit about anything but what he was doing.

I don't know how he managed it without biting into my pubes, but somehow his lips pulled my briefs down and freed my dick and he began sucking on it, his hands constantly caressing my ass, and I nearly fainted from the waves of beauty that now crashed over me from his rolling tongue and prying nose and invasive fingers. Then my balls were freed to be juggled and his tongue slashed up and down me as his free hand explored the crack of my ass and I drifted into some world of pure sensation that so closely paralleled the act of flying I honestly thought I was in the air gliding through heaven until a breathtaking surge gripped my thighs and swirled around my scrotum and shot to my tits and ricocheted across every nerve in my whole fucking body and my balls shrieked and I came like I'd never cum before, over and over and over and over and Jake wouldn't stop wouldn't stop wouldn't stop sucking and playing and feeling and pinching until I was whimpering from the perfection of it all.

Then he had me take hold of the bars holding the stall to the ceiling and lifted my legs up to his shoulders and stepped down and let his pants drop and sent his briefs after them and slipped his raging dick between the cheeks of my ass and shifted his hips to rub it between them back and forth and back and forth and leaned in to whisper, "I'd fuck you, but my father would know," as he kept going back and forth, his hands gripping my ass, my legs in the air, his lips crushing mine and mine crushing his and it was so brutally erotic I got hard, again, but then he tensed and pulled me tight against him and kissed me, hard and mean and so full of love, I couldn't breathe, and I felt him shoot and jolt and twist until he couldn't anymore — and then he rested against me for a never-ending moment that was all too brief and I knew I could never experience this nirvana, again, unless it was with him, no matter what I might do or tell myself, and when he came back to life, he made it perfection by softly gasping in my ear, "Come back. Come back — for that."

Oh shit. Oh shit. Oh...shit.

Just let the motherfuckers try and stop me.

— SIX —

Jake rented a car and we headed straight for La Défense, thanks to very nicely detailed instructions from this adorable clerk who I think was thinking naughty thoughts about the both of us. And I lounged in the passenger seat like a pregnant cat in the sun, all but purring as I watched Jake drive. Jesus Christ, his profile was classic — the perfect blend of Persian and Irish that seemed even lovelier behind a pair of Ray Bans. I let my fingers trail from his elegant chin down over his neatly curved Adam's Apple to tickle the hairs peeking from behind his shirt. I ached at seeing him, now, my Jake, back in control and sure of himself, once more. Knowing his way forward. Casual. Easy. Heartbreakingly beautiful in his darkness. Like Collie had been in his bright light. My lovely Collie, whom I couldn't protect. Well...I'd protect Jake. I'd commit murder before I'd let anyone hurt him. He cast me a smile, as if knowing my very thoughts — and I wouldn't have been at all surprised if he did. I chuckled and stretched like that silly cat would stretch.

"So," I all but sighed, "I'm not to see daddy when I've been fucked, but it's okay when I got sucked."

"Rule number one," he smiled.

"How would he know?"

"I don't know, he just does. He told me he could smell it on me. I thought that was bullshit, but that's how he found out I was gay."

"Now who's bullshitting who?"

"Seriously. I came home one day, found him on the couch talkin' to mom and he came over to hug me and jolted back and said, right in front of her, that I smelled like I'd been fucked. And it spooked me 'cause I had been. By a teacher. So he got me to confess. And threw me out of the house and all my things with me. Which is funny, 'cause he and my mother'd been divorced for twelve years and it was her condo."

"Son-of-a-bitch."

He shrugged. "She let him do it." He drove in silence for a moment then added, "Y'know, for years, I figured somebody'd outed me to him. That that's why he'd come into town. Turned out he'd just come to tell her he was gettin' married, again. Dad believes in tellin' people important things face to face, not by letter or phone call or e-mail. It's how he was raised. Manners are important — except when your kid's a fag; then fuck him. Never mind how good he was and I was a good kid. Accepted into a top college. Scholarships. Part-time job for extra cash. Didn't mean shit when I wasn't a hundred percent like what they wanted." Another bout of silence.

"Is that why you went to work for the city?" I finally asked, my hand lying against his arm.

He nodded. "They canceled everything. Wouldn't pay a penny to the college. For years I hated them both — until one day — 'bout a month after I was out on probation — my mom said somethin'. She was on one of her cryin' jags and had called me to try and convince me to turn back to the straight and narrow."

"She didn't put it like that!"

"Yes, and didn't even notice the pun she was makin'."

"That's pathetic."

"No argument from me. But she was *born again* at the time, and any sense of irony vanishes when that happens so — so she said — she told me — no, she wondered if what had happened to dad in the Shah's prison was the reason I'd come out queer. Now, I didn't know what the hell she was talkin' about, and she immediately swore she never said anything and insisted what she *had* said meant nothin' and yak, yak, yak, but I think what she meant was — I think dad was raped by his interrogators. There were stories about that happenin' — even under Khomeini. And I've seen pictures of him from the time of the revolution. He was fuckin' gorgeous."

"Like his son," I said.

He cast me a quick smirk then got serious. "That's why I cut him so much slack, Tone. It makes sense if he went through that — him hatin' fags. Shit, if I wasn't gay and — and I'd gone through what I did..." His voice trailed off. His grip on the wheel tightened. I put the palm of my hand to his cheek. He finally sighed and his voice grew full of emotion. It hurt to hear him. "You're right, y'know. I do want to be part of the family, again. It's stupid, but..."

"Jake." I cut him off to keep him from drifting into a display he'd hate me for seeing, if everything turned out like I was afraid it would. "Ain't I your family?"

"Aw, Tone — you gotta even ask?"

I smiled and left it at that — but I was boiling with anger at the motherfucker who sired Jake and the bitch that bore him for not taking their responsibility as parents to the max. And now I was nearing the entrance to a fresh, new office tower to rip some new assholes — and even in my foul mood couldn't help but notice that, *damn*, this was a weird one. Never-ending sheets of silvery blue glass twisted into shapes you'd think impossible on a building, like it was trying to do the Mambo and had frozen in the middle of a turn. I'd noticed it from a distance and thought it fascinating; up close it was like the future imagined by a drunk video game designer with no depth perception.

Jake had finally agreed to let me try and meet his father alone so the two of us could be (as I put it) as open and honest with each other as need be. He parked the car in an underground garage and set himself up by the Thumb next to the Tour SFR. He was actually sketching it — but doing so in a way meant to show me he was trying not to care about what I was doing even while letting me know he really did. I halfway think the reason he gave in so easily was, he was a bit nervous at what might be revealed and things were too tenuous between him and his old man for him to just shrug anything bad off.

And you know — I honestly hoped I'd turn out to be wrong.

I stopped at the main reception desk to sign in, told them who I was and whom I wished to see, and after a call upstairs was directed to a bank of elevators that shot up to the top of the building. No hesitation on anyone's part. No security guards. Nothing. Looked like they wanted me to come up without any interference.

I stepped into a sleek reception done in chrome and black Lucite panels — big and quiet and dressed to impress, but I wasn't surprised. What little research I'd been able to do showed me Faraz Darya-Bandari had a hand in a dozen different companies in a dozen different businesses — from transport of goods to manufacturing to publishing to real estate. He'd done good, our Faraz, which added to my hope I was wrong about him.

But then I noticed the floor shift just a little, like I was on a ship in a quiet harbor, and I just sighed. Of course. Dubai was part of the bullshit. Matt and I both had been imprisoned somewhere on an upper floor of this building.

Look, I've never thought of myself as all that brilliant or even super-smart or anything; I just make connections that make sense when I make them, and ninety percent of the time I wind up being right. But this — this was just silly. I mean, yeah — they probably didn't expect me to leave the building alive or even to come back here, but I *was* here; surely they'd consider the possibility that I'd figure out that I'd already been in this building and want to keep me off the top floor. It only made sense if they were halfway intelligent. Instead, they'd invited me up. So either they were arrogant in their certainty of their mastery of the situation — or they just plain didn't give a shit...and I had a feeling it was more the latter.

Sure enough, an elegant young woman in a little black suit and fuck-me heels strode up, very proprietary about this being her space. "Monsieur St. Lazarre? Je m'appelle Charanne. Je comprends que vous êtes venus voir m. Darya-Bandari?"

The bitch thought to intimidate me with her French. I just smiled and said, "Je m'appelle Antony, seulment, et je suis très heureux de faire votre connaissance, mademoiselle. Où est ce monsieur?"

She blinked and almost smiled then motioned down a short, neatly-lighted corridor of Lucite walls holding original artwork and a marble floor to a wide set of steel doors and said, "This way, please," in perfect British. As she led me to them, she added, "I'd no idea you spoke such excellent French."

I just smiled and said, "Thanks," as the doors swung open. No sense in letting her know I'd exhausted seventy-five percent of my repertoire in firing back at her — well, the *acceptable* repertoire; "les mots mal? Merde."

I stepped into a massive office of black leather and rich mahogany and a continuation of the marble floor. To one side was a sitting area of overstuffed couches and settees with glass tables in their midst, a flat screen TV that was as wide as the wall and a bar stocked with everything you could think of to drink; to the other side was a long conference table with matching chairs; and in the middle of it all was a simple table-like glass-top desk clear of everything but a few sheets of paper, a sleek black wireless computer monitor and keyboard and a pad to write on. Knick-knacks dotted the room, more artwork hung on the walls and curtains framed windows that offered exquisite views of The Eiffel Tower, Notre Dame, The Louvre and anything else you could think of in the glorious city of light.

Of course, a man was seated behind the desk, wearing the latest in top designer suits. His eyes were dark and sharp, his nose hawk-like, his hair black and flecked with silver, his skin olive and his face so much like Jake's, I felt like I was seeing him in twenty-five years. The couches held two other men — Gentle Voice and Boss Man — and both of them had their eyes fastened on me so tightly, I felt a bit like Gulliver after he's been tied down by the Lilliputians. So I was right — it's *don't give a shit* mode. The double-doors whispered closed as the guy behind the desk rose, not smiling, not frowning, just gazing upon me with a cold calculation.

"Mr. St. Lazarre, I expected you this morning."

"It's Antony, Faraz," I replied, not bothering with nice and wondering why he'd let me know he had a way of tracking my credit card. My research on him hadn't shown anything about a bank or financial institution under his control — not that it meant anything, considering the number of shadow companies he owned — except he didn't seem to be aware of my side trip to Copenhagen. Which could mean the information was second-hand.

"Would you care to be seated? Some refreshment, perhaps?"

I shook my head and sat in an elegant chair facing the desk. Faraz returned to his seat, his eyes locked on me.

"So — Antony — why are you here?"

"To make a deal," I said.

"We have one already," said Gentle Voice.

"I want to renegotiate."

Boss Man chuckled. "He speaks as if he has something to deal with."

I kept my eyes on Faraz as I asked, "Am I talking to you — or am I talking to them?" He made the slightest movement to indicate he was the alpha-dog. "Then you should train your puppies to be quiet."

Gentle Voice sneered. "That was not a very smart thing to say — "

"Kazem." The word sliced into him and he shut up. So, Kazem *was* Faraz's errand boy. I almost smiled. Faraz eyed me for a moment then said, "What deal do you offer?"

"I'll take down the judge if you'll let Jake back in your family." He blinked. I think he expected me to demand he shut down Greco'd or make threats if he didn't leave me and Jake alone or something dramatic and childish like that. Something he could understand and handle. Instead, I was asking him to do something that was completely against his nature. Because the second I saw him I knew he was brutally unforgiving of anyone who stepped out of his norms, and whatever bullshit he'd been handing Jake up till now, I could see he was prepping to crush his dream of being back in daddy's good graces — and I'd crush the fucker before I let that happen.

Sure enough, he leaned back and without giving it much thought said, "And if I say no, you will allow Judge Gilbert to become a United States Senator — and perhaps even run for president. Truly?" Bitch had been doing research on me, too.

"Oh, I can stop that without much trouble. But you want somebody who can take all the heat while you regroup...shut down...rearrange...whatever. And that I wouldn't help you with. And you need me to see to it *His Honor* is the dead end in this game and not merely the on-ramp to an investigation into your company, worldwide."

"What company is that?"

"Greco'd."

"I have no affiliation with any business by that name."

"Really? That's not what my research tells me."

Boss Man popped in. "If you refer to what I told you — ?"

Meaning he was an actor reading a script, of course. I waved my hand at him, dismissively. "Yeah, yeah, it was all bullshit. But Matt swallowed it and Benny believed it, and that's all that really matters. For them, anyway. But I found the link that called bullshit on it all."

"Antony, there can be no link for something that does not exist," said Faraz, casually.

"Man, I thought I was dealing with somebody smart." I turned to Kazem. "Maybe I *should* be talking to you."

Kazem glanced at his boss, startled but covering it well.

Faraz tapped his finger on his desk. I turned back to him. His voice was still in complete control. "Is this how you negotiate? Insult the client?"

"Faraz, the day Officers Thomas and Marquez questioned me in my dorm room, I burned some CDs of all the data I had on Collie's murder, Nussewald's connection to it, notes I'd made about it — everything. And I mailed them to myself. I know you guys got hold of at least one, probably two of them — but just for the sake of argument, let's say you got hold of all four that I made." Never hurts to beef up your point with a little lie. "You know the information I had and have available. And you would also know it's information that can easily be replicated, right down to the little notice in a weekly paper about the forming of a corporation under the name *Greco'd.*"

"Which I had nothing to do with. I haven't been to Texas in ten years."

"But you been to Miami." He shrugged a *so-what.* "At the same time Benny Marquez was visiting family — on leave for bereavement and Judge Gilbert was in town." This was something Matt had found out while checking Gilbert's court cases (tracked out in a very illegal-hacker way). He'd suddenly cleared his schedule the same week a convention of GOP scum gathered there, and Benny's grandfather died just a few days before it started. This was still a huge *Hail Mary* because I didn't really know that Faraz was there at the same time, but it made sense.

A flicker in his eyes and the slightest narrowing of his brow told me I'd scored. "You see, I got a buddy at Homeland Security and he told me — unofficially, of course — where you and Gilbert have been all based on airline and passport records. It won't take much to put you kids together in one city at one time once Interpol and the Justice Department know to look." I smiled, proud of my bullshit, but Faraz smiled back.

"You have no friend with HSA," he said. "And you know perfectly well this ad you refer to means nothing. Is this why you are taking up my time?"

Okay, Antony, a good kick in the ass would work, right about now. He'd just played you. That little frown was meant to send the wrong signal, and the amusement in his eyes and dancing around the edges of his lips was the tell. He'd seen the data and taken care of it, probably the second he decided to pull back and lay the blame for everything on his three little pigs. So...Plan B.

"Okay, fine, I was trying to keep Jake from learning you're the guy who set him up to be the first one they brutalized in that cell," I said. "That his own father had him raped because he turned out queer — and because you really, really hate fags. And I think I know why."

Man, if his eyes had been razors, I'd have been sliced to bits. "Shahin, have Jacob brought to me."

Boss Man pulled out his iPhone and hit speed-dial. So, they knew where Jake was. Meaning they *did* know about my side trip. Again, this little player got his little self played like a fucking idiot. Well — I can't say I was shocked, so up popped Plan C. "Kazem, I assume you've seen the uploads from yesterday; have you checked today's, yet?" I heard him shuffle. No specific answer meant, No. "Take a glance at who I offer as the second and third parts of the bargain. I'd say they're more interesting than some Czech porn actor pretending to be a Russian soldier nobody cares about." Not that I really knew that, but it sounded right.

This made Faraz offer up a real frown. He put up a hand and I heard Kazem and Shahin rise and come to the desk. Faraz hit a couple of keys on the keyboard and they watched the monitor...and I studied them, keeping as casual as I could.

And then I saw it. The tiniest flicker of a smirk dance across Faraz's lips. And dumb-fuck Antony gave himself a *serious* kick in the ass, then. No wonder the shit had been able to fuck with me. I mean, I knew the Iranians were motherfuckers when it came to gay men. Hell, one of the things that freaked me out after suicide boy was hearing about two Iranian boys who'd been hanged for nothing more than jacking each other off. I even saw a photo of them as the nooses were being put around their necks, and they looked like two terrified kids still in high school, and I'd actually gotten ill from understanding just how much the world hated gay men and women. Shit, look at Uganda and its *kill the fags* law, designating execution for anyone gay, all pushed by the American Talibangelicals. Small wonder so many queers stayed in the closet; they had more to lose than just the respect of society and their peers.

So I'd built Plan B around Jake's interpretation of what happened to Faraz as the man wanting to keep secret his own abuse while taking out a sort of revenge against the world for it happening while making a buck off it. Kind of Freudian (or would it be Jungian? I never could tell the difference) but it worked within the concept of what had happened. What I hadn't considered was Jake might be wrong about his dad. And oh-my-god was he — and that's when Plan C kicked into gear, my scorched earth policy. The plan of last resort.

I actually felt my pulse quicken, like I was some fluttery Southern Belle who just got the palpitations. Because this ripped all of my lovely plans away and stomped on them into the dirt, and I let it happen with a casualness that startled me but was also devastating. All I had to do now was keep Faraz from noticing. So I asked in as steady a voice as I've ever had in my life, "Did you like what we sent you, yesterday?"

The only response from Faraz was a slow intake of breath,

enough to give me my affirmation. Shahin actually curled his nose, a bit, while Kazem — I guess this *was* just a job to him.

I rose and joined them to take a casual glance at the monitor. Good old Matt — he'd done exactly what I'd asked. They now had elegant video of Grady Lowenthaal in a blue and black striped Speedo practicing his exquisite dives. His powerful body and his blond hair mingled together to make him the perfect image of beauty in motion as he flipped up and over and down in textbook form to cut the water with barely a ripple.

Kazem spoke to Faraz in Persian, but I could make out one word — Grady. They knew who he was, and Kazem almost seemed happy; he must think he has a client for a guy like this. If only he really understood. Faraz looked at me, wary.

I very matter-of-factly said, "He's famous in sports circles. Probably headed for the Olympics. Expected to win a few medals. And he's not at *all* ashamed of his homosexuality. He proclaims it in interviews and attends gay pride functions and raises money for AIDS services. Imagine a guy like him, bound and gagged and fucked by somebody like me, all on video. And then there's Joe. Is he up, yet?"

Kazem clicked a couple of keys and another video streamed up — this one of a young, dark-haired college dude who wasn't so much buff as just cute and well-put-together in a healthy-boy-next-door sort of way — Joseph Stanton, only son of that motherfucking ADA. It was a wide-angle shot of him leaving his fraternity house with a couple of his buddies, all dressed in some form of cargo shorts showing off lots of nice calves as they piled into this new red Charger parked before a nice big colonial-style frat house, and I knew exactly which one it was.

Then I stopped breathing. One of the guys with Joe was Shane Nussewald. Shit, I'd figured he'd graduated, already, but there he was, all buff and beautiful and being dragged into little Joe's car to ride shotgun, the seat of best-buds only. And even from a distance I could tell Shane wasn't really up to joining them; his eyes were too hurt. Probably because his father had recently died. It's funny, but until that moment, I'd been so busy hating on Wilbur Nussewald I hadn't once considered there might be people out there who truly loved him. And yet, there on one of his sons I could see real grief.

And it fucking pissed me off. How dare anyone feel bad that the son-of-a-bitch was dead? After what he'd done to Collie and Jake and almost had done to me? Considering how many lives he probably ruined, and if there was any justice was burning in hell for? Fucking shit. Well...now I had video of both Joe and Shane — and could choose either to help me play out this game.

"So which?" Kazem asked.

I jolted, thinking he had read my mind, for a second, then thought to say, "Guy in the brown t-shirt and camo-shorts, who got behind the wheel."

"This one is not familiar."

Excellent. "He's a prick tease who dicked me around. I'll get both of them, fulfill my end of the original deal and also use them to crush Gilbert, if you'll let Jake back into the family. Let him know his brothers and sisters."

Faraz leaned back, examining me like he would a bug he's trapped. "You place too much importance on yourself," he finally said, his voice still in complete control.

"Do I?" He waited for me to continue. Guess it was all or nothing, so I dove in, head first. "You need me to make this work — to see that the investigation into Greco'd dies with Gilbert going to jail. Without me, it stays open."

"How can you achieve this?"

"He can't," said Shahin. "You're not so experienced or wise as you think, Antony. You'll be caught so easily."

I returned to the chair, fighting to keep myself looking as calm and cool as I wanted them to think I was, and sat down. I looked from one to the other and said, "What if I am?"

Faraz was instantly on the uptake as to what I was planning but his boys weren't quite as quick.

"How will you free yourself?" asked Kazem. "Keep from being sent to prison?"

I leaned back to accept my fate. "I won't."

Faraz had already put two and two together and come up with ten million. His eyes grew sharp as diamonds and as wary as a hawk. Kazem took a moment but finally caught a glimmer of what I was planning. Then Shahin got it. The stillness in the room enveloped me and I felt a bit like I was floating.

"Officer Arlen Thomas," I said, "of the Texas Rangers, already suspects me in one kidnapping and rape. I may let drop something about what I did to his partner, Officer Benjamin Marquez. You do know that's who we used the other day?" No reaction from any of them meant, Yes. "Under interrogation, I will finally admit that the honorable Nathaniel Carson Gilbert, the Third hired me to make movies of myself raping guys like myself so he could keep selling these videos to some shadow company in Switzerland for their special clients, all just to fund his campaign. I chose Marquez because he handed me over to Nussewald, and Grady Lowenthaal spurned my advances — I had him in a couple of classes — and little Joe there was a trick I picked up at a frat party and sucked off, and who then stole my stash of pot. I will be forced to link Gilbert to Greco'd and probably sent to jail, and the story will end. So long as you let Jake be part of your family."

"Why is that a condition?" Faraz asked, finally intrigued.

"Because if I do this, if I let myself be sent to prison, he'll come back to the States to be with me, and that cannot happen. He'd wind up inside, too. But if he has family who love him and need him, here, I can talk him into — into building a new life, without me."

"*Without* you?" Shahin asked, in a near mocking tone. Motherfucker wanted to twist the knife.

"Yes."

"This does not make sense," Faraz said.

"Doesn't have to; that's the deal. You make Jake part of your family, and I'll — I'll fix your little problem."

"You still have not told me why you want to do this."

"Is it that important?"

"If I am to believe you."

I hesitated. Looked at Kazem and Shahin then shot my eyes straight back at Faraz. He understood and made a simple move with his head. Both men stiffened. Obviously they weren't used to being sent from the room. So they would think I hadn't noticed, I walked over to a window to look out over the city of light, making their exit easier. Not that I really gave a shit; I just needed a moment to allow my thoughts to form.

Paris is a beautiful city. I wondered if Jake would move here to be near his brothers and sisters; I could see him doing that. Taking a little apartment in Saint Michel or Montmartre. Living the life of Gene Kelly in *An American in Paris*. Happy and content that his family belonged to him, again. He'd miss me, sure — and God knows I'd miss him — but there was no other way it could be — not and have him safe and happy.

I've known him for over a year — thought I understood him and had figured out his moods and fears and quirks — yet it took me this long to finally understand how deep banishment from his family had cut him. How much of his silence and secrecy was him not wanting to pick at the scab covering the wound. That doing so would be too much heartache for him to bear and he'd have to face the reality that he had brothers and sisters he'd never know, so he'd growled his warnings to back away and licked at the scar, in private, all the while pining to know his blood, again. To have what Uncle Ari had. And seeing his cousins' happiness, in Copenhagen, is what had made him begin to think he could actually approach his father and beg to be allowed to return — like it was him who had done something wrong.

He'd never have that with me around. Faraz was obvious in how barely he held his contempt of me in check. I'm the bastard who ruined his sweet little arrangement. I'm the proof his son slept happily with men. I'm the cocksucker who dared confront him in his own territory after he'd crushed their connection to someone in the Texas Rangers, because no way in hell would Benny deal with this motherfucker, again, no matter what he promised or paid. God only knows how much that had cost Faraz, and Jake would be guilty of everything I had done, just by association. And the only way that could end, the only way he could separate my actions from Jake's life was if I ended it with him — and the thought made me sick deep inside.

But I knew — without question I knew there was no other way to handle this, now. In my anger and arrogance, I'd fouled the water too much.

Faraz's reflection appeared in the glass, watching me like a cat watches a bird it's about to pounce upon. I didn't dare turn; he'd see me weak and hurt. I just made myself smile at his reflection, and finally let the words escape me. "I'm doing this because you hate Jacob Darya-Bandari — and I love him."

"You love him...but you would inflict my hate upon him?"

"He wants to know his brothers and sisters. You'll let him, and you'll make him think you like it." I was finally back in control and could turn to look at him...and try to keep from getting angry. "That's your punishment for helping get Collier Winston-Royce killed."

"Which was from Nussewald's stupidity — "

"I don't give a fuck," I snapped. "You'll let Jake return to his family, never knowing what you did to him, never knowing what you did to others, happy and thinking that everything's worked out, at least in that area. You'll do it because — because maybe — just maybe I'll be able to arrange to have more videos made for you." He blinked, and not happily. "From a real prison. Committed against real convicts. Big buff guys like Collie — or maybe slimmer and tighter like Jake. I mean, that is what you like. Right?" I all but licked my lips.

His face tightened, and his eyes held death in them. "You dare to suggest I enjoy watching such — ?" His voice died in disgust and anger. Maybe I'd pushed a bit too far, so I stepped back and got ready, just in case I'd need my Aikido. But there was no question in my mind I was right about him, now.

"Nobody needs to know what you enjoy," I said. "So long as you keep Jake happy."

"You have no idea what you're talking about." The words drifted out of him, almost like a toxic sigh.

Wanna bet, motherfucker? Because now it was screaming at me, it was so obvious. I leaned against the wall and said in the most even-handed manner I could, "You were a fucker in the Shah's prison, not a fuckee. May even have been helping the Shah and his secret services. Fuck a guy, tell him you had to do it, get his trust, and suck him dry of details about the opposition. That's why you had to leave the country. That's why Khomeini's people were after you. You were a total fucker."

Fury boiled up in his eyes — mixed with a sudden caution. You could almost see the questions play out in his mind. How much did I know? Whom had I spoken with? Had I written it down, or left it with someone like Matt for security or blackmail? Is that why I dared go nose-to-nose with him?

I kept talking. "I bet you played it careful. You weren't the first or second or fourth guy to shove his dick up inside a struggling man's ass, but you were one of them. Maybe even set it up. And it worked out great except for one thing — you found out you liked it. Loved it. That doing it made you feel powerful and fed your core — and made you ashamed. Because it's sick and disgusting — but you need it to feel whole."

"So — you see me as homosexual." He was almost sneering.

"No," I said, "I'm not that limited. I see you as a guy who enjoys the sense of power and control raping a man — hell, raping *any*body brings. Sex is just a fun by-product. It's overwhelming, being able to force a human being to subjugate him-or-herself to you. To slip your dick inside them and punch it in and out and in and out for as long as you want, over and over and over. Enjoying every stroke. Every touch. Every sensation. Every twist of their body as they try to get away. To roar with pleasure as you near your peak. And then to make them like it. Enjoy it. Get off on it. Whether it's cumming all over your hand or wetting the sheets. It's the epitome of power. It's control. It's nirvana. It's stronger than any drug ever developed. It takes you over. Body and soul. Nothing even begins to approach the rush of it."

His face grew a bit flush. The sneer vanished. He absently licked his lips.

"But it only works if your partner doesn't want you in him," I continued. "If he fights you. If he must be held down to be used by you. And buying someone to let you do it isn't the same thing. It doesn't carry the same sense of danger and derision and disgust at their weakness. That's why you love the idea of men being fucked. They fight harder. The win is better when it's done against their will. By half a dozen other men, each taking his turn. The tapes of those guys in holding cell six were made for you. This 'clientele' and 'special order' shit was just a screen for you to hide behind, and all these little walls and subdivisions were built to keep anybody from finding that out — even your boys." My voice was lower, more full of emotion as my predator mindset took over.

"I know what it's like," I added. "You know that. I've felt the same rush, and I know that when you come — when you finally give in to the mind-bending ecstasy — it's the most absolute pleasure there is. It's God and the Devil, combined. It's eternity. It's hideous, soulless perfection. And it's hell on earth when after you've tasted it, you can't have it, anymore."

He was frozen, now. Eyes still locked on me but filled with something evil trying to hide in his shadows.

I kept on, my voice low and melodious. "And you can't have it. Yeah, you're a rich guy. You can afford to buy someone to be used that way, even if they don't want to be. You know that men, women, anybody can be bought and used for any purpose in this world. You can even keep it quiet. For a while. But you're smart enough to know things like this — no matter how rarely you do it — people catch on. It builds into gossip. Innuendo. Hidden smirks. Humans don't need much detail to start talking, and talk can kill more than just a reputation."

His eyes drifted into a thousand yard stare, his expression stunningly close to that same one Matt had shown after raping Benny.

Son-of-a-bitch, it was point, set and match.

"You can't have that," I continued. "Can't have anybody knowing you're anything but the perfect family man. The perfect success. You can't even have a fag son; it might look like you failed. Might be bad for business in the Persian community. So you had to abandon the beauty of true rape and cope like a junkie who's trying to go clean...but who spends the rest of his life craving one more fix of the pure thing. Yeah, there's videotapes and websites that can be watched in secrecy, and they almost satisfy the beast. But they're too staged and usually wind up being kind of silly...and you need the reality of it — the truth of it, again. The animal in your shadows demands it."

277

His breath was tighter. More shallow. His eyes returned to me and I had a pretty good idea if I kept this up too long, he'd show me exactly what he'd done in that prison. So I casually wandered over to his desk. The two videos of Grady and Joseph & Shane were paused, side-by-side on the monitor.

"So was it good for you — the video of me raping Orin Tedesco? It wasn't very high quality, but the emotions were real and I did get a couple of good shots of my inserts. Did that bring back memories? How about all the images of Marquez fighting me and Matt? That must've really made you cream."

He didn't move, meaning, Yes. "You...are...a devil," he finally whispered.

"And the pot calls the kettle black."

He shifted, his eyes still sharp and wary. "And my son loves you? What does that say about him?"

Straight to the heart. "It says that I can also be an angel," I snapped out before I could stop myself. I gulped in a deep breath to regain control, but the words escaped me, anyway. "This isn't all there is to me. At least, it didn't used to be. When I was with Jake — he was my drug. He was my life. And I loved him more than I love myself. He sees that in me and he knows that I'm someone who'll do anything to protect him."

"Even to the destruction of yourself?" Lobbed the ball right back at you, Antony. Match ain't over, yet.

"Sometimes that's the only way to win," I said.

Faraz let the smallest of smiles crease his lips. He'd found his weak spot. "That could be seen as very romantic. But I think it's a lie. I think you prefer the idea of Jacob pining for you, like an abandoned dog. It's selfish but typical of someone like you. Pretentious and self-important. It is your own needs that guide your actions, no one else's."

The bastard knew which buttons to push. "Think what you like," I shrugged as I took a deep breath to pull away from the emotions building inside me. It was a weak return but better than saying nothing.

"Of course, it works only if Jacob is willing to do this pining. To hold himself in wait for you. I wonder if he will?"

Good serve, motherfucker. Fast and cruel and slamming into my own questions and doubts. I honestly had no response.

I started the videos playing, from the beginning. They were only about a minute long, each, but showed some great images of three completely different young men whose lives were about to be shattered by the casual evil I was perfectly willing to commit. I felt sorry for them...but the truth is, their pain was less important to me, at that moment, than Jake's happiness. So I sat in Faraz's chair and watched them. "What do you want, first? Blond or brunette?"

He cleared his throat. My non-response had cut his momentum. Finally said, "The diver will quickly be missed. Better to go for the other young man."

"Really? 'Cause I say Grady first, then Joe — and this guy for dessert." I tapped on Shane's image. Faraz was taken aback at that offer. I smiled. "I promise — it'll be good. As soon as I see video of Jake with his brothers and sisters."

"I — I have to think." Meaning I'd really thrown him off his game and he wanted to find some new strategy to use against me. Fuck that.

"Think about what? I'm offering you an ongoing service, Faraz. Dozens more videos from prison. It's not hard to set up. Rape is an unspoken part of a felon's sentence in the US — hell, most of the world — and mobile phones have cameras that are amazing in their quality, so the video can be shot then shot straight to you. You can kill Greco'd, completely. Kill the whole charade of selling these movies to 'special investors.' Give me a secure line to a secret laptop and you got everything you could want. Big, buff, young, tall, slim, blond, brunette, redhead, black, white, brown, you name it. We're a country that *loves* to throw people in jail, and sooner or later every kind of guy'll pass my way. And I'll have my alliances set up and I'll share every moment with you. And all I'm asking in return is you make your own son happy. You have to *think* about that?"

"And that is the only reason you wish to ruin your life?"

No, but there's no way I'm ever telling you, motherfucker. It'll have to be enough for me to say, "I told you — I love Jake. And I would kill to protect him — and you're right, even if it meant killing myself. And I finally see that short of that, this is the only way to remove him from this situation. Because every other way I've looked at it, there's too great a chance he'd wind up back in jail — and that would destroy him. And I will. Not. Let. That. Happen. But if they got me — and they got Gilbert — and they see the chain's been shut down, the link to you dies along with their interest in the case. And Jake'll be here, out of their grasp."

"But you offer more videos. The link still will be — "

"Unseen. You know as well as I do, prison's a whole different world. People don't see anything they don't want to. And there's ways to make sure they don't want to. So what do you say?"

Faraz slowly returned to his desk and sat on its edge, his eyes never leaving me, his mind back to working at its cold calculations. I glared at him, not daring to look away or even blink if I could help it. He finally leaned in close and whispered, "Double-cross me and I will have Jacob castrated and his balls sent to you. And I will see to it you live with that for a very long time."

The cold-blooded motherfucking son-of-a-bitch. How the hell had Jake been begot by this scum?

I shrugged my agreement to his terms, then he smiled to let me know the deal was in place.

And there it was — finally. Jake would be separated from any connection to me, and so long as I fed Faraz's need, he would provide any proof I wanted to show he was keeping his end of this devil's bargain. So — now that I could see what my real choices were — all the swearing I'd done that I'd never leave him, all my protestations of love and plans to live my life with Jake...they fell away like childish dreams, and the deal to save him and end my future roared in to take their place.

And the weight of the world lifted from my shoulders — and sent my heart straight to hell.

— SEVEN —

Now in the interests of full disclosure I have to admit there was another reason for me to separate myself from Jake. Subtext, if you prefer. And while the main intent, the one true reason I was willing to offer up this deal was that I really honestly wanted him safe and happy with his family — well, I wasn't bullshitting about rape being a drug as strong as heroin. And I'd been caught by it. Orin then Rattler then Benny...shit, even me being taken by Matt — they'd all given me a taste of the incredible high it can bring and filled me with this — this craving to experience it, again. And my silly little comment about rape not hurting anybody? I'd begun to believe it.

Yes — I know how evil that sounds. I know it's a bold-faced lie; that in truth, the reality of rape is destructive in ways unimaginable. I was aware enough to understand my sudden need was *not* something that should be considered acceptable in any way, shape or form. That its whole idea was built upon the crushing of another human being's spirit and sense of self. But there it was — the real unvarnished truth of it. My happiness in Denmark may have distracted the beast and would probably have done so forever if we'd been left alone to live our lives together, but what I'd been through over the last week or ten days (I still wasn't sure what exactly happened while I was drugged) had rattled its cage with a vicious fury, and it was howling to be fed.

Now whether I like to admit it or not, Faraz had seen this in me as completely as I'd seen it in him. Two creatures of the same species circling and sniffing each other out as enemies who could still hunt together for a mutual benefit. I just couldn't decide if we were jackals or hyenas — though the latter was more appropriate.

281

Anyway, he accompanied me down to find Jake — and embraced his son like he *was* the prodigal returned. Jake's confusion jumped into wary happiness when Faraz bought both of us coffee at a nearby café and invited him home for dinner, that night. Hell, he even provided detailed directions on how to get there from De Gaulle.

As we drove back to the airport, Jake did his best to get me to tell him everything that happened, but the closest he could get to an answer was, "It wasn't anything like I expected." And as he saw me off, he held me close to whisper, "You — I dunno how you did it — but thanks. Thanks."

I nearly crushed him, holding him tight as I could, not wanting to let go...and not wanting him to notice how I was shaking. Because I knew — I fucking knew that this would be the last time I held him.

"Have fun," I murmured. "Don't go in with expectations. Let the evening flow. I think you'll be happy."

He already was. His dark beautiful eyes actually seemed to glow. "I don't think I'll ever really know you, Tone, but I hope one of these days I understand you."

I chuckled. "Don't bet on it." Then I stepped back and made myself head for security, my own eyes never leaving his.

He must have seen something in them, because he frowned and called, "One week, Tone! I mean it! I don't see you in a week, I'm comin' after you!"

"I know," I called back, knowing full well Faraz would see to it he didn't.

I walked down the passageway like I was drifting in slow motion. My emotions were on hold. My life no longer was real. I sat in my seat and did not move until we were off the ground, and before we'd left European airspace I'd kicked back four shots of Bourbon, telling the flight attendant in my very broken French it helped me with my fear of flying. She understood. I zonked out and slept right through to the landing, not dreaming or waking up till we were about to touch down. And Matt met my plane, just like we'd planned.

The second I saw him I said, "We may have to go through

with at least one of them."

His face went white and his big eyes nearly doubled in size. "You — you're not really gonna — ?"

I nodded. "I don't want you to be part of it, because what I'm going to do is not pretty."

He looked away. "Listen, I — I don't — shit, I gotta pee." Then he headed for the men's room. I think I freaked him out with the casualness of my statement and he needed a moment alone to regroup. When he came back, all he said was, "You — you drive. I gotta think."

So I took the wheel and headed back to the motel told him everything that happened. And I mean everything except the final agreement between me and Faraz; but the rest? He was filled in from beginning to end.

"So Jake wasn't really — ?"

I shook my head. "His dad set him up to be held by the security guards then had him released, and that's the video they used. I'm pretty sure the Russian — he was just an actor."

"I never saw him. And we were in Paris the whole time?"

"Faraz showed me the rooms. They're on the top floor, in the utility area. He owns the building and had them built to match the guards' holding cell. None of his staff know about them — well, except for Kazem and the bodyguards."

"That guy who was Boss Man — he's gotta be Jewish. He speaks Hebrew better'n me."

"I speak enough French to fake it, and I'm hardly fluent."

"So it's all bullshit. The whole fucking thing's just bullshit. Faraz was just yanking our chain." He was deeply wounded by the realization he wasn't part of something heroic.

"C'mon, Matt, it doesn't change what you did. You stepped up and — and you were doing the right thing. You did what you did for all the right reasons. Don't let go of that."

He looked at me, his eyes still hurt. "Even with Marquez?"

"I told you, he was set up for us. He knew what he was getting into." Though to be honest I'd begun to wonder if he really had, or if he'd been lied to, as well.

Matt finally sighed. "This isn't right."

"Matt, I mean it — I only want your help up to a point; then I want you to get the fuck back to Florida."

"And leave you to handle this by yourself? Fuck that."

Oh, fuck. He didn't understand just how bat-shit crazy I could become. I'd have to dump him without letting him know my plans. Or what I figured would happen.

We got to the motel and I checked my e-mail — and there was a link to a QuickTime movie of Jake with his brothers and sisters, all six of them wary but smiling. Even wife #2, a lovely woman in the latest fashion, was smiling at seeing them all together. I'd had a feeling Faraz was lying about her hating Jake. That or he had such complete control of her he could make her go along with whatever he told her to...but I doubted it. She actually seemed to like my guy, and when the camera caught them talking, alone, in his halting Persian — I could tell he liked her, too. A lot. It nearly broke my heart, seeing him so at peace.

Matt noticed and put a sympathetic arm over my shoulders as he said, "Jesus, he is so beautiful." All I could do was nod. "I'd kill to protect him, too."

"It's not going to come to that," I said.

"You so sure?"

"Yeah. All I have to do is finish Gilbert and Stanton, and that'll be it."

"Stanton? The frat guy?"

I nodded. "His father's an assistant district attorney who was part of it."

"Antony, these guys you had me tape — they haven't done anything to you. What're you gonna do to them?"

"Just use them to lay a trap."

"How?"

"You don't want to know. Trust me."

"You're not gonna hurt them, are you?"

I looked at him. Saw serious concern in his eyes. Human concern. So...the drug hadn't taken hold of him, yet. Maybe it never would. Some people just don't get addicted to things. They can smoke or drink themselves into oblivion for years and stop cold-turkey. Or they can channel their addictive natures into something positive, like helping charities or rock climbing or collecting blue bottles or crap like that. Maybe that was Matt, a guy who'll never lose sight of who he is and who he can be, even when he's done things he can't really explain.

So I told him, "No. I won't need to hurt anybody." And he seemed to believe me. Hell, I almost believed myself.

Matt laid out everything he'd learned — Grady's course schedule; that he was prepping for a championship meet in three weeks so was practicing his dives until all hours; that he was ranked in the top ten divers, internationally, and was pushing to be *the* top guy before he graduated and hit the Olympics.

"He lives on campus," Matt told me, "so he doesn't have to drive and can be at the pool as late as midnight, when it shuts down. He usually has somebody with him — his coach or another diver. Last class is at five but he's got a lab on Wednesdays till eight."

"Where's his dorm in relation to the pool?"

"He's in Findley Hall."

I nodded. Not even five hundred yards from door to door. It's where my quarterback had been living. "What about Joe?"

Joseph Stanton was even easier than Grady. He lived in the frat house with over a dozen other guys, had all his courses in the afternoon and loved to laze by the pool, even when it was cold. "Prepping for Spring Break," said Matt.

"What about the rest of the guys in the house?"

"Their courses are all over the place; he's usually the last one to leave for class, but the place is never empty."

Matt's voice took on a slightly gentle tone as he spoke about Joe. And when he showed me all the video he'd shot, his face grew open and focused on the guy's actions. Apparently he'd developed a bit of a crush on ADA Stanton's kid...and I really couldn't blame him. Joe really did have those boy-next-door looks and lean clean limbs going for him, all of which was in perfect view when Matt snuck some tape of the guy lounging by the pool on a sunny day in a pair of red board shorts. I even noticed how golden and lightly touched by hair he was, reminding me more than a bit of Leon Cartucci. Then he rolled over to sun his back and showed his lovely little ass. My growler started up, since Leon had never let me touch his butt. I wondered if I could make this kid my proxy for that.

Grady had another practice session scheduled for that night, after his late lab, so I asked Matt to keep track of Joe for the next day while I scoped Grady out, myself. He quickly agreed and just before dark, I dropped him off near the frat house with the promise to pick him up in two hours then drove over to park near the sports complex.

What Matt didn't know was, I'd just dumped him. Because it was going down, tonight.

You see, I'd bought a workout bag, combination lock, rope and a pair of swimming shorts at a sports store while out picking up lunch, and I'd left them in the trunk. Then I'd snuck a towel from the motel into the bag along with one of the cameras while Matt was taking a dump; since he already had video of Joe, he didn't feel the need to ferry a camera with him. I'd told him I was going to check out Grady at the lab before his practice and maybe talk to him about helping us. He wasn't a hundred percent sure I was telling him the truth but he accepted it since he never thought I might abandon him. I had no idea what Matt would do once he realized I had; I just hoped he was smart enough to vanish once he heard what happened.

I pulled into student parking, near the sports complex and got as close to the pool entrance as I could. Needless to say, I wasn't worried about having the proper permit. Then I pulled the gym bag out of the trunk, slung it over my shoulder and headed for the complex. I was hoping this old guy who manned the night desk was still there and would remember me, and let me in without my student ID. If not, I had a Plan B — but I got lucky. He was hunkered over some paperwork, gripping his pencil as if he'd like to break it in half with his two fingers.

"Willard," I called out, using my best *Lady-Bird-Diction*.

The second he looked up his face brightened and he said, "Lazarus, ain't seen you in a 'coon's age." The first time he'd said that to me I had to ask him what it meant, and he told me it had something to do with how long raccoons can live...but a black friend of mine said it was racist. I never did find out exactly how, or which was the truth.

"Been comin' in early, thanks my schedule and work," I shot back at him. "But now the job's ended and I can go back to bein' me, again."

I went straight for the sign-up sheet, not even bothering to offer him any ID — only there wasn't any sheet. So I faked just collapsing against the counter to hide my surprise.

"Got your card?" he asked.

"Aw, I don't even have my wallet, Willard. Can I just sneak in some laps to clear my head?"

"Big boys're real hard-assed about that, now."

"It's after eight on a Wednesday night. They're all workin' on their fourth cocktail or snort of coke or somethin'. Please. I don't wanna have to crawl all the way back to my dorm. I mean, it's not like you don't know me."

It took him a moment but he finally worked up a visitor's pass with his name as my sponsor. "Just in case. Tell 'em you're my sister's kid an' thinkin' of comin' here."

"You are a gentleman and a scholar."

"Bullshit right back at ya," he laughed then buzzed me in.

I grabbed a locker next to the toilet and shoved everything in. The one sure thing about being in the water is, it makes you want to pee — and I figured that would be the perfect time to jump Grady. Plus it wasn't that far from the room where Quarterback and I had our first rendezvous and using that for my next *fling* would be poetic justice — well, in my own mind.

I changed into the shorts. I wasn't too crazy about the loose pouch liner, but they were on special and I was nervous my card wouldn't have enough left on it to pay for everything (I think I just squeaked by). Once I was adjusted, I strode to the pool, wetted myself and dove in.

It wasn't until that moment that I realized I hadn't been swimming since I joined Jake in Denmark. It had already been edging into winter, so the beaches were too cold, and while they had heated, indoor pools like this one — and I'd been using the indoor tennis courts and backboards to teach at — it had just never occurred to me to go to one. But the second the water enclosed me, I felt as if I'd returned home, and I swam half the length of the pool before coming up for air then slipped into a slow and easy stroke to just luxuriate in the wonderful feeling of it. I loved the sensation of water gliding past me. Loved the near-weightlessness it gave me. Loved the push and pull of it all. It washed everything away and for right here and right now, it was just me and the water surrounding me. And my building turmoil and fear drifted close to peace.

I got to experience that for ten minutes before Grady and a posse of groupies — both male and female — appeared, and I jolted back to my new direction in life. The pack poured off in one direction to sit on the bleachers as Grady bounced down to the locker room — and watching him pass, still full of his own sense of self and all golden and elegant in attitude, I found my critter purring with anticipation.

The posse waited for him to come out to begin his warm-ups, chattering amongst themselves and ignoring the other members of the dive team as they got into doing their thing. When Grady finally did make his appearance, it was in a lovely black Speedo with slashes of color across his crotch and ass that added to the bulge and shape of them both. Damn, he'd grown better-looking since I'd seen him, last. His muscles defined to just the right degree. His waist slimmed just the right amount. His hair was cropped differently, in a way that offset his surfer-boy style. I had to studiously ignore him, even while still casting him quiet little glances as he strode around the pool to the diving platforms — and I grew almost breathless at the sight of his solid ass rocking atop those colt-like legs...which was *not* what I was expecting from myself.

His coach and the other divers began a patter that I couldn't follow, but I didn't care. Nor did his groupies — for the first half-hour; then they began drifting away in ones and twos. Practices like this can get pretty boring if all there is to watch is lovely men jumping into the water, over and over and over — unless you got a fetish for that...and I think for the first time I caught a glimmer as to why some men would. The way these boys paused at the top of the platform, feet together, deep in their own manner of visualizing a perfect dive, then stepped up to the edge in movements surprisingly like ballet, took another even more elegant pose and sprung into space to twist and turn and float down to the water until at just the last instant they'd jolt into a straight-edge and cut through the surface like it wasn't even there. Over and over and over, so that even the less attractive guys on the team took on this almost inhuman beauty.

Of course, Grady was the most glorious. I started doing the Australian Crawl when I was heading for the platform end and the backstroke for my return, going as slowly as possible so I could watch him climb the steps to the high board, station himself and take dive after lovely dive — each and every one of them exquisite. Why he hadn't already hit #1 in the rankings was beyond me.

Problem is, he just kept on going. And going and going, like that damned rabbit in that battery commercial. Soon I was beat. It had been too long since I'd done this many laps in the pool, and my shoulders and legs were not happy about it. I kept thinking, he *has* to take a piss soon — because I was about ready to bust and I hadn't had anything to drink; but he was holding it in like he was a fucking camel. Shit.

Finally I couldn't wait any longer, so I just got out of the pool and pattered in to the toilet and let loose, and oh my God, how wonderful it felt. So as I stood there and did my own version of going and going, I decided to shift to Plan B, which entailed grabbing him en route to the dorm and using the bushes. *Not* something I looked forward to. But as I was finishing off, he appeared beside me, gave me a glance that seemed to nearly recognize me then whipped out and started pissing.

My heart jumped. I immediately tucked away, slipped back to my locker and looked around. Nobody else there. Okay — everything was in place. The cops had a way to ID me. So now all I had to do was go for it, wait till someone came looking for him and make sure there was enough of a commotion to get their attention. Nice and easy.

Except that's when my inner beast began yowling at the

thought of making his perfection my own personal property. The creature was hungry and feeling proprietary and letting me know it from my head to my tits to my balls, but that was *not* the way I wanted to go so I kicked him back into his cage.

I powered the camera up and pulled out a towel to act like I was drying off but twisted it in readiness. My plan was to let him pass me, whip the towel around his neck and get control of him before he could say anything, then drag him and the camera into the steam room and — well, whatever happened, happened...until people noticed he was missing and came looking. Then would come the *nasty story* of how I'm linked to The Right Honorable Nathaniel Motherfucking Gilbert. Nice and easy...and no serious damage to Grady beyond getting felt up.

But then I looked at him, again — standing at that urinal, his feet planted apart, his elegant legs gliding up, the Speedo gripping his gorgeous ass, his slim hips and broad shoulders and clean arms, the whole image so fucking erotic my beast smashed through the cage, still howling with hunger.

Holy fucking shit, he was gorgeous. Too fucking beautiful. My breath grew shallow and my dick began to itch and I had the first glimmer of an idea that I was about to go a hell of a lot farther with Grady that I'd planned. After all, he and I had history. I'm a damn good-looking guy and he was gay and he'd blown me off when I made a pass at him, like I was a troll or skank or some two-bit queen out to tell the world she fucked a rock star. What the hell was wrong with him? Well — maybe this fucking faggot would do some fucking, after all. It'd be a hell of a lot more damning if I was caught with my dick up his ass and him begging for help, and fuck him for not wanting it to begin with; he would by the time I was done.

That last thought shot every nerve ending in my body straight to bat-shit crazy. I could just feel his tight, taut body twisting against mine, fighting me as I shoved him into the steam room. I could picture myself groping him and kissing him and tearing that Speedo down to his knees and ramming myself into him so hard, he'd think I was trying to come out his mouth (pun intended). I just knew it would be better than anything I'd ever done before — not even Orin would compare, and his had been gloriously fulfilling — so the very thought of it made me feel light-headed and on the edge of madness.

By now, I was hot and full and ready for it. Grady packed his dick away, pointing left, and turned to wash his hands and showed me, once again, just how fucking gorgeous he was and how big he promised to get when I got onto him since I knew exactly how to get him going, even if he was freaked out, and DAMN, can't Speedos be brutally sexy on the right body, with all that golden skin to rub and grab and touch against mine and —

"Hey, Tone. How's it goin'?"

— slammed into me. I jolted around to find Jake leaning against the lockers opposite me, dressed in the same clothes he'd been wearing the last time I saw him, his hands in his pockets, his legs crossed at his ankles, looking like sex incarnate.

For an instant, I lost track of reality. I actually thought I was seeing a ghost or hallucination. But then I saw the expression on his face, and while it would have looked nice and cool to anyone else, and everyone else would have heard only the gentleness of his tone of voice — I knew him too damn well. He was pissed as shit.

"What're you doing here?" snarled out of me faster than I could form a thought, my critter screaming from this new threat.

"No, Tone, question is, what're *you* doin' here?"

"You should be at home — with your family! You got no reason to be here!"

He stood straight, his dark eyes locked on me and blazing with anger. "You think I can't tell when you're up to some shit? You think I'm gonna sit around and let you fuck things up worse than you already have?"

"Dammit, Jake, you don't know what you're doing."

"The fuck I don't."

Then Grady pattered by, casting us a quick, wary glance as he headed back to the pool — and I was so shaken, as gorgeous as he was I didn't even watch him walk away.

But Jake did. And nodded. And called out, "Dude — doin' good!"

Grady looked around, surprised, caught a good look at my guy and smiled. "Thanks." Then he backed away, drinking him in before he spun around and vanished out the entrance. I guess Jake was anybody's type, he was so perfect — the little fuck.

"So — that's Grady Lowenthaal. Hot." He looked back at me. "But I never would of thought he's what you go for."

"Jake, shit — I had it all worked out, I had it set — "

"Yeah, that's you, Tone," he sneered. "Five steps ahead of everybody and so busy pattin' yourself on the back for it, you don't notice when it's you gettin' fucked over — shit, *won't* notice till it's too late."

He was leading up to something, and normally I'd have let him lead, but I was way off kilter. Seriously — him being here? Now? Just as I'm about to do what I agreed to do to keep him safe? What the fuck was going on? "How did you find me?"

"Matt."

"MATT?!" That little fuck. I'll rip him a new one. "How'd he get hold of you?"

"He didn't. When you and I did our little thing in the men's room, I saw a piece of paper fall out of your jacket pocket. It had Matt's mobile phone number on it, so the second you entered dad's building, I called him. You spooked the shit outta him."

The little fuck'd be lucky if that's *all* I did to him, now. "What did he tell you?"

"What *didn't* he? Shit, the poor guy's about to fall apart from all your crap, he's so afraid you're gonna hurt somebody." Shit, Matt *hadn't* spilled everything. "And you're sayin' you're open and honest with me. Bullshit."

"Jake, you don't know what I had to do to — to — "

"Get my dad to take me home, last night? My father, the sneaky-assed control freak? Who never did shit for nobody he didn't want to?" I nodded. He almost relented. "Well — y'know, I gotta admit, I really did *want* to think he was being straight with us. Even after talkin' to Matt and hearin' what you had him doin', I was hopin' it was just bullshit stuff. And most o' the night was really cool."

"I know," I said. He raised his eyebrows in question. "He sent me video."

"Why?"

"Proof. Part of the deal."

"And your end's takin' out that diver?"

I shook my head. "I — I wasn't going to — "

"Tone, please — don't lie to me. When I come up, just now — that look on your face — I've seen it before. That day in my gramma's house? When you chucked me 'cross the room?"

It felt like a fist slammed into my chest. I'd nearly broken his back. Then I'd snuck off like a dog, leaving him to his own thoughts about me. Yet he'd still come looking for me. I felt like shit. It seems no matter how hard I try to keep from hurting him, I wind up hurting him.

"I — I was just going to drag him into the steam room — and let someone catch me — catch me — "

"I told you — don't lie to me! You promised not to lie to me!"

"I'm not. That was the plan. But then I — I saw him and — and something inside me — there's something that I can't — something animalistic and I can't control and it came roaring up and — " I couldn't continue.

"Uh-huh. Why were you doin' this, to start with?"

"Judge Gilbert's running for the senate. I — I'm here to stop him."

"Aw, Tone," and he actually seemed disappointed.

He came over, pulled my clothes from the locker and handed them to me, telling me to get dressed without a word. Like he couldn't even think of what to say to me. That cut deeper than his anger ever had and ninety percent of my anger dissipated. I pulled my jeans on, shaking. I was finally beginning to wonder if I *had* screwed up, if I'd gone too far, if I'd driven him away — and if I had, I didn't know if I could keep living.

I know, I know — I'd been planning to cut off contact with him, but that was when I had a greater purpose to it. That was when he'd be back with his family and had a chance at happiness and would still be thinking of me. Faraz was right, but only to a point. I didn't want Jake pining for me; I just wanted him — hell, I just wanted him to be thinking about me so I could draw strength from that and now that this illusion had been snatched away, Jake cutting me off would be worse than death.

He seemed to notice how unstable I was so took the towel and finished drying off my hair. "So, Tone — while you were havin' fun thinkin' you were as smart as my dad, did he mention he's been to Texas recently? More than once?" He must have seen my eyes saying, Excuse me?! Because he added, "Didn't think so. But then the only reason I found out is, when Mira heard I'm from this fuckin' state — she's his wife — she took me aside and asked if I'm the reason he kept goin' there. He thought she didn't know, but only an idiot thinks he can keep shit like that secret from the woman he's married to. She was afraid he wanted to get back with my mom, he'd been so sneaky about it. You know what I think it was?"

He didn't have to tell me. That last bit of data had shattered all my stupidly-blind-self-certain-mental-finagling and brought me straight down to earth, just like Icarus only faster than having my feathers melt out from under me. "He was helping Gilbert prepare for his Senate run."

"Maybe you ain't as dumb as I thought. But of course, that ain't all. I figure he was also preppin' to neutralize a possible problem for Gilbert. And I wonder who that is."

Oh, shit. Me. Of course. I was the guy who'd go bat-shit crazy to stop the fuck, even if it meant the end of me — as I'd so willingly told Faraz. I'd have raised issues that would hurt Gilbert's campaign — like him refusing to let Collie out on bond and letting a number of men who'd been assaulted make deals with Stanton to keep their rapes secret. Suddenly I wondered if they hadn't actually targeted straight men, after Jake and up till Collie, since they're the type who'd be inclined to want the whole thing to just vanish. Whether or not Gilbert had done anything really illegal was immaterial; merely being part of that would stain his self-proclaimed *law and order* reputation.

As for me — I'm the nut case already accused of raping one guy, suspected of raping another, had brutalized and assaulted a young Texas Ranger, had flipped off the Texas AG by going to Denmark to live with Jake...and now I've come back to jump the bones of a major sports figure. And I was dumb-ass enough to think people would believe me when I told them I was doing it all for Nathaniel Carson Gilbert, the Third? That would render anything I said against the prick meaningless crap from a skank, and all evidence would become questionable, at best. And then everything could be laid off on Nussewald and Stanton, and Gilbert's campaign might even benefit from the *attempt at smearing his good name.*

Oh, and if you think Stanton wouldn't sit still for being made the current goat, consider this — I'd even provided Faraz with video of the man's son. It wouldn't take all that much to convince him if he didn't play ball with Gilbert, little Joe would find his way into that holding cell and his end might be as hideous as Collie's. And Stanton had helped set it up so he wouldn't even know till it was too late. On top of that, I'd already gotten the impression Faraz had adjusted the data I'd gathered and had it all ending with those two. I'd have nothing to back my story up.

Shit. Jake was right. I *was* a total fucking idiot.

I grew weak and leaned against the lockers to keep from dropping to my knees. "I — I was just trying to protect you."

"Tone, since when am I that easy to break? I been through worse 'n you and I'm still here."

The last of my anger vanished into nothingness. The critter slunk back to his shadows without even so much as a whimper. My brain slipped into neutral, and all I could say was, "I'm sorry. I'm so sorry."

"Y'know, I think that's the first time you ever said that to me."

"Bullshit."

"Said it and meant it. Now — will you be honest with me?" And the way he asked gave me no choice.

I nodded, drained. I was finished dressing so everything else went into the bag and I slipped it over my shoulder. It wasn't until then that I finally had nerve enough to look Jake straight in the eye. And my heart leapt for joy — because he had this What'm-I-gonna-do-with-you expression that told me maybe — maybe things weren't over, yet. All I had to do was tell him the truth and — and he and I could work it out.

"Guess we better go pick up Matt," I said, "so I don't have to tell the story twice."

Jake rolled his eyes. "He's outside, waitin'. And you're gonna pay me back every fuckin' penny this bullshit's cost me."

I almost laughed as he and I headed for the door. My dear sweet cheap-assed Jake. Could he be more perfect? I turned to walk backwards so I could watch him. "You got here fast."

He shrugged. "I was supposed to stay the night at dad's, but Matt called so I snuck out and caught an early plane. I spoke to Matt the second I landed, found out what you were up to and made it over to that frat house in ten minutes to pick him up. I figure by now my dad knows I know what he pulled."

I stopped. He stopped with me. "Jake — do you?"

He looked at me and the curtains pulled away from his eyes to reveal anger and pain and betrayal and I knew before he told me, "If he was part of this from the beginnin' — yeah, I got a pretty good fuckin' idea."

"I wish you hadn't found out."

"Why not?"

"You wanted to be part of your family, again, and — "

He looked to the heavens with a huge sigh then slipped a hand around to the nape of my neck and shot his dark eyes deep into mine. "Tone, why do you have to be such a meddly-assed control freak?"

Straight to the gut. "Like your father?" I snapped.

"Yeah, like my dad," he snapped back. "You always gotta be into stuff. Always gotta be managin' stuff. And on top of it, you take on responsibilities that ain't yours to take. What — you can't just let things be?"

"I want you to be happy."

"And cuttin' yourself out of my life's gonna do that, how?"

"Jake, I've hurt you — made things worse for you in — in ways you'll never understand. I'm not good for you. Or right for you."

"You stupid fuck," he said, back to being weary and sad. "You got no idea what's right for me."

"I know you better than you think. You're decent and real and

— and shit — why would a guy like you even want to be with some psychotic fuck like me?" I was so damned close to tears.

"You want an answer to that question?"

No. "Yes."

"Do you? Really?" I pulled in a deep breath and looked him straight in the eye. He nodded. "Did you know my dad had a wolf for a pet?" On that, I gave him a definite *what-the-fuck's-this-all-about* look. "Uncle Ari told me. He found it as a cub on our country estate. Raised it. And treated it like shit. Hit it. Played tricks on it. Ignored it. Chained it to a post and left it without food or water. Showed it off to his friends in Tehran. The only reason that wolf lived is 'cause Uncle Ari fed it and cared for it — probably ninety percent of the time. And the wolf liked him — but every time it saw dad, it yipped and howled for joy. You wanna know why? That wolf — he saw dad as part of his pack — and that is where a wolf's loyalty lies. With his pack. With his mate. No matter how much of an asshole he turns out to be."

Ouch.

"That's me with you, Tone. You're my mate. I knew it the first time I saw you followin' me down the street. I knew it when you came into my gramma's place. I knew it when you knocked me on my ass for tryin' to fuck you. No matter how much of a shit you are, no matter what happens from now on, I'm always gonna — shit, I'm gonna yip and howl for joy when I see you. And dude, you need to understand somethin' — it's all on you as to how you treat me, from now on. Shit — forever. Because I can't end this, Tone. You say you can't, but you just tried to. Me — I'll never be able to. Even if you *do* end it, I'll never be able to. And you never understood that about me?"

His eyes brimmed with tears. His face was so completely open and vulnerable and wounded. His hand shook a little on my neck. He was my Jake, he'd always be my Jake, and I'd never — *never* ever doubt him, again. No matter what. No matter what. And Jesus Christ, I wanted to hold him and tell him I'd never do anything — *any*thing ever again to hurt him — and mean it.

But as sure as I was of him, I was just that unsure about myself. Scared to death I would hurt him some more. Terrified of

297

letting him down, again. Because I knew me. I knew if something came along and hit the right buttons, I'd go bat-shit fucking crazy, again, and might crush him without meaning to — like I'd almost done, just now — all the while thinking I was doing what was right. I really was this — this stupid, fucked-up junkie locked into his own special needs. And here was this wonderful guy — this great guy telling me it didn't matter, that he'd always be there for me — and I finally understood why he didn't want to tell me this, because it put responsibility for us on my back and the weight of it so overwhelmed me, I almost stopped breathing and my heart stopped beating and my mind went blank.

It was all I could do to smile at him and whisper, "Okay."

"You're gonna have to prove it," he said, smiling. "Prove how good a boy you can be. Every day."

I pulled him close and let the words whisper from me, "With you — I'll always be good."

His voice went sing-song. "That's not what I mean, Tone."

I took a deep breath. "I'll be as good as I can be. So long as you're around to give me a good kick in the ass when I threaten to go crazy."

He gave me a peck on the cheek and smiled. "I don't believe in domestic violence. Maybe Mira can help you figure out how to change your ways." I looked at him in askance and he added, "My step-mother; I told you her name. Turns out she's a psychiatrist."

"You want me telling the mother of your brothers and sisters about me?"

He grimaced. "Okay, point taken — but she's good for a referral."

"For you, anything."

Then he grinned and opened the door and we bounced outside — to find half a dozen patrol cars surrounding the sedan I'd rented, with a dozen cops standing around chatting. Matt was talking to one of them, his big eyes even bigger. And the second they heard the door, they all looked at me and Jake — and I froze.

Because in the middle of it all was Officer Arlen Thomas, looking very pissed off. He saw me and came strolling over with a snarling grin that would have fit on a hyena as it was about to rip your heart out.

And he said, "Hey there, son. Mr. Blaine. Looks like you boys and I got some things to talk about."

— EIGHT —

The three of us were taken down to police headquarters, each in a separate patrol car and each put into a separate interview room. And me telling Thomas neither Jake nor Matt knew anything meant zero to him.

"I'll decide what you know an' what you don't," he snarled in his lowest, steadiest voice, yet. But as hard-assed as he was, he wasn't really ready for Jake's push back.

"Fine," my guy said, nice and even and with no malice in tone or attitude. "Please call this number; it's the Danish Consulate. They're open to handling Iran's consular necessities and will see to it that a representative is sent to be with me during the interrogation." And he handed Thomas a business card. Shit — plus I was *really* floored at how precise his English suddenly was; my dude was, like, totally educated.

Thomas all but smirked at him. "You're American."

Jake sneered back and raised his hands, saying, "May I show you something?" He carefully reached into his back jeans pocket and pulled out his Iranian passport. "This says otherwise."

Thomas took it and looked it over. "Okay, you got dual citizenship. No entry stamp. You come in on your US passport?"

"Doesn't matter. I'm also a resident of Denmark and I've applied for citizenship there. And please don't think you can ignore my request. I informed the Danish authorities of where I was going and what my past situation has been with the state of Texas' legal system. The Danes take situations like this very seriously. They even faced down the Nazis over their Jewish citizens. You think you're tougher than them?"

"Denmark was overrun by Germany."

"Which shows how stupid and limited you are in your awareness."

Thomas fielded the insult without much more than an intake of breath. It was obvious his instinct was to tell Jake he's full of shit, but he was in an area of so many grays it was better to take the safest course. So Jake, Matt and I were held as material witnesses to something he'd make up later, and now I was waiting for the interrogation to begin.

Of course, there was only one way for this to go, so far as I could tell. Me taking full responsibility for everything and promising to cop any plea so long as Jake and Matt were released. They knew nothing. Nothing. It was all me and if the DA or the AG didn't go along with it, I'd mess their cases up so badly, they'd wish to God they had. And since we'd already been through something just as complicated before, I figured they'd know enough about me to expect not only could I do it — but I was totally willing to.

What surprised me most was how calmly Jake had taken Thomas on. Nose to nose from the first word without even so much as a hiss or spit. Maybe he was right. Maybe I was trying too hard to protect him from things he could easily handle himself. Problem was, he didn't know how focused Thomas could get, and how willing the powers that be would be to make up charges against him just to get themselves out of a jam. What Nussewald had pulled was childish crap compared to what Texas would do. Shit, we'd had a governor who'd allowed an innocent man to be executed for political expediency's sake, and been re-elected by a huge margin. Once you're into killing prisoners for something that evidence shows wasn't even a crime, you know they'll have no trouble messing with your world to cover up a crime of their own. So the only thing I could do was threaten to mess with them worse. And boy, would I.

After I'd sat there for nearly two hours, Thomas strolled in with a man I'd never seen before — not in person, anyway — Judge Nathaniel Carson Gilbert, the Third. He was shorter than I expected, and thin, but you could see the resemblance between him and Nat-four. What surprised me most, however, was his face was light and happy and his eyes sparkled with humor.

"You're younger than I thought you'd be," he said without bothering to introduce himself, letting me know up front he'd been keeping track of me as much as I had him.

I shrugged. "My mother says I was born fifty years old."

"I can see it. So — basically what we're dealing with here is a sociopathic personality. Interesting."

"Some would agree with you."

"But not your boyfriends, I assume?" And he waved a hand to indicate Jake and Matt were still being held.

I shrugged. His smile widened. He really was having fun. Okay, fine, motherfucker. Let's have fun.

I leaned forward and asked, "Tell me — were you smiling when you helped murder Collier Winston-Royce?"

"I didn't help kill anyone." His manner told me I hadn't made a dent in his pleasure.

"Liar."

"You have no evidence of that."

"Who needs it? These days, all you have to have is some good innuendo backed by some glorious gossip and the right media outlet to get it going. I prefer liberal bloggies, myself."

"And you think people will believe I had something to do with that child molester's death?"

So...the motherfucking son-of-a-bitch wanted to play dirty. "The so-called victim was in his twenties and admitted to lying about the abuse and getting his cousin to set the murder up. Which you knew. In fact, you knew Collier was innocent of any crime. But I guess that don't matter in Texas, now does it?"

He leaned forward and rested his chin on his folded hands, still having fun, the motherfucker. "He was homosexual, so I'm certain people will care." Said in a voice that dripped with honeyed condescension.

Suddenly I felt like I was playing chess against a computer. No matter what you do, the damned thing's electronic brain had access to a million variations of every move you might want to make and could parry, instantly — meaning, you can't beat it. Because he was right; the only way the majority of Texans would give a shit about anything I'd say now is if I could prove this prick wanted to have their white virgin sons carried off to be butt-fucked by black men in the Congo — and even then he'd have his very loud defenders who *believed* he was a good man and any comment against him was slanderous, no matter what the evidence, since everybody knows proof means nothing in the court of public opinion.

So I shrugged. "Okay. They won't. So what do we do now?"

That brought the hint of a frown to his face. "You're not putting up much of a fight."

"We were fighting? Really?"

That made him think, for a moment. Then he said, "Very well. Tell us everything that happened and I'll see to it your sentence is as lenient as possible."

"Okay, on one condition."

And that brought a blink. "No conditions."

"You release Jake and Matt."

"I told you, no conditions."

"Then no deal. I'm innocent of all charges. See you in court — and please try to explain why the judge overseeing my case came into the interrogation and tried to make me take a deal before I was allowed to see my attorney. His name's Angelo Castillo and he's damn good. And he belongs to the ACLU, too."

"What good do you think that will do?"

"None."

And *that* actually surprised him. "Then why do it?"

"To fuck with you."

"No need to use that kind of language."

I smiled, laced my fingers together, propped my chin upon them and said as sweetly as I could, "Oh, I guess I *will* start fighting, now — just to fuck you up."

Any offer of cooperation vanished completely from his face. He leaned back and said, "I'd been told you were an intelligent young man."

"I'm told you like to watch men get raped by lots of other men. Gives you a real rush."

"Once again you threaten me with something no one will

believe."

"Won't they? Look what happened in Florida, and to a good decent member of the GOP. There's lots of people willing to latch onto the idea that anyone even vaguely associated with homosexual actions is deep-down queer, no matter how right-wing-nut they are. I wonder how many people'll wonder if you're really one of them closet fags, out to get into office 'fore he comes out and changes to one of them-there libruls pushin' their fuckin' homo-sexual agenda?"

"And you'll even go so far as to claim we had sex?" His smile was back.

"Naw, nobody'd believe I was that desperate — unless it's for money, and that'd make me a whore which you'd have a hell of a time proving beyond your self-delusional base of supporters."

He chuckled. "You'd be surprised at the size of my base."

"Pun intended?"

His grin widened — and he rose and left the room. Thomas just shook his head.

"Son, you are an idiot."

"Of course. It'd be *so* much better if I trusted you and came clean and told you everything I've ever done that's wrong and believed you'd keep your end of the bargain and not hang Jake and Matt out to dry."

"Jake Blaine — or Dayra-Bendario, whatever his name is — got released just before we came in here. He wasn't kiddin' 'bout them Danes."

Shit, was that why Gilbert had come in here? To see how much trouble I'd make for them on top of a budding international incident? I mean, I'd applied for Danish citizenship, too. And Thomas knew Jake's real last name; how could he know that unless the Danes had come in and — wait, he'd seen Jake's Iranian passport. No — I still didn't know if I could believe him, so I didn't relax. "And Matt?"

Thomas shook his head, disgusted. "He's on his way to county jail an' — "

"No," shot out of me.

"Yes. He's bein' charged with kidnappin' an' assault on a

police officer, an' he'll be — "

"Thomas, he didn't have anything to do with that!"

"The hell he didn't. You ever hear 'bout this thing called DNA? That boy's is all over Benny."

What the fuck? "He gave you a DNA sample?"

"He will. An' you an' me both know how it'll come back."

The son-of-a-bitch, he was going to nail Matt for Benny, all thanks to me.

"You can't do that, he'll die," I shot at him. And the bastard knew it. He knew Matt'd be brutalized by the guys they have in there — hell, it may even be the same style setup as before and he'd be attacked and he couldn't handle it like me. Shit, he'd nearly come unglued just thinking about me going after Grady and Joe.

Thomas shrugged. "Should've figured that out 'fore he attacked Marquez."

"Matt didn't do shit, you stupid fuck! It was all me!"

"Shut up with that language!" burst out of him, and he was close to hitting me. "What your little buddy did to Benny's unforgivable. The guy's catatonic and — "

What? Wait a minute. Benny was in a catatonic state? "What makes you think Matt's the one who fucked Benny over? Why don't you think it was me?"

"Don't matter, son; it's either you or him since nobody else was there an' you damn well — "

"You don't know! You haven't found out which one of us butt-fucked your buddy. Who told you it was Matt and not me?" He hesitated, finally realizing he'd said the wrong thing and suddenly a memory sliced into my brain — McNeil Shirripa, one of the guys who'd been abused in holding cell 6, had been arrested by a Texas Ranger. BAM! All the connections cascaded into place. Benny hadn't told Thomas a damned thing. Hell, he's already been slipping into a nasty shock when I left and probably *was* catatonic, especially after what I'd done to him. So how could Thomas know it was just me and Matt there? How could he know the other guys had left? Simple.

"You're part of it. You know what Benny did and who he's

working for and he was set up and you're helping 'em get away with it, you son-of-a-bitch! You're FUCKING PART OF IT!" I bolted to my feet and jumped at him, screaming, "IF YOU SET MATT UP LIKE YOU DID COLLIE, I'LL KILL YOU, MOTHERFUCKER, I'LL FUCKIN' KILL YOU!"

He slammed me against the wall but I twisted and sent him over the table. Before I could dive after him, other cops poured into the room and fought to hold me back but I was seriously bat-shit crazy and still fighting hard to get at Thomas and slung a couple of the fuckers off me before I felt a slam to my back as I was tasered for the second time in four days. But this one was like a thousand pins being shoved into my skin as the same time. I dropped to the floor and they piled on and secured my hands behind my back, tight. Then I got tasered twice more, just for the hell of it, before two of them yanked me to my feet.

I saw two others helping Thomas up. I was shaking from the intensity of the explosion in my nerves but I still spit at him, "You call yourself a cop? You call yourself a fucking Ranger!? You're a fucking disgrace, you motherfucker!"

Thomas glared at me then snarled, "Hold him for transport. I got enough to take him back to Austin." Then he cast me a wicked smirk. "I told you you're an idiot."

That rattled me, a little, and kicked a small part of my brain into gear. Had he said what he did just to piss me off? Was I that easy? No, it made too much sense, now. I didn't know when he'd become one of Faraz's boys — if it was after we'd met the last time or if he'd been helping them all along, maybe even helped them set up his partner — but he was definitely one now. Him letting me know it was just me and Matt in that warehouse with Benny — that had been proof positive enough for me. Because Matt was smart enough and scared enough to have lawyered up to keep from telling him anything, and him mentioning Benny was catatonic had been too true an off-handed revelation. So what did his last comment mean?

Whatever the reason behind it, Thomas had succeeded in setting the beast free, and it was pissed. Snapping and snarling and just fucking *daring* anybody to be dumbass enough to mess with it.

I was ready to scorch the earth around me, and I didn't care who got caught up in it. So it took three more taserings to get me into a police cruiser, and then I only let them because it felt like my heart was about to explode.

I was driven straight to county jail, cursing the drivers the whole way, unable to stop the spew of *fuckers* and *assholes* and *mother-fucking-sons-of-bitches* and such. It was nearly midnight, and in the darkness I caught an even better idea of the intimidating reality of the jail as we passed unlit, run-down buildings and vacant lots cleared of trees up to that pair of long, four-story brick structures with tiny slits of light for windows and a black outer wall separating them from the area, and drove by the well-guarded entrance, zipped down the sharp, small incline between the two buildings and backed into the tiny loading dock. But this time, instead of impressing me with just how powerless I was, it only made my beast angrier.

Two cops dragged me from the car through the thick metal door and down that short bland corridor to the intake area. The same two deputies as before sat at computer terminals behind the counter and I was shoved to one of them, where the same fat bored slug ignored me.

"Antony St. Lazarre," snapped one of my cops. "Hold for transport."

"Got nobody on the manifest by that name," came the dead-as-can-be reply from the slug (Huerra?), who once again didn't even look up. Man, to say I was experiencing the déjà vu-ness of it all was an understatement.

"Why don't you check, first, asshole," I snapped.

He looked at me with the same dead eyes — and smiled that same hideous smile. "Put him in *F* till I pull things together."

I got the feeling he'd be taking his time, again, so snapped, "Put a rush on it, motherfucker. Don't wanna be here a week, like last time."

His eyes lost their deadness and he tried to make me scared of him with this really, really mean look, but I was still angry so just stuck my tongue out at him and laughed.

I was taken straight to the cell. No inspection for contraband.

307

No changing into the jailhouse issue jump suit. Just through that thick door and down the hallway that lead past the thick-barred cages backed up to a concrete block wall, and thick-barred sliding doors cut horizontally by a narrow slit for meals, each holding the same scary guys awaiting arraignment or transport or just being held till it was decided which area of the jail they'd serve their thirty-day sentence, all of them still a mixture of black, brown and low-rent white-trash with the occasional Asian. There weren't as many as last time, but they still yelled the same shit as before and I yelled back and kept it up until we got to the last cage — from which there came this dead silence in counterpoint to the nastiness of the boys.

Because it was empty.

I was shoved in and my hands were left flex-cuffed behind my back, and they were starting to hurt. "You gonna take these off?" The cop just slammed the cell door closed and left. I screamed after him, "Fucking *cunt*! Fucking motherfucking CUNT!"

He cast a glare back at me but kept walking and exited the area, even as the other prisoners yelled the same thing after him, laughing and jeering in fellowship. It was royal.

Then Bored Guard wandered through the door and took a couple of prisoners away, leaving the first cell almost empty. I barely paid attention.

I looked around. They called this one *F*? It was the same fucking cage as before...except there was no pane in the ceiling for the camera. So — they'd renamed the cells, but why not leave the camera? All the other cells had those glass panels in the ceiling.

Then I heard Bored guard come back and take two more prisoners away. The noise was growing lighter.

Shit, I needed to pee, again, but first I needed to know — "Matt?" I screamed. "Matt, it's Antony. You in here?"

The remaining guys in the cells screamed and raved and ranted back at me but I ignored them. Waited for them to quiet down. And I heard nothing, in response.

"Matt? Are you here? It's Antony, man. C'mon!"

More noise from the scum. Nothing to tell me Matt was around. Maybe Thomas was lying about him. Maybe Matt was still back in an interrogation room. Maybe he'd said that just to add to my provocation. I now wished I'd broken the bastard's neck.

I still had to pee but needed my hands in front to do it. So I sat on the table with my feet on a bench, slipped my hands under my ass and got them down to about my knees, then drew my left leg up tight and twisted my foot and managed to slip the cuffs past it, then I did the same with my right foot. It wasn't easy and I felt like I was about to pull my arms out of their sockets and slice through my wrists near the end of each one, but I managed to at least wind up with my hands in front of me so I could use the toilet.

I noticed Bored guard taking away a couple more prisoners and wondered if they'd started up a night court system here. Last time, I'd had to wait till the magistrate came to get a bail hearing. Maybe Collie's death had effected at least one positive change.

I shook off the pain, went to the commode — and nearly pissed my jeans with fright. Someone was huddled in the table's shadows, shivering and quiet. "What the fuck?"

"Please, please, I didn't do anything," whimpered out of him, and he sounded brutally pathetic. The beast snarled but didn't feel very threatened.

"Dude, it's okay," I said, fighting to be soothing. I couldn't really see him but it was obvious he wasn't a regular, like me. "It's okay. Neither did I." Liar that I am.

"I — I shouldn't be here. I shouldn't."

Then I noticed he was in street clothes, too. I glanced at the other prisoners; they all wore jump suits. Okay, creature got wary and wondering — but immediate needs had to be met.

"Uh, listen — excuse me a second, okay?" Then I stepped over him and unzipped and whipped out and took my leak, and when I was done I turned to look at him, saying, "Man, I needed that so bad — " And my voice died. I finally got a good look at the guy, saw he was dressed in old K-Mart special pants and tennis shirt with a pair of ragged Topsiders on his feet — and I knew him from somewhere. "Dude, what's your name?"

He looked at me, his eyes dark and sad and beautiful, and recognition flared through them followed by fear. And then it hit me — "Sean? Your name's Sean, right?"

"You're that guy — the one that got Rattler — got him so pissed. Oh, shit. Oh, shit. Don't touch me! Don't come near me!" He scrambled up and bolted for the bars, screaming, "I don't belong in here! I didn't do anything!"

The other prisoners screamed and ranted and laughed at him as he called down the hallway, even as Bored Guard took a couple more of them away, leaving only a few behind. He didn't even glance over.

I went to Sean, trying to be soothing. "Sean, it's okay. It's okay. I'm not gonna do anything to you, buddy. C'mon, what happened with Rattler was — "

He jolted away, shaking with fear, his voice quivering. "You're that guy — that guy — you made me — you made me."

"Made you what?" What a stupid question; I knew exactly what I'd made him do. Hell, I could still picture what a lovely image he made, fucking the prick.

"You made me. You got Rattler pissed and he don't believe me. But you MADE ME!"

I sighed and sat on a bench. He was hysterical and I had a feeling if I'd done anything more than just sit there, he'd have lost it completely. Instead, he crouched in the corner where the bars met the *L* part of the wall, his eyes locked on me, shivering. Jesus, he was a mess, and it made my beast want to wait to see what happened. So I didn't say anything for a good ten minutes, just let him settle down.

And I heard Bored Guard take away more prisoners, twice, but still didn't think anything about it.

Finally, Sean stopped shivering and just cowered, his eyes never leaving me. Looking at him, I could see he still had the same basic looks — hell, it was almost like he'd gone into a holding pattern, physically. But his sad eyes were laced with a flittering, unfocused panic and his nails were bitten to the nubs. He was obviously close to a complete collapse...and it hurt to see him like this — hell, to see anyone like this.

I sighed. "You're still doing drugs. Dude, I told you — if you didn't stop — "

"He made me." The words were sharp and quick, more like

they were escaping him than anything else.

"Who made you?"

"He did. So long as I said okay, he wouldn't do it to me. Too. He did it to them. But he said. He wouldn't to me."

This was beginning to sound spooky. "Are you talking about Rattler? Uh, Vernon?"

He nodded, sharp and jagged. "Your fault, you know. He went crazy. Really pissed off."

Man, I did *not* like the direction this was taking. I shifted to another bench to get closer to Sean, and he pressed back against the bars, shaking again. I held up my hands, showing him they were still wrapped in the flex-cuffs.

"Look, Sean. My hands're tied. I can't hurt you in any way. See? See? I can't do anything." He slowly relaxed and turned his sad eyes on me, confused. "Tell me what happened to you," I continued. "What did Rattler do to you?"

"Not to me," he said, finally. "I — I made him money. The other. Other guys. One after the other. Started with Nick. He's in jail. Nick. Beat a guard up. Rattler's friends got him. Couple times. Other guys. Every one. Got a new posse. They have fun. Lots of fun. Lots of fun."

Holy shit — it sounded like Rattler was getting revenge against the guys I'd talked into fucking him over a year ago. And indications were, he was being brutal. And all because I'd turned the tables on him. Shit, I'd never thought about that being a possibility.

Then another possibility hit me — that Rattler was the guy who coordinated all the attacks in this cell. If he had guys he usually works with, now, maybe he was the guy who built a crew to jump the designated victim. Fake an excuse to book 'em, put 'em all in here and let Rattler direct the show — like he'd planned to do with me. Which made it sound more like a porn shoot — and yeah, that's what it basically was but still, you couldn't pull it off every time. So could that be what happened with Collie? Rattler hadn't made it and things got crazy and — and now that it'd been done to him, he was out doing it to anyone who'd crossed him?

Just like me?

Shit.

"Everyone?" I asked. Sean nodded. "But not you?"

Sean shook his head. "I make him money."

"How?"

"My dad. Got a nice business. I work there. Ship stuff for him. For Rattler. In boxes. To South Africa. He gives — gives me — "

"Tina?" I asked. "Is that what's screwed you up?"

He shook his head. "Can't do that. Messes me up. Makes me crazy. Too crazy. Gives me 'ludes."

"What's that?"

"Quaaludes. Bar — bar-bit — uates."

"Oh. Wait — those're addictive, aren't they?"

He shrugged. "Help me sleep. Can't sleep. Can't sleep. Folks had me on — on Ritalin. Since kid. Doesn't do it. Now. Nothing helps. Make me easy. Nothing."

Oh, shit. "Sean — how long've you been in here?"

"Yesterday. Since — uh — yesterday."

"Yesterday? Wednesday?"

"Too — uh, Tuesday."

"Alone!?" He nodded. Shit, no wonder the guy's freaking out; he's probably in withdrawal, sleep deprivation and paranoid psychosis. "What'd they arrest you for?"

He shrugged. "Just did. Won't let me. Call my dad. Get his lawyer back."

"*You* were the guy whose lawyer showed up?"

He nodded, jerky and really out of control. "Won't let me call my dad. Won't let me — won't let me — "

"But they have to! It's the law."

"So fuckin' what?" came this little growl behind me.

I jumped and spun about — and here was Rattler, same ratty goatee, same tatts, same hard-muscled body, looking as lean and mean as ever. And my heart dropped to my stomach. I now understood what Thomas had meant by me being an idiot.

I'd given him the excuse, in front of witnesses, to be arrested and booked and put in the county jail — right back in holding cell 6.

— NINE —

Okay, I know they call it *Holding Cell F*, now, but mingled in with this startling moment of absolute clarity about my situation came this stupid understanding of the significance of that letter. *F* is the sixth letter of the alphabet. Cute. And it's also the first letter in *fuck*...as well as *forced* and *fear* and *faggot* and *fun*. I actually wondered if the powers that be had chosen this particular cell with its silly designation as some kind of inside joke for them to chuckle over as they viewed the tapes of the men whose lives they'd ruined. To top it all off, *F* was also the first letter of *forgotten*, and I had a feeling that was about to happen to me.

Bored Guard brought Rattler up to the cell along with three other guys I didn't recognize — a pair of skinheads who looked like they spent their lives in the gym working on their muscular muscles and who wore tight t-shirts and even tighter pants with Doc Martens on their feet, and a guy dressed as a preppy frat brat but who was probably more comfortable in the same clothes as his buddies. Rattle wore a wife-beater under a cowboy shirt, casual jeans and his boots, and the closer he got the more he looked like he'd been working out, too. All of them were in cuffs, all of which were removed as they were herded through the door.

And then I noticed there were only two other prisoners left in the whole set of cells — that the place has been all but emptied — and after he closed holding cell 6's door (excuse me, *F*'s door) Bored Guard took those last two guys away. And the second they left the room, Rattler and his buddies moved out to flank me.

Okay, Thomas was right — I *was* a total fucking idiot, because not only had I put myself here, right where he and his bastard handlers wanted me, but even though I'd caught a glimmer of how nasty things could get within the state of Texas I hadn't understood just how deep the corruption ran. Clearing out the entire holding cell block? Bringing me and Sean in without so much as a real booking, so there'd be no paper trail, and in complete violation of our rights? Leaving Rattler and his boys in the same cell as me, despite knowing full well there was history between us? Not even Gilbert had that much pull. Nor did Thomas. Nor did they have the balls to do anything like this unless they knew it would be kept quiet...kept secret from the media...and have whatever happened explained away with some obnoxious flip-off of a press release that everyone would love.

And even if somebody *did* find out and raise hell about it, keep in mind — some prison guards in California were tried for arranging the rape of a prisoner, hit with plenty of evidence but they still got off. Same for any number of cops who get caught beating prisoners, even once the guys are subdued; I don't know of one who's been sent to jail for it. There was even an instance in Miami where a man called 911 to report that a couple of plain-clothes cops were beating a suspect and wound up being arrested by those cops and had charges made up against him, all of it caught on the 911 tape. They're still on the force. And in the Texas state prison at Huntsville, a teenage boy's pleas to be protected from the men who kept raping him were ignored, so he killed himself...and nothing happened to the guards or prison officials. So Rattler and his buddies could do anything they damned well wanted to me or Sean and odds were good they'd never even get charged for it. And here I was, hands cuffed, four against one.

Well — never let it be said I got smart in the face of my annihilation. My critter stood up straight and snarling. Teeth bared. Ready to go down fighting. And deep in the still-caring part of my brain I thought, Sean's right, he doesn't belong here — and I'll do whatever I can to protect him. So I backed away from them, spitting, "Hey, Vern, long time no see. Lookin' good, dude. You been workin' out?"

Rattler's buddies began edging around me. I guess he'd had warned them about what'd happened, last time. But him? He just strolled over to Sean, which was *not* where I wanted him to go. So

314

I said, "Looks like gettin' fucked did wonders for you."

Rattler just sneered at me and leaned against the bars, right by Sean. "Lessee what it does for you, cocksucker."

"Hey, buddy...it was YOU who sucked MY cock, remember?"

His sneer became a snarl. "Well it's you gonna take it in the mouth, today."

"Cool. Can I do yours first? It looked tasty when you shot your wad." And I licked my lips.

He chuckled. "Yeah, I'm a dumbass. My dick between your teeth? Fuck. Nope — you're gonna suck off Sean-y, here." Then he ruffled Sean's hair in a tender way, scaring the shit out of the poor guy.

Sean looked up at Rattler. "No, I — I — I — please, Rattler, I can't, I can't — "

Rattler pulled him to his feet by his hair.

My critter growled a warning. "*Vernon*! I coerced him into what he did. You know that." I turned to his buddies, who were pacing my slow move backwards. "You know, Vern's been fucked by half a dozen guys — and — and he came, twice. Really got off on it."

The most I got from any of them was a shrug off the Preppy one.

"They know what happened," said Rattler. "They're here for the game."

That didn't sound good. "What game?"

"Who gets to fuck *you* twice. Been playin' it a while. Fun, ain't it?"

"Fuckin' fantastic," said the skinhead to my left.

"I won, last time," said the skinhead to my right.

I hit the wall so raised my hands, smiling. "Okay, guys, just 'cause my hands're tied, don't think I can't break some bones."

"You won't," said Rattler.

"Don't be so...sure." My voice died. I'd just noticed Rattler was holding up a buck knife. He grinned and opened its gleaming blade with his thumb in one simple practiced move. It clicked into place and he pressed it to Sean's neck. His three stooges also pulled out knives of varying sorts and opened them. Okay...I guess

315

*none* of us got the cavity search. Well — one or two of these assholes I might be able to take, but all four and still keep Sean from being sliced to ribbons? No way. So I held my hands higher and said, "So — which one of you's cuttin' these things off?"

They just shook their heads. Talk about a bunch of sissy poseurs.

"Don't work like that," said Rattler. "Goes like this. You're gonna suck on Sean-y, here, while we fuck you. If you get Sean-y to cum while one of us is in you, that guy gets to fuck you, again. If he don't cum before we're done, we all get to fuck you, again."

"I see," I said. "What's in it for me?"

"We let you go," said Preppy.

"Till we wanna play, again." That came from Skinhead-left. "Remember that blond fucker with the great ass?"

"Nice tits. His buddy didn't cum. We all got him, again."

"And again," said Skinhead-right.

"This — this is what you're doing to Travis and — and Bryce and — and — ?" I had to fight to keep my voice level.

Rattler nodded. "Travis gives *good* head. I almost couldn't hold it till after my buddies were done."

"He the one we got three times?" asked Skinhead-right.

Rattler shook his head. "He's the dark-haired one."

"Right."

"Fuckin' wimp cried like a baby," said Preppy.

"I liked it when he came in his buddy's mouth," said Skinhead-left. "What was that shit's name? DJ? He was my favorite fuck."

"Lessee what you think o' this one," said Rattler. "Now, c'mon." Sean fought to keep from dissolving into tears as Rattler guided him to the same table he'd been fucked on. "Lie down, face up," he snarled. Sean did, shaking.

By this point, the three stooges were right up against me, each with his knife pressed against my torso. Preppy even began using his to slice the buttons off my shirt. I didn't move.

"Okay, Tony," said Rattler, "we can play it another — "

"It's ANTONY, motherfucker," I snapped.

"I'll call you what the fuck I want to, cunt. Now listen up —

you don't wanna play our game, fine. We'll take our turns fuckin' little Sean-y here." And he slit his knife up the length of Sean's tennis shirt, parting it neatly down the middle. Sean nearly screamed in fear. "An' you can watch."

"No, please, please — I didn't do anything — Rattler, I made you money — lots of money — "

"Not as much as I'm gonna make off this." He nodded to the ceiling.

I looked up and thought, Is there a one-way panel? No, it couldn't be. So why leave the damned camera in that spot? It couldn't — it wouldn't pick up — and then I noticed something I'd missed — little black plugs spaced at various points round the ceiling — and a couple of wires running up to similar plugs along the bars — with little holes in their tips. Were those lenses? Holy shit, was this cell loaded with tiny cameras feeding back to a laptop or two or three-dozen?

"You guys're makin' a fuckin' porno!" I shot out.

"That's what we're bein' paid for," sneered Preppy.

"Gay for pay," laughed Skinhead-left.

"You mean rape," I shot back.

All three of them shrugged in response. Okay, it really *was* rape for pay. Shit. Shit. Shit.

Rattler slid the two halves of Sean's shirt away to brush his knife over the poor guy's tits — and I could see the son-of-a-bitch had gone commando, because it was turning him on in ways that left nothing to the imagination. Sean began gasping and shaking with fear. Not the way for this to go, no sir.

"VERNON!" I snapped, loud and harsh. He looked at me. "He's *my* part of this game!"

Rattler stopped, wary. "You sayin' you'll play?"

I nodded. "But if you want me to get him up and get him off, if you cut him in any way, that becomes impossible. Or are you one of those cunts that cheats?"

Sean looked around at me, wildly, "No, I can't, I can't — you won't be able — "

"Sean, SHUT UP!" I shot at him. "You don't know what I can do. Hell, look at last time — I made you get it up and shove it in

Rattler's ass and cum. You think I can't do that, again? You got that little faith in me?"

Sean swallowed. "But — but, I'm not — "

"Doesn't matter," I said. "Just relax. You're mine, not his — not if he wants a real game."

Rattler stood up straight. "You really wanna play?"

By this point, Preppy had sliced off all my buttons and was caressing my exposed chest with his knife. So I looked at him and said, "So long as he's the first to fuck me." Then I blew him a kiss.

Rattler smirked. "Fine. Strip him."

BAM, the three of them grabbed me and tore at my shirt and jeans, mauling me as they went and using a combination of knives and hands to expose first my body and then my legs. The deck shoes vanished and my jeans lasted about two twists longer, and it seemed like in seconds I was naked and being hauled to where Sean lay, hands groping and probing and slapping and pinching me all over the place.

They slammed me face down over the end of the table, my ass exposed and my face in Sean's crotch. Rattler got up on the table and straddled Sean's belly, then used his knife to slice the guy's pants open, revealing another pair of flimsy briefs. He slit those off at the hips to reveal Sean's pretty, sloping, ringed dick all scrunched up and terrified of being touched. Rattler slipped a hand under it and held it up for me to examine as Sean cringed. "Good luck," Rattler sneered, then he climbed down off Sean and pulled out a mobile phone to record it.

Preppy's hands were digging into my ass like you wouldn't believe while Skinhead-left focused on my left leg and Skinhead-right focused on the other. None of them went anywhere near my dick, so I guessed they weren't into boys — just fucking people who can't fight back. I hoped Faraz liked what he saw.

"Hey, asshole," said Rattler, then chuckled at his own stupid pun, "they don't start fuckin' till you start suckin'." Thinks he's a fuckin' poet, and the hell with the pun.

So let's get it over with. "Sean, scoot down a little closer to me."

"What?" His voice still carried more than a little panic.

"Scoot down a little," I said. "I can't quite reach you." He hesitated, then shifted closer, to where I could run my lips over his dick. He cringed. I maneuvered my hands up to touch his balls, which was a weird position to be in because it looked a bit like I was praying to the great scrunchy penis. I chuckled at the stupidity of the thought and caressed the hair on Sean's legs. He jolted. So I whispered, "It's just a blow job, Sean. Just a blow job. Close your eyes. Picture the best blow job you ever had. Something long and luxurious and elegant."

"I — I don't — I never — " he gasped.

"Shh...shh...relax. It's all on me, dude. It's all on me. It's my fault you're here. I made you join us, remember? I molested you. Forced you to get hard and put you into Rattler's ass. Remember?" I didn't look at him as I spoke, just nuzzled his balls and lovely sloping dick. He smelled a little like roasted peanuts. "So relax. Dream. Think of where you'd like to be. Who you wish was doing this to you. My mouth'll be their mouth. My tongue'll be their tongue. My hands, their hands. This is not hate, Sean. This is not to be feared. This is giving satisfaction. This is making love."

I worked my hands up around his crotch to caress the hair on his lower belly. Felt Preppy's paws dig into my butt cheeks. It sent my stomach into flips of anger and my heart racing. I wanted to hurt all of these fuckers. Not Sean — no, I'd grown proprietary over him. He was my creation. My responsibility. So I focused on making it as easy for him as I could.

It took a few moments, but Sean's shivering lessened. His squirming ceased. His breath grew less and less ragged. He finally lay still and his dick began to shift about, gentle in its movements. His balls danced up and down as he became more and more relaxed. I nuzzled him, some more.

"Do you see it, Sean?" I whispered. "Do you feel it?"

His breath was steadier. Deeper. "Yeah."

"Describe it to me."

"The beach. At Cabo. Spring break. Went with. Bunch of buddies." I heard Skinhead-left snicker. I'd have killed him, right then, if I could. "Ran into Jennifer Marsh. Beach was crowded so we. We wandered off. Down to a cove. Nobody around. Always

319

liked her. She liked me. Till I junked up."

"Shh," I said, softly. "Back to the beach. C'mon, buddy. What happened?"

"Talked. Had a couple beers with us. I — I wasn't used to drinkin', yet, so I got buzzed. And I kissed her. And she kissed me. Felt so good."

"What was she wearing?"

"Swimsuit. All one piece. Scarf around her hips."

"What were you wearing?"

"My boardies. Board shorts."

"How was the sun?"

"Hot. Good. I burn easy so. I always have lotion. She put it on my back. I put it on hers."

He was beginning to respond, so I ran my tongue the length of his dick. He clenched his ass but definitely reacted.

"She do this to you?"

"Yeah." His voice was breathless.

"And this?"

I circled its head with my lips. He almost gasped. I shifted my hands back to where they could play with his balls and he squirmed a little, but this time from pleasure. And his butt clenched and his dick whispered up his thigh, bouncing a little. I watched it and thought, How lovely.

But the truth is, Sean was a beautiful guy. Not in the classic mode, sure, but on his own terms. Everything about him fit together from his slim body to his sloping legs to his sad eyes to his hair flopping in his face to the look and feel of his dick. And to think such beauty could be so brutalized and ruined and left to waste away — it cut me — brought me close to tears. It wasn't right, hurting something so fragile and lovely. It was evil. Pure evil. And it was my fault this was being done to him.

I didn't care that the three stooges were so busy with my ass and legs; I deserved whatever they did to me because I'd set Sean up for this — just like I'd set Matt up with Benny and — and even Travis and Bryce and DJ and Nick and the others. Each of them lovely in his own way, and I'd lead them to be hurt and damaged and maybe even destroyed, if Rattler and his crew used Travis as many times as he claimed. Even if they'd all agreed to do whatever was needed to keep from being hurt, such a thing would be soul-destroying. I was evil and deserved my fate.

You see, by this point I'd pretty much figured they were going to put an end to me, here. It'd be easy to do, and I almost welcomed it. But the way Rattler had been with Sean — both rough and loving — made me think he would *not* want to kill him. I might be wrong (I have been so many times throughout this story) but it was the only hope I had, and I figured half that hope would be showing Rattler Sean could be got off, making him useful for future revenges.

So I slipped my mouth around Sean's dick and began to suck on it, and let myself focus on making him feel everything I could make anyone ever feel — until Preppy rammed himself into me, all in one movement. The pain was so sharp and hideous, I had to yank my mouth off Sean to keep from biting him as Preppy humped me like a rabbit — whupwhupwhupwhupwhup. I could barely stand it and had to force myself to concentrate on Sean and get back to sucking his dick, using every trick I knew to get him harder and pull him close to ejaculation. Swirling my tongue around his shaft as my lips caressed it. Lingering over his head in a twisting motion as I flicked my tongue against his slit. My fingers constantly tickling at his balls or playing with his pubes or the hairs dancing over his legs. He began to let out little moans of pleasure, and that is all that kept me going, because Preppy's whupwhupwhupping got faster and harder and more painful until he slammed himself deep into me and began to cum and I could feel him ejaculate into me.

Well...I guess safe sex wasn't part of the game.

He yanked himself out and finished onto my back, then a moment later, Skinhead-left took his place and pushed into me. Fortunately, he was nowhere near as big and I could handle it better. Plus he was more of a grinder, scrunching his hips around like he was trying to brush his teeth or something. It actually tickled and took my focus away from Sean's dick, for a moment...until I realized he might also be a quick one. He was crushing into me too fast and furious so I got back to Sean and a moment later, Skinhead-left was cumming, too. The big difference is, he wrapped his arms around my hips, grabbing his elbows and locking me into place as he fired into me and fired into me and fired into me and I got to thinking he was never going to stop. Then he lay on top of me, nearly crushing my groin into the side of the table, and gave my dick a couple of yanks. Damn, *gay-for-pay* my ass, for this little fuck.

Then Skinhead-right took his place — and he was a slow one. Pushing in deep — deeper — deeper until he was at the hilt then pulling back and pushing in almost like a metronome — tick-tick-tick-tick-tick-tick. The rhythm of him helped me get back to Sean — and I seriously worked the guy, pumping and caressing and licking and touching...and soon I could taste him getting close. His breath grew faster. His butt began to clench and press up. His belly gripped in on itself and heaved and spasmed, involuntarily. He put his hands on my head to keep me in place as he began to pump into my mouth. I let him set the pace — and he shoved himself up and down and up and down and then he grunted and I pulled back and used my hands to manipulate his dick and balls and he began to spurt up and over, like little geysers, one after the other after the other, all done in the open so Rattler could catch it on video.

Skinhead-right finally joined him, ramming himself into me then pulling out to shoot onto my back. He was all but crying out from the pleasure he was getting. I was just relieved he was finished.

"Shit," said Rattler. "I thought we'd all be havin' you, again. Shows what I know."

Yeah," I said. "Yeah. So you're next, huh? And then this guy, again? And that's it."

"We'll see," he said as he kept taping. He smeared Sean's cum across his belly, making him jolt. "You been in here since Tuesday, huh, Sean-y?"

How the fuck did he know that?

Sean nodded, still a bit out of it.

Rattler ran his hand up Sean's torso and across his chest. "Well, don't you worry, none. It'll all be over, soon."

Fuck, I did *not* like the sound of that. "So," I croaked, "you're

gonna leave him alone, right? You're gonna let Sean go?" Rattler
was silent. I looked up at him. His expression was unreadable. Oh,
the motherfucking-son-of-a-bitch. "You let him go, Vernon, right
*now*, or you don't get to do shit in me."

"Who the fuck you think you are?" he snarled. "You don't tell
nobody what to do, faggot. Get outta the way, Sean."

Sean looked at him, a bit lost. "What? You — you're not
gonna hurt him, are you?"

In answer, Rattle grabbed Sean under the arms and pulled him
off the table. He crashed to the floor then Rattler turned to me.
"Turn him face up," he said as he shoved the phone into his pocket
and unzipped his jeans. "I want this bitch to watch me fuck him."

Preppy and the Skinheads jumped to flip me onto the table,
but with Sean out of the way and them being bumbling idiots, I
was able to twist and slam my elbow into Skinhead-left's nose,
crushing it. He howled and fell, blood pouring from it.

Preppy was on the table, his hands gripping my shoulders, so I
rammed my fists into his crotch. He crumbled up like a little boy,
screaming with pain, as I kicked Skinhead-right's legs out from
under him.

Then Rattler was on me, punching me — and he had a nasty
fist because it hurt like shit — but I rolled off the table into the
area between the bench and the wall, kicking at him and Skinhead-
right as he kept grabbing for me but I couldn't get my balance, all
of a sudden, and the floor was slippery and people were screaming
and I was getting cold and weak and I saw Sean grab Rattler from
behind, roaring, "You're killing him! You're killing him!" and
Rattler slammed him around and against the bars and I saw his
knife flash I thought, *Oh my God, I got him killed!* and the door
down the hall slammed open and guards and cops scrambled up to
the cell and I was so cold — so fucking cold, all of a sudden and I
actually thought I caught a glimpse of Jake and something in me
screamed, No, not here, he can't be in here, not him too, please,
please not him, not in here, they can't bring him here, because if
he's here then I've killed him, too, I've killed him and I can't live
with that, I can't face that, but there was Matt, too, and I didn't
understand it but I wanted to but I couldn't because I'd killed Jake

and Sean and God knows how many other people and I belong in hell but I was so cold and I just wanted to get warm again and don't let Matt be hurt, too, please, please don't let him be hurt like I hurt Sean and Travis and Bryce and Nick and so many other people and now Jake...Jake...Jake, I said over and over and over as men in suits poured into the cell and someone screamed like a madman and I think it was me and the iciness overtook me and I slipped into darkness.

— TEN —

I sat on a rock, backed against a hillside overlooking a golden meadow that stretched for miles down to a massive lake, its banks ragged and elegant. Thick forest covered the hills to my right; a drop off or cliff allowed me to see mountains and more less-dense tree coverage rising to my left. Deer wandered about, casually feeding, and I caught glimpses of squirrels dancing along the branches of the trees, like they were playing games. The simple blue sky peeked gentle between white feathery clouds, with eagles and hawks and flocks of swallows dancing around it all. I wore my heavy tan cargo pants, woven from wool, a black cotton t-shirt and somebody's fleece jacket, with comfortable hiking boots on my feet, and the breeze was a hint too cool, just the way I like it.

I knew Jake would appreciate seeing this beauty — this elegance. He'd have hugged me close and watched it just be — then he'd want to head on. Collie would have stayed here to drink in the tranquility until it was *me* who wanted to leave. So that's why I was here — alone — so I could set my own time frame and do as I pleased — and I ached at having all of this perfection, and only me to see it. That wasn't right.

But nothing was right in my life, at that moment. Nothing made sense. Oh, I could connect the dots like you wouldn't believe — Nussewald and Stanton and Gilbert branched out to include some sheriff's deputies in the jail, a couple of Texas Rangers and maybe even the Attorney General of Texas. I could now see that interrogation in my dorm room and in the jail shower were really a scoping out of the danger I presented and finding out how real it was. That they'd first tried to minimize it made sense; the less mess involved the better. But then Gilbert got stupidly ambitious and the problem threatened to rear its ugly head, again, and plans were made with Faraz to eliminate the possibility of more trouble.

I was still 90% sure Faraz was addicted to watching guys get raped, but now I doubt he was the only one who got off on that, because the line to him just kept expanding. I could see that the whole deal in holding cell 6 or F or whatever the hell you want to call it was managed with more than just a few people involved, and that the media, even if they found out, would do nothing about it. Which meant a *lot* of money was involved and I couldn't see Faraz being willing to put that much cash out just to yank on his dick. So I didn't know why it had all happened because none of it added up.

Of course, if I'd told Jake that, he'd just have shaken his head and said, "It ain't meant to, Tone. Life don't make sense." And dear God, I wish he was here to tell me that, right now. I'd believe him. I'd accept it. I promise I would.

I heard footsteps approaching, soft as if to keep from disturbing me. I turned to look, hoping for Jake — but it was Matt, dressed in all in black — t-shirt, jeans and sneakers — seemingly unaffected by the chill, his big eyes focused on me — and they held disappointment. He squatted next to me, ignoring the view, his lean arms crossed over one knee, one hand holding his chin. And he shook his head.

"You are a real asshole," he sighed, "dumping me like that." I could only shrug in agreement. "The only reason I went along with it was, I knew Jake was on his way."

"And you knew he could stop me."

"Somebody had to. I'd of got caught up in it."

"No — you wouldn't. You're still capable of decency."

"So're you, when you want to be," he grinned.

I looked away, smiling. Knowing better.

"What do you see?" he asked.

I could barely form the word. "Peace."

"Is that all?"

"Heaven."

"C'mon, Tone — what do you really see?"

Only Jake can call me that, so I turned to correct him — and it *was* Jake squatting there, same clothes, same position, same disappointed look in his eyes.

"Don't you see it?" I asked.

"I like how you describe it to me," he said as he slipped his right hand up to caress my face and I all but melted into it, the feeling was so wonderful. The tenderness behind it. The love. The joy. It's like I was waiting my whole life for that one simple touch and I never wanted it to end.

"It's where I want our home to be," I whispered. "Yours and mine. A world where no one hates and no one weeps and no one is alone. I never want to be alone, again."

"You won't be."

I gazed into his dark beautiful eyes. "You hate me, now."

"I do." My heart sank. "And I love you. And I want to kill you, sometimes. And I'll kill any motherfucker who ever lays a hand on you, again. You're my mate, Tone. You'll never be anything else. I wish that was enough for you."

"You and me? Like a couple wolves?" I sort of smiled.

"More like a pack. I think Matt's one of us, now."

"He likes you. Have you slept with him?"

"Naw, I just beat the shit outta him for fuckin' you."

"Aw, Jake — he's a good guy and he only — "

"I'm jokin', you shit. Jeez. You think I'm an asshole?"

God, I was so relieved. I tried to reach for Jake but I couldn't move and I flashed back to that chair in Faraz's cell and suddenly the beautiful vista vanished and I was with Jake in a hospital room with my hands strapped to the bed and an I-V dripping fluid into my left arm.

Oh, fuck. Oh, fuck. I glanced around and Jake was there, but he was seated in a chair next to the bed, his laptop open, his eyes locked on me. "Are you back?" he asked.

Back? Wait. "Weren't we just talking?"

"Nope — I been listenin'. Quite a conversation you had goin' with me, in that fucked-up head of yours."

"Wasn't I conscious?"

"Nope. Just chatty. But don't worry, I agree — Matt's a cool guy. And he really is sorry for fuckin' you an' he told me why he did it an' all that shit. So I'll let it go. I'll fuckin' let it go." He set his laptop aside and came over to me. Brought me a cup of water.

I sipped then croaked out, "How long have I — ?"

"Two weeks. Two fuckin' weeks on that hillside, ignorin' me, Matt, the doctors, the crap they were shoving into you..."

So I had described it to him. That was how he'd known where to find me in my own mind. It just made sense that I would trust him enough to share my hiding space. I looked at him. Saw pain in his eyes. I took another sip of water and it felt so good on my lips and throat, then I said, "I'm sorry."

He slipped his hand behind my neck in a sort of embrace and he whispered, "Liar. I take it you're back. Completely?"

"What do you mean?"

"Do you remember anything?"

"Uh — being in that holding cell. Rattler and his friends — them using me. Fighting him — and you — you were there? And Matt, right?"

He nodded. "You remember anything else?"

"Uh — Sean. Guy named Sean. He was so scared — but he was — he tried to stop Rattler."

"Sean Driscoll. He was fightin' Tidwell when we came in. Anything else?"

"How cold it got. So cold. And Rattler — he's got a mean fist. His punches hurt like shit."

"Punches?"

"Yeah — he kept hitting me and — and — " Punches? No. No, he wasn't just hitting me. I looked at Jake.

He nodded and said in a voice close to tears, "You got knifed. A lot. So did Sean — his arm and his side — but you — you nearly fuckin' died on me. And then you wouldn't come back and — and the doctors used a lot of crap words to explain it, but what it boiled down to is, you had a psychotic break, and — uh, your brain — it had to reconnect itself."

"Where am I now?"

"Where the fuck do you think?"

I looked around at the pale blue walls, all blank and godless. Bars on the windows. A prison hospital. My time in the beautiful dream was done; now came the nightmare of reality.

"I guess I got a little explaining to do."

"Little? Shit, Tone, you got a *lot* of people pissed off at you."

Probably an understatement. I looked at Jake. "You, too?"

He lay his head on the pillow, looking at me. "You drive me fuckin' crazy — but no, not right now. Later, okay?"

Oh, shit. "Okay. But if you want to rip me now — "

"No time. There's some guys outside threatenin' to break down the door to talk to you "

"No doctor, first?"

"He's comin', but — shit, the rules're different in here. You dunno what I had to pull to just be able to sit here — and — and dude, if you've done half the shit they say — " His eyes held a world of pain. I ached at having caused it. "I — I still don't know you, do I?"

"Jake, I — I promised you — I'd tell you the absolute truth, from now on. So this is it. Fuck the doctor; let 'em come in. And I'll spill everything — if you'll stay here with me and keep me honest." His eyes bored into me. "You'll hear things you don't want to hear — and — " I had to fight to keep talking. "And they'll make you hate me and pack or no pack, mate or no mate, I — I'll understand if you — "

"Will you shut up?" I did. "One of these days, Tone, you're gonna catch on to the idea that it ain't always about you. Well, yeah, maybe it is right *now* — but not always. Do you finally understand the concept?"

I nodded. "I think so."

He touched his forehead to mine and whispered, "You sure you don't want the doctor before I let in the jackals?"

No. I could face down a herd of hyenas with him at my side. So I shook my head and said, "Let 'em do their worst."

"They'll try — but I got your back, you — you fuck." Oh boy — *later* was going to be fun. He tapped my heart three times then went to the door and opened it and grandly said, "Gentlemen, start your engines."

Of course, first through the door was Officer Arlen Thomas, acting all innocent and pure, the AG right behind him, and I thought, Oh, shit. But with them were representatives from the

Department of Justice; they'd been called in by Jake and the Danish consulate, thanks to his near arrest, all to make certain everything was kept legal and correct. Apparently the only reason law and order had prevailed — hell, the only reason I was still alive — was because the Danes turned into first class assholes and threatened to loudly and publicly complain to the World Court, and that might be embarrassing to the DC crowd — and they don't give a damn what the Texas crew might think, say or want to do, not if it means them not looking good.

Well, I started off by announcing my suspicions of Thomas and the AG. The DOJ boys asked them to wait outside while they interviewed me, which both men had to do since FBI guys were right there, snarling at them. Then the doctor arrived and checked me over and proclaimed me fine, and I proceeded to tell the DoJ everything, just like I've told it here. What I did. To whom. What I'd planned to do and to whom. Why I did it. Where, when and how. Gave them Greco'd's website address — shit, gave them access to the deepest regions of my soul. It took hours and hours and by the time I was done, I was drained of all my hate and anger — and the animal of my shadows was curled in a dark corner, silent and sane and ready for a long, long hibernation. I saw quite a few shaken expressions and some very pale skin on a couple of them. Guess I was evil incarnate, to them — like they would *never* have done *anything* like I did if they'd been in the same situation...and please never you mind all the bullshit about torture and illegal wiretaps and such that's still being revealed in doses by the DoJ. However, it did look pretty much like I was bound for prison.

Except — I'd tried to protect Sean, and he'd already given a deposition to that effect. I'd also uncovered a shadow group in Texas' so-called system of justice involved in the deliberate serial-violation of a number of men...and women, it turned out; assholes posing as angels, bastards claiming to be the guardians of justice who'd been complicit in Collie's death. And for what it's worth, I had neither killed anyone nor harmed a true innocent. My fate was put on hold till they sorted everything out.

Which began to happen when Benny 'fessed up, resigned from

the Rangers and returned to Florida. Seems he'd told the truth about Gilbert vouching for Faraz, and a little bit of cross-referencing *did* put those two together a number of times. Last I heard, Benny'd joined Miami-Dade's Police Force (and don't try to tell me they would give a shit about his illegal activities, please; they're American cops and cops stick together, forever). He was probably very happy in his new career; the PD hates fags there and the city lets them.

Gilbert quietly dropped his bid for the Senate. He wasn't going to but then three men whose names I'd given to the DoJ — David Luka Hersk, Andre Yelvin and McNeil Shirripa (guess which older well-respected Texas Ranger was his arresting officer) — came forward to discuss what had happened to them in holding cell 6. They weren't going to until they found out they were not the only men it happened to. Of course, Gilbert still had his supporters, but even they began to fall away once people saw all three guys were married, straight and had children. The DoJ hinted at five more men they'd talked to and were willing to detail how this particular judge helped convince them to do as Stanton asked. Apparently being straight *was* a requisite for being raped for the camera. That Collie'd been gay was a stupid blunder on Nussewald's part made worse by Orin's mother, little Ms. Loreen, who'd decided on her own to *let the guards know* he'd raped a child. "That'll show the faggot," was how she put it in her diary. The cunt was still comatose, last I heard; I hoped she stays there, caught between heaven and hell, forever.

Gilbert finally resigned his bench and joined the faculty at a California law school known for hiring scumbags to teach law (like this right-wing freak of an investigative counselor who'd forced the impeachment of a president for lying about cheating on his wife). The AG managed to wiggle out of the scandal clean, but Stanton and Thomas stupidly forced the DoJ to indict them for assault, conspiracy, prostitution, kidnapping and distribution of pornography — and then insisted on being tried in open court. It got nasty, and both men are currently appealing their guilty verdicts; it don't look good.

Joe Stanton vanished before the trial. The gossip was he and his mother returned to her home of Pittsburgh and he was now at a prestigious law school under her maiden name, thanks to his grandfather being a legacy. If he *was* at that school, one hoped he would turn out better than another legacy...a dysfunctional idiot who bumbled through life and finally stole the presidency.

Shane Nussewald's now a deputy sheriff, proudly following in daddy's footsteps. I halfway think it's too bad I didn't have a chance to connect with him before everything blew up.

Now Orin, that little bastard's an aide for a right-wing-nut Congressman who's said gay men ought to be castrated. The assumption being Orin agrees with him, so I'm still glad I fucked the little prick.

And I *was* glad I'd never gotten near Nat-four when I was revenging. He joined Doctors Without Borders and is currently working in Bangladesh. Once again, scum begat a decent human being. It makes no sense to me how that could happen.

Travis, Bryce, DJ and the others vanished. I can only imagine what sort of hell they went through with Rattler and his boys, so small wonder the best way to escape him was to drop out of sight. I hope they were able to get past it, but statistics are not on their side.

As for Rattler and the lads — they copped a deal on the rape and attempted murder charges, gave depositions against Gilbert and testified against Stanton and Thomas and wound up at the Federal Prison near Austin instead of at Huntsville. Dumb move on their part; Nick the muscle queen got transferred there because the guard he beat up was a Federal one, and he had it in for Rattler. I wished Nick all the luck and fun in the world.

The worst that happened to the jail guards was reassignment to another branch of the sheriff's department. Of course.

On the positive side, this ordeal had so traumatized Sean, he went into rehab and kicked his habit. He's now an anti-drug counselor for the school district and got married a couple months ago. To Jennifer Marsh. She contacted him after hearing about what he'd been through (the media made his bit sound a lot nicer than it was, and made me into the anti-Christ, but that's to be expected). To flip off the gossip rags who wanted to make this into an evil versus good story (guess who was evil), he asked me to be his best man; I was proud to stand up beside him.

Sure enough, Matt hit it off with Jake and wound up joining our little pack. Dumped his dull life in Florida to live here and work online with Uncle Ari in building websites for his clients — and to be honest, I'm not at all sure how I feel about Jake being so understanding as regards what happened between me and Matt in Paris. Jake's response? "You pulled some real shit and I'm still with you."

I hate it when people get logical on me.

What's funny is, when the two of them go out together (I can't, yet) Matt always gets lucky with some hot little number. Seems they think this sweet slim guy must be a killer in bed to keep a stud like Jake happy, meaning they think my boys are a couple. If only they knew — and I doubt any of them *did* find out; Matt's learned to keep secrets — and don't forget, his blowjobs are perfection. So now he thinks he's the perfect stud, and he's even grown a perfect strut. I almost feel proud.

Jake's become a Danish Citizen — giving him three passports, though I doubt he'll renew his Iranian one when it expires, next year. Same for his American in four years. He jaunts over to Copenhagen twice a month to meet with Ari then drops by Paris to see his brothers-and-sisters. He always lets his father know when he's coming, so the prick can be elsewhere.

Somehow, since Greco'd was formed in Texas, Faraz's lawyers convinced Interpol and the FBI his connection to it was so tenuous, it wasn't worth the effort to prosecute him. So he still has his office atop that twisted building and God knows if he ever takes men or women to those penthouse cells for...let's say, a little fun...though it wouldn't surprise me a bit. Nor would it surprise me to find he's built up a new version of Greco'd in a part of the world that's just as pliable as Texas is when it comes to money. Brazil, probably, because Rio has some beautiful men prancing around the Copacabana in tight little Speedos, and the authorities have just as minimal a concern for humanity as my fucked up state does.

As for me — I testified against Thomas and Stanton (boy, were their lawyers' cross examinations vicious; but my critter woke up for them and we *all* came away from that little fight bloodied), then I wound up on probation with a monitor on my ankle. Jake gets a real kick out of it and we're planning a major celebration for when it comes off, in just under two years. Then Jake and I can move back to Copenhagen and he can finish his graphic novel. The Danes have been decent enough to put my application for citizenship on hold till then. I hope it'll be okay; I just don't want to live here, anymore.

Matt's indicated he might even join us...if things don't work out with this doll of a Jewish guy he's dating. I hope they do (I've caught hints they both like to role-play) but if they don't and I can get hold of that tennis pupil who'd come on to Jake, I might introduce them. I think they'd hit it off.

Of course, Jake said if I do that, as much as he hates domestic violence, he'll hit me. "No more meddlin', Tone."

I promised him I wouldn't. And I keep my promises, now. Because by the time I was done telling the DOJ everything in that prison hospital, Jake...he was shaking...and he could barely look at me. And that came close to destroying me. But he was true to his word and stuck it out. And now at the end of every day, if I've still done right by my guy, he'll look at me proud and I'll just about die from happiness. Then he'll put on a little show as he showers, slowly soaping his sleek arms and buff chest and flat belly and exquisite dick and balls and just-round-enough ass and all the way down his beautifully-formed legs as steam fills the room and suds cascade by in gentle waves. And it seems like he's happy that just seeing him fills me with joy. Then he'll invite me into his world and wash me in the same luxurious manner (which is awkward because to keep the monitor dry, I have to stand with my leg outside the curtain). He caresses my scars and lingers in places just long enough to let me know what we're doing that night. And I do what he wants, every time — because just being with him heals me — makes me whole, again.

We still never fuck in the shower (hell, we couldn't if he wanted to), so it's all deep kisses and hands caressing and nipples touching and dicks sliding against each other and legs maneuvering until we're close to madness, then he'll turn off the water, grab a pair of thick towels and we'll dry each other in sexy ways that still amaze me and wind up on the bed and I'll crush him so tight against me it's like I'm melding him into my body as he all but roars in his need and flips my legs in the air and slips himself into me and pinches my tits as I let my hands drift all over his body and shoulders and arms and ass, driving him crazy until he explodes inside me (figuratively, not literally; I'm making him use a condom until I've tested negative for HIV five times, because I wouldn't put it past Ratter or his boys to be passing the disease along). Half the time, I'll cum with Jake; other times he'll whisper his lips over my dick till I shoot — and it is still always like the first time we'd been together.

I really do want to think he's forgiven me for my lapse into madness, but some nights — some nights the idea of what I almost did to Grady and thought of doing to Nat-four, and the chaos I brought to so many lives — it just plain overwhelms me. These moments explode out of nowhere for no reason other than — hell, they just come. What makes it worse is, my plans for Joe and Shane are never a part of my self-flagellation, and what I actually *did* to Orin and Rattler seems immaterial. And I know in my head and heart that's wrong, just not in my soul. And it's this — this irreconcilable division of deeds in my brain that sends me careening close to madness, again, and I wonder how anyone could ever love me, considering the hideous things I've done.

But then Jake seems to notice and he takes hold of me and he smiles at me as if to say it'll be all right and my heart leaps and my soul howls for joy and I hold him and I know I'll never be able to leave him, again, or hurt him or do anything he might not feel proud of me for doing. I give him my complete and total support in anything he wants to do, and earning his full trust and respect is my one true goal. No hate can shift me away from that mission. No sense of being wronged can lead me down the path of revenge, anymore. You see, he's the only thing that matters to me now.

Because he's my pack.

He's my mate.

He's my Jake.

And, dear God, how I love him.

Kyle Michel Sullivan is an award-winning writer whose sole purpose in life is to tell stories that make his characters more real than the people he actually knows. After all, only fictional humans can truly understand him and be willing to talk to him at any time he wishes. He also sketches and paints and dreams of making movies.